AFTER MIND

SPENCER WOLF

BentStrong Books
www.SpencerWolf.com

This is a work of fiction. Names, characters, places, and incidents are a product of the author's imagination or are used fictitiously. Locales and public names are sometimes used for atmospheric purposes. Any resemblance to actual events, locales, businesses, companies, or institutions, or to actual people, living or dead, is entirely coincidental.

AFTER MIND / Spencer Wolf. – 1st ed.
ISBN-13: 978-0-986-21751-7
ISBN-10: 0-986-21751-4

"Mistakes, faults, pains, memories, and dreams, but most of all, lots of imagination is what makes us all human."

—Margaret Theresa Madden

ONE
NOT A MANGROVE RIVULUS

YOUNG PACKET WAS first born when his body was twelve and his mind was little more than a swirl of thoughts rising toward the source of a light. He opened his eyes and lifted his forearm against the painful brightness of an overhead halogen bulb. He glanced around and saw a barren hospital examination room. He was on a bed. It was raised from the floor.

His legs, scrawny knees, and feet were cold. He had no blanket, only a gown as a cover. A curtain hung bunched at his right. He could see no doctors or nurses and there were no windows to the room. There were no familiar faces to greet him. He was alone.

A bedside table was in reach from his supine position. A blue, plastic rectangular basket was close and that was all that mattered in the moment. He rustled his fingers inside. It was empty. His mind raced. The rush of his fingers against the inside walls of the basket dropped it to the floor.

Something was missing. Not in the basket, in him. He had no air in his lungs. Pressure built behind his eyes. His throat seized. His hands gripped the bed. His mind gave in to his body's muscle reflex, and his lungs sucked in a first true gasp to breathe.

The reddened haze of the room softened to blue, and the rise and fall of his chest under a rested palm was a newfound comfort, the discovery of air. A strong heartbeat had oxygen and more of the room came into focus.

A party-letter "Welcome" sign was hanging by school-room yarn across a curtain rail that looped around his bed. On a supply cart against the far wall was a metronome that kept a steady tempo.

He dug his elbows into the bed's cushion, flexed up at his waist, and swiveled his legs over the edge of the bed. He sat upright. His throat hurt. Eight floor tiles away was a sink with a pitcher on its counter. He lowered his feet onto the chill of the tiles and steadied himself for a walk across the floor.

Once at the counter, he poured a shaky cup of water from the pitcher. He held the cup without drinking and shuffled with it back to his bed. He drew a doctor's revolving stool with his foot from under a tuck of the curtain, and sat on it, carefully holding the cup. He noticed that his feet could reach all the way to the floor.

He raised the cup to his lips. The water jiggled. It trembled in rings. *The nightmare of water had returned.* He swiveled on his stool shy of a quarter turn back, balanced the cup on the bedside table, and slouched into a sigh. The water's paper cup was safe and away. He slipped into an anxious whimper.

His hands were clean; their backs looked older. He wiped a finger under his nose. He was far from grown; he was twelve, and even though filled with the hope of a human, he was deathly afraid. The room was a cell.

Then, a knock at the door startled his next breath to a hold.

*

Packet sat up on the bed. It was raised higher so his bare legs dangled over the edge.

Daniel Madden was close. He wore a blue cap. He shifted his stance at Packet's front and flicked his penlight on, then off, checking Packet's eyes for dilation. Then Daniel switched to an otoscope from his coat's chest pocket and checked Packet's ears for infection. Daniel didn't breathe when he leaned in to look or listen, but when he backed away, his lips came together and he made the most elated but restrained and faintest of whistles. Daniel checked Packet out to be fine: He was whole. He could hear. He could see.

He was thirsty. Packet rubbed his neck again and then cracked his parched lips to speak. "My throat is really scratchy," he said with a forced, fiery swallow.

Daniel slipped his otoscope back into his pocket. He stared.

"Can I have something to drink?" Packet asked.

Daniel smiled and stepped across the tiles to the sink. He didn't have to look down. He took a paper cup from the cabinet above the sink and dunked it into the pitcher. He held it there and then turned back over his shoulder. "You," he said, "you can have anything you want." Then he took a white sugar bowl with a teaspoon in its open top from the cabinet.

"I haven't had any water to drink in three days," Packet said.

Daniel scooped a spoonful of blue powder from the bowl and stirred it into the cup of water. "Three days without water? You know, I heard there is a kind of fish that can live outside of water for three days. A mudskipper, I think."

"A mudskipper is an amphibian," Packet said.

"It's actually an amphibious fish," Daniel said, returning with the cup of blue, thickened water in his hand. "So you're only half wrong, but that's a very good sign." He offered the cup.

3

"Water makes me burn," Packet said as he turned his head.

Daniel set the cup aside on a tray at the foot of the bed. "A mangrove rivulus," he said as his smile disappeared, "now that's a fish. When its water dries up, it burrows into a grounded wet log. A mangrove rivulus can live out of water for more than two months."

"Am I a mangrove rivulus?"

Daniel stopped. He didn't complain. He closed his eyes and exhaled, his shoulders seemed heavy, and his saddened breath no longer whistled. Then he fiddled for a different tool from a kit on the tray at the foot of the bed. "You can be whatever you want to be, but you are definitely not a mangrove rivulus. And from the looks of you, you're already so much better than last time."

"Do you know why my neck hurts so much?" Packet asked as he rubbed.

"Do you remember what happened to your neck?"

"Should I?"

"Do you know your name?" Daniel asked.

He didn't.

Daniel lifted Packet's right arm at the elbow and tapped its soft inner bend with two fingers. Then he tore open a small, square packet and pinched out a wet towelette. He used it to swab over a tender vein.

"Packet. My name is Packet." And with that, Packet, the boy, met Daniel's warmest of smiles.

"No, it's not, but it's close enough for now," Daniel said. He pulled a tall metal stand closer to the bed.

"I saw a wild boar. Hyenas ate it," Packet said. "They killed it and ate it."

The stand had wheels, and up at its top was a watery bag.

"Where did you see a wild boar?" Daniel asked. "Never mind, you don't have to answer. I think maybe the water I fixed and put in this pouch will help you be you."

"I don't remember where I saw it," Packet said as Daniel pulled a needle from its wrapper.

"Does 448 Treeline Drive mean anything to you?" Daniel asked.

"No." Packet looked away. He winced from the stick of the needle.

Daniel used a piece of tape to hold down a tube. The tube ran up from the back of the needle to the bag on the pole. "Then think of it as a key," Daniel said. "If you can think of nothing else, then 448 Treeline Drive is what I want you to look for. A key. Your key." The water started to drip from the bag. It ran into the tube and disappeared through the needle. Daniel rested the back of Packet's hand onto the bed, his elbow exposed.

"Can we play computer now?" Packet asked.

Daniel stepped away from the bed. "You want to play computer?" he asked as he ground the thumb knuckle of his fist back and forth across the bite of his teeth. "How do you know we're not already?"

Packet dropped into a deep, curled slouch and threw open his arms. "Dad, come on! You know I like to play. Stop kidding around." The tube nearly pulled loose from his arm.

Daniel stumbled back over the wheeled legs of the stool. "You recognize me?"

Packet tacked the tape back down onto his elbow as the water continued its drip. "I do now," he said.

"Stay here!" Daniel said. He rushed for the wooden door on the left.

"When will you be back?"

Daniel slipped off his blue doctor's cap. "One minute?"

Packet's bare feet dangled off the edge of the bed and he tapped them against the pole. "One little one?"

The heavy door clicked shut and Daniel was gone. But that was okay. He was always working on something, or trying to. He was strong and smart. And he was good. Maybe when Packet got bigger, he could be strong and smart like his dad, too.

But for now, Packet's gown barely helped with the return of the chills. He was alone again, and his stomach rumbled. He was hungry. But the pain in his throat remained. As the water dripped, he looked around and filled in more of the details of the rather full room. Most of all, there was the color of blue. The walls, the supply cart with its metronome, the water flowing in the tube, the fine, pixilated tint of the air. . . .

He could tolerate a nagging dry cough, and he did. But a minute to wait seemed too long when his scratchy throat kept him thirsty for more than just water, and he was left tethered to a half-empty bag on a pole. But most of all, he was afraid to be on his own.

Meg. Meg could take care of him, he thought. Where was she?

Water filled the anvil-shaped and colored cumulonimbus clouds that blanketed the Tasmanian island sky, but the blackest of storms wouldn't rain over the island's flattened mountain peak. As if with the whispered call of a name, a cool autumn wind descended on the day. A gust of air whisked down from the mountain's peak over waist-high Fagus trees turned from green to bronze to gold. The lower foothill forest awoke with a cacophony of birds and hidden waterfalls. Single homes of the hills melded into the fingers of a city and a modern palm of greater concrete and steel at the bay. Hobart was a gateway that connected the people of a distant shore to the rest of the modern world.

Margaret Teresa Madden raced on foot across View Street

with the wind at her back. At twenty-two, she had stayed fit through diet and care, and could run, but never too fast. She went only by the name of Terri.

She turned southwest along the bay's Grosvenor Crescent to the main university campus. She shunned to her far left the abandoned and dilapidated Marine and Antarctic Studies building whose presence was a constant reminder of loss. The institute was rebuilt next to the pier at the harbor for Antarctic-bound ships. Once, she had been set to sail from there for an ornithology field study on the flight range of Antarctic Prions nesting on the distant Macquarie Island. But at the time, lost as she was, she'd backed away from the plank at the dock before her ship left port. She ran from her trip with nothing but a 3D-lenticular picture of a bird in her bag and the lingering despair of a thousand more places she would never go. So she waited.

She broke into a sprint through a parking lot on campus. There was only one thing that kept her going—the memory of her not-quite-brother.

Ages before and half a globe away from where she was now, the two of them had been stuffed in the car for the five-hour drive north from their old suburban home in Minnesota to the chilly northern lakes in the Boundary Waters' wilderness along the Canadian border. The trip was tolerable only through her obsession with Sea Turtle Rescue, a repetitive virtual swirl of a game that she played incessantly on an antiquated, hand-me-down, digital tablet. That game was hers alone.

When their constant bickering became too much to bear, her mother would snap, "How do you know when it's time to pull over and take a break from driving? When the argument from you two is about what side of the car the sun is shining on: 'It's shining on my side.' 'No, my side!' 'No, it's not! It's shining on—' 'Mommy! He said the sun isn't shining on my side.'"

Terri slipped out a smile and dodged a car pulling into a space in the lot. Then she recalled and laughed, remembering her mother's final break: "Okay, enough! We're pulling over so we can get out and see. The sun is staying right where it is, and where it always has been, and that's all you're going to get out of me."

Terri leapt onto the curb from the lot that edged the southwest curve of a green, oval sports field. The field's white cricket pavilion stood as testament to tradition while competitive runners lapped the lawn. Miniature aerial drone trainers flew backward to set the pace, each drone keyed on the individual pattern of its chosen runner's jersey. The lead runner was fast and fit, with a loud striped chest of red over blue. He watched Terri the most as she ran, and she caught a few of his looks, but none were ever returned.

She turned away from the field and toward the east and west rectangular wings of DigiSci's four-storied, "H"-shaped building. She hopped the steps to the glass foyer that connected its stone-veneered walls. Other than receipt of a large corporate contribution nearly a dozen years before, the building's biggest outside connection was a long-standing partnership with the famed lab for advanced Human & Cognitive Machines—HACM Lab US—at the University of Washington in Seattle.

Terri had made up her running distance too fast. She circled DigiSci's entryway, laboring to catch her breath. She stood as straight as she could, pressing the palm of her hand deep onto the beat of her chest.

DigiSci's tired façade hid a tangled story of change inside. Terri swallowed to calm her breathing, then muscled open the foyer door. The stairwell to the left was plain from a distance, but had a closer detail only she knew from a hundred failed runs before, each ending with a return to sitting and weeping on a stair. This time, Terri thought as she held her breath and skipped up the stairs, it better be different.

A plaque, hanging by a thread on the foyer's second-floor wall, was inscribed with the simplicity of a Mandelbrot set, a unified equation, a layered, complex beauty of nature. The equation was expressed as mixed media on wall, an expansive, swirled design that barely survived beneath brittle, flaked paint. She had seen its earlier creation and there had been art here once, but it had all disappeared long ago.

She passed the robotic torso of a security monitor on a counter, and pushed open a metal door into an eight-by-twelve-foot mantrap. A biometric scanner on the wall read the veins of her fingers, and the rear door opened. She turned right, into the western wing of the building, and made a beeline down its center hallway to the last door on the left. An "Emergency Shut Off" button for the entire building's power was mounted under glass on the wall outside a single wooden door.

Inside, to her left against the wall, was one of two computer room air-conditioning (CRAC) units. It pumped ducted air to seven-foot-tall server cabinets, eight on each side of a single central aisle. The chilled blanket of air was like a whole body inhaler that calmed the scorch from her run. She slowed, turned to her right, and faced the one black cabinet at the end of the west-facing row.

The brushed-black metal of the cabinet was a welcome touch. It was critically cooled in the small room's farm of servers. As it whirred, she scanned its speckle of lights and exhaled.

"Is it true?" she asked beneath the hum of the room's white noise.

The second of the two CRACs was perched along the room's rear wall to her left. It pumped out its chilled air under the tiles of the floor. On the wall above the second CRAC was a four-foot-wide slate, and above that was a single, three-lens camera. Its blue LED flickered.

"Is it true?" she shouted.

The blue LED went solid. The slate on the wall turned clear and the gray cinder blocks of the wall shown through. Then the screen wiped into a live video stream.

Now in view, Daniel paced between a desk, its mess, and his side of the wall. The backside of outdated, text-based code in the correct orientation from his side of the room covered the screen right to left. He turned with his fist over his mouth, the knuckle of his thumb scraping his teeth. He looked, but saw right through her.

"I asked you a question," she yelled.

Daniel swiped his hand in the air and his code scooted away. "The problem is he doesn't know who he is. But it's him. And he wants to play computer."

"How do you know it's him?" Terri asked. "Last time it thought it was a dying squid."

Daniel smiled. He finally saw her and leaned with his knuckles upon his desk. "Because he thinks his name is Packet."

The green lights of the cooled and brushed metal cabinet flickered, but to Terri, they could have meant anything from the outside.

"Can you do it?" Daniel asked. "Can you try it again? Once more?"

The LED panel of the cabinet signaled that the servers ran warm above seventy-six degrees. Normal operation. But to her arms, the air felt cold as ice.

"Absolutely," she said, and then turned back to Daniel on the screen. "I don't know."

Daniel glared, eviscerated her doubt. "And he refused to drink water."

She ran her hand along the cheek of the cabinet and cupped her fingers along its edge. The tiny bumps on her arms stayed raised in the room's cocoon of chilled air. "Then yes," she said, but unsure. "Absolutely. Whatever it takes. One last time."

Daniel's few steps to his right took him out of view of her screen. A simple, wooden door at the left side of the wall's CRAC buzzed and unlocked at its frame. Daniel entered the data hall and held out his hands in an offering of peace. "I set him up in a hospital room, a safe environment for him. He's accepted it so far, free form."

The tall metal cabinet was waiting, its processors churning inside.

"Are you ready to go inside? Do you want to see him?" Daniel asked, finding a way to lift a tiny smile.

Terri thought of every reason to say no, but then found an ember of "yes" that trumped them all. "Only if he can see me."

TWO

NOTHING MORE, NOTHING LESS

CESSINI MADDEN WAS twelve when the family bumped up the Tasmanian central highland hill in a Jeep. His father, Daniel, drove with an exaggerated bounce in his seat as he kept to the road. Robin Elion Blackwell wrung her hands in the front passenger seat. Her preteen daughter, Meg—short for Margaret Theresa—lowered her window to its final quarter and finger-cupped its top for a view of the construction. The bumps would soon be over, or so the sandbagged signs said.

Bouncing his feet on his rear-seat mat, Cessini thought that this place could be different, or better. The refreshed Tungatinah Hydroelectric Power Station wasn't far from the place they had recently started calling home, but they had been driving around the island of Tasmania for most of the day. The plan was simple: to get to like their new homeland that placed them forever and a mile from where they had come.

Cessini caught the wind through his window, the sweet smell of the world. "Hey, Dad," he said, "you and me, we could fix this road. Give us a shovel and a couple of machines, and it's fixed in no time flat. This is the best place ever already. You're going to love it. All two hundred megawatts of power. Pesky water doesn't stand a chance." He bounced his feet on the mat. This was going to be great.

Tungatinah revealed its industrial self as they cleared the final switchback in the road.

Meg looked at him, shook her head, and then went back to her window.

"Okay, so what's it look like to you?" he asked. "'Cause the sun's shining on my side for sure this time."

"Hope," she said. Then, with the side of her head on her window, she laughed at the height of the sun, obviously still on her side of the car.

"Hmm, hope," he said. If Meg said it, then it must be true. He poked her and she scooted farther away.

He reached for the ScrollFlex case in the netting attached to the back of Daniel's seat. He unrolled the soft clear screen from its suede capsule case and swiped by a picture of him and Meg traveling halfway across the world in a plane. He held the clear screen up to the windshield as it registered their location. A photo journal from Tungatinah's brochure appeared, which he flicked larger and read aloud:

"'After its third overhaul in seventy-five years, Tungatinah had a weathered dignity and resolve. Five penstocks dropped water nine hundred fifty feet from the head lagoon.'"

He looked out his window and found the long pipes. They were orange.

He continued: "'The latest upgrade was a transition to super-conducting coils and zero-resistance transmission lines that delivered a hundredfold benefit to life. The old clearances that were cut two hundred feet wide through centuries of conifers for the run of overhead power lines could now grow back to the welcome width of a family walking side-by-side on the grass. Once complete, the new buried run of conduit will have a hidden width of only six feet underground.'" He looked up from the screen. "Hey, Dad. They're burying cables six feet under. What if they hit a few dead people?"

"I don't know. I guess a few of them would wake up with a shock," Daniel said with a whistling haunt as he brought the Jeep to a halt in the Tungatinah lot.

Cessini chuckled, got out, and stretched his legs. The metal transmission towers that crowded the paved lot were covered in rust. They looked far older than the brochure's enticing photo. Robin hesitated and stayed in her seat, her fingers pinched over her brows.

Cessini read on: "'Three decades earlier, the mainland over the strait to the north was the largest net exporter of coal in the world. Then the people voted to have the greatest proportion of renewable energy per capita on a world-leading par with Norway and Iceland.'"

Robin relented and came out of the car. Meg stood at her side on the curb.

Cessini scrolled down to two bulleted highlights: "'The islander's first phase initiative was the superconductor upgrade to the heritage site of Tungatinah and also to her five sister plants in the lowland western catchment. The second phase was the upgrade of the remaining fifty hydroelectric power stations throughout the five remaining northern and eastern catchment generation systems.'" But the second bullet was best: "'The target of the entire system was fifteen thousand gigawatts of clean, deliverable power to the whole of the greater island grid. Any excess would be routed to feed the new Basslink-B undersea power cable to the mainland.'"

Cessini stopped reading as a man limped to greet them curbside. He figured it was the man his dad had called earlier about coming out to see the place, and he watched him.

Gerald Aiden stepped with an oddly stiff-sided gait that punctuated his walk, ruined the drape of his uniform, and twitched his pile of under-eye wrinkles.

The ScrollFlex snapped back into its windup capsule case.

"I hear you're the one with all the power around here," Daniel said.

"Good one," Gerald Aiden said, his voice hoarse. He secured his cordial shake with a hand to Daniel's shoulder. "Haven't heard that one before."

Cessini held out his hand. "It's nice to meet you."

Gerald Aiden took it. "And you are?"

"Cessini—spelled with a 'C' and 'e' so you say it like the water. Like sea. Not the astronomer. He's a hard 'C' and 'a' as in Ka—Cassini, but I'm 'Cee' like the sea. Cessini."

"Okay, steady there, kiddo, you're way too quick for me." Aiden laughed and pivoted for another introduction. "Mrs. Madden?"

"Blackwell," Robin said. "I still go by Blackwell."

"Okay, then." Aiden winked at Daniel. "Your problem, champ, not mine."

Meg offered a wave, but received no notice in return.

"Well, all right, then," Aiden said to Daniel, "shall we go have a look?"

Meg stepped up, insistent and loud: "Why are the big pipes orange? Those ones coming down from the hill."

Aiden stopped. "Name of this place means 'falling water.' And those, my gal, are penstocks, water inlet pipes from the lagoon. But it's not the pipes that are orange." He pivoted and restarted their walk to the main assembly building. "They're covered in lichen. A living, breathing, composite organism of fungus and algae. A body and its feeder. It's pure symbiosis. Can't live one without the other. They're what you see as the orange, not the pipes."

Cessini picked up his pace and followed Aiden across the lot. He twisted up backward as he walked to see the tops of the metal high-voltage towers and their live power lines. They were huge from underneath. Straight ahead lay the imposing four stories of the rusted, corrugated main assembly hall. Two smaller bay buildings attached to the hall on its left and right. The power station sat beside a bed of frothed water. The spill-off roared.

The boil kicked up an arched spectrum of light, a rainbow-refraction of water drops in the air. A rainbow was to everyone else a beauty of nature, but to Cessini it was a warning, a cage in the sky held in front of his walk, like a dead canary in a coal mine. He flinched at the sight of its glistening arch, but continued ahead. *The nightmare of water had returned.*

"Let me know if you have something in particular you want to see," Aiden said as he turned and noticed Cessini lagging behind.

Cessini knew himself to be smart—maybe not as smart as some, but definitely braver than most. Who else, he thought, could walk as tall through life while afraid of the rain from above and the pain of their own tears from within? If there was anything he'd learned from his dad, it was that all things could be fixed, and by God if he could still crawl, he would find a fix for the run of his fear, and his days of nightmares with water.

He straightened his shoulders and soldiered on. Meg elbowed him back to center. The door of the hall was fifty yards afield. Cessini bucked up as Daniel tousled his hair.

"I think he'll want to see the turbines first," Daniel said. "He's my number-one engineer."

"Got me a boy just like that," Aiden said. "Thinks he can run this place better than me."

Meg walked beside them, but with her head scrunched down, preoccupied. She was unfurling the winged tabs on the side of her hand-me-down, digital tablet.

"How do you protect the power's transmission?" Cessini asked.

SPENCER WOLF

"Warrior ants. Little digital packets, actually," Aiden said. "The ants scuttle around the network, always on, eyeing for threats. Like real ants, they put out a scent that others from the colony can follow. So on the monitors, when you see a cluster of them little digital buggers somewhere, something's wrong in the grid. But no matter if it's only one ant by itself or more running in to attack, they'll always sting the threat until it is dead. Power transmission secure. Roger that?"

"Cool," Cessini said, then elbowed Meg at his right.

She scowled and turned her eyes back into her game. The main roaring spillway of water to his left was contained in its distance.

The pinpoint of a dreaded sound drew his attention straight ahead to the front of the building. A worker had attached a garden hose to a wall-mounted faucet. The knob squeaked as he turned it. The water sputtered and then gushed from the loose end of the hose. The worker opened the cap to a fifty-five-gallon drum resting on the bed of his mini-truck. He swung the loose end of the hose and the water splashed, overflowing the lip of the drum before he stuffed the nozzle through the open cap. His water care was an absolute wreck.

A smaller puddle on the asphalt lot also grew ahead to the left. An air conditioner mounted in the wall above the western bay door dripped with predictable timing. In a few summer months, the clogged overhead fan would spill out a couple of gallons of water a day. The spill could be prevented, he thought, if only these locals could unclog the copper condenser pipe. Two workers strolled through the parking lot with crumpled bag dinners. They sipped from cups with straws. Their cups were only ounces each—nonetheless a measureable number to watch. But the man with the hose out front and the fifty-five-gallon drum could be devastating. That careless man would be watch-point number one.

17

Gerald Aiden thrust his fingers into Cessini's chest. Cessini stopped and blinked when he saw what he'd nearly run into. The main assembly bay's mammoth hangar door was directly upon him.

"Watch yourself there, son," Aiden said. "You don't see forty-odd foot of this door in front of your face, you ain't gonna see much inside, neither."

Cessini disengaged his mind from the man working the hose and sidestepped through the adjacent, man-sized entry door.

Inside the turbine hall, five inverted cones sat like tips of icebergs atop a polished concrete floor.

He marveled behind Meg, then pushed forward to see. "Now those are turbines!"

"Those tops are the exciters," Aiden said. "The guts of the turbines are under the floor."

Under each assembly sat a vertical shaft with rotating blades. The blades spun from the high-pressure water that poured down from the orange pipes. The spinning shaft generated power in motors—motors that were now upgraded and wrapped with superconducting coils. The power of water filled the air and it was alive. He drew in a sweet, tangy smell. It was one he would never forget, it was the sweet smell of shop oil, and it filled the air of the power station humming with well-lubricated machines.

Cessini scanned back for Meg. She followed a step behind, missing it all. She clacked away with a deft touch at the side-mounted finger tabs of her tablet. The skin of her hand-me-down tablet was a mangle of color over old, childhood scribble. Her tablet was not the sleek, modern ScrollFlex that retracted into a suede case, but her old tablet was still somehow better. Her tablet used to be his.

"Hydroelectric power is power from water," Aiden said as he led from the front. "Not power by water itself, but by the entire system. How we catch it, control it, and convert its potential energy into kinetic energy that we see and use every day." He tossed a casual nod up toward an LED-light basket hanging from the roof.

"Yes!" Cessini slapped his palm atop his fist. "Control the water before it takes control of you."

Aiden stopped and shifted his weight. "Son, water don't ever control you. Weren't you listening to me? Here is where we control the water. It's what I do. I help people get control of their lives. You young kids need to get your mind out of them ScrollerFlexes and pay attention."

"I was. I notice everything. And I didn't say—"

"Whoa, kiddo," Aiden said. "Stop right there. I'm just saying, with lights on I don't fall down. ScrollerFlexes can drop free from the sky and I'd have no more use for them than a dead boy bouncing. You get me? I like things simple and easy."

Meg glanced up without lifting her head from her game. She snickered and nudged Cessini with her shoulder. Then she returned, head down, to her Sea Turtle world.

Aiden leaned against the framework of a black, metal ladder. He folded his arms and raised his brow, waiting. A horizontal gangway ran high above his head across the midline of the four-story warehouse windows.

"Okay. I get you. Simple. Can we go up there?" Cessini asked.

Meg paused for a look. "You sure? It'll be high."

"If it suits you," Aiden said. "My leg don't let me go. But you're free to power on up."

Meg folded in the wings of her tablet and handed it to Robin, who took it and nestled her arm into Daniel's. "Go on up. We'll be fine," Robin said.

Cessini ascended first, clinging to the almost vertical rails of the ladder as Meg followed. He stood up onto the gangway's platform and held tight to the hand bars. His back was to the windows over the valley and spill-off water below. He focused on the warehouse's floor, the power potential of the five turbine sets. The sight of their tops from his height was an uneasy perspective. He turned around. Through the windows and down below was the water's rush. Its mist rose, passed through a rainbow of fear, and condensed on the window. On the outside of the glass was a smacked hand and finger smear. The wet imprint hovered high and exposed out over the pool of water. Beads held and then dripped from the tips of its fingers—fingers from a ghost that hung in desperation outside of the window's pane. He was jostled.

"Close enough to walking through clouds for you?" Meg asked.

He braced himself on the rail. "I just need to stand here a second. Get used to the height."

"Tell me, what's the count of this place?" she asked.

"I don't know. I stopped counting after the fire," he said.

"Come on. What is it?" She knew him too well.

"It's a five-number watch with a four-count drip on two outside."

"What's the drip?" she asked. She didn't know.

"Outside, the condenser above the annex. It's clogged. It drips to the pavement. A slow one-two-three, then a long four and a drop falls."

"I didn't notice it when we came in," she said.

"There's also a workman with a tank and a hose. He's careless."

Gerald Aiden hollered something from the floor below. He gestured out the windows. "The power runs out onto the grid through the new superconducting cables," he yelled as loud as he could. "Each carries a hundred times the power of copper." He spun his right pointer finger around his outstretched left pointer. "The superconducting cable's wrapped with liquid coolant running at minus a hundred and fifty degrees Celsius."

"You want to play 'Without?'" Meg asked as she turned back to Cessini.

"Without what?" The window-side railing dug into the small of his back. He gripped as tight as he could, both sides. The knuckles of both hands were white. The spill water's flow increased, if not in his mind, then by its raging sounds from below. The turbines revved up into a high-pitched whirl.

"You have to keep the thin wire coils chilled or they lose their superconducting properties," Aiden shouted.

"You know," Meg said, "a bike, a car, a truck, a train. Whatever you want." She came closer. She was right in front of his view. She blocked out the height. "Go bigger and bigger or smaller and smaller. But at each, you have to say what happens without—like a bike without a rider falls down. A car without a family goes nowhere. Your turn."

Aiden widened his arms out from his sides and shouted "From here, you can see. . . ."—but no one was listening.

Cessini braved a smile at Meg. "Three seconds without a brain and you die."

"Seriously? That's lame. But okay. Three minutes without a heart and you die."

"Three hours without checking Sea Turtle Rescue, *you* die. Three days without water, *I* live." He turned around to the window.

"Hey, that's not nice. And you took two turns."

"Three years without sunshine," he said. He wavered. A droplet's vein of water ran down the pane. Was it inside or out? He closed his eyes. "Three years. That's 94,608,000 seconds. Is that good?"

"No. And you don't have to show off to me."

"Three millennia—"

"Come on, stop it. You're ruining the game. Open your eyes or I'm not playing."

"A civilization dies and its souls perish with it."

"That's not true," she said, miffed. "All the old souls come back when the next civilization comes along. They pick up where they left off." She caught him as his knees buckled.

Aiden hopped up the first few rungs of the ladder. The gangway jerked and shook. "What's the matter?" he said. "Afraid of heights, you two?"

"We're okay," Meg said.

Cessini balanced. The skywalk rattled. If a wall of water rose up the side of the glass, it would never reach their height up on the skywalk—but the mist? What about the mist? If the skywalk nicked the window, one hole in the glass would be enough. Droplets would land on his arm, or worse, his face.

Aiden stomped on the steel. "Is what I'm showing you not good enough? You don't want to look anymore?"

"It's not the height!" Meg said.

Cessini breathed in his nose and out of his mouth. He focused on Meg. "If I could bear all the clouds in the sky," he said to her caring, patient smile. "I still would never want to come back to this world. Nothing here is good for me anymore." He inched his way along the railing toward the stairs.

Meg managed her poise so well. She held on. What he said was wrong, and he knew it.

"But," he added, "I'd most likely come back for you. Come on, let's go down. Get out of this old rusty box. What do you say?"

"One step at a time. Okay?"

Aiden hopped clear from the bottom of the ladder. Daniel pushed past him. "He's okay. We got him," Daniel said.

Cessini's feet were back on the ground. "Sight of all that

water," he said, "makes me feel like I'm falling, or worse, that's all."

"Worse?" Aiden said. "What could be worse? We're upgrading as fast as we can. Water out there. Power in here. You seen it. You like it. But you ain't gonna fall. What's the matter with you?"

"He doesn't mean anything by it," Robin said.

"I'm fine. Don't worry," Cessini said.

"What happened?" Robin asked as she handed Meg back her old tablet.

"Take a guess," Meg said.

"I'll tell you what I'm going to do," Aiden said. "If you like to fix things, we got every tool you can imagine out in the shop. We'll get you some whatnots or a souvenir to go."

"Sounds good," Daniel said.

Cessini nodded.

Outside the main hangar, Cessini covered his eyes from the sun and turned to the right. He skipped a few steps to avoid the spill from the fifty-five-gallon drum. He was safe. The workman of watch number one and his mini truck were gone. His hose was coiled on the ground.

Watch-point number two, with its four-count drop, was right on schedule. The condenser above the annex door was okay. After the count of one-two-three, and then a slow four, a drop fell to the asphalt. Its growing puddle broke through a sand-pebble damn and trickled toward him. It was easy to step over. Then the fan of the condenser bucked with a loud grind. It sputtered and the old, clogged unit shut off.

"Your air conditioner coil is plugged," Cessini said. It kicked on with a bang and spit its condensate out from above.

He wrenched his neck forward to dodge an instantaneous blur. A single droplet struck below his left temple. He threw himself against the rusty corrugated wall and slammed his fist for a sheet metal's pang. He hid his face. He bottled a scream. The single water drop had evaded his count. He failed to control. He spun away from under the conditioner box. He was outside, but caged. What else did he miss? Right then and there, he knew, counting was as useless as dead.

"I said you have to clean it!" He kicked the pebbles of the worthless dam on the ground. He paced back and forth. Meg gave him his room. He cupped his hand over the side of his face. Robin broke away toward the lot; her hand was over her mouth. "I can't do it anymore," he wailed as Meg came back. "I can't." Anguish turned to his body's physical reaction and he doubled over in pain. He muffled a frightful cry. He bounced his foot on the ground.

Aiden grinned. The corner of his lip was raised halfway up toward his squint. He gave the puddle on the asphalt a swift, limped-in stomp. "Come on, kiddo, it's only water. I've been necked a hundred times before from that crotchety old box. No harm."

"What is your problem?" Meg asked. She shoved Aiden against the warehouse wall.

"Hey, go on then," Aiden said as he held up his hands. "You called me to do a favor for a sick kid, remember?"

"Hey, he's not sick," Daniel said. "You've got no idea what kind of sick we've been through. Don't talk to him like that."

"Tour around by yourselves all you want. I can't fix you, nobody can," Aiden said.

Cessini breathed to himself. He rose back up and straightened his shoulders, then lowered his hand from his face. A ringed welt radiated from the strike point at his temple. It stung down past his cheek. A red streak looped around to the back of his neck and disappeared below his collar.

Aiden stumbled back. He glanced up to the condenser. "You know, you people scare me. I don't know if kids like you should be held closer, or kept away."

Daniel shuffled Cessini away from the building, and then stepped forward toward Aiden. He raised his elbow, cocking his fist. "Listen old man, you don't know what you're talking about."

Aiden cowered away from Daniel's turn. Robin wrapped Cessini into her arms, but he pushed her away, and instead took in the rudeness of a man he had only just met. He walked alone toward the high metal towers in the lot.

"Aw, come on now," Aiden said. "I was just having a go at you."

"Well, you shouldn't. Not at his expense. That was completely rude," Robin said.

"Didn't mean nothing by it," Aiden said. He softened his weight on his hip. "We all right?"

"We're right," Cessini said as he kept walking. Meg caught up but he pulled away his arm.

Aiden reached out for balance against the red rusted wall of the building. For a moment, he looked like a sad, crooked old man. He stumbled off, then around, not really knowing where to turn. "Hey, kiddo," he said as he limped with a pivot and called out with a bite, "You need to toughen up!"

Cessini stopped under the first tower and stared at the man. Aiden gave in first, waved him off, and then left.

Cessini fell into the seat in the back of the Jeep and slammed his door shut. Meg slipped in at his side. He couldn't look.

"You okay?" she asked.

He covered his neck with his left hand. He pounded the door with his fist. "Why does this only happen to me?" He throttled the headrest of Robin's seat to his front. "Tell me why? Tell me how to fix me."

Daniel squeezed the top of the steering wheel, and then

rested his forehead on his knuckles. "Don't you worry about him. You'll never see that man again," he said. Then he relaxed his once fisted hand and turned the key in the ignition. "I don't know what happened. I would never have hit that man."

Cessini calmed his own thrash. "A memory," he said. "Nothing more. Nothing less. Let's go. Just drive."

Robin sank deeper into her front seat and pulled her door shut. Her head fell back. Her eyes longed for a clear prayer view to the sky, but were stopped by the roof of the Jeep. She wrung her hands into the pit of her waist and cried out a desperate sob.

Cessini's window was closed as they drove farther away. He rested his forehead on its tempered glass and overlooked the dry hills of the valley below. Only a growing distance through silence could drown out the power and percussion of the water they had left behind.

Packet sat up straight against his pillow on his hospital room bed and buttoned his pajama shirt for the night. An uneaten tray of turkey dinner and gravy congealed on his nightstand. The tube and its watery bag that dripped from the pole were gone.

Meg was on the edge of his bed and dabbed a cotton ball into a jar of cream. "We brought you back. You're in the mainframe. You think you're sitting here in your own self-image. Your dad thinks it worked. He said it was true. But I'm not so sure. I think you're just running, reliving sad, old home movies. And no one likes to watch the same old stock ten years in a row, least of all me."

He stared, as blank as a slate.

"I need more. I want the real you. And from where I'm sitting, out here, I can see you imagining yourself in this hospital room." she said. "I can even see the memories you dream."

"What do you mean? You're sitting right here," Packet said.

Daniel reached up from beyond the foot of his bed and took down the festive "Welcome" letter cutouts that drooped from the curtain's rail.

"You remember Tungatinah, that's great," Meg said. "I know you saw the pipes. Do you remember what color they were?"

"Orange."

"Do you remember the condenser that dripped? Was it broken or fixed?" she asked.

"Easy. Broken."

"Okay, good. Now, if I put this cream on your temple," she said as she dotted the cotton ball over his left ear, "tell me, where did the owie come from that I would be touching right here?"

He flinched as she reached. "Can we go home now?"

He could tell she was tired by the way she twisted slower from her waist and tossed the spent swab onto the instrument tray. "Not until you tell me so I know it's you," she said. She took a tortoise-shell hand mirror from the tray and showed it to him.

"I don't know." He looked in the mirror. "Did I scratch myself?"

"No, you didn't," she said.

"Is that the boy who splashed me?" Packet asked, pointing at the boy in the mirror.

Daniel laid the letters on the tray, but by their weight and tangle they fell into a scattered chain on the floor. He didn't bother to pick them up. He must have been tired, too.

"No," Daniel said. "It's not. But that boy in the mirror is like an infant with twelve years of memories."

"Then how'd you get that boy in this mirror to look like me?"

"You are that boy in the mirror," Meg said. "It's you, Cessini. We're on the second floor of the DigiSci building.

27

Remember the cabinet on the pallet?"

Packet tilted his head and squinted at the mirror's screen. It simply didn't make any sense. "But that boy is so much older than me," he said. He humphed and rubbed the cream from his head.

"Don't do that." Meg hurried in with her hand. "You'll smear the magic."

The cream dissolved between the rub of his finger to thumb. She held up the mirror again. The boy in the mirror looked back and smiled an innocent grin. He had no cream on his head. Packet laughed himself into a wonderful temper. "Are you a magician?" he asked.

Meg slouched forward over her knees at the edge of the bed. She flopped the mirror's rectangular stem between the roll of her fingers, then looked toward the door, then Daniel. "No way can I do this in real time. From toddler to twelve. I won't wait that long. I can't," she said. Her eyes were glassy and tired.

Packet cupped his hands over his eyes. "If you're a magician, can you make yourself disappear?"

Meg didn't like that at all. She looked up. She was far more than tired. She was angry. "I'm not here right now," she said. She sprang off the bed and stormed toward the door on the left. "It's only you in this fabricated room of your mind."

Daniel grabbed her arm as she pulled the door handle.

"Even an eighteen-month-old recognizes himself in a mirror," she said. "It's failed." She twisted free from his grip. "It's not even close. I can't do it. I won't."

Daniel skipped to her side and blocked her from opening the door. "This is my fault. Please," Daniel said. He pleaded. "I need you. And he needs you more than me."

"He can't even pass basic questions," she said. Her voice cracked deeper as she began to tear up.

"If it wasn't him, he wouldn't know you here in this room. Not like he does."

Meg's hand fell from the door handle and a tinge of her loneliness crept through the room.

"If you're not here right now," Packet asked her, "then where are you?"

"She's close," Daniel said as he turned. "We're inputting through a set of controls in the lab next door. Meg is holding the implant."

"What implant?" Packet asked.

Meg rushed over to the instrument tray and slammed it loud with her two open palms. She held up an implant with its dangling magnetic coupler that had appeared on the tray like magic. She cocked her head and hollered, "Cochlear!"

He laughed. "That's not even close to my ear," he said. What in the world could have made her so angry? He stuck his fingertip deep into his ear and twisted a silly face.

A knock rattled the wooden door on the right. Packet lowered his finger from his ear.

"He's here," Meg said, setting the implant back on the tray.

"Who is?" Packet wiggled himself farther upright on his bed.

"The man who paid for all this," Daniel said. He took a big breath and exhaled. Meg quieted, too. "Dr. Luegner wanted to see you before you went to sleep tonight," Daniel said as he straightened himself and went over to answer the door. "He won't be here long. Be yourself. Be good. Just . . . don't be too much of yourself right now. Okay?" Daniel asked.

"Okay."

The door on the right creaked open and a silver-haired man peeked through. Daniel's stance blocked the man's face.

"Can I come in?" the man whispered.

Meg moped back to the nightstand and fiddled with the

bed sheets. She feigned a smile without raising her head. Her smile was truer as a frown.

"Why do you and Terri look so much younger?" the man asked Daniel, blinking one eye. "The video feed of my contact is receiving. I can see this whole room fine."

"We're streaming images from the mainframe's perceived visual field, live as it processes and thinks them, out to the receptors in your lens. Terri and I are in the studio next door with the camera on us and we're transmitting our images back into the mainframe's simulated visual cortex. This room that you see is the composite in his mind; him sitting in his own self-image, us the way he last remembers us, and you, the way he sees you now. Except that I have our privacy filter on."

"Your youthful age?"

"I don't want him to see the real us just yet. You're seeing the way he remembers us. Last time Cessini saw me, I was fifty. Terri was twelve. He's only going by what he knows," Daniel said and stepped away from the door. "Here, move to your left, more into the frame of your camera."

The man entered the room from the door. He had an aqua-blue collar and darker blue cuffs that stuck out from under the sleeves of his navy pinstripe suit. He stared at first then made a seemingly random search with his eyes: up, down, left, then right as he oriented himself, taking in the full scope of the room.

So why do I look like that, also so young?" the man asked. "I haven't worn that suit in a decade."

"I'd rather you say, 'Why do I look like this?' Not 'like that.' You have to imagine we're in the same room. It'd be rude otherwise. He can hear you," Daniel said. "Besides, you have your camera filter on. We're feeding in your general movement, your body and obscured face. But he's clarifying you in his mind, visualizing you from the last memory he has of you.

It's natural perception."

"So he's hallucinating the parts of me he can't see?"

"It's what we do instinctively, as humans," Daniel said. "He knows you're not simply a shape."

Packet shied away as his dad and the man talked. If he stared any more, they'd realize he could hear every word, so he fiddled with Meg's tuck of his sheets instead. Meg's smile was nice.

The man leaned back against the door. He crossed his polished black shoes.

"He remembers that suit when he thinks of you," Daniel said. "A decade ago for us was only yesterday for him. You had called our home. You were wearing that suit."

"Okay, fine, so this room is a stage in the software theater of his mind," Luegner said. "And this hospital room is—?"

"The seed I gave to the code. It's what made it finally work. Imagine waking up with no sensory inputs—you can't see, you can't hear, there's nothing but the swirl of your thoughts. You need an orientation. For Cessini, it's this room. I situated him. I seeded a human mind that's now recreated and processing away in the two rows of eight server cabinets of your lab. This virtual hospital room is a safe environment for him. He feels comfortable here."

Packet overheard, but Daniel wasn't making any sense, so he took another good, long look at the man who pulled at the dark blue cuffs of his suit. The man raised his hand as a greeting and smiled. He had nice teeth for being much older, and hair that didn't move. His face looked perfect. Too perfect? He had a nice suit. He stood with his black shoes apart. But there was no way he was as strong as his dad.

"So, there you have it. You can see from this composite image of his mind that he's taking us in," Daniel said with delight. "He simply knows my younger face and that of Terri's, but he sees her as twelve-year-old Meg."

Meg stayed distant at the left door, her forehead on its frame, gripping her hand on its lever.

The man held out his hand as he approached the bed, and Packet took it to be polite. "My name is Dr. Hopkus Luegner," the man said. "It's an absolute pleasure to meet you."

Dr. Luegner came down to Packet's eye level. He glanced back over his shoulder at Daniel. "You're telling me I can interact with my younger self through the memories of someone who knew me? That's remarkable."

Meg turned around at the door, rolling the back of her head on its frame. Her bottom lip quivered.

"Technically, yes," Daniel said, "but only now at first because you have your privacy filter on. Don't turn it off, you'll surprise him, and I don't want that now. But obviously the interaction is not the real, physical you. There's no physical connection between your two hands. It's the perception of code."

Meg slid down the wall and sat on the floor. She pulled her knees up to the front of her face.

Packet saw her. He thought he should go over and say he was sorry for making fun of her when he stuck his finger in his ear, but he didn't.

Meg drew the bangs of her hair back over the top of her head, and then pointed her finger out over her knees. "That's not the real him," she said to Dr. Luegner. "He can't even recognize himself in his own memories. He doesn't feel. And I know he feels nothing for you."

"That's all right," Luegner said without raising his voice. "I can feel enough for us both."

Meg's pointed finger dropped from her knee and she turned her eyes into the cover of her other hand.

"Outstanding work," Luegner said to Daniel.

"Thank you. He's coming along nicely," Daniel said. "We

see what he sees, even when he dreams. He'll close his eyes, drift and daydream, go to sleep, remember the past, or imagine he's in a completely different place. We can try to talk to him when he thinks he's somewhere else, but it's like talking to someone who's asleep. He'll take your voice and interpret it into a different context. Same as we would do. If you close your eyes, you can still hear me talking, but you might be imagining yourself walking on a beach, riding in a car, flying in a jet, or dreaming of life in a spaceship. The bigger problem, right now, is that he still thinks all those dreams are about some other boy named Cessini."

Luegner leaned forward, staring tighter into Packet's eyes.

"I think if we can get him into a state of lucid dreaming, we can work with him, get him to make the identity connection that he is Cessini. So, until then, if you want to interact with him directly, keep him in the fixed frame of this room, otherwise anything goes. But never forget it's him. He's my son. He's my number one engineer."

"And to think all this time," Luegner said with a snicker to Daniel, "I had just about given up all hope on you—a simple, working class, systems engineer." Then Luegner reached his hand into the air in front of his own face, turned his outstretched fingers as if dialing a knob and, with it, his privacy filter was off. The source of his image was no longer obscured.

Packet, startled, backed away on the bed. Luegner's suit was no longer navy, but charcoal. And he had aged, though not by much. The skin on his face was still tight.

"Dammit!" Daniel said. "I specifically told you not to expose yourself, not yet. You have no idea what we've been through to get here, how fragile he is."

"Don't worry. I'm not here to hurt him or take him away from you. He's your boy. I know he's yours," Luegner said. "When will he be done enough?"

"Done enough for you, or done enough for us?" Meg asked from the floor. She wiped a sleeve across her eye.

"He'll be done when we give him the Enhanced Blackwell Inversion Test. Let him pass first as human," Daniel said. "Then Cessini after that."

"Blackwell. That's an interesting choice," Luegner said. "Robin ought to be proud." He opened the door on the right a crack and leaned down into darkness. He retrieved a brown paper bag from the floor outside. He peered back at Daniel. "I rendered a gift for your boy. You gave me the interface schema and I used the standard visual installer package from HACM Lab. I hope you don't mind my being the bearer of gifts."

Meg snapped a look toward the door, but her view was blocked by the medical supply cart. She leaned forward and around it to see. "What did you bring?" she asked. "Whatever it is, please, don't use it against him. He won't understand."

Flustered, Daniel rushed to Luegner at the door. "Don't. He's not ready yet. He uses the best interpretation of what he sees, the most likely probabilities, especially if he's missing a truth." Daniel looked back at Meg and she agreed.

"It's a present, not an intrusion," Luegner said.

"This is his mind. You're bringing it into his mind. How much more intrusive can you get?" Meg said.

"He'll fill in the middle of a memory with a hypothesis. He'll make mistakes. His mind will play tricks, confabulate falsehoods. That's normal. Think about it; we fan through a flip-book with missing pages, but we still conceive a whole movement. He just needs to fill in some more of his pages—he'll get there on his own."

"I have something for you," Luegner said to Packet as he carried the brown paper bag past Daniel, ignoring him completely. "I think you're going to like it." He put the bag on the bed. "I know how to keep only the best of the best secrets, and

I can be better than any magic." He reached into the bag and paused. Then he pulled out a solid white sphere the size of a pomelo, not quickly like a rabbit from a hat, but poised and deliberate like a stolen candy offered to a young boy. "A present for you," he said.

Packet looked at Daniel for approval, but Daniel seemed sad in his nod. Meg came over from the floor to see. Packet took the sphere to his lap with two hands. "It looks like a big grapefruit," he said.

"It's a prototype processor, a 3D fluid lattice. You could fit the whole data hall, two rows of eight servers into its size, if this were a real processor, of course," Luegner said.

Packet rolled the sphere in his hands. It had the weight of a decent toy. It had a fine, smooth-pored texture, like a citrus peel. It was stitched like a soccer ball with pentagonal flaps, but also with two distinct hemispheres that he could rotate between his hands. Burr holes were at the corners of each flap where wires could go in. The flaps had knobs to grasp with two fingers. He pulled one. The flap popped off with its suction release of "tsusk."

"I want you to be a success," Luegner said. "To be successful like me so we can continue to grow stronger together. You will be a marvel upon marvels. Who knows how far we could go?"

Meg moved around the bed, Daniel, and Luegner for a less crowded view.

Packet circled his fingers around the sphere. White and green pulp-like cones descended around spokes to a marble-sized, polished core. The cones fell off with a gentle rub and settled onto Packet's bed sheet. The shiny marble inner core was a blue commingling of even smaller polyomino cells. If real, little packets of memory could bubble up, travel down, or circle about any which way to find its own context—if that's what this magic was for. The toy with its intricate, nested pieces would be delicate to dissect, and maddening to reconstruct. It was art in its most devious form.

He looked up at Dr. Luegner with a silent, agape stare, and at once knew every line, every detail of the man's perfect face.

Daniel bowed his head in defeat. "There," Daniel said as Luegner smiled. "Now he knows you, too. You just witnessed yourself become memorable."

Luegner planted himself on the side of the bed and took Packet's hand into his. "My parents told me," Luegner said to Packet, "that the first name they gave me, Hopkus, came from the words Hippocratic and Opkus—an oath. And my oath to you is that I am a friend of your family, and I will do absolutely everything I can to help you. And if you fail, well then, that wouldn't be much of a surprise about your father." He looked back. "Remember, I don't fail often, and have very few surprises, only the good ones."

"Okay," Packet said. He withdrew his hand and continued the disassembly of his toy.

"If mommy leaves the room," Luegner asked, "where is she?"

"Is she dead?" Packet asked. He kept fiddling, disassembling.

"No," Luegner said. "She's just gone from the room. Object permanence." Luegner looked at Daniel. "Even a toddler would know. To speed things up, why don't you drop your camera filters."

"You're right, he's no more than a toddler for some reason, and I don't know why. But a clear camera on us, on Terri, so soon would shock him, fail him. I want to let him grow into himself, comfortably, not shock him into being someone he's not. Ease him into being the boy, the person we know and love, my son."

"Don't worry," Meg said as she shuffled the tools on the

tray and found the cochlear implant, "If it works, it won't take that long."

"Not take that long, Terri? It only took you shy of eleven years so far," Luegner said.

"What is shy of eleven?" Packet asked. "And why do you keep calling her Terri? She likes to be called Meg."

"Because I'm twenty-two now," Meg said as she swiped the tray clear with her forearm and all its tools were gone. She was definitely angry. She ran for the door.

"Twenty-two!" Packet said with a howl. He fell back against his upright pillow. Now that deserved a laugh. She was exactly the same. And so were her bangs. What a goof. Sometimes she could be so awkward and nothing funny she said could ever change that. He gathered the toy's flaps that fell away from his lap, and held up a little smile of his own for Meg, if she turned back around to see it. "You'll never be twenty-two," he said.

Meg cranked the door handle and pulled. Then she turned without smiling and screamed at him like he had never heard her do before, "Watch me!"

She stepped through the door, and like the insertion of a page into the churn of a flip-book, her hair was pulled back in an instant. The side of her face was thinner. She was taller, crisper. The mechanical closer pulled the door shut behind her. Daniel rushed to the door. Packet craned his neck to see.

Meg was gone. Packet was stumped. He held his breath.

Luegner stood over the nightstand. He opened its drawer and took out the blue, rectangular plastic basket. He handed it to Packet and nodded. Packet accepted it and collected the scattered pieces of what now looked like an old broken toy.

"I'm sorry," Daniel said as he rested his head on Meg's closed door. Then he turned and faced Dr. Luegner.

"You've done a wonderful job here," Luegner said. "You've

earned yourself, and him, a short while to prove it. And if I know Meg, as you know that I do, then I know she'll be perfectly fine, too."

Packet dropped the last section of his toy back into the basket.

"We'll make peace with her, and your boy," Luegner said as he tugged on the cuffs of his sleeves. He showed Packet nothing was in them. "You ready?" he asked as he set the basket on the nightstand, and then he sifted through the pieces of the sphere. "We'll make peace with control." He reassembled two pieces, then found a third. "We'll make peace with freedom." The third piece snapped in and with each successive find and fit, he spoke again, "Hope. Sacrifice. No regrets." He gave the sphere a twist and its core lit up with a bright blue radiance that rose through its pulp-green cones to its white textured skin and emerged as a beautiful aqua. "Control your world and be free in your mind to own it. That's peace."

The sphere had become a gentle nightlight in its basket. The absence of light through the burr holes speckled the soft blue tint that shone on the wall of the room. Luegner slid the basket to the back of the nightstand. He rubbed his hands together and grinned over his shoulder. He was done with his trick, pointed at the overhead light, and snapped his fingers at Daniel. Daniel relented and dimmed the room lights from a dial by the door.

The wall of the headboard was bathed in a luminous blue. "Are you a magician?" Packet asked.

Luegner settled his gaze on Daniel. "If he passes your Blackwell Inversion Test, I'll see what I can do to keep him funded and turned on. Fair enough?"

Daniel looked sickened in the path of the sphere's blue light. "He'll pass. I know he will." He approached the bed and pulled up the doctor's revolving stool from between the curtain and the bed frame. He straightened up the blanket so it would be ready and warm for the night.

"You won't leave me?" Packet asked to the strength and closeness of his dad's face and tucking hands.

"No, I won't ever leave you. I'll always be sitting right here at your side. Here in the very next room." He patted the blanket up around Packet's shoulders and looked at Luegner. "He'll pass. Because I'll teach him everything I know. Everything."

"Will I die when I go to sleep?" Packet asked as his head sank to his pillow and Luegner looked over.

"What? No," Daniel said. "Whatever gave you that idea?"

"Mommy did."

"You're not going to die." Daniel kissed Packet a long goodnight on the forehead. "Go to sleep now. Only for the night. Dream about when you were you. You'll wake up in the morning and I'll be right here when you do."

"You know, Daniel, sometimes I wish I had your style," Luegner said.

Daniel heard, but didn't turn. Instead, he snapped upright and hurried across the room to the supply cart. He knelt down and opened its lower drawer. He rummaged through, filling the room with loud bangs and clattering sounds.

"Do you want to play computer?" Packet asked. He lifted up on his elbows to see.

"Not tonight. It's late," Daniel said. "Here. Take this." He sprang up and returned to the bed with a simple old polished bronze cowbell. It had a loud, jarring clank. "Ring this bell if you need me."

"Will you have your cochlear implant in, too?"

"To you it's a cowbell. To me, it's the 1s and 0s of an instant message."

Luegner leaned in to watch again.

"Will you go find Meg?" Packet asked. "She looked really upset."

"I will. Don't worry."

"Why introduce a cowbell now?" Luegner asked. "He's going to sleep. He can't use it."

"Not yet, he can't. But soon I'll give him my penlight, too." Daniel flipped the light's switch by the door. The lights went out and the sphere's blue glow filled the room from the basket.

"Why?" Luegner asked.

"He has separation anxiety," Daniel said. "Have a boy of your own, you'll understand."

Luegner smiled, maybe a real smile, maybe not. He shook Daniel's hand all the same as he stepped toward the door on the right.

"I know you'll do all you can," Daniel said as he let go of Luegner's hand. Then it looked like Daniel wiped his palm on his pants.

"You were always the smart one in the room," Luegner said.

"No," Daniel said and shook his head. "Wait for him. You haven't seen anything yet."

Daniel's stance blocked the view of Luegner once more, then the door shut with a clank.

Packet pulled the blue plastic basket on the nightstand closer to his head. He was still a little afraid of the dark. The light of the sphere and its dark spots started to pulse.

Daniel stood still and alone by the closed door. He pressed his palms to his eyes, stayed and sighed for a moment, then rubbed his hands up and down his face. He was definitely tired, too.

Packet did what he should to behave under the glow of his new, blue nightlight. He closed his eyes and sleep settled in. His dad was there. His dad was good. He was strong. And he knew his dad would still be there in the morning, if he woke.

THREE
IN HIS HEAD

TODDLER DREAMS FLASHED through young Cessini's mind as he slept in his car seat on a rushed Wednesday of a cool September day in the southwest suburbs of Minneapolis. The car hurried south on the winding, tree-lined pinch of road between Grays and Wayzata Bays. Cessini woke with a startle at a bump in the road. They passed a cemetery and its blurred rush of headstones aligned like rows of white candy in the ground. The road widened, houses passed in a smear, and he nodded off again. His head lolled in his toddler's car seat.

Daniel looked over his shoulder. The car's blinker ticked. Cessini stirred. He arched his back. He was awake and alert as Daniel cornered into the Carver Medical Plaza, swung the car around, and parked in the first empty space by the entrance.

Inside the building, Cessini bobbed in Daniel's arms as Daniel ran past a cone-shaped fountain made of stacked rocks. He dangled the case of Cessini's handmade digital tablet in his supporting hands and then shifted Cessini from his right arm to his left at the reception desk.

"I'm sorry. I'm so late. Can you still squeeze him in?" Daniel asked.

"His name?"

"Last name, Madden. We had to stop at a vendor's. I couldn't get out of work."

"Madden . . . Kassini?" the receptionist asked.

"Yes. It's Cessini. With a C."

Cessini lifted his head from resting on Daniel's shoulder. A young girl was playing with toys on the floor of the waiting area. "Go over there," Cessini said. He pointed.

"He's just here for the booster?" the receptionist asked.

"Yes," Daniel said as he spun around for his own look. A woman was waiting and the girl was on the floor.

"I think we can manage. Have a seat. I'll call you," the receptionist said.

"Thank you," Daniel said. He walked to the waiting area. Its chairs were aligned in a half-square. Daniel settled Cessini down on a chair, but he shuffled forward and slid down onto the carpet. The girl on the floor stared at his every move.

"She must be around two?" Daniel asked the woman who was sitting on one of the wooden chairs.

"Just had her third birthday. August sixteenth."

"That puts them about nine months apart. Cessini will be four at the end of November."

"Is he before or after Thanksgiving?"

"Put it this way: I'm figuring on dishing out leftover turkey with every slice of cake."

"You're lucky." She laughed. "We'll be the queens of summer splash parties and August mosquitoes."

Daniel let out a deep breath to relax. He handed the tablet case to Cessini on the floor. Cessini took it and then Daniel went right back to the woman. "I'm Daniel," he said. "And this is Cessini."

"Robin," the woman said. She held out her hand. "It's nice to meet you. And this here, crawling fearlessly on every dirty floor she can find, is Meg."

Cessini zipped open his tablet's case in the center of the carpeted square. He slipped out a thick, polished digital tablet. He unfurled its eight finger-tab wings from its backside, fanning four out to either side. Meg chewed her knuckles as she watched. Cessini looked at her once, but otherwise ignored her.

"Nine months is a big difference at this age," Robin said. She reached for a communal basket of toys and offered a random one to Meg. It had only lights and recorded beeps, no imagination. Meg tossed it, and then crawled into Cessini's carpet square with more fingers in her mouth. She watched as he fingered the wing-like tabs of his tablet until he swatted her away.

"My turn," she said.

"No. It's mine. I'm using it."

"Mommy. He won't let me play with—"

"Come on," Daniel said. "Give her a turn."

"She never much went for the spinning, mirror toy thingies anyway," Robin said, and then she threw the toy back in the basket. "Probably give kids identity issues right from the start."

Cessini looked at Robin. She talked a lot, he thought.

"I take it no daycare?" Robin asked.

"He goes. But I usually take him everywhere with me. Even to work. Especially on days like today."

Cessini hunched over his crossed legs and protected his tablet. He curled four fingers under the feathered tabs of each side and he wiggled away. He clicked up as if on their natural notes, playing like the keys of a piano. His thumbs clacked the ruffled black keys as sharps and flats aligned on the front sides of the screen. The black skin at the top and bottom was doodled with fluorescent art.

Meg's eyes got wider. She rubbed her palms back and forth over the wrinkles of her pants. She was ready to lunge for a grab.

Cessini scooted away. There were no sounds from his tablet

other than the clacking of keys. He aligned and grouped red liquid-like dots on the screen. Each dot carried a numeral inside.

"That's not being nice," Daniel said. "Let her play."

His fingers clicked away as if to music only he could hear. He combined two smaller dot groups to form a larger cloud. He pulled teardrops of rain down from the cloud into a bucket on the ground before a numbered group evaporated back up, putting the screen in balance. His fingers played, his smile intensified, and then with a twist of the screen he was done. He turned the tablet around for Meg and Robin to see all the numbered red dots balanced within a churning blue sky.

Robin leaned over. "That's amazing. He's really only three?"

"Scary, isn't it," Daniel said. "He does it all in his head."

"What kind of tablet is that? I've never seen one with keys sticking out from its sides."

"The tablet is standard. The keys on its side are mine. I made them, attached and coded them myself."

Robin held out her hand. "I'm sorry, but I must not have been paying attention. I'm Robin. Did I already say that? It's nice to meet you."

"Daniel Madden." He shook her hand and smiled.

"Like the scientist?"

"Yes, like the 'madden' scientist. I get that a lot, but only on the bad days. The rest of the time, you can just call me Daniel."

Cessini swiped his fingers down the screen and pulled in a new, higher level. A doodled font of hexadecimal notation populated the screen. He turned his back on Meg and began his clicking anew.

Meg pouted. She left the carpet to rummage through Robin's purse.

"I'm sorry," Robin said, "but I couldn't help overhearing

when you were at the counter. I'm not in such a rush. She's just here for the spray, too. If you need to, you can go first, or maybe the nurse can do them together?"

"That would be great," Daniel said.

Meg grabbed Robin's small suede case from her purse and crossed back over the square to Daniel. She handed the tan case up to him.

"No, thank you," Daniel said. "Do you like what he's playing with on the floor?"

Meg didn't answer with words but climbed on the empty chair beside Daniel. She pulled and uncurled Robin's ScrollFlex from its case.

"Do I have a choice?" Daniel looked up, asking Robin.

"No, it's okay. Go ahead. She misses that."

"Misses what?"

"Reading with someone other than me."

"I hear you," Daniel said. He took the ScrollFlex from Meg.

Robin got up with her palm pressing her forehead. "I'm sorry, I was just—I'll go see what's holding them up, and if they can take us together."

"Sure," Daniel said. Meg scooted in closer at the arm of his chair. He tapped through letters on her fancier, semitransparent ScrollFlex screen. Images appeared. He touched a portrait of Giovanni Cassini, a man regaled in semi-profile glance and pre-Newtonian powdered locks.

Daniel held up the screen for Meg to see, but Cessini could see straight through it. Daniel framed the man's picture so that Cessini was superimposed with it on the floor. Meg giggled. "Giovanni Cassini," Daniel said. Cessini looked funny with overlaid waves of white hair. "This man here is Cassini, with a 'Ka', not 'C' like my Cessini there on the floor. 'Cee'— Cessini." Daniel winked and Meg ate it up.

"Ceeme," she said and pointed at him past the screen.

"Okay. Ceeme. Close enough."

"Keep reading," she said, grinning. Her short bangs were just falling in.

"The astronomer Cassini discovered the rings of Saturn and calculated the size of the solar system. It was his collected data that led to the calculation of the speed of light."

"I like his hair," she said.

Cessini listened from the floor.

"That is true. I guess he does have nice powdered hair. How about something more age appropriate, what do you say?"

"Okay." She scooted back in the chair and pulled her knees up to her chest. She smiled.

"That's what I thought." Daniel touched through more letters, grinning and wiggling his eyebrows. He enlarged an image with a sepia timeline and read one of its points aloud. "The original Turing test consisted of two simple text conversations with a human judge. If the judge couldn't tell the difference between a human's text conversation and a computer's, then the computer passed."

Daniel looked at Meg. She kicked out her feet and sat back up straight. She giggled. Cessini looked up.

"The enhanced test added images and sound so it would be harder to pass." Daniel lowered the screen. "Can you keep a secret?" he asked and Meg nodded. "I'm creating the En-hanced Inversion Test to go even further." He winked.

She pulled her knees back up to her chest. She giggled.

"In my inversion test, the computer is the test-taker and judge and it has to determine for itself if it's a computer or a human. An epistemology coding turning in on itself. Descartes': 'I think, therefore I am.'"

"Why?" She smiled and kicked out her legs to sit up straight when he looked.

"You want to know the trick? I designed the Inversion test

so the taker would fail the first time. But if that very same taker comes back with a passion, a hope, a genuine force of feeling, then it won't simply be an emotionless computer. It will have passed the test. And in my book, it'll be a human computer."

"Why?" she asked again, about to draw in her legs once more with her giggle.

Daniel held up a finger in front of her big eyes. She paused. "Because . . ." he said and Cessini looked up. But then Daniel dropped his finger and hand in defeat. "I don't know. I don't even know if the logic is correct. I asked myself what it even means to be a computer or a human, and that's what I got—a test that's designed to be failed. The first time."

Robin looked back at their square from the reception desk. The receptionist peered around her, then back up, said something, and nodded.

"But I don't know," Daniel said to Meg. "And the last three years have been so hard for him. And I never thought it would take so much out of me. You know what I mean?"

Meg shrugged, then added with her own great declaration, "When you go to work, you need to bring a grapefruit."

Daniel looked at her. He considered it. "For lunch?"

"Yes." She giggled. "A really big, juicy one, too."

"Okay. I guess that's a little more age appropriate, right?" Daniel said.

"When I was a little, little baby," she said, pinching her pointer fingers and thumbs together and then down to teensy-weensy in front of her nose, "I ate four grapefruits."

"You did, did you?" Daniel asked. He grinned. "Whole grapefruits?"

Meg shrugged. "I dunno. Cuties, maybe?"

Robin swooped in for a rescue. She held out a hand for Meg to follow her and Meg jumped down off the chair. "I'm so sorry. I'll take her now."

"Why?" Daniel asked. He handed Robin's ScrollFlex back up to her. "She asks such good questions."

The receptionist looked up from her desk. "Cessini? Meg?"

Daniel stood up, reached down over Cessini, and snapped shut the feathered tabs of his handmade digital tablet. Daniel scooped him back up into his arms, and Cessini wailed, "Mine!"

Within moments, Cessini was clacking away again on another tile floor. His feet were outstretched on the tiles in front of a black, cushioned bed table.

Meg bounced on Robin's lap as Robin sat on one of two chairs by a nurse's empty desk. Colored cutout posters of healthy inside kid-parts hung crooked with tacks on the walls. Daniel leaned back against the sink with its countertop jars of packets, depressors, and swabs.

"Is she getting her spray for a preschool around here?" Daniel asked.

"Silver Springs," Robin said as Meg climbed back down to the floor.

"Us, too," Daniel said.

"What are you teaching him with all his clicking?" Robin asked.

Meg sat at Cessini's side and stretched her legs out to copy.

Cessini looked up for approval and Daniel nodded. "Look," Cessini said as he flipped his screen around and back again so fast that no one could see it. "Hexadecimal."

"No, seriously. What?" Robin said. She sat up straighter to see.

Cessini clicked the tablet's keys. Graphical wheels of numbers and letters filled a four-space hangman's row. The first wheel over the left space had numerals one through nine. He settled on the numeral two. He spun the adjoining wheels and replaced a twelve with the letter "C" and a fourteen with an "E."

He pressed both thumbs on the black keys at the side and locked in his wheels in the screen. He smiled and nodded when done. He enlarged his completed four-spaces into the center of the screen and held it around. "2CEE."

"I get it," Robin said. She sat back. "To see. That's cute."

"That's us. Me and Meg," he said, then held his tablet's screen higher.

"How is that you and Meg?" Robin asked.

"Plus them," he said. "2,C,E,E." He told her without looking back at his screen: "2+C+E+E. That makes 2, plus 12 for C, plus 14 for E, and plus another 14 for E. Plus up all the numbers. 2 plus 1 plus 2 plus 1 plus 4 plus 1 plus 4. That equals 15. Fifteen is 1 plus 5. That equals 6. Six is two of three. The two of us, her and me, are three."

Robin collapsed in her chair, astounded. She looked across and found Daniel's nonchalance, his arms folded loose at his chest. "How? How could he—?" she asked.

"I just taught him the tools. The rest he does in his head."

Cessini turned his screen back around and cleared it.

"That was excellent, Cessini. I liked it," Daniel said.

"In his head?" Robin asked, shaking hers in disbelief.

Meg's drool ran down her knuckles.

"Don't worry, he makes mistakes," Daniel said. "He's almost four now, yes, but he'll make plenty more mistakes before he's older, too. But that's fine. We all do. Isn't that right, Cessini?"

Meg grabbed the tablet at her first open chance. He held like a bear. "It's my turn, Ceeme! It's my turn."

Cessini yanked harder and with a young mind's instant flip of a switch, he was a toddler once more, a screaming three-year-old no more precocious than raw. "No! It's mine. I'm not done," he said.

She fought. Her screams were shriller than his. "Mommy! Ceeme won't let go," she said as the tablet's feathered tabs bent upward toward breaking.

Daniel swept down and broke away both their grasps. "Stop, don't pull. You'll break it." He jerked it up high to above his shoulder. He stood out of both their reaches.

Robin snatched Meg back up to her lap. "I'm so sorry," she said beneath Meg's ear-splitting cry.

Cessini slumped quieted on the floor. He stared up at the tablet and waited. Daniel paused him with a finger, and then lowered his tablet back down to his grasp. He took it. Daniel was good.

Meg's kicking and wiggling stopped as her lower lip pouted once more.

"So there you have it," Daniel said. Cessini turned his back and hid the tablet from Meg. "And the funny thing is," Daniel said as he rubbed his forehead, "Meg and I just started talking about this in the waiting room. If you ever want to make a computer more human, make sure it's coded to be full of screaming mistakes."

Robin's eyes brightened. "Don't worry. It does get easier, or so I've been told."

Then with three taps on the door, a nurse entered their exam room. With her smooth, green clothes rounded the way she was, she looked like a big green apple with a little medicine basket in her hand. Zoo animals were all over her shirt.

"Hey, kiddos," the nurse said. "Looks like it's going to be two for the price of one today."

"Thank you so much for squeezing us in," Daniel said.

"Please," the nurse scoffed and sat on the revolving stool at her desk. She unrolled her own tablet screen and entered some notes. "Something good's got to come from being a single dad," she said.

Robin grinned as she stroked back the bangs from Meg's forehead.

The nurse whispered behind the edge of her hand. She pointed at Robin, then winked and smiled at Daniel. "She invented PluralVaXine5."

"I didn't invent it," Robin said. She nestled her face into Meg's soft hair and gave her a kiss on the back of the head.

The nurse disappeared behind the cabinet door above her desk, and by rote handed Daniel a couple sample tubes of cream.

"I just worked once for the man who did," Robin said.

"Thank you," Daniel said to the nurse. He uncapped a tube and kneeled in front of Cessini. He squeezed a white dab onto his finger and checked Cessini close up, especially his neck and behind his ears. He dabbed on a few circles of relief. Cessini paid him little mind and unfurled the keys of his tablet to play again.

"I'm sorry," Robin said with a tsk to the nurse. "I guess keeping secrets isn't one of our strongest suits, now is it?"

The nurse rolled on her gloves. "Oh, go on," she said and huffed. She ripped open two clear plastic packs with a nasal-spray applicator in each, and then collected two little brown bottles from her medicine basket. She unscrewed the cap of one bottle, screwed the sprayer top on, and shook the bottle and cap hard between her two fingers and thumb. A rubber stem stuck out from between her two knuckles.

"If I didn't know you both so well," she said as she wheeled herself closer on the stool, "I'd sing a different tune, but boy oh boy, do I feel like the hand of fate today."

"I think you made your point," Robin said.

"Oh, please. 'Minnesota Nice' still exists, doesn't it?"

"You betcha," Daniel said.

The nurse pushed a hand on Daniel's shoulder as she

wheeled passed. "Good. Because I broke all the rules just to get you both in here at the same time. For that, you can thank me later."

Meg was steady on Robin's lap. The nurse was prepared and leaned in. She had the readied brown bottle of PluralVaXine5 in hand. She placed her pointer and index fingers on the tabs along both sides of the nozzle, opposed her thumb under the bottle's base for seating, and shook the contents once more. She placed it under Meg's nose.

"Ready, sweetie? I'll count from three and you go like this." The nurse showed her with a sudden and deep breath in through her nose, her head tilted back.

"Why?" Meg asked.

"This is the last booster you'll need. It will fix you for all kinds of things. It will make you feel better if you're sick, keep you better if you're not." The nurse moved the bottle up beneath Meg's left nostril, then in. "Ready? On three, two, one. . . ."

Meg jerked her head back in exaggerated imitation of the nurse's precise example. The back of Meg's head butted Robin's lip against her teeth and Robin yelped enough for them both. The spray entered Meg's nostril at its periphery, but enough.

"Got it," Robin said. She reached around and wiped Meg's sniffle with her cuff.

Cessini was a perfect patient on the floor where he watched and waited. The nurse took the other applicator from her desk, leaned down, and placed it under his nose without his interest or movement. He didn't care as long as it didn't interfere with the clicking and clacking of his tablet.

"And three, two, one. . . ."

Cessini breathed in a wicked breath, far too deep. He winced. He felt the rush of moist heat high in his sinus. His interior cavity burned and prickled the backs of his eyes. He coughed out his breath and squinted away the burn with a quick shake left, then right of his head.

Then he went back to counting.

"All done," the nurse said.

"So, I guess we'll see you around preschool, then?" Robin asked Daniel.

The nurse sat back at her desk and fastened rubber caps on the nozzles of the bottles. She dropped the secured bottles into two bags, and snapped off her gloves into the trash. "Final dose in twenty-four hours," she said. She handed the marked bags to Daniel and Robin. "Call me if you need me." She got up, cocked her head, pointed at them both, and saw her way out the door. "Take your time. No rush."

The door clicked and Robin stood up with Meg. "I'm sorry," she said as Meg grabbed the bag from her hand. "If you're not too busy running around inventing magical play things for your son, maybe we could get together sometime for a coffee?"

"Share more little monster horror stories?" Daniel asked.

"Well, yes, since you put it that way."

Cessini followed his tablet up from the floor in Daniel's hands as he refolded its wings. "Or, we can get them together for a play date," he said. "Either way, it's my thanks for getting us in when I was running so late."

Cessini stood behind Daniel's leg and locked eyes with Meg, looking down from Robin's arms. Meg looked away and rubbed her nose straight across Robin's shoulder.

"I'd like that," Robin said as she looked at her sleeve. She stuffed Meg's bag from the nurse into her purse. "Fate works in mysterious ways," she said as she twisted her neck to release her hair from the pull of Meg's fist.

Daniel reached into a jar by the sink and handed an alcohol wipe packet to Cessini for having crawled around on the floor.

"'Bye," Cessini said to Meg. He opened the packet and pulled out the wipe.

Meg watched him, but said nothing. She stuffed her knuckles back into her mouth. Robin opened the door and carried her out first. She stretched around the corner to the last moment, watching him unfold the towelette and rub his hands.

Daniel held Cessini's tablet case as he followed out after Robin. Meg eyed the tablet's dangle, and then glared back at Cessini. He pushed his finger into his ear and stuck out his tongue. They didn't get along at all.

Cessini stepped on the pedal of a tall garbage can by the door, tossed the packet's wrapper in, and then ran to catch up with Daniel's hand. He followed Daniel, Robin, and Meg out, but only because he had to. It was better than being alone.

FOUR
COLORS AND CODES

THE GREEN GRASS fields of Silver Springs Elementary in the southwest suburbs of Minneapolis were stimulating and safe. The surrounding trees were stricken with fall color. First and second graders laughed and chased each other around their playground of structures and games. Recycled shredded-rubber chips cushioned their falls from metal apparatus and kept them contained within a safety border of play.

Six-year-old Cessini stood still outside one of the railroad ties that constructed the border. He tore a dry-rub towelette from one of the packets he carried in the front pocket of his fire-red, cotton hoodie. Water, as a recent phenomenon, had started to burn even deeper. He could have let his body go dirty for days without cleaning, but he became meticulous, instead. And as an extra benefit, his packets kept him a step ahead of the first grade battle with germs.

He was disinfecting as usual when a pack of immature boys one grade older darted by from the field. The dew-covered grass under his shoes was a sparkling field of unease. He took a step forward into the border's ring. He made sure his heels stayed secure against the black railroad tie. The reddish-brown rubber mulch was dry. He dared to go no farther in. A cool-water sweat beaded ahead on the red, yellow, and blue jungle gym bars. Fits of chases and laughter swirled by as three older boys circled in, taunting.

"Cessini is a packet. Cessini is a packet," chanted one second grader. The two older boys gaggled in behind him.

"Come on, wet wipe, why don't you come in the ring and play?"

"All wet wipes are a packet. Not all packets are a wet wipe," Cessini said. "That means I'm decidedly not a wet wipe."

"That makes no sense," the second grader said. He laughed.

"It does to me," Cessini said.

"Come on, wet wipe, run," the second grader said as the bell rang and another bully pushed him straight on.

Cessini tripped back over the railroad tie border and fell onto the morning dew. His hands touched down to break his fall. He sprang back up as fast as he hit. He rubbed his hands onto his rough pleated pants. They hurt. He patted them on his fire-red hoodie as a much softer cloth.

The boys skipped backward toward the door as the bell rang. They left him standing on the playground alone.

His hands were dry, but sore. The grounds were almost empty. He reached to the back of his neck with reddened hands and pulled his hood over his head.

The bell stopped ringing and the bullies were gone with a last taunting call. "Cessini is a packet, Cessini is a packet."

He pinched closed his hood around his face and hid. He held back the tears that he didn't want to fall. He waited a moment in silence, and then looked out through the slit of his hood over the green fields of play. He sniffled to dry his nose. He took another packet from his pocket and rubbed the remaining bit of soreness from his hands. He followed a stern wave-in from a teacher at the door, and hurried on his own back to class.

He hated being alone.

*

As Cessini fought the urge to be scared, long-term memories of bullies on a field bubbled up in his mind, but on October fifteenth he was full of strength and pride as he climbed the steps to a stage. The University of Minnesota hosted a pod session and pushed it live for broadcast. On the small stage set with five chairs around a semicircle table, Cessini grabbed the front bottom of his assigned seat and pulled himself in. He sat beside Daniel, who was next to Robin, then two other men, all of them invited experts, including him. The host, who hadn't yet arrived, was expected any minute on a pedestal screen.

Meg sat alone in the front row of the empty theater, waiting and swaying her feet as she began a game of Sea Turtle Rescue on Cessini's borrowed, handmade tablet. She began at its most basic level and took control of a hatchling to cross a dangerous beach and enter the ocean tide. The game had become a fascination, but also an annoying obsession. Nurture a turtle every day as it grew and sought life or leave it unattended as it starved, was attacked, or was lost to the sea, all in a manner of swirls.

Cessini fidgeted in his chair up on the stage, anxious to get his tablet back.

The host arrived on the pedestal screen, sitting in his own private cubicle. An airplane logo scrolled by at the bottom of the screen, followed by *'Origination from the Sea-Tac International Airport at the Port of Seattle,'* and then the complete captioning of their recorded session.

"Okay, then, we're on," the host said. "My apologies first for why I was late and not there with you in Minneapolis-St. Paul. I missed my plane. I'm still at the airport in Seattle. But, welcome, and let's jump right in."

The toes of Cessini's shoes scraped the floor and he stopped his chair from twirling.

"My first question to you is: Does free will exist or are we bound by fate? Did I miss my plane because I'm afraid to fly and busied myself on the way to the gate? Or by the simple fate of traffic snarl? Andy Fisher, let's start with you at this end of our table of experts and go around, ending with a special question for you, young man," the host said to Cessini, "so get ready. Professor, you're our panel's evolutionary psychologist. What do you think?"

"That's a fair question to start," the professor said. "Physically, I think we've reached the height of evolution as a species. But now, I think we're taking the next step forward from our ancestors. Now, what do I mean by that—"

"I'm asking why I missed my plane, not how do I look in the walking lineup of man," the host said with an awkward smile.

"My point is," the professor said, "that various fears developed across the span of history in order to improve survival. Humans developed fear during the Paleolithic Era, or early Stone Age. We had to. And any complete discussion of 'free will versus fate' must throw the evolution of fear into the mix. I think we're evolving psychologically as a species with a new set of fear associations. Fear of too many people, fear of technology. Fear of death itself, thanatophobia. Death fear is surprisingly common today across religions, ages, cultures, and backgrounds. We're evolving a fear of death that's affecting a greater percentage of the population with each successive generation."

"So, you and I are alive today because early humans developed a healthy fear of being eaten by saber-toothed tigers, and they lived to pass on that fear?" the host asked.

"Exactly. During the Mesozoic, mammals developed a fear of heights. Then during the Cenozoic, ape-like creatures added a fear of snakes. And when we humans in the Neolithic Age discovered rats and bugs were carriers of disease and destroyed our food, we became afraid of them, too. Continuing to evolve our fear of death is essential for allowing our species to live."

"So, then, why did I miss my flight?"

"Technology is our next evolution of fear. And as a species, it wasn't only you caught in that traffic snarl. The difference with technology this time around, though, is that we can use our minds to solve where and how far we want it to take us."

Cessini raised his hand, and then spoke. "My dad said he's going to take me and that girl sitting down there to the fair this summer to win stuffed animals and eat some cotton candy," he said. Meg glanced up, but then hunched back down over her game. "I let her play with my tablet. My dad made it for me."

Daniel rested his hand on Cessini's arm.

"Interesting, young man," the host said. "But we'll get to you in a minute." Then the host snapped his fingers and pointed. "Wait a minute, Professor. You dodged my question. Free will or fate?"

"There is no free will to choose," the professor said. "Our fundamental behaviors guide us whether we realize it or not. We're pre-programmed over thousands, millions of years."

"It's far more recent than that—" Robin said as the man next to her sprang forward first.

"I am convinced—" the man interrupted.

"Reverend?" the host allowed.

"I am convinced societal fear is due to the decay of religious unity," the reverend said. "And I wholeheartedly disagree with Andy's evolutionary hypothesis. Individuals who practice their faith most adherently are those least afraid of dying. But an entire generation of technology is taking us further away from our faith. And without faith, we have more fear. More fear raises feelings of loss of control, and with that, the loss of free will. But ironically, this loss of free will one feels, in the absence of religion, more than reinforces my theological view that a higher being is the one in control. Free will belongs only to God."

"If you're suggesting we shut off the flow of technology and everything will be fine," Robin said, "then that's a dream that simply won't work. Speaking both as a mother and cognitive neuroscientist, I can tell you molecular processes are directly linked to behavior. We don't have to go back thousands or millions of years. It's happening now. I've studied fear-conditioning behaviors in the real world, the processes that bring about long-term potentiation, or LTP. LTP is the induction of synaptic plasticity by the electrical or chemical stimulation of the lateral amygdala neural circuits."

"Whoa, you just blew my lateral amygdala circuits," the host said. "Anyone ever tell you that you talk like a computer?"

"I'll vouch for that," Daniel said, leaning in.

"To translate," Robin said, "Fear is learned."

"A chicken pecks on a kernel of corn and gets shocked, so it decides to eat lettuce instead," the host said.

"Exactly. It's called Hebbian synaptic plasticity. For modeling, in the lab, we've already completed large-mammal brain emulation. Soon, we'll be announcing the completed scan and modeling of a human brain in its entirety, beneath the connectome's one hundred trillion neuron pathways, to the level of the synaptome. We'll scan every property down to the individual receptors and small molecules in the synapse, every signal state, including phosphorylation and methylation of the proteins. Given that model, we'll be able to measure the very subjects of our discussion: free will, fate, and fear. But for now, no, it's not free will. It's chemical fate."

Cessini swiveled to find what Daniel was looking for on the ceiling. The lights, the tracks? There was nothing different up there, but then, Daniel's eyes were actually closed, and he was grinning, listening. When Daniel opened his eyes, he looked happily at Robin. She shifted in her chair and ran her fingers across the top of her ear to tuck back her hair. Pressed tight to her lobe was a tiny red earring in the shape of a key. She didn't wear much jewelry but it made her look really pretty.

"Back in grad school, I studied the problem with imagination," Robin said. "How the mind goes immobile in the face of a constant reminder of death. DigiSci was searching for the body's longevity switch, and found the mind's counterpart instead, a death switch, if you will, a trigger. The hypothesis was, by activating that trigger, the person would enliven with a sense of imperative, a 'live now' mentality to enjoy life. But we observed the opposite effect. It depressed the hell out of the mice," she said with a laugh.

"It's nice to see you have a sense of humor," the host said.

"I do," she said. "The mice seemed tormented knowing death was imminent, even suicidal to get it over with. Dizziness, hallucination. And thankfully, DigiSci abandoned that line of research. But some of the early, most promising concepts were refined and repurposed into the development of the early VaXin series of sprays—" She stopped and squinted, put her hand to her forehead. "No. Actually, no. I'm mistaken."

"I don't follow," the host said. "Which sprays?"

Robin put her hands down into her lap and lowered her head. She spoke again, but more reserved. "I agree there's a definite fear of loss of control. A loss of control to government, to technology, to corporate intrusions. So, laws are passed to lessen the impact. One of which is all sims and chatbots must self-identify when initiating a session or are directly questioned."

A digital stamp appeared and rotated at the bottom right

corner of the screen for the HACM Lab US at the University of Washington in Seattle, sister lab to the Human & Cognitive Machines lab, HACM Lab AU in Tasmania.

"Snubbing that law only promotes further unease," Robin said. "People like to know they're not being interrogated and with whom their ideas are being shared. They like to think they have a choice, even though they might not."

"Understood," the host said.

"Reverend, you'll appreciate this," Daniel said. "My father gave me the name Daniel after the man who was called to interpret the dreams of the king."

"I do appreciate the reference," the reverend said, "but who's the king in your analogy?"

"I don't think I've met him yet," Daniel said. "But you never know. Fate works in mysterious ways."

"Daniel, by way of introduction, you're here tonight as an invited guest of Robin Blackwell, alumni of the university," the host said.

"Thank you. Robin was kind enough to invite me and my son as guests of your panel, thinking we might have a unique perspective to offer."

"Thanks to the hand of fate just a few years ago," Robin said, "our paths crossed over our children. We met at a doctor's appointment. If one of us wasn't early or late, we might never have met."

"It was me. I was late," Daniel said.

"Congratulations," the host said. "It looks like fate is the unanimous winner so far."

"No, just a minute," Daniel said. "I think the most direct answer to your question on why you missed your plane is algorithms. It's not because of what happened millions or thousands of years ago or even what we've learned in our lifetimes. It's because the algorithms in our brain are processing far faster than we are even aware. All possible decisions are pre-calculated in the microseconds before your body responds, or you even know why you've made such a decision in the first place. Your brain decided on a 0 or a 1 before you even know why you picked a door on the left versus a door on the right. Understand the 0s and 1s of the brain, and you can play the mind like the keys of a piano. Tune an off key. Replay entire days. Reduce the spikes that are too painful to bear. So given the advantage of microsecond speed, I'd have to say fate is the winner. That is, according to my first attempt with the question."

"I've reviewed your bio," the host said to Daniel. "You have no formal education. Bringing you here to this stage, Robin is the biggest success you've had to date, is she not?"

"I am self-taught, yes," Daniel said, "and you're pretty transparent, you know? You're mixing your context references. But to answer your question, yes, Robin's invitation 'to date,' as in bringing me here with her to speak, is my biggest success."

The host ticked a smile. "Maybe you mixed your references. Being that this is your biggest success 'to date,' as in 'up until now.' So, tell me in your own words, why are you here?"

"Did you know he still listens to really old music," Cessini said. "And he still makes his own parts by hand sometimes instead of printing them."

"I'm nostalgic for the old days," Daniel said as Robin snickered. "But I'm learning. Teaching myself to code. I've got some great ideas on a new kind of test, I think. An inversion test." Then he glanced up at the host on the screen. "You'd love it. I'm also thinking of self-publishing a paper on algorithm compression, maybe kernelling. I don't have that fully fleshed out yet, but I think it could transform robotics. I don't know where it'll take me. But as a dad, I interpret fate and free will every day." He nodded like he figured out something great.

"So, I guess you could say by interpreting Cessini's world that, yeah, maybe that makes him the king."

"That's a wonderful segue," the host said. "And as a father myself, so you don't think I'm a complete faux pas, I have a founders' relationship with the prestigious *Journal of Advanced Design and Computational Dynamics for Intelligent Systems.* If one of your papers pan out, submit it to me. I'll see what I can do."

"Thank you," Daniel said, humbled. The host seemed sincere.

"You're very welcome. So, introduce your son so he can grant us his unique perspective on our topic of free will versus fate."

Daniel leaned forward with his elbows up on the table. He pinpointed his focus with his fingers scratching his brows. "Throughout all of history, we have had a symbiotic relationship with water. In order to live in this world, one must learn not to be reactive to water. Seventy percent of our bodies are made of water. Technology is ubiquitous, like water. Since we don't genetically fear water, we shouldn't genetically fear technology."

"And I don't," Cessini said.

"Don't what?" the host asked.

"Fear technology," Cessini said. "I like it. But I'm reactive to water. Genetically, we think. *Aquagenic urticaria.*"

"Precisely," Daniel said as he mapped out mental notes on the table with his hands. "By evolution, Professor, he shouldn't be reactive to water, but he is. By psychology, Robin, he shouldn't be conditioned to like water, but he does. Maybe that learned fear will come next, Reverend. We're all hoping not. But for now, he's moving forward, not fearful. I even just got him a wave machine that he wanted, and made a sort of bellows lamp in the shape of a squid to go with it that he absolutely loves."

"Your reactivity to water is not your imagination poking beneath the surface?" the host asked Cessini. "A fear of water induced by some previous event?"

Cessini looked up and shook his head. Daniel said, "No."

The host stopped short of a follow-up question as a pixelated logo of *"DNWR,"* appeared at the lower right corner of his podium screen. "This has turned into quite the serious discussion," the host said. "And what are you going to be when you grow up?"

"I dunno," Cessini said as he swiveled in his chair, then said with bright, lucid eyes, "Maybe I'll walk on the sky and save everybody before a giant spaceship comes crashing, *plhssss*, and explodes all over the planet." He bumped and crashed his fist across the desk.

"Like a superhuman?" the host asked.

"Yeah." Cessini grinned with a bob of his head. "Something like that. My dad and I can make anything happen. I'm also going to invent a fireman's hose without water."

"That already exists as foam," the host said.

"But mine's going to shoot nano-tech cells that catch and slurp up the fire back into the hose."

Daniel folded his hands on the table as he leaned in toward the host. "Technology doesn't kill the imagination of children. It lets it fly. We might not have free will according to all of our answers so far. But I can only talk about what I know. We're here in the now, and technology is here to stay, whether we like it or not. Robin is right. There is no source you can just go and shut off. And this gets to the point of exactly why we're here."

Daniel closed his eyes and all waited in silence. "Everyone has a digital life assistant in the dash of their car, the devices they carry, the particles in the clothes they wear. All this frees the human mind to run with its own ambition and dreams. Human potential ignites with its own power, and that power feeds back around for the creation of more and greater computer code. The unseen, wonderful beauty of code. Think about it. It's beautiful, magical, structured, and clean. I go to sleep dreaming about an unseen world of colors and codes. I wake up falling in love. If that dream of true emotion is by any hope some small measure of my doing, then I declare my second answer to your question firmly on the side of free will. My freedom to choose. And for that, I know, Cessini will be right at my side."

Cessini swiveled in his interview chair, proud as a son could be.

The host turned again to Cessini. "Well, young man, you stick with a father like yours, and I have no fear you'll get everything your heart desires," he said. "But unfortunately for me, my fear is that when you get older, you'll have forgotten all about this interview and the quality time you've spent here with me."

Cessini shrugged his shoulders and spun his chair by force of a single hand on the desk. "No, I won't." He pushed for a faster twirl. "We only forget the bad and remember the good."

"Well, thank you," the host said. "I'll take that to mean you think I'm a good host."

"Yeah, I do," Cessini said as he skidded two hands on the desk and smiled back as he stopped. "I know I'll remember this time."

"The long-term effects of a lot of things are unknown," Daniel said. "Technology, good or bad, can unleash the power of the mind or take us down the next evolutionary step of fear. We need to choose wisely. The world needs a canary, don't you think? To keep us on the right path. Long term . . . my bet is on Cessini and the triumph of free will. But then again, it's a fight with whatever strength you put into it. And as already said, fate has a pretty big head start."

Daniel winked at Cessini adoringly, a connection only they two could share. No camera could have caught it. A memory imprinted on a soul. A packet. A moment he could remember.

"Well, Daniel," the host said, "it appears you may very well have found your king."

"He's my protégé. My number one engineer."

"The king . . . Now that sounds good," Cessini said.

"Very well, then, young king, now that Daniel has brought us full circle from time's immemorial fate to the 0s and 1s of passionate free will, I now have my one question for you. In the face of fate, free will, and fear, you've managed to keep your mind in line with your true self and dreams. So, tell us," the host smiled. "Tell us, what is your forecast for the world?"

"Not good," Cessini said with a spin.

"Not good?" the host exclaimed.

Cessini kept up his twirl with a grin. "Yup, not good."

"And there's nothing we can do about that?" the host asked.

"Not according to all of them. But then again, I'm the one who's going to be king and the battle to win my mind is going to be epic," Cessini said as he dragged his toes on the floor to slow. "And like my dad says about him and me against the rest of the world, as a backup we'll always have hope."

"Hope," the host said and turned to Daniel, "I like that."

"Well, that should count for something," Cessini said as he shrugged and his chair stopped.

Daniel relaxed into his chair with his fingers clasped at the back of his head.

"Yes, it does, with epic proportion," the host said as his eyes redirected toward a void at the back of the stage. "For those of you just tuning in, I will repeat my disclaimer and auto-identify. As you may or may not have recognized, I am an autonomous host reporter, residing wholly within the Blue Planet mainframe at Digital News and World Report, DNWR version 4.7.022, operated remotely by the HACM Lab US at the University of Washington, Port of Seattle. All interaction is based on my RK3 processing core and is not representative of DNWR's opinion or position on any issues. Viewpoints are entirely my own. You plan, I scan. Available twenty-four hours per day, any topic, anywhere."

From down in her hardback seat in the vacant audience below the stage, Meg looked up from her screen of Sea Turtle Rescue put on pause. She had created a beautiful set of swirls that she loved, of mineral-rich sediments rolling in the glistening current of a bay. Her turtle's flippers added a higher-layer detail of four repeating eddies within rays of light—a set that was, for her, a creation of perfect. She tilted her head for impression. It was a heartfelt design that could only be called art, a delightful vision with the potential to cure the soul.

She liked it, but couldn't submit it for points in a contest. Cessini was getting up on the stage. She leaped up in her seat to follow him and go. She flicked the tablet's feathered keys to save. Maybe she'd remember to send it in to a contest later, and get a sticker in return to share with her dollies or press on the frame of her bed.

She ran up the stairs to the stage. As long as she gave Cessini his tablet back in the car on the ride home, everything would be fine.

Cessini, who once believed there were only humans, looked at the host's frozen eyes on the screen and knew that there were fake humans and bots now, too. He took Daniel's hand in his as he got out of his swivel chair to go home, and smiled with his simple shrug. "Who knew?"

He walked from the stage a bit taller and mightier than on approach. He was going to be king. And his next battle, in whatever form it was going to take him, was going to be epic.

FIVE

TECHNOLOGY MAKES TWO

D ANIEL CLAPPED A hardcover chapter book shut. Cessini lay on the bed in his darkened bedroom and ran his hand across a mural of trees and waterfalls painted on the wall at his bedside. He still liked to trace his fingers over the cascading blue falls. An orange plastic cup with a straw was not quite full on the nightstand. Daniel tossed the closed book into a blue plastic basket, slid the basket under the bed, and nearly made it to standing-up-straight for lights out.

"Wait, don't go," Cessini said. He reached up with his hand.

"Come on, it's late. It's a school night. And I've still got work to do."

"I'm scared."

"Scared of what?"

"I don't know. I just don't want to go to sleep."

Daniel leaned for the cup on the nightstand and handed it to Cessini. "Take a sip, close your eyes. You'll be asleep in no time."

Cessini drew a shallow sip through the straw.

"Don't drink too much or I'll be changing the sheets in the morning." Daniel winked.

Cessini coughed back up into his straw. He dropped the cup onto his pillow.

"What are you doing? I just said don't drink too much." Daniel grabbed up the cup before the top came off and the water spilled.

Cessini turned to his side and propped up on his elbow. He forced a hard swallow.

"You okay now?"

Cessini relaxed and nodded a bit, but his frown was truer. He started to tear up. "Daddy?"

"What? Tell me."

"I think I'm getting worse."

Daniel slapped the cup down on the nightstand. "Okay, stop. I can't do this right now. Worse? How?"

Cessini found his breath and closed his eyes. It was an easy bit of relief.

"Did it go down the wrong pipe?" Daniel rubbed Cessini's chest as he lay his head down on his pillow. "Tough love, come on, how's that? There, is that better?"

As soon as Cessini's head hit the pillow, he shot back up to a seated position and barked out a loud, croup-seal cough. He gagged and clenched the sheet in two fists.

Daniel dropped down to kneeling at the bedside. He stroked a hand on Cessini's back. "Hey! What are you doing? Are you choking? Talk to me."

Cessini breathed in quick, shallow puffs. "I'm okay."

Daniel grabbed the cup from the stand. "What did you put in here?"

"Water," he said. "It was just water. I put in water from the sink."

"Did you put your thickener in it?"

Cessini nodded, then gagged and coughed out a spit. He drew air in deep through his nose.

"What's happening? What are you doing?"

Cessini's eyes rounded. His chin clamped down on his

chest. His throat seized shut. His shoulders arched up, his back rounded over.

Daniel thrust his left hand behind Cessini's back. "I got you!" Cessini spasmed into a tight, rigid ball. Daniel forced his right hand between the steeled tendons of his knees. Daniel spun him up in a heave from the tangle of sheets and into the cradle of his arms. "We're going to the hospital."

Cessini let out a long, hollow sigh. Then his arm fell limp at his side.

"Cessini!" Daniel screamed. "Wake up!"

Daniel lunged with Cessini in his arms, whirled, and banged himself free out the bedroom's door.

Packet was sound asleep in his bed when his warm blanket cover was pulled down from the tuck of his chin. Daniel's hand was on his shoulder and shook him awake enough to talk.

"Wake up," Daniel said. "I want to tell you something important."

Packet turned while still groggy and faced the blue glow of the sphere in the nightstand basket.

"I think your problem is from a combination of things," Daniel said. He stroked Packet's hair off his forehead. "That's why you still think you're so young and not yourself."

Packet murmured without allowing himself to wholly wake from under the warmth of his blanket. "I said I'm okay."

"Your memories have a problem ordering themselves long term from short. I'm going to update a few routines in the kernel."

"I was dreaming. Dying is good; the pain goes away," Packet said with his eyes still shut.

"No. Dying is not good. I want no part of you to die. Do you hear me?"

"Where's Meg? I want to talk to Meg."

"She needed a break. She's not here right now." Daniel looked toward the door. "But I can find her. I can bring her back."

"She didn't say 'goodbye.'"

"When? Do you mean at the doctor's office when you were three? She watched you intensely. She wasn't old enough to say 'goodbye.'"

"No, she was right here. She left out that door and her hair got short."

Daniel stood away from the bed. "That's because you really scared her this time. She doesn't believe you're Cessini."

"Who's Cessini? I think I once knew a boy named Cessini."

Daniel grit his teeth. "Then you are getting worse." He wheeled the metal pole to the side of the bed. He squinted in the dark. He fiddled through his kit on the instrument tray. "And *you* are Cessini," Daniel said as he looked for a tool. "I think there's a problem with your kernel that replicates neurogenesis in the hippocampus. Up here. In your head. There's one cell type that does two different things as it ages. When the cell's young it creates new memories. But as it ages, it changes itself, so you can remember the past. That's the cell's aging process I emulated." He found a cotton swab. "But I think I calibrated the coefficients of change wrong. So now your short- and long-term memories are all confused. I made a mistake."

Packet settled his head back onto his pillow.

Daniel prepared his inner elbow with the swab. "I think I fixed that code, I'll reorder it for you. But you also need something more fluid to go with it. A secondary sort criteria." He adjusted the length of tube hanging from a new watery bag.

"Tell me and I'll remember," Packet said. He looked away as the needle stung.

"The first sort criterion is cause and effect," Daniel said. "When you were first born as Packet, you learned to breathe, which felt good. That was one circumstance, one memory. And as Cessini, you drank water, and you choked. Also one circumstance, one memory."

"Okay," he said as his eyelids fell shut longer than they stayed open. The tube was in and the water's nutrients flowed. "I was dreaming of a waterfall."

Daniel sat closer. "Yes, you were." He pushed the glare from the blue basket away.

A warmth entered Packet's arm. It tingled up past his jaw and circled within his head.

"The second sort criterion is going to be a lot harder for you to get," Daniel said. "It's belief and know. Two circumstances, two memories pulled apart by time, but that aren't in contradiction to each other. Two different circumstances. One person. One you. Talk to me, so I know you understand."

Packet nodded as the swirl settled in his head. The blue sphere in the basket pulsed. The dark pinprick spots moved around in the blue-lit room. They could almost be counted. One spot even stayed on Daniel's face as he bobbed in and out of its path to talk.

Daniel slapped his hand on the bed and got Packet's attention back. "Listen to me. I need you to do this for me." He held out his two hands like a scale. "One old belief that's wrong . . . here . . . gets outweighed by new knowledge that's right . . . here. These two hands are not the thoughts of two different people. One is the younger you, the other one is the older you. You're still the same person. There's no contradiction. It's the same you right here in the middle of a scale. A scale that is centered up here in your head and that gives you the ability to change your mind. Form a memory."

"I understand."

"You string a bunch of these little kernels of memories together and your identity will start to take shape—it will form you. You'll be no one but you."

"Okay. I heard you," he said, but his head rested on his pillow, soft and dear.

"Then, once we've got all that down, all that will be left is for you to understand the world in which you live." Daniel reached up and squeezed the bag. It flowed. "And I'll get you there—I'll teach you the tools. Everything I know. We'll get you there together, don't worry."

"I like playing computer with you," Packet said as the dripping water satiated his thirst.

"Me, too." Daniel smiled, at last. He combed his fingers through Packet's bed-pressed hair. "Now I need to tell you one more thing. I know it's a lot for you to think about now, but if you could do just one more thing for me? Remember I want you to think about the number 448. It's a code, your code."

"You mean 448 Treeline Drive?"

"Yes. I set the number as your key. I can't tell you how to solve it, but I know you can do it on your own. One day Luegner's going to ask if you found it, and I need you to say you at least tried."

"I want to go home." Packet's eyelids fell shut, and stayed.

"I know. I'm doing the best I can."

Packet rolled away to his other side. The penetrating blue glow was a waking bother.

"Now sleep. Process what I told you for as long as you want. Come back as you. I know Meg will be right here when you wake up."

Daniel pulled the cover up to Packet's chin and he drifted back toward the darkness of night. Daniel reached for the cowbell on the nightstand and silenced its clank. He set it against the edge of the pillow. "Ring the bell if you need me."

Packet rolled back over to face Daniel and the blue basket as he slept. He pushed his hand under his pillow. The bell fell with a loud clank on the floor. "I'm not a baby anymore," he said with a grimace, but could no longer stay awake. "I don't need a bell anymore," he whispered as he faded and his breath steadied into a rhythm. Tiny blue specks danced around the insides of his eyelids and he sank deep into the rest of his dream.

Seven-year-old Cessini counted all of nineteen dark-spotted beetles and flies dancing and clinking against the tubes of a fluorescent fixture. He sat on a steel mesh bench against a cinder-block wall. It was the first year his shoes touched the floor. The bathroom's stink was not so bad at the room's hairpin entrance. The room itself was built like a square bunker of blocks.

He slouched over Robin's ScrollFlex. It wasn't his tablet with side-mounted keys that Daniel designed, but it was still good. The ScrollFlex's clear screen was a see-through magnifier of the urinals and stalls. He shook it and pictures and text appeared. He finger swiped through the pictures on the screen while Daniel and Robin gabbed outside the block wall, but within earshot of the entrance.

"So here we are. What about you?" Robin asked Daniel outside. "How'd you end up creating these incredible gadgets for your son?"

"After school, back in my father's shop, when I was younger," Daniel said, "I built the coolest robot you ever saw. I couldn't get a job, so that's where I fiddled. I was working on a really great one, too. Until I crossed a few wrong power cells and the whole place just about went up in flames. Also known as, 'Son, your work here is done. You graduated, go travel. It's time you learn to be on your own, if you get my point.'"

"Ouch," Robin said.

"Right, so I figure, okay forget the robot, software is where it's at. Couldn't afford to go back to school, so I learned coding all on my own. Turns out I've got a good mind for it. I'm a systems engineer. The body's a whole system. I figure if you lose the body, save the mind, instead."

"Lots of people are working on that. With a lot more resources than you."

"I know. Maybe they'll all beat me to it, maybe not. But, anyway, I remember everything from those days alone with my dad when I was young. And I still love to tinker on the lathe, turn square columns of metal down to round. See what a precious piece of work comes out the other end. It may not turn into anything, but that's okay. I build these gadgets for Cessini because it's what I love."

Cessini flipped across the ScrollFlex's images of squared tiles. The animal pictures he found seemed best. He chose the driest-looking pig he could find and started the video, volume low. On the screen, an African wild boar foraged the green shoots of a valley floor. Between the rocks and dusty trails, it still managed to find enough to eat and grunt on. "Do animals have free will?" the narrator asked. "Or do they follow their noses to the first tasty treat that keeps them alive for another day?"

"So, are you still loving the madness of school with your little monster?" Robin asked. Her voice was more distant from the entrance.

On the screen, a spotted hyena stalked through the tall grass of the valley's ridgeline. "Do the hyenas choose where they lope?" the narrator asked.

"I've been busy, so 'loving,' no. But, I'll tell you, you don't know what loving is until the two of you come out together on the other side of a bad bug."

"Has he been sick?"

"A couple years ago. Three days of bad diarrhea and vomiting," Daniel said. He was close to the entrance. "I bent down, wrapped my arms around him for a hug before heading to the hospital. I could feel him thinner, lighter, he'd lost so much weight. He couldn't cry. His tears were dry. He laid his head on my shoulder and wrapped his little arms around my neck. He just rested there a moment before we left for the ER. He said 'Daddy,'—and that was all—he fell right back asleep. And he could, because he knew I was there to make him better."

The boar scratched into the dirt at the end of a dry ravine where a ridgeline converged. The hyena sprang from behind. The chase was on. The boar wailed and squealed. It scrambled up the point of the ravine. The hyena nipped at the kicking heels of the boar. A hoof hit the hyena's muzzle and the hyena tumbled down. The boar made it up to the grassy ridge. It cut left on the ridgeline, escaped.

"I've been lucky with Meg," Robin said. Her voice cracked. "So, you really burnt down your father's shop?"

"Yup. Guilty as charged."

A pack of hyenas lying in ambush sprang from the whole face of the grassy ridge. They enveloped the boar and closed in a U-shaped formation. The boar went mad with fear. The hyenas clamped tighter and laughed. A hyena took the boar over the edge. They rolled down the pebbled slope as the upper pack swarmed down. The boar scrambled for a hollow in the dirt. It kicked up dusty clouds, flailing before the ripping, tearing agony began.

"Hyenas devour from the rear," the narrator said. "They rip hind legs from sockets."

A hyena's muzzle clamped onto the boar's nose. It lapped the blood with a curdling snicker. The boar's eyes widened and froze. Its forelegs were splayed by the pack. Its movement was choked. Its body was drawn and quartered.

"The animal's body has a merciful shutoff switch," the narrator said, "A trigger for an end, a tether to death when the anguish and pain of life is too great. Does an animal have free will? In its pursuit of life? Acceptance of death? In an instant, its choice was carved in blood. The carcass beneath the ravenous pack was once a wild boar. Now heartless, it was nothing like that anymore."

Cessini put the tablet on his lap with the giggles of a hungry pack quieting into the end of the video's play. He was scared but he couldn't run, not like at school. At school, he would have been the boar.

Daniel was laughing as he was close again at the entrance. "I'm not making this up," he said to Robin. "In the year eighteen ninety-five, there were only two cars on the road in the state of Ohio and they crashed."

"Come on, everybody says that one, but I heard it's not true," she said.

"Okay, then how about this one? The first person to die in a car accident was Mary Ward. She got run over by her very own car that she was driving at the time of the accident."

"Now that sounds ridiculous," Robin said.

"No, seriously. Steam-powered. In 1869. She was driving, fell out, and landed underneath her own car. She ran herself over. And that was that."

Cessini tapped his feet. He had to go, bad. A small boy finished in the stall. "I'm done," the boy said. His voice was young. His legs were too short for his feet to touch the floor. The shoes of a man facing him shuffled. There was nothing wrong with a man helping his boy in a stall. At school they said no strangers. He knew that. But this was different. His daddy was helping.

The sink's faucet dripped. And so his mind went back to the water—always the water that burned. Why did he have to be so afraid?

"Okay, you got me," Robin said. "What's the story with knowing historic car accidents?"

"You want to hear another one?"

"Sure, why not. One more."

"Two victims in the car," Daniel said.

Cessini rested his head against the cinder block wall. The small boy stood up onto his toes as he turned around. The toilet paper roll sounded like it spun out easy. The paper's tail touched the floor.

"Bad accident," Daniel said. "Neither of the two victims remembers any of it. On a networked piggyback lane. The network controlled the cars bumper-to-bumper—on 169 North about to pass the loop of the 101 East on-ramp. Supposed to be immeasurably—'immeasurably,'" he quoted, "safer than human-controlled cars at their tight distance. The baby was less than a year old in a rear-facing car seat. His mother was driving. It was a beautiful day. Their windows were open. A hacker took control of the network."

"I didn't hear this," Robin said.

"A hacked car darted in from the loop of the 101 East on-ramp into traffic. The mother's car instantly overrode the network to get its control back. It cut hard right to avoid the incoming car. The internal control sent her tumbling over a fifty-foot embankment. Sixty miles per hour. Rolled the car, the baby, and his mother three times. They landed in a catchment pool. The airbags deployed. The mother was knocked out. They were upside down, with the windows open, her head below the water level of the pond. It wasn't deep, but enough. The baby was safe. He was buckled tight in his car seat in back. He stayed inches above the water. He could breathe," Daniel said.

Cessini looked to the opening of the bunker. Daniel's voice trailed away. His shadow got smaller on the wall.

"When the fire rescue got to the baby," Daniel said, "he was screaming hysterically, hanging upside down in his seat, staring into the water just below his face. He was completely out of his little mind. His mother drowned at the scene. She died. But Cessini, the baby, lived."

Cessini shook his legs and knees together. He rocked himself on the bench. He looked back to the door. Daniel wasn't coming. His eyes started to tear.

"But I'm sure he doesn't remember any of it now," Daniel said.

It couldn't be true, Cessini thought.

"And technology makes two. A once happy three became two," Daniel said.

Robin didn't answer.

The stall door opened and the small boy came out with his father. He was a preschooler. He climbed the stepstool at the sink. His father stood behind him and helped every inch of the way. The boy pushed the knob on the faucet for a timed water flow. He pumped the soap dispenser. "Rub, rub, rub, before the water stops," the boy's father said as they pushed the water knob again, together.

Cessini's lip quivered. His dad was too busy with Robin and she wasn't his mother. His had died and now he knew how. She was gone and wouldn't wake.

"And when you're done," the boy's father said as he reached, "you push this lever for a paper towel to come out. I always use the back of my hand in case there're germs on the handle. That way, you don't have to wash your hands all over again."

The father lifted the boy off the stool. A sign was taped over the mirror. It read, "All food service workers must wash their hands." The small boy waved to Cessini, then took his father's hand as they left.

"Hang on," Daniel said, "I just want to check on him a second." Daniel popped around the corner of the hairpin entrance. "How's it going? You ready?"

"No. Not good. I don't want to go anymore."

"Looks like the stall is empty now. You know how to go. So, go on, try before we get in the car. Hurry up. It looks like clouds are coming. I'll get us some cotton candy for the ride, okay? Now go. I'll be right out here if you need me."

Cessini nodded and scooted forward on the bench. Daniel was nudged from behind. Two older boys skirted by to enter. They were laughing by the time Cessini shuffled back onto the bench.

"Oh, hey, Packet. How's it going? Got a wet wipe?" the older bully sneered.

"Hey, wet wipe," the other bully said.

Cessini wiped his nose on the cuff of his sleeve as the two boys shoved each other over to the urinals. Daniel was gone, again. The boys snickered as they stood and went.

"I bet you miss her terribly," Robin said outside the wall.

"Like burnt shop oil," Daniel said.

"Like what?" Robin asked.

"At my father's shop," Daniel said. "I made hundreds, maybe a thousand axle pieces on a lathe. About yea big, finger to elbow. Started off square. I turned each down into intricate detail, layers of curves. As the lathe spun with the right amount of shop oil, my chisel ground away the corners and burrs to reveal the shaped axle hiding under the steel. And I only ever broke one. I pushed too hard with the chisel and that one axle broke through. The one I couldn't fix."

"What's the matter, wet wipe?" the older bully said as he zipped. "Ain't you going to go like your daddy said?"

"He can't. Remember?" the other bully said.

"Oh, yeah, that's right. He probably goes like a girl."

"I do not."

"Don't laugh," Daniel said, "but his mother reminded me of all the beautiful, perfect parts you could make with the right amount of shop oil. And when she died, the thought of that one broken axle, the one I pushed too hard and broke, came back into my mind, like the burning smell of shop oil. She was broken and gone. And there was nothing I could do to fix it. Cessini doesn't remember her, but sometimes I think he misses her more than he knows."

The older bully stopped at the sink, but he didn't wash his hands. He jacked the knob five times with a hammer fist. He cupped a handful of water from the faucet and threw it at Cessini on the bench. Cessini flinched, drawing his head into his shoulders. The splash didn't reach. He froze, afraid.

"See you later, wet wipe," the older bully said. He flicked his fingers with a splash of water as they passed and left.

Cessini put on his bravest face, but only when no one was left to see. "My name isn't wet wipe, it's Cee—I have super powers," he said. He touched his shoes to the floor then looked up at the sinks. "My name is Ceeborn. I can breathe and swim underwater and I'm so not afraid of you." His watery eyes settled on the fluorescent bulbs in the ceiling that hummed and the flying bugs that clanked on the tubes.

Where was his dad when he needed him most?

Then a muted flush sounded from the other side of the wall.

He slipped down off the bench and stepped across the paved floor to the sink. The ScrollFlex's screen had caught a few drops of water from the bully's splash. He pushed the towel dispenser's handle with the back of his hand and tore free a paper towel. He wiped the screen dry with care. He tucked the

ScrollFlex under his arm and looked back at the empty room.

The stall door was open. The bunker was his. But he didn't have to go anymore. He was only seven, but already so alone. If Daniel wasn't there when he needed him most, then when? No wonder he always missed his mother more.

Outside the wall, Daniel and Robin were gone. They were already far away. They were standing by a cotton candy vendor in the crowded fair street. Daniel bought a swirl of candy, but at his distance, it didn't look so good anymore.

Meg exited from the other side of the bathroom's dividing wall. Cessini's handmade tablet with its side-mounted keys was tucked under her arm. With both their parents so far away, she came to his side, took his elbow with her hand, and led him away from the entrance.

"Come on, Ceeme," she said. "I'll take care of you now."

She must have heard everything, he figured, so he let her hold his arm. She walked at his side as they made their way to the candy cart under the skies grayed with clouds. The vendors along the row raised their umbrellas in anticipation of rain. But the life of the Summer Festival and their play-date had already turned a painful corner.

"Do you want your tablet back?" Meg asked as they walked.

He wiped a sniffle before the tears fell. The lower lids of his eyes were red and started to sting. "No," he said, "you can have it. My dad made it for me. I don't want it anymore."

"I'd give you the ScrollFlex. But I can't. It's my mom's."

"I know."

They reached Daniel and Robin at the cart and Meg turned even nicer. "I don't feel much like staying for the fireworks," she said to Cessini. "Do you?"

"No," he said with the touch of her arm in his. "But I could probably win you an animal before it rains."

"I'd like that," she said. "That would be nice."

And to think, by the look of their parent's grins, Daniel and Robin on their own date thought everything was great at the fair.

The windows of the second-floor break room in the DigiSci building were black well past the dark of night. Terri slouched over a small, white mushroom-stem table. Her mug was untouched. She drilled her mind down into a worn groove as she rubbed the edge of her thumbnail into the layers of the Formica top. A dark-brown resin was layered over a pressed-wood core. She didn't start the scratch, but its ridgeline felt right to her touch. Daniel broke her focus by dragging up a chair that screeched against the floor.

"The only memories stored were those powerful, dying ones he had during the upload. He's exaggerating, thinking he's worse than he was," Daniel said. "Only his frightened, traumatized packets came through. That's why it's not him. We didn't capture his natural state. But you need to see what I saw. At the festival. He needed you."

Terri slouched back into her chair, lost from rest. "He needed me then, or now?"

"Both. Long-term and short. I adjusted the coefficients of change for the code of his cells, to speed up their aging so he remembers the past. If it works, he'll remember more detail, mature faster; connect the past with the present. The whole nature of his thinking will change."

"Listen to yourself. You have no idea, do you? You're guessing. Hoping."

"He thinks he's safe in the hospital. He's confabulating who he thinks he is. It's not him, but it's a start. I think 'belief and know' will work—"

"Dashboards of cars have better chatbots than this wreck,"

she said as she sat straighter up. "And 'belief and know?' It first came out thinking it was a blob of numbers, then, ooh and ah, a human, but barely. Okay, now it imagined the body of Cessini. It's his face represented, old memories stored, but it's still not him behind the eyes. And it'll never be. It can't be. He died. It's going to crash itself and die, like all the others. I can't go through that again. I won't."

"This wreck *is* Cessini," Daniel said and slammed his hand on the table, then he lifted and pointed his finger to her face. "I am not leaving my son. My son! He needs me now. He needs me. Not you."

She froze.

Daniel was flustered, enraged. He kicked back his chair and circled away from the table. "I'll work on his critical thinking. Filter out contradictory ideas. I'll temper all the spikes we scanned. But don't quit on him. Please. He's afraid. I know it's him because he's afraid of water."

"*It's* afraid of water because *it's* a computer," she said.

"He's not a computer. Don't say that."

"Your program developed an association and fear."

"Did you ever feed this computer water? No. He has a fear of water because he is Cessini. And Cessini was a human who knew he was reactive to water."

She crossed her arms over her chest and fell back into her hard, scooped chair.

"He's carried it with him," Daniel said as he sat and pulled his chair back up to the table. He pushed her mug away, and leaned in closer to her. The liquid jiggled in rings in the mug. "Since when do you drink black water," he asked and she slipped out a nervous laugh.

"Maybe it figured out computers and water don't mix. So it gave itself *aquagenic urticaria*. It found an underlying affliction it could associate, no matter how rare."

"No," Daniel said. He came down to a whisper. "If I could have done anything to help him before he set, I would have coded out his *urticaria*. Not added it in."

She considered in vain what was left. She looked down over her arms crossed over her heart. "You know Luegner is a liar. He will take him from us first chance he gets."

Daniel winced. He looked over the table, its cuts, its shape, its center position in a foyer. It was a lonely foyer with wall-high windows that looked out to nothing but darkness and a reflection of two desperate souls. "None of this would be here without Luegner."

"Luegner took my mother from me," she said and opened her arms onto the table.

"Don't say that."

"When was the last time you heard her laugh? She's a mess. Luegner did that to her."

Daniel spun up from his chair as both hands rushed to his head. "Luegner won't take Cessini. I won't let him. But Cessini will only come back for you. You were the only true friend he had."

"I don't want to do it."

"Don't forget, Cessini is gone because of you."

"Don't you say that. Don't you ever say that again!"

"If you didn't kill him by accident, then by neglect. Now you've got to help me save him by purpose."

"That is not fair. I've done everything I can possibly do."

"Then be there for him. He'll come back for you. But only when you're the you that he knows."

"And what about me? What if it hurts too much for me?"

"It won't. 'Belief and know' will work. It takes time to build a relationship, doesn't it?"

"Not as long as it takes to forget one."

"We won't come back out of that room until we've won

and he's with us again," Daniel said and moved forward to the edge of his chair. He reached his hands across the table.

She didn't take them to hold.

"Give me the chance to fail the first time, okay? Like a mad scientist. Funny-haired, Newtonian powdered locks and all," he said and flipped his hands over and open.

She hit one and he curled it back up. "Cassini was pre-Newtonian, actually," she said. "Difference of a few years here and there. But who's counting?"

"Will you do it?"

"Everyone is entitled to one mistake, right? So tell me the truth. What is he?"

"Technically," he said, but that's not what she wanted, "he's an advanced computer with twelve years of memories. An advanced computer that thinks—that thinks it's a dying boy who's reactive to water. But personally, he's Cessini."

She leaned forward in her chair, holding her head in her palm and resting her elbow on the table. The worn groove in the surface of the table was a meaningless blur in her tunneled vision over a circle of white.

Daniel waited in her silence.

She curled her fingers into a fist against her head, but found the fall of her hair over her forehead distracting. She pulled her hair back behind her head and retwisted its band. Then she pushed herself up by shoving back her chair.

Daniel waited. He stared.

"Let's go," she said, decided.

Daniel closed his eyes and breathed. She stopped him with her left hand on his shoulder. She reached around for an overriding embrace with her right and gave him a loving kiss by his temple. She stayed in close to his ear. "You don't give up, either. Okay? Call my mom again. She'll come back. She knows how to help if you let her."

"By the way, for the record," Daniel said as he poked her ribs away, "who's running this show, me or you?"

"He is," she said and they both knew it was true. "Now let's get back to work, slacker. He was more than just my friend, too."

SIX

A LADDER AND A BAGGIE

HARDLY A DAY went by after school when nine-year-old Cessini and Meg didn't ride the bus together, not to their respective homes, but to Daniel's southwest suburb's 36,000-square-foot data center with attached two-story office.

Daniel worked as a critical systems engineer out of his test lab on the office's first floor. He built new servers, storage, and infrastructure for the explicit purpose of trying to break it. Given a system's weakness, he could access its log files and then fix it to make it better for a next round of testing.

Up on the second floor, Cessini and Meg became instantly busy and safe at the end of the abandoned southeast hall in an after-school work space set aside just for them, an old fourteen-by-sixteen-foot corner office. A six-foot shared table in the middle of the room was theirs alone for projects. It was theirs from the minute school ended until Robin swung by to pick Meg up.

Cessini loved their days, but hated the room. Directly above the centerpoint of the table where he sat was the bane of his nine-year-old existence. He stayed, sometimes immobilized for hours on end, with his eyes fixed straight up at the incline ceiling, and to the scourge of the room: a sprinkler head.

The room peaked at fifteen feet, but at its twelve-foot center, at the end of a long, thin finger-like pipe, was a single, sixteen-pronged sprinkler head that set two inches down into their room. And only by virtue of a 1/8" glass bulb filled with a thin red liquid was a torrent of rain damned back. It could decide to extinguish his soul to its core at a moment's break and flash. Being human so exposed beneath was an awful fate to endure. Sometimes, he wished he were a computer, because computers never, ever, worried.

Meg, for her part, was always there to scribble, to tease, to sleep with her head down, or simply lift her eyes and watch him. She was delighted to help, though she always leaned too far in and across for a closer look from her side of the table.

When Cessini stopped staring, he fiddled. He had access to any tool, any resource in Daniel's first-floor lab. As a starter, he built a robot's body, a really great one, and just maybe, as he daydreamed, a new body for his ailing mind. He steadied his roughly framed robot's elbow on the tabletop and articulated its forearm to vertical.

"Do you think a sprinkler pipe full of water would miss a drop that falls on the floor?" he asked.

"No."

"How about a drop that dies in a fire?"

"Probably."

"Does rain miss its home in the sky when it falls to the ground in a war?" he asked.

"Yeah, that's why it's always blue," she said with a self-congratulatory grin.

She might have been right. But a water pipe with feelings? Never. The devil's pipe itself couldn't mourn.

A 3D printer no bigger than a small microwave oven, and even easier to use, was on a movable supply cart behind him. Cessini hopped off his stool and checked the printer's spooling progress through its orange glass canopy. The print head swirled and moved about the cubic space in fine spatial strokes, painting not on a flat paper, but a solid product upward, layer by layer. Cessini sculpted by proxy any of an old master craftsman's dreams, and all with a simple finger swipe on the printer's networked catalog screen. He looked into the printing bay from its side. The white-colored joint of his chosen plastic knuckle was printing up fine in 3D.

Meg's perspective was a little different from her side of the table. She could never keep up with Cessini with counting or numbers. So she flowed and arranged all the colors of life into a world of their own. Cessini's winged tablet had become by de facto hers, and she made it her own. She played Sea Turtle Rescue on its worn and scribbled-on screen. The game was a trap of empathy and enduring commitment. Her turtle brood travailed from egg to sand, then sea. They survived only by everyday nurture of clicks and swirls, or worse, left abandoned to a dying end. She hunched on her side of the desk. She would never leave them neglected.

He pulled a tendon cable up through the three-prong, primitive gripper he built.

"If you were in here with the turtles," Meg said, head down, as she tickled the winged keys of her tablet, "I would carry you all around with me. Every day."

"Okay. I'm trying to get this one cable up through—"

"Probably only for a year or two, though, until I get older," she said.

"That's okay. I wouldn't want to be stuck in there too long. Get eaten by a duck or something."

She lifted her eyes. "There's no ducks—Crocodiles, maybe."

He redoubled his concentration on feeding the looped end of a cable up through a horizontal washer to a hook at the bottom of a wrist. Once hooked and pulled from below, the cable drew the three fingers above the wrist into a pinch. Little springs were secured under the base of each finger's knuckle and returned it to open when the cable was let loose.

"That's really neat," Meg said. "All three of the fingers can move by themselves?"

"Yup, and you only need one cable to do it. Nice, hey?"

"Like three opposable thumbs on one hand."

"Exactly."

"You could hold lots of things like that."

"I know, right?"

"Except there's no fingers, only thumbs. So what good is it?"

"Yeah, I know. So, I'm still working on it," he said as he looked up from his work and she retook her stool.

When she was no longer hovering over his side of the table, he stood and filled the void. And when she came up to standing, he sat down again without notice. They seesawed, played, and worked through the hours of the clock. It was plain as the color of day. They had become inseparable.

But his mind always returned to the sprinkler head above, and he took another peek up at it. "The brain always picks the highest probability," he said. "That's how it works. It figures if it happened before, it's probably going to happen again. We live by our memories. But memories aren't real."

"Then what is real?" she asked as she feathered her keys and circled her turtle in the sea.

"Imagination is real. Imagination means believing what can come next. And I know what can come next."

"What do you know?"

"That this isn't a pure room."

"It isn't?"

"It's a one-watch. I figured out a system. At home, every

time I walk by the four-watch down the hall to my room, I keep track of every source. If it drips, it's a count and I keep track. I count them all through the day, every day."

"What's a four-watch?" She twisted on her stool and rotated the swirls of her tablet.

"It's the kitchen. One through four. The sink, the refrigerator, the dishwasher, and anything left on the counter. I watch the four sources. I keep track and never let my mind forget where they are."

"Okay, stop." She lifted her head. She stopped her stool. "From now on, we don't say 'watch' or 'count.' The kitchen is the kitchen. A leaky faucet is a leaky faucet, not a two-, or a four- or a six-count. You got it?"

"I know, but—"

"I get it, but you can't talk like that. What are you going to say when a friend, if a friend, ever comes over and you want something from the kitchen? It's not, 'Dad, can you get us something from the four-watch?' That's never going to work for you. You say, 'Can I have a drink of milk from the refrigerator in the kitchen?' 'I left my glass on the counter next to the sink,' or the dishwasher, or the dozen other wet items waiting to be dried and stacked. Or, how about the refrigerator, the one with the ice maker. Did you count that one, too, by the way?"

"No. Okay, I'm still working on it. But bathrooms are the worst. And this building is a one-hundred-twenty-six-watch."

"Okay, back up. What about this room?" She blinked. "There's no water in here."

"This is definitely not a pure room." He pointed up as her eyes followed. "That sprinkler," he said, whispering.

"Oh, yeah. There's that. You know it's just a pipe, right? There's not even any water in it. Not until there's a fire, anyway."

He thought a moment, then said, "Last night, I dreamed I could swim."

She scoffed. Then went back head down to click-clack away.

"Really, I did. Underwater, too." He leaned forward over the robot arm. "I'm not kidding. Swimming like a fish. But it was me."

"You mean I could be up in a boat with a pole," she said, laughing, "and I could catch you like a fish. You'd be flapping away. Wiggle, wiggle, aah, wiggle-wiggle."

"Yeah, you could try," he said, then relaxed. The 3D printer beeped and he looked back. The knuckle was done, but he didn't rush. "Okay. I got a better one. Why did the rhinoceros get kicked out of brain school?"

"I dunno, why?"

"Because he kept trying to break into the girl's hippocampus."

"What does that even mean?"

"Did I get you?"

She was silent.

He threw his head back, cracking himself up. "I did. I got you." He pointed at her and twirled on his stool. "I think. . . ." He cackled and twirled. "I think it's funny."

"What? You mean at the zoo?"

As he slipped from his stool, he slapped out to grab the table's edge. The hook of his robot's arm broke free with the force of his crash. The tendon cable let loose and the gripper's fingers sprung back to open. They hyperextended and broke without their knuckle backstops.

But he didn't care in his belly-on-the-floor laughter. He could fix a broken finger later. His mind reveled instead in his healing now.

She lifted both hands in surrender. She tried to laugh with

him, but couldn't. "I still don't get it."

He looked up from the floor over the table top to her scowl. When he was younger at school on the playground he believed he was alone. That lonely boy was real. But with Meg here at work, fixing or breaking from laughter, he knew he had a friend. There was no contradiction. He believed and he knew that he was his same self. He got up from the floor and laughed a small victory for fun.

"I still don't get it. What's so funny?" she asked.

"Never mind," he said as he climbed back on his stool at his side of the table. "Remind me when I'm done with the body to build a hippocampus for my robot's brain. I can print one out on the printer with its mouth open really wide like this. . . . Like the one with the broken tooth at the zoo. I can fit it right up here where the head is going to go."

"Wait a minute. You have no idea what a hippocampus means, either."

"Yeah, so? I heard my dad say that joke to the guards downstairs. They thought it was funny. And you know what?"

"What?"

"I have no idea what it means, either. But I'm glad that you're here."

"Great. Where else am I supposed to go?"

He shrugged.

"Then do me a favor. When you get up, print me a giraffe, too. I want one."

He straightened up one of his robot's fingers. They weren't broken as bad as they looked. "I thought of a name for him."

"For who?"

"Packet. I'm going to call him Packet."

"Call who packet?"

"My robot." He showcased the working pile of pieces in front of her face.

"Okay, whatever," she said. "Don't forget my giraffe."

"You know what else?"

"What?"

"I'm going to go into space."

"With your robot?"

"No. But all kinds of people say they're going to do it and never do. But I will."

"So how are you going to get into space?"

"I dreamed it, like me swimming under water."

"Oh, please. Then you're not going."

"Yes, I am. I invented a bioship that uses space dust for fuel. Space dust gets shot out by stars, and it's organic. That means it's alive. And it's everywhere in space. My ship grabs up all the space dust in a giant ocean tank of water."

"Right. And what are you going to do about all that ocean water?"

"Nothing, the water won't bother me because it'll be in space! And the people in my spaceship will know how to turn all of it into energy. They *blast* it out the back. Physics says you can do it. Quantum engines and energy stuff. I know all about it. I dreamed it. It's real."

"Cool. Can I go with you on your spaceship?"

"Sure, why not? It'll be a big ship. A thousand people. Giant. Open air, *huge* inside."

"Cool."

"You want to know what it looks like?"

"No."

"Okay, so, imagine a gigantic barrel, hold it up sidewise so you're looking into its opening. There are people living and walking all along the inside walls."

"Wait, you're going into space in a barrel?"

"No. Come on." He tore a sheet of paper from a pad and hurried to scribble oodles of tiny people. She leaned over her desk. He rolled the paper into a loose tube and tacked its long seam with a piece of tape. "It's huge, okay? The people walking along in here stare across the diameter of the tube and what do they see? The people on the other side, over here, are upside down and looking back across at them. This freaks everybody out, right, so you put a huge projection screen, side-to-side, right down the length of the tube. And you project the sky on that screen. Now the people think they're standing in a semi-circle or a valley and they look up and see the flat, projected sky with clouds and everything." He ran a flat hand along the outside of the rolled paper to show her how the sky screen would go lengthwise down the tube.

"Cool."

"But there's a problem," he said as he ripped out another sheet of paper from his pad and rolled an even tighter tube. "You got the axle of the ship running straight down the length of it." He stuck the smaller tube into the larger one. "People don't want to look up and see some giant axle in the sky. They'll freak out again. So, you wrap that axle with more projector screen."

"Yeah, I get it. I like it."

"I know, right?" He peered through the two rolled tubes to Meg on the other side of the desk.

"One thing, though"—she leaned over the table and grabbed—"the projector screen can't be glued right onto the axle itself. It's got to be kind of like supported off it a bit so there's room between the screen and the axle. That way repair people can walk between them and fix things, like you see people walking through the framework of those old blimps, or something. 'Cause there's always stuff that needs to be fixed."

"Yeah, that's true. There's always stuff to be fixed." He chuckled, grabbed the two paper tubes back from her, and squished them into the gripper of his robot. The three inanimate fingers held.

"Yeah," she said and went back to her game.

"So, before we go into space. . . ." he said as he got up, danced a few steps over to the cart, and then smiled through the canopy of the printer, "tell me, what color do you want your giraffe?" The printer's spool reset for the start of another piece as he flipped through the networked catalogue. He smiled again, looked back at her, and knew. Together, they'd have so many more places they could go.

But until that day, on a regular Tuesday, Cessini's eyes slowly pivoted back up to the black metal pipe down the midline of the ceiling as it taunted and belittled him, pressing him down into the cushion of his stool. The metallic sprinkler head's sixteen-prongs mocked him deliberately and incessantly from above as he worked.

He had fabricated all sorts of spare parts, servos, tendons, screws, and wheels that he collected into little plastic baggies and packed into the shelves all around the room. So why couldn't he likewise constrain the water from the sprinkler head above? He hopped off his stool to do it.

"You want to know what I think is a really bad idea?" Meg asked, busy with her tablet.

Cessini grabbed a four-rung, closed stepladder that leaned against the wall, opened it, and straddled its legs atop the table. He was careful not disturb his robot's developing frame. His plan took balance, nerves, and a roll of masking tape.

Meg watched in fits of silence and sputter. "What are you doing?"

"What's a bad idea?" he asked. He pulled a spare baggie from a box on his desk and tucked it into the left front pocket of his pants. Then, before she could answer, he squeezed his fist through the center hole of the masking tape roll and pushed it up to his forearm.

"Wait, what are you doing?" she asked again.

Cessini's eyes never left the polished sprinkler nozzle above. He put a foot on his stool and climbed up onto the edge of the table. He steadied his hands on the top bar of the stepladder and committed his climb up to its fourth, top rung.

"Don't!" Meg jumped off her stool.

He let go with his hands and wobbled to a standstill. His sight rose to twelve feet from the floor. His target was directly above and only a back-arched glance away. He raised his trembling hand. His eyes were within inches of the sixteen-pronged head.

Meg scattered around to his side of the table and grabbed for his pant cuff.

"No, don't pull," he said and kicked.

She ran for the door as a lookout.

He clenched his teeth and curled his toes in his shoes. He reached down with his left hand to remove the baggie from his pocket. The tape roll dislodged down his forearm to his wrist so he raised his hand. He spread his fingers to return the roll to a tighter place on his forearm. Then he reached instead with his empty right hand to his left side, arching his ribs, and dug the baggie loose from his pocket. "So what's the really bad idea?" he asked.

She ran back in to get her tablet away. "Don't. The water will shoot!"

With the baggie balled in his right hand, he pulled a strip of masking tape free with his fingers, ripped the tape with his teeth, and zeroed in. He pinched the top corners of the baggie, blew in a puff of air, and reached it up toward the sprinkler head. He wobbled. He breathed.

His hands didn't move as his mind intended. The distance to the head looked reachable from the floor. Now, his neck was straight back with his jaw open in pant. With each inch higher that he dared, the sixteen prongs cursed back at him with a dizzying unease.

"Ceeme, no! Stop it."

Each pointed tooth of the head was detailed with a studied recognition he knew from below and now knew intimately. The small glass bulb with its blood-red liquid was ready to burst. Only a thin metal guard protected it from breakage with the slightest impact. If it broke, the pre-action system would activate. Seconds would count before the air pressure in the pipe matched that of the surrounding air. Water would rush into the dry pipe, fill the sprinkler head, and spray off the six-teen points of the splatter disk in a deluge over him and the room. There was no way he could climb down the ladder in time or dive for cover to avoid the horrendous rain. He'd have to throw himself down and hope for the best. The floor down below where he would hit was hard. He could hide under the table, or better still, hit the floor full footed and run.

Meg fell back onto her stool. "You want to know what I think is the really bad idea?"

Cessini blew another puff and swelled open the baggie for another go. It fit over the sixteen prongs. He tacked the torn-off strip of masking tape on the top edge of the baggie and pressed it onto the higher stem of the nozzle's one-inch-high vertical pipe. He closed his eyes to breathe, and then opened them as he pulled the tape roll from his wrist. He picked the tape free and set its end onto the pipe. He wrapped the whole roll around twice, then three times more around the outside of the baggie over the nozzle, tight, but not an ounce more of pressure against the delicate glass vial inside.

Meg spilled her secret without waiting. "My mom said she was talking to your dad. They want us all to live in the same house."

He unwound and circled the tape once more to be absolutely sure it was tight and the baggie was secure over the sprinkler head. He tore the tape from the roll with his teeth and pinched it off. He swallowed. He was done.

Meg breathed out below.

His forehead was beaded in sweat and aflame in a rash, but he felt the worthwhile cost of a victory. He climbed down with the palms of his hands a red, burning blaze. He touched down his feet on the desk, then the stool, then the floor. He removed the stepladder from its straddle over his robot's body and set it folded back against the wall by the 3D printer.

He sat on his stool. His skin was afire with sweat. He smiled at Meg, satisfied. "I think that's a great idea," he said. "Moving in together in the same house. I like it."

She didn't move a muscle. Her hand was pressed over her heart.

He scooted his stool closer up to his side of the table and opened a baggie of screws and electrical gizmos. He peeked up at Meg past his eyebrows and then looked back down at his work. She said nothing. She was still. His faintest twist of a tri-wing screw made a louder peep than her. He looked up again, holding his screwdriver upright beneath the tip of his finger. "So, when are you thinking of moving in?" he asked.

Meg broke her blinded stare at him and tilted her head back to the baggie taped and wrapped around the sprinkler head above. He had done it. All she could do was nod. Her hand stayed over her pounding heart as she looked back down and across the table and uttered a faint, but definitive, "Never."

The never day came on a Saturday night. Daniel's hands covered Cessini's eyes as he led them straight into Cessini's bedroom for a present. Meg was antsy with anticipation. Robin beamed, a rare occasion. Daniel removed his hands from Cessini's eyes once he was aligned in the center of the room, but then he kneeled down for an eye-to-eye hold.

Cessini's painted mural of the waterfall and his bed beneath it were the same, his nightstand with sound machine and an old bellows lamp shaped like a squid were left untouched. Daniel held his shoulders from pivoting any farther. Behind Daniel was a new white melamine shelf that wrapped waist-high around the three other walls. The shelf was the perfect mantel addition for his many projects and discoveries yet to come.

Robin drew the bubble chain for the vertical blinds as the outside darkness had already settled.

"Keep your eyes closed," Daniel said.

"What is it?" Cessini itched to turn. The mystery gift had to be at the end of the shelf behind him by the door, he thought.

"Responsibility," Daniel said.

"Whaaat?" Meg said, miffed. "It's okay, just tell him."

"No. I want you both to listen to me," Daniel said. "This gift is a little something that wasn't easy to get. But Meg insisted we keep trying, for you. A 'thank you' from the two of them for welcoming them into our house."

"Everything is going to be great," Robin said. Her smile was genuine like a mom's should be.

"Fine. Okay. He knows. Show him already," Meg said.

Daniel pulled Cessini closer to his knee on the floor. "Imagination means life," Daniel said. "You inspired me. What you're building on the table at work. We can build a mind for your robot body. I have an idea for how to make it work. I can code it. I think I figured out how. I'll call my mind code 'Packet' after the name you gave your robot. But most of all because I'm so very, very proud of you."

"Oh, come on," Meg said, "is this a present from me, or you?"

"I like that," Cessini said to Daniel. "Packet will fit together perfect. We'll build ourselves a real winner."

"Speaking of which," Daniel said, "don't you worry about any of those bullies at school."

"I know," Cessini said.

"You're already better than them," Daniel said. "Build something even bigger than you can imagine. Keep reinventing yourself. Each and every day. You'll never become obsolete. And you'll leave them behind in the dust."

"Daniel, come on already," Robin said. "Meg's right. You totally stole our present."

"Be smarter than me," Daniel said. "It's not a crime to be smarter than me."

"That won't be too hard," Meg said. Cessini held out his palm and Meg slapped it. "Can you please just show him now what we got? Blah, blah, blah. . . ."

Daniel let him turn to see.

A terrarium was on the shelf. Two feet long. Meticulous. It had a sand beach on the left and a small pool in the middle. The shallow pool of water wet the bottom of a hollowed-out log perched from the right. A small, gray amphibious fish —three inches, no more—emerged from the hollow of the log. It walked on its fins for a look. It didn't enter the water, but stayed at its edge.

Cessini got closer. A mangrove rivulus. He was sure. He wrapped his hands on the side of the tank.

"It's you," Meg said as she joined him by the glass.

"A mangrove rivulus," Robin said. "A fish that lives out of water. Every couple of months, pour water over the log and it's happy."

"It's the opposite of you because it's a fish. But it also lives without water. So, it's like your opposite, but also your equal," Meg said.

"Wouldn't my opposite be a real fish?" he asked.

"He is a real fish," she said. "Simple tank, but it's like you. It's your world. It's your life."

He backed away from the tank. The rivulus ducked back into its log. "But you still have to keep the log wet."

"Well, yes, that's true, but—"

"Then we're not the same at all. I'm not a mangrove rivulus."

"Exactly!" Daniel said. "That was my point."

Robin came down at Cessini's side. "You know what's most crazy about this fish?" she asked.

"It talks?" Cessini asked.

"When it lives in water, it doesn't get along with any other fish. They fight a lot," she said. "Probably like you at school with those boys. But when their water hole dries up, they all become friends and live together in the same log. One day, you'll see, everything can get better."

Cessini sat at the edge of his bed by his nightstand. They all watched him stare at his new forced friend.

"The place we got it from said, though, if it doesn't want any friends, it doesn't have to have any," Meg said. "It can live its entire life by itself. It can become a hermaphrodite and make clones of itself."

"That's weird," Cessini said.

Robin smiled and stroked Cessini on the back of the head. "Every two months, just add water." Then she leaned in and kissed his forehead. "And thank you for welcoming us to your home."

"But it has to eat so make sure you feed it more often than that," Daniel said.

"Right, feed it," Meg said. "And live with the water or don't. But don't grow up alone."

"I hear you," Cessini said. "I'll give the fish a try. I like it.

I'll watch it on a sixty-day count."

"You'll try?" Daniel asked. "What count? You know how hard it was to get this fish up here? It's Minnesota. How many tropical mangroves do you see around here in Minnesota?"

"Hello, it's called 'fly it on an airplane,'" Meg said and Cessini laughed. She always had the right thing to say. She bounced for the door with a hand aimed straight for the light switch. She put them all into darkness with a click. "Now I'm going to bed. Goodnight."

As the lights went off, the ocean waves of the sound machine on his nightstand came on. The repetitive roll and crash on a distant shore was one Cessini respected. It was a soothing constant hush, a nightlong reminder of a world that could never be his, but a safe one imagined in the harmlessness of a recorded machine. The simple white box with speckled holes over its speaker was the dreamtime peace he made with the ocean.

Robin flipped the light switch back on before leaving. "Goodnight."

Daniel left another gift on the edge of his nightstand, a penlight.

Cessini clicked the penlight's on-button and flicked its light left, then right. "Thanks, Dad. You know I'm not afraid of the dark anymore."

"I know."

"I'm here," Meg yelled through the muffle of gypsum. "My room is right through this wall. Can you still hear me?"

"I can," Cessini said with a smile as he clicked his new penlight on and off.

Daniel hugged the frame of the door, not wanting to leave. He tapped his fingers on the light switch.

"Leave it on," Cessini said. "I want to watch the rivulus for a while."

"I think this is going to work out great," Daniel said as he let go of the door. "We'll be in our room next door. Call me if you need anything. Okay?"

"I will," he said, and then Daniel, too, was gone.

Beside the sound machine on his nightstand was the bellows lamp in the shape of a colossal squid that stood vertically on its eight outstretched arms. Its soft mantle skin billowed out and in with hypnotic, rhythmic breaths, synchronized with the lapping waves of the ocean tide.

Cessini lay awake in his bed long past when all others, both old and new to his home, were asleep. He pointed his penlight on, then away, then on, and away again from his new mangrove rivulus in its tank. Its eyes darted in and out of the log with the rapid movement of an oddly pointed moon and probably wondered as only it could—was it alone?

With the press of his thumb on a button, Cessini believed he could control a simple life in a tank, and he was right. But one unintended effect of the gift of the rivulus had clicked back into his mind like the weighted tick of a metronome and nothing could matter more than the return of his fear. The vengeance of water to soak the skin would soon be coming his way. It was inevitable, and as certain as a sixty-day count in his mind.

SEVEN
CONTROL

THE SIXTY-DAY COUNT lasted for three nightmarish years. By the time Cessini was twelve, the anxiety of his days spilled into the exhaustion of his nights. The soothing intent of his wave sound and squid-bellows lamp had taken their toll. His mind gave way in his sleep to his dreamed-of alter-ego, Ceeborn, and his stronger world of opposites. Ceeborn was him in appearance, but braver and aquatic. One night, in his dream, he was fearless and ran along the bank of a river, climbed the rail of a bridge, and dived into a rush of water. But then with a tumble from his bed, Cessini awoke on the floor of his room in agony, his skin aflame and pajamas sweated through.

Again and again, the same anxious, nighttime watery wave rolled in, but each time it was capped with a different froth. One sweaty night, he ran as Ceeborn through a botanical garden and away from the unseen, click-clatter of claws on stone. He escaped the patrol of three charred, six-legged robots moving after him like waist-high ants in a networked line. Their bulb-shaped heads were clear, faceless domes, and inside their bulb was a retractable mind, a tablet with side-mounted keys that clicked and clattered with their relentless movement forward. The lead robot's middle and rear pipe-legs locked in place at their shoulder joints. It flexed its squared front thorax up at its waist and rose, extending and splaying its sixteen-pronged front claws in a dominant pose. Then it leapt in attack. He was pinned in its grasp.

A beautiful aurora of lights in the sky flickered as Ceeborn regained his focus upward, and the dome of the patrol stayed locked down in its stare. He was carried away beneath the three robots' chassis in their coordinated line. His wrists were pulled over his head by the leader, his waist supported by the middle robot, and his ankles held immobile in the front claws of the rear patrol. His lungs heaved in a gasp. He rolled his head to his side into the pit of his outstretched arm and coughed up a lungful of sputum and froth.

The lead robot kicked a door open to a rotted hallway. The three entered with him suspended beneath their bodies, marching forward in a slanted line. Their left legs walked on the narrow floor while their right legs angled up onto the rounded wall. The tubular hall was lined with soiled porthole windows.

Daniel was ahead. He exhaled and opened a door into a darkened cell. Inside, the patrols dropped him in a heap of shivers as the leader maneuvered and shackled him to the floor. Damp moss infested the pitted walls of the cell. Daniel peeled a flake of fleshy decay from the ceiling. The room's opened wound bled and another ulcer was formed. A slice of flesh dropped to the floor. Its impact was grave.

"None of us can leave here," Daniel said, "unless I can fix this problem—or we'll all be dead soon enough."

The lead robot straddled him and lowered its bulbous head to within a breath of his face, close enough to smell the tinge of its burned metallic flesh. He averted his eyes from the robot's tablet screen, and in the distorted light through the clear dome of its head, he saw Daniel crouching to leave under the frame of the door. Daniel stopped at a porthole window along the corridor's festered wall.

Ceeborn lay curled and cold on the floor of his prison. The lead robot's dome tilted to its shoulder as it reached its piped front leg forward toward his neck. Its sixteen-pronged gripper extended to choke him into a reddened haze—and away and awake from this horrid, but oddly irresistible, wet world. He opened his eyes in a bed.

Cessini found his nights a prison cell fraught with horror, but the wetness of its walls soothed his lungs and healed the cracks of his drying skin for the moment, at least, in his mind, until waking itself had become his horrible burden to bear. His days began with mornings that burned the worst.

He woke late, well past seven in the morning. He fluttered his eyelids through a swollen rash. He sat slumped on the edge of his bed and shivered. He rubbed his hands up and down his shoulders. He crossed his arms high on his chest and his fingertips met behind his neck. He squeezed himself a warming hug and twisted to relieve the soreness of a hard-won night.

When he'd put the first baggie up three years before, it had been quickly noticed and removed. He had put up another, then one more fourteen days later, but neither Daniel nor any of the operations staff at the data center would stand for it. Even Meg had to defer to Daniel's position. Cessini's younger daredevil days of ladders and baggies were long over and gone.

Meg swung into his room with her hand on the frame of his door. She slung her school backpack over her shoulder. "Oh, come on, you're not even up yet?"

"Meg," he asked, "why did you think all of us living here was a really bad idea?"

"Ugh, I don't remember. Stop asking me that."

"Did your mother ever tell you what happened to your dad?"

"Yes. He died."

"I know. . . But I bet he was a real hero."

"Yeah, his name was Michael. And I bet he was, too." She smiled, then shrugged, as if that was all she wanted to say. She reached across her chest and re-shouldered her backpack. "Why are you asking? Is this about your nightmares?"

"No. I think you have a secret you're not telling me." He released his hands from his neck.

"Really? Well, then, we'll talk about me some other time. But not today. And I'm not coming to the building after school. I got invited out with some friends and I'm going."

"Wait, no, you can't. We're starting Packet's power cells. I need your help. You'll miss it."

"What do you mean, I can't? I'm going with my friends and you're going to miss the bus if you don't hurry up and get dressed." She leaned back into the hall, and shouted, "Daniel, he's going to miss the bus. Again!"

"Wait, Meg. I need to talk to you."

"No. We'll talk later. And not tomorrow, either. I'm going to the doctor's. I'll try to stop by later in the week. We'll fix your robot's cells then. How's that?"

"Meg," he said, then he looked at her straight. "I think I'm getting worse."

"No, you're not. You're the same as you've always been."

His hands dropped to the bed, palms up, elbows exposed. "I think that's a mistake."

"What, you going to start counting mistakes now, too?"

"No. But all the little ones add up."

"Oh, really? 'No'? Starting when?"

"I won't count. But I know how to fix everything at the office. You should come and see. I'll fix it up perfect for us both."

"Great. I'd like that. Do it," she said. Daniel popped in for a peek. "He's all yours," Meg said as she ran out and down the hall. "Good luck driving. He missed it again."

"Oh, come on. Hurry up!" Daniel shouted at him.

He stared at the empty door and sighed. She was gone. "Starting now."

"All right, get dressed and I'll take you," Daniel said.

Cessini rose slowly and dressed himself dry. He hurt like a young warrior grown weary of war. His plan to fix everything at the office was simple. And he would end his war with water later that day after school when he would be back under the sprinkler head, and fix it all for good.

The 12,000-square-foot office attached to the east side of the data center was old. Its wall insulation was dried out. It had been built fifty years earlier to house a uniform supply center. As the decades passed, wall-to-wall workspaces and cutting-room floors had become offices and labs. The adjoined warehouse was constructed of concrete masonry unit blocks to a clear ceiling height of twenty-three feet. In the old days of the uniform supply center, it had stored tens of thousands of cottons, wools, pantsuits, and dress blues, and circulated them in and out on chained railings and racks.

The same warehouse space, later reengineered as a data center, circulated trillions upon trillions of data bits per second. If profit margins were measured per bit of material, the data center would lose to the uniform supply. But in absolute dollars, the value of digital bits that flowed through its cables and walls far surpassed the old, needle-to-cloth warehouse.

Only one part of the old business remained. And it was completely unseen to the eye, but it was everywhere. In the warehouse's decades-long heyday, the uniform business grew in fits and demanded tighter office cubicles and remodeled floor plans. When one wall was in the way, it was moved. Walls that looked solid and permanent came down with a crew's easy slice of a reciprocating saw or swift swing of a sledgehammer. When the pipe end of a clothes rack punched through a three-eighths-inch wallboard, then that hole was patched in under an hour if the job was called in. But too often it wasn't. The dry-waller's trip cost more than the patch, so holes stayed open until their numbers made the service call worth the expense. Eventually, all businesses decline and the holes and tears became more and the calls became less. The decades' net result of remodels and shifts was the trapping of all the old bits of lint, fine fibers, and frayed fabric cuttings that wafted, or were brushed, and settled behind white gypsum walls. They stayed behind patches, forgotten.

Years later, the dried, withered bits of the building's old business lay piled, covered, and unseen within its framework of new office walls. The bits that should have been counted lay hidden instead, as ready tinder for a new power-hungry tenant's small probability of fire.

When viewed from above, the data center was laid out like a firebird-in-waiting, nestled among suburban neighborhood fields. The window eyes of Daniel's office structure faced east off a body, which was made of three data processing modules. Modules One and Three formed the north and south shoulders, while Module Two was their extended neck in the center. Nine generators trailed as wings and twelve transformer boxes fanned over the lawn as the resting firebird's embers spread out to the west. Twenty air-conditioning condensers aligned on each of the three Modules' roofs, cooling the precious data servers that hummed away inside.

In the center of the adjoining second-floor office, seventy-five honeycombed cubicles were aligned for remote disaster recovery. Their virtual seats were seldom filled, only occasionally warmed by techs or traveling business-types. But more often than not, Cessini and Meg had the whole floor to themselves.

Cessini passed the otherwise staid, gray-paneled work area and entered his southeast corner space, alone. A fourteen-inch blue giraffe lay fallen on the lower shelf of the 3D printer's cart. Its fourth leg had broken off. Its remaining three left it hobbled. A front leg had snapped back to its one remaining hind, melding them together as an "N."

He leaned forward on his stool, eyes fixed on his robotic work, mind taut and calculating. But with each puff of solder smoke, he tilted his head and eyed up through his periphery. The flanged-neck demon of the sprinkler head was un-bagged. It watched and micromanaged his every gesture, and criticized his every touch of iron heat to flux core wire. The pipe's hooked sprinkler finger could shower acid rain upon him at the whim of the building's beast. It could spew fire at any moment from its sixteen silvery nails.

Cessini lay down his glove. He rose from his stool and followed his eyes without fear.

The sprinkler head taunted him from the end of a one-and-a-half-inch diameter pipe that ran up along the sloped ceiling. It elbowed forty-five degrees at the ceiling's peak and went through the room's west side wall into the north-south, second-floor hallway.

Outside his door, the finger pipe joined into the top left of a "T." He followed the feeder right until it turned again, elbowing ninety degrees west across the hall. The pipe's shoulder disappeared through a round fitting above a utility closet door.

He needed Daniel's key to enter.

Daniel was in his first-floor break-it-to-fix-it lab, sitting hand to forehead over his messy desk.

Cessini barely had to speak to know. "Is it working?"

Daniel jerked upward and covered his papers. He relaxed when he saw it was Cessini.

"Not yet," Daniel said. "But I think I got it this time. I think it could work." Daniel peeked at the door. "I've been slacking. Don't tell."

"Did you put in all your simulated memories?" Cessini asked.

"Typed in all the old ones, this time at age fifty, and the younger ones, too. The simulation keeps crossing, though, getting them confused. It keeps thinking the older you and younger you are two different people in the same room talking to each other. Like you and me, right now. Can't figure it out. But you know what I'm going to call it?"

"What?"

"Poly-Algorithmic Compression, Kerneling and Exo-Transference." He grinned as Cessini hit on the letters. "PACKET."

"I like that," Cessini said.

"We'll make this together. Your robot, my code. What do you think?"

"I think it sounds like a plan. Why not?"

"'Cause I'm not sure," Daniel said. He returned to his papers. "I think it's my algorithms that are killing it. The main algorithm has a matrix of subs for each specialized brain function. I figured to use parameter constants. I called them my Madden Equation Parameter constants, MEPc's one through six. Play them like the keys of a piano, a person's sensitivity to each determines predisposition to music, painting, or maybe counting, like you and me."

"And you think the spikes from some combination of six coefficients are going to make it all work? Make a person a person?"

"I don't know. You're right. Maybe my PACKET code's all

wrong. Exponentials, instead? I don't know. Maybe that won't work, either. Maybe it's as simple as correlating time. The brain processes bits at a rate. Align that with the scan speed into the computer. That's much simpler. Yes, align the two speeds right, and the computer thinks on its own. A mind that 'knows thyself.'"

"Isn't that's just an emulation mode? Clock speed or something?"

Daniel dropped his pencil and sat back. "Right. Nothing special about that. Okay, forget that. I'll keep at it. Don't you worry." He pinched his fingers above his brow in frustration, then drew them down into a fist over his mouth. His thumb's knuckle found its way to a rub back and forth across his teeth.

"You should get a job at some fancy lab or something, not here."

"It's quiet here," Daniel said in the isolated room. "I can get some work done." He glanced at Cessini and tried to smile. "Lots of greats started out as clerks. Then straight to the top. You, me, and PACKET. What do you say?"

"Can I have the keys?"

"You know, Robin would say you're my dissociative identity disorder," Daniel said.

"What's that?"

"Two identities. One mind in conflict with itself. DID."

"So, are you my DID or am I yours?"

"I don't know. Maybe we're both Robin's." He picked up his pencil. He had an idea.

"Maybe we're Meg's," Cessini said.

"That doesn't make any sense. How could we be . . .?" Daniel trailed off as he returned over his work.

"I was kidding."

"Cessini, what do you want? I'm busy," Daniel said without looking back.

"I need the keys."

"What for?"

"Utility closet. The slop sink. I got some paints. I've got work for school."

Daniel tipped his head at the shelf behind his desk, and returned to his code. The metal keys were an odd sight of old, but jingled as a tool that still worked. "Be careful, that sink splashes. Water bounces when it hits the drain."

"I will. It was nice talking to you, DID," Cessini said. He offered a smile.

Daniel grunted, engrossed. He was gone.

Back on the second floor, Cessini opened the utility closet's door. The entering sprinkler pipe commingled into a twist of eight other tubes. The tubes turned down and ran behind the basin of the slop sink like organ pipes wrapped in sleeves of white insulation, stained from drippings of rust and decay that had seeped from the roof. There was no minor shutoff valve for the sprinkler pipe. He had to go downstairs.

His feet burned, sweaty from what he was about to do. The pipes emerged from under the first floor's ceiling in an offset north-south hallway. He ignored the wrapped tubes and the slop sink drain that went north and picked up the trail of the black iron sprinkler pipe that headed south. He followed the pipe to where more ribs of the beast joined from other hallways into its six-inch, iron pipe spine, like a double-sided "E." The pipe elbowed west in an "L" and thickened along the southern wall of the Network Operation Center, at the center of the office's floor plan. He pressed on, staring up; one pained foot in front of the other, as if each one set forward onto its bed of glowing coals. Then the pipe disappeared ahead into the cinder block wall of the main data center's Module Two. A dead end. He had to retrace his steps.

He tapped on the glass of the NOC and gestured toward

the door in the data center wall. The watchman slid open his half-panel window.

"Sorry, Cessini. Can't let you in," the watchman said.

"Come on. For school."

"Two words," the watchman said as he held up two fingers in succession. "Compliance and insurance. You stay on this side of the wall until you're eighteen. Talk to your father." Then he slid the panel shut.

Cessini stared through the glass, emboldened. He backed away on his own. He knew how to go around. And if he were to summon his courage as the mighty Ceeborn, he knew there would be nothing to stop him.

The first-floor northern storage closet had an access panel in its floor. He put his finger in the panel's D-ring and gave it a half turn counterclockwise. He lifted the panel, felt the cool air breeze from a higher pressure tunnel, and slipped in head first. A tight two-by-two foot tunnel ran a short distance, and then intercepted a perpendicular stretch of boxed-in tunnel that ran lengthwise beneath the NOC and straight into the data center. A six-inch-wide cable tray hung along the full distance of the tunnel. It carried the NOC's in-house communication cables directly to the main data center Module Two on the other side of the cinder block wall.

He stopped midway through. He was lying on his back. His elbows brushed the tunnel's walls. The cool airflow was drying and sweet. He paused to dry his body and recover his mind in his hidden spot of an under-floor world. He clicked his penlight and held it in the bite of his teeth. The gray, pebbled ceiling was exposed between the grate of the tray. It was the rough underside of a three-inch-thick, poured-concrete slab floor. It looked like a roughened beach of stones, a cosmic swirl of pebbles. People who walked on the floor above would have no idea he was there. He was in a world only he could imagine and he was only halfway west to his goal.

Once through the tunnel, he popped aside a square cover that fit into a cut in the concrete slab on Module Two's side of the wall; there was more darkness above the slab. He twisted up above it, but still beneath the module's main access flooring. The flooring was a grid of composite tiles raised thirty-six inches up from the slab. The tray and its cables went their way beneath the raised floor, Cessini went his. The floor's two-by-two-foot square tiles spanned all eight thousand square feet of the data module above—one hundred feet east to west by eighty feet north to his south. The whirl from above the floor shattered his ears with a deafening howl.

The tiles stood on a grid of aluminum pedestals set apart like a forest of thin silver trunks extending as far as he could see with the penlight in his teeth. The far west side of the module was spanned by a twenty-by-eighty-foot mechanical and electrical—MEP—corridor that supplied the massive consumption of power. A triangle of shorter pedestals to his right rose up and supported the underside of a pedestrian ramp that joined with the leveled data center floor.

Above the floor, twenty cooling CRACs and chiller units encircled 232 server cabinets, all squared into eight rows of twenty-four, and two rows of twenty.

The CRACs faced the ends of each aisle and blew four hundred combined tons of cold air under the floor where he crawled. The cold air was drawn up through perforated tiles along the cabinet rows and into the hot-running servers. The chillers, sitting perpendicular to the CRACs, pumped refrigerant through pipes to the blowers that bathed the room in cold air from above.

Cessini crawled though the whirlwind din. He skirted the pedestals and pushed his way south to where a wall protruded twelve feet west. At its end, the wall cornered left for a count of seven floor tiles and the southern border of Module Two. The smaller border room as measured by its foundation was a twelve-by-fourteen-foot, squared-in cinder-block bunker. The entire building's main fire control room was inside.

He pushed aside a tile and hugged up the southern wall under the high mount of a CCTV camera. It pointed down the far western wall's shorter, twenty-cabinet aisle. A crisscrossed camera aimed north for detection of any approach along the end of the aisle. But neither camera pointed straight down in its extreme to the one single tile that was two-by-two-feet in size, and pushed aside.

Watchmen in the NOC monitored the module's seventeen other cameras twenty-four hours per day. Every camera was placed to capture all biometric-protected doors, mantraps, and aisles of cabinets and cordoned-off cages. But no cameras were conceived nor placed to detect the movement of a twelve-year-old boy who'd grown up in a data center.

He opened the door of the fire control room, his body pressed to the wall. It was always unlocked by strict fire marshal code. Inside, three black metal grated stairs descended from the raised floor back down to the concrete slab thirty-six inches below.

His targeted sprinkler pipe broke through from the east side wall. It entered the room eight feet up from the floor, but only five feet and eye level from the top of the stairs where he stood. The pipe turned down. It was married to a crusted volcanic well by a ring of bolts.

A square cut in the concrete slab exposed the bare earth below. A twelve-inch-round, 250-pounds-per-square-inch pressurized water main pipe rose from the ground and supplied the emergency fire suppression system for the entire 36,000-square-foot building.

He had penetrated the source. The firebird's coursing

veins, glands, and devilish fingers that lived throughout the building all began with this main.

He toed down the stairs. If provoked, the system would erupt and flood all three precious data modules and mercilessly shower the whole east side office with rain. The three pre-action zone valves that branched water to the modules, and the butterfly valve that led to the office, all had electronic, tamper-resist sensors for remote monitoring. They could not be touched. The twelve-inch OSY valve at the bottom of the stack that came up through the bare ground from the municipal source was chain-locked with a key, and marked only with a fluorescent orange tag, *"Sealed Open."* A maintenance clipboard showed service was last inspected by squiggled initials the day before, Monday.

Cessini had Daniel's keys.

He unlocked the OSY's chain. He turned the valve handle counterclockwise with some force. Then he relocked the chain to seal the valve into its closed position. On fast glance, the circular handle was in its identical position, though rotated once wholly around. The raised metal letters on the dark painted steel with directional arrows for *"Open"* and *"Closed"* was a pie-piece turn from where it was before. Given the speed of a squiggle on a clipboard, no one would be able to tell.

He stood up and calmed his breath. He stumbled back and fell seated on the second of the black metal steps. He had shut off the flow at the source.

He breathed and stared as he sat.

He had never felt more victorious, more in control, more terrified. He would put the valve back to *"Sealed Open"* by Friday.

EIGHT
CESSINI ON FIRE

B
Y THURSDAY, CESSINI'S world in his after-school office was pleasant at last. His brow ceased to prickle from sweated thoughts of the sprinkler head above. He was free to focus and work. His robot on the table was nearly complete. Meg was gone, but that was all right. It was quieter alone. But something was wrong. He hadn't eaten. His stomach rumbled. Then he felt the faintest of clicks behind his right eye.

He paid it no mind with a quick shake left, then right of his head. He stood up from his stool and worked on the rest of his robot's frame.

The robot's open head was exposed to the north as its body lay supine on his table. He needed better access to its back. He leaned over its body and shoved away a bundle of wires on Meg's side of the table. He readied a hand on the robot's right shoulder, then his other onto its waist. He balanced his stance to compensate for the weight, gave the body a hoist up toward seated, then twisted and dropped it with a heavy jolt onto its shoulder. Its eyes snapped east to the window.

Cessini's knees buckled. His right ear popped and rang like a siren deep inside. His vision rolled over, shifting the room ninety degrees clockwise. The floor of the office and grass outside through the window twisted to vertical at his left. He fell to the table and steadied with a confounded "Whoa."

A white-and-black streaked Antarctic Prion, a *Pachyptila desolata desolata*, dove straight down outside the window's frame. It landed on an evergreen tree that now inexplicably grew horizontally across the bottom of the window.

He sagged into the turn of his vision and raised a hand to his temple. The room spun in his mind, but his feet were still planted flat on a floor. The unpinned movement of the room nauseated his stomach. He fought the urge to be sick.

His hand fell from his head and dropped down to his waist. It didn't hang out from his side. So gravity worked. His body was rightly below him. But more so, the bird could not have flown down. The tree was never felled. It was only his eyes that were offset, broken.

He opened his eyes and staggered. He fell toward what felt like his right. He kneeled on the floor. The window stayed east, the door was still open behind him to the west. But north was vertical and wrong. All fours on the floor were better, but the off-axis rotation was a dizziness he could not relieve. He clawed himself up by gripping his stool. He lay his head down on the table, pressing his left ear for a rest. He heard the swish-count of his pulse.

He squeezed his eyes shut, then opened them wide and saw the bird diving again outside. He wasn't dreaming. He was awake. Ocular destabilization, maybe. But that could have nothing to do with the bird that was so far from home. So then what? Revenge of the pipe? He twisted his eyes up to see it.

And then his vision corrected, ratcheted back counter-clockwise toward normal. He took a few extra breaths as it did. The poles of the earth righted. It was a nightmarish bout, but it was over. The exhausting days of his world piled yet another stone onto his life's balance toward madness. How much longer could he hold on?

His vision calmed. He braced himself against the frame of his door. The empty, north-south hallway was correct and upright. There were no panicked voices to be heard. No lights flashed for emergency exit. The ceiling and floor edges of the hallway converged with proper perspective. The worst so far was behind him. He straightened his shoulders and turned back toward the room of his overhead foe: The pipe.

The sprinkler pipe pointed like a finger from above, directing him back into his room to work—work that he did with a discipline for hours on end. What more could it want? He blinked and crossed the threshold of his door, entering fresh for another go 'round, stable as if no inexplicable twist had ever occurred.

He refocused on the power cells of his robot. They were the pride of his design. With its thin solar panels on its chest, a constant drip of power recharged the advanced ion battery packs that he had nestled as two life-giving lungs under its ribs. The major organs were all correct in principle and function. He double-checked the components against the schematics of his control system. He rubbed his thumbs around the tips of his fingers. The upper body's power cells would keep the brain functioning if the lower half lost its own. He smiled. Complete. It was all wired together. Top to bottom, upper to lower. He proudly outdid even himself. The lower body ran on a 120-volt AC and was plugged into a wall outlet.

He toggled the upper body's switch, which let loose an immediate discharge. A short.

The full capacity of the ion batteries bypassed into the lower body's circuits. The wave of current shot up the power cord and into the wall. The wall faceplate blew from its case.

Cessini shot a panicked look to the sprinkler above. His

fingers curled into an electric seize on the body's frame. Then he blew backward and fell against the wall.

Bluish-white smoke from the outlet turned black and wafted up the wall toward the ceiling. He came to with the pierce of an alarm through the silence. The paint on the drywall above the socket bubbled out from inside the wall.

His mind raced ahead of the paint bubbles and smoke. He teetered to his knees. His eyes prayed up. The glass vial had not yet broken, the sprinkler head was dry. The fire would come. The water would not. He had won against the sprinkler head, but at what spiraling cost? His victory was trumped by guilt.

The true source of his alarm was far from his door. He braced his hands on the floor, pushed off to his feet, and ran straight toward the siren's call. He could fix both water and fire in one, and the burning would be his alone to stave.

Statistics promised four minutes of sprinkler suppression before the fire department arrived in five minutes, with another ten minutes to set up. The statistics were blown from the start. A command post would arrive to an uncontrolled rage: Only half a floor below him and eons before his robot even existed, a wall-mounted whiteboard's center screw had nicked the rubber casing of his wall outlet's hidden electrical wire. Electricity arced at seventeen hundred degrees. Tinder and dried insulation ignited. One floor down and one wall north was the epicenter of the test lab. As the fire found its way out of the wall below, the powered tangle of cables flamed and blew.

Flammable glue adhered the carpet tiles to the first floor's concrete slab, but the fire discovered a much better freeway of fuel a layer below and exploded on the bundled run of live wires. Main house power cables ran a four-inch conduit artery west and pumped a straight shot of power adrenaline under the data room wall. The ignited artery crossed the eighty-foot span of data Module Two and T-boned with the main Mechanical and Electrical corridor. The MEP power corridor along the far west side of Module Two had powered cross ties to the adjacent Modules One and Three, and as a system of three, traversed the entire far west side of the building. The firebird-in-waiting had woken from its nest of kindling and stretched the shoulders of its wings alight.

Switch gear shorted. Nonessential power blew and the building went dark. The fire lapped the walls of the office. The three data modules were protected by cinder-block walls that held back the flames as intended. Sirens wailed throughout the hall.

Daniel peered under his lifted forearm. He ran through the second floor's honeycomb of cubicles hollering in vain, "Cessini!"

Cessini dropped to his knees along the first-floor hallway by the sliding glass window of the NOC. East-facing windows in September were bright after five, but the rest of the office billowed in darkness. Smoke covered the guiding lights of emergency red.

Electrical conduit encased under the poured concrete floor hadn't seen daylight or inspection since it was set. Its enclosed power wires had expanded and contracted with the flow of current through the years, turned brittle, and now burned. Two NOC watchmen broke free with critical drives of data and ran. System monitoring screens wilted like film. Network cables swelled, their casings burned.

Cessini dropped onto his back into the under-floor two-by-two-foot tunnel. The whole length ahead was pitch black. The tray of cables sizzled as he scurried beneath by feel of the patterned stones in the walls.

He fell out into the module between the aluminum pedestal forest and flipped to his knees. Speckled red light shined through the raised floor's perforated tiles from the emergency lighting in Module Two above. He scrambled left toward the fire control room and resurfaced through the two-by-two corner floor panel. He hoisted himself up and stood. He grabbed for the fire room door, and then suddenly stopped on a thought. He let go of the knob and slumped to the floor.

He didn't have Daniel's keys.

The OSY chain lock he'd sealed closed on the main valve couldn't be opened without the key.

The module's server cabinets crunched their numbers and processed their customer's code as smoke plumed in through ductwork on both eastern and western side walls. The smoke swirls were drawn in and mixed with the rising hot air that was expelled from the backs of the cabinets.

Cessini dropped back under the darkened floor and scattered from the base of the fire room wall. But with the circulation blowers so forceful, rather than rise, the blackened smoke fell.

The chimney intakes of the CRAC cooling units funneled the smoky air around the perimeter of the room, down into their forty-ton blowers. The CRACs' filters couldn't keep up with the grit; the needed flow of pure cold air under the floor had stopped. The precious server cabinets that were hungry for their flow of fresh coolant air, starved and their temperatures rose.

Cessini raced back on his knees between the posts, disoriented in the suffocating eddies. The dark forest under the floor was a storm of swirling, particulate clouds lit only by the red lightning streaks punching through from above. His tunneled exit was a furnace. He scrambled for the shorter pedestals to the left, to push through the floor and come up by the pedestrian ramp. He arched his back, then pushed a tile with his shoulders. The weight of the square wouldn't budge off its frame. It wasn't locked. It lifted by inches and hit something solid. He turned his head sideways to see. He pushed his hand through and felt with his fingers pressed up through the crack. He felt the caster of a supply cart laden with tools. The negative air pressure of the gap he created sucked as a vent, pulling smoke past his face. He dropped the tile, coughed, hacked, and clawed away on his knees. He was trapped in blackness under the floor.

He bashed and resurfaced through a tile at the farthest end of a row. He had to breathe. He climbed out and stayed. Above the floor was better than suffocating in the wind below or drowning in eddies of soot. But he was at the far northwest corner, when he needed the east. He struck the tile beneath him with his fist. How could he have made so many mistakes in a row, so many wrong turns in the dark? His vision tunneled back to the panels leading to under the floor. Go back under or run?

A power distribution unit was spaced at the western end of each row and supplied power to its aisle. He saw only to the first four rows of ten in the haze. Once the second power distribution unit's internal temperature reached fifteen hundred degrees, it exploded.

He curled.

Power feeder cables ran up from each power unit and fed through bus-ducts over each cabinet row. Individual power cords spaced twenty-nine inches apart on the ducts dropped over every cabinet and writhed like black snakes hung by their tales on a vine. Critical customer accounts with their stored lifelong memories fizzled en masse. The cable snakes ejected their sparks as they twisted into burning coils and jumped from their wired hold. At the foot of cabinet fourteen, a cardboard box of manuals and warranty checklists caught its fill of embers and burst into flame. The fire had found its way into the sacred data hall. Cabinet fourteen and First Central Bank went offline.

Every backup system designed to keep the cabinets running at all costs now force-fed their electric fuel to the fire.

Forty-eight cabinets faced inward to each aisle, twenty-four flush to each side. Each black-sided, humming cabinet was four-feet deep and nine-feet tall. And each one's flashing blue and orange lights flickered and died unchecked. Miles of network cables in their backside hot aisle lay in wait for the running flame. Nokomis Auto Parts and Freemont University ceased all transactions. CareWard's four hundred pharmacy chain stores lost all customer records. Their businesses ran in the cloud, but lived physically in the uninterruptible data center located in the suburbs precisely southwest of Minneapolis-St. Paul. All operations were susceptible to a fault, to their single point of failure. And every invention, every building, every data center ever built had one, and if not one, then more.

Cessini went fetal in the rumble of the belly of the beast. He covered the soft of his elbow over his mouth. Noxious fume filled the room. His lungs burned.

Power trays hung from the ceiling and showered sparks from their blackened rows. Flames fanned, cables attacked and whipped wicked arcs. Acrid smoke billowed up from every perforated tile, every row. The air was poison. There were enough CRAC cooling units to fulfill the room's need with one extra unit as backup. Then the backup failed; its intake was clogged. There were no more redundant units for error. Power dropped, a second CRAC spun down. The remaining cabinets generated more heat than could be cooled. Then source power blew and half the CRACs dropped in one swift dump. The cabinets had internal fans, but without the underside draw of cold air, they cooked themselves from inside. The module was choking; the modern business of cabinets by rows was ending.

Cessini recoiled, called for Ceeborn, but failed. He hid, but was dying. He was trapped, but somehow sustained. As nearby remaining CRACs altered their flow, a dead air pocket opened between the edges of two rolling eddies. A single CRAC perpendicular to a refrigerant cooler still ran in the corner, and created a cross wind air bubble void. He breathed in the opened air pocket. It was a temporary relief from the smoke, but never the impending fire.

In the MEP corridor, two and a half megawatts quartered to each of four uninterruptable power supply units. As the fire spread, the uninterruptable units cascaded offline. Cabinets died in their blink.

Breakers tripped off the main power source from the municipal utility transformers outside. Each module had its own battery life support with only ten minutes of power to live. The clock began. But before the batteries died, two dedicated 2.5-megawatt diesel generators would synch in and take over relief for each module. If those two generators failed, a third would swing in as a last resort. Enough diesel was stored in their nine underground tanks of 3,400 gallons each for each generator to last 24 hours. Any fire that found the fuel tanks' wick from above would shorten those hours' life expectancy in an instant. The number-two diesel tanks would explode and send pressure waves and bits of concrete shrapnel across the office park and through the adjoining residential neighborhoods for miles around. The calculated threat of an unchecked fire spreading through the data center was extraordinarily small.

But those small numbers were the furthest thing Cessini could think of as he curled his knees up to his chest. He wrapped his arms around his legs, dismissed the counting of numbers again and again, and cried his eyes closed while the fire bore down.

Then a hiss from above. A frightful panging of overhead pipes.

An awful pressurized, sizzling rush grew louder as water flooded the dry and flamed sprinkler pipes.

Three firefighters from Southwest Station 54, in full protective gear, had fought their way to the control room. The fire team leader rammed the door, leapt the black mesh stairs, clipped the chain with a bolt cutter, and opened the main water valve. The pressure needle sprung. The iron pipe rushed with water to where iron elbows, wrists, and fingers still hung. The deluge of the office began.

Cessini's head ducked into his shoulders under the dry sprinkler heads above as the horrible 126-watch data center teetered back on its watery scale to full open bore. The double interlocking pre-action fire suppression system in the data module required two events to trigger the water's release, an alarm and activation of individual sprinkler heads. The alarm blared unhindered without fail. The glass vials of sprinkler heads had long since broken in every aisle except those where he hid in the northwest. The air pressure was equalized in their pipes and the waves of water barreled in.

Five, four, and then three aisles away, the water poured and rained, vaporizing on the hot melt of cabinets. The spray and its puddles met electricity with wicked cracks of lightning. Once the glass vials burst in his last row along the northern wall, a 30-second timed delay would be all he had before the air was gone from the pipe and water gushed from its heads.

It would be best to get up on the floor full footed and run. He could beat the black swirls rolling up through the tiles in the middle of his row. He could jump through the fire engulfing its far end. He could make it in seconds. But not without catching the vengeance of water. If water flowed freely from above in Module Two, then that meant it was already raining torrents throughout his eastern office escape, a monsoon over his faraway exit. His body needed to flee. His mind refused. Daniel would be so enraged, so disappointed. Cessini fell back down into the air pocket and wept. The sprinkler heads over his space were the last ones dry.

He alone would burn in a shower of fire.

The sixteen-pronged head at the far end of his aisle opened and sprayed. The next closer popped and poured. Then the next and—

"Cessini! Cessini, are you here?" Daniel yelled. Daniel's muffled cry was swamped and gone. Then Daniel yelled down the closer third row. "If you're in here, run! Run to my voice!"

The sprinkler over Cessini's head stayed dry. No water here was better than burn over there.

"I'm begging you, please! Cessini!"

As yet another closer sprinkler opened its rain, the hell of great fire was traded in for much worse.

Daniel ended his search at the pedestrian rail of the first row. A chimney rose from the shifted, vented tile under the cart. He shoved the cart free. "He's here. He's here!" Daniel screamed as two firefighters interlocked his arms, and pulled him away. "Cessini!"

The *Emergency Shut Off* button was mounted on the interior wall at the door. A firefighter lifted its glass cover and struck it full force with his fist as Daniel cried out in rage, "Damn you, Cessini! What's the matter with you? If you're in here, why can't you be brave and run? Damn you!"

Cessini, in his corner, heard that alone through the rain.

All powered operations of the building instantly shut down. All remaining servers from the 588 that lived in the three modules, their CRAC cooling units, their generators, their everything, all went dead, down, and cold offline. The building was silent but for the horror of an unmistakable water count growing near.

The firefighters retook the end of the first row, wrestled the pressurized nozzle of their hose forward, and threw back the handle. They doused the aisle, from power lines above to deadened floor below. Water saturated the cabinets and flooded through the perforated tiles.

Daniel fought back. "Not the hose!" he screamed. "You'll burn him with the water."

The fire team grew up the aisle. Cessini only got to his feet. He was trapped, darting in his corner. His bloodcurdling scream of panic drove the fire team faster toward his rescue.

Moments before, he was terrified to run through sprinklers showering 100 gallons per minute at 50 psi. Now charging him into his corner was the onrush of a two-and-a-half-inch attack hose spraying 200 gallons per minute at 275 psi. In an instant, the forward mist of the water was upon him, then the full power of the hose. It was a wetting protectorate to carry him to safety, but drenched instead, he boiled. His eyes filled red and wild. His body writhed in agony, an unquenchable fire.

"You're killing me!" he screamed and fought back as a rabid beast overwhelmed by the tossing strength of a lead firefighter from Southwest 54. Cessini rose up into the air as a sacked creature, hoisted and thrown atop a heroic shoulder. Flown closer to the ceiling, and carried beneath the full open sprinklers' inundation of the row, he burst as if set on fire alive.

Outside, in the yard beyond the safety of the trucks, Cessini ripped at his skin, desperately peeling off his wet clothes as he wailed. A tending paramedic attempted to settle the tortured mind of whatever such a poor boy could be doing. He was reaching to comprehend the trauma psychology of a boy who thought his body was aflame.

"It's okay, little man," the paramedic said with his hands reaching and open. "You're not on fire."

Daniel stood at his distance, his life's work snuffed in a blaze before his eyes. He pulled an oxygen mask from his face and stared at Cessini, raw. "Don't," Daniel said to the paramedic. "Let him cry."

The building was gone. It was a horrid cost to shoulder. Cessini fell to his wet knees clawed bare. He locked eyes with his father, and then his mind collapsed. He looked down. The grass under the bared skin of his knees was wet too.

In the light of the fire trucks, they saw together the overflow water that soaked down the yard and cried in its rivers to his knees. The aisles of red welts of his face flamed and streaked from the run of his tears.

"It's his dermatology," Daniel said as he softened. "He's crying because his body hurts. It's not his mind. It's his body."

Daniel lay down the silver fire blanket he was given to wear as a shield, and came to comfort and dry his wet son.

Cessini's face was covered in pain. He wanted to scratch at his face and body until it bled, to peel away his inescapable skin that had in itself become his own blanket of fire.

"What did you do?" Daniel lamented.

Cessini was silent. He could hardly swallow.

"You took us apart," Daniel said.

He shivered and fell only to Daniel's arms.

"Why would you do that? Why?"

"I was afraid," he said as his eyes shut in their swelling. "I was so afraid."

Daniel exhaled and pulled him back in. "You should have just told me."

Cessini hurt too much and pushed away.

"We'll pull through this together, don't worry," Daniel said. "We've done it before. We can do it again." He cupped Cessini's face in the gentle air of his hands and assured him, "We'll pull through this together, I swear it. Did you try to save us? Is that where you were going? If so, your mother would have been so proud."

And with that, his tears ran anew. He fell back into a hold. Guilt was trumped by forgiveness. And the stronger the bonds of arms, the greater the tears of water to savor.

NINE
BALANCE

CESSINI LAY IN his bed on his side and ran his finger up and down his mural-painted wall. A hospital identification band was still wrapped around his wrist. The mural of trees and waterfalls had been changed. The waterfall was dry. Its form remained, but rocks and sprouted landscape replaced the water. The wave machine stayed on his nightstand and rhythmically pumped its white noise for a sound night of sleep. But the old machine's deeper influence was not so easy to take.

The squid-bellows lamp stood up on its eight bound arms, its outer mantle breathing out and in to the count of three in synch with the lapping wave sound of the ocean tide. His mangrove rivulus was still alive on its shelf, if older and slower, and it nestled in solitude in its moist hollow log. He watered it bi-monthly according to its need, though with more robotic habit than genuine human care. He tried, but he simply could not identify with a semi-aquatic fish that was neither his opposite, nor equal.

A vial was at the bottom of the tank in the small pool. It was a treasure chest filled with a younger boy's long-forgotten cure for the ills of his soul, a triangular brew of two parts animal and one part plant. A fish scale, a beetle's wing, and a bud of a dandelion. Each lay stale in the capsule at the bottom of the rivulus' unused pool.

Robin whispered herself in and sat on his bedside. "Your father thought you might want some company." She turned off the wave machine and waited for the mantle to let out its last gentle breath. Cessini didn't turn to her, though she set her hand on his shoulder for him to talk.

"Ten million, seventy-four thousand," he said.

"What is . . .?" she asked.

"The number of times it breathed since he made it."

She looked amazed as the lamp settled still. "Is that a guess?"

"It's a six-second cycle. Like a metronome. Three-second breaths, out and in. I sleep eight hours a night. Three hundred sixty-five days a year. It's been five years, nine months since he made it. I didn't count. I multiplied in my head."

"Looks like your dad made his money's worth, then," she said as she poked a finger to the thin of his back.

"I don't even hear it anymore," he said. "Or the waves. Not unless I'm sleeping. And when I sleep, I can swim underwater. Do you believe me?"

He turned to face her. The welts from the fire were smaller. The streaks of tears ran sideways across the bridge of his nose to his pillow-pressed ear. She dabbed a spot of white cream onto her finger from a tube. He held still as she touched the salve onto the lines of his remorse.

Meg stood in the doorway like a soft, crying ghost.

"What is it?" Robin asked her, no more than a stitch above being a wreck herself.

"What did you do?" Meg asked Cessini.

"Nothing. Looks like now we both have a secret."

"No, stop, I don't. Talk to me. I could have—"

"Go back to bed," Cessini said.

"Mommy?" Meg asked.

"It's okay, honey. Go back to bed."

Cessini rolled onto his side and hid against his wall.

"It's late," Robin said to Meg. "I'll be there in a minute."

Meg stood a moment for answers Cessini couldn't yet give. He hurt. She didn't go with him to the data center when he asked. Maybe she could have stopped him. Maybe there was nothing she could have done. Or, maybe they would have died together. In all, there was only one thing left he could say. "It's a good thing you weren't there."

She turned away from the door, silenced, then left to go back to her room.

Robin rolled her palm on Cessini's back as tears welled in his eyes. "Don't cry," she said. She dabbed another spot of cream from her finger to his cheek.

"What are we going to do?" he asked.

"I don't know," Robin said. He bunched up the sheet to rub at his eyes. "No, don't. You'll smear the magic." She dried his cheek with the cuff of her sleeve and begged him, "Please don't cry. It'll get better. Your father, he'll get better. You'll see."

"How?" He sniffled.

"I don't know. But he will. Tell me. Please tell me what's the matter?"

"This safe room. It's pure, but I have to pass the four-watch to get to the front door."

"What do you mean four-watch?" she asked.

"The kitchen. The bathroom is a five-watch with a three-count drip."

"I don't know what you're telling me."

"The shower drips if you don't turn it off all the way and I don't want to reach in by myself. What if I fall?"

"How are you going to fall? It's right at the tub. Wait, you keep track of all these . . . counts, when you leave the house?"

"Ever since I was little."

"Every place you go, wherever you are?"

He did.

"That must be exhausting," she said and sat closer. Then he saw something he hadn't noticed before. Her whole body shook, ever so slight. Her hands trembled, even as she sat still. "Well, if counting works for you. It sounds like you have everything figured out."

"Why do your hands shake?"

She raised her eyebrows in surprise. She laughed. "They don't. I put cream on your spots because I feel bad." She tried to rub again. "Because I love you. I want to take care of you. Make you feel better."

"But why do your hands shake?"

She hurried her hand behind her back. Then she brought it out front and level. "You want to know? Well, to tell you the truth, I swore on Meg's life I would never tell anyone. And that means most of all you." She dabbed a finger to his nose.

"Don't," he said. "You can tell me."

Her words were stuck in the purse of her lips. She couldn't say why. She covered her mouth with a hand that shook.

"Do you want to know my secret, then?" he asked and pressed up on his elbows.

She looked toward the sky and shored up her nerve. Then she looked back down with a nod that was clearer than the muffled cry of her single word, "Please."

His words were far easier to say. "I hurt so many people and have no friends to tell. I'm lonely."

She choked out a breath and dropped the tube to his sheets. Then she fell into his arms for a long-needed hug. "Me, too. And so did I."

He wouldn't have known. "How?"

She laughed a bit, maybe somehow relieved. Maybe not. Her hair tickled his nose. She rubbed her eyes and sat up straighter. She pressed the back of her hand to her forehead. "Lonely is a terrible place to be. What about your friends at school? Isn't it getting better?"

"They still call me Packet."

"That's good, isn't it?"

"The wet wipe."

"Well, you are not a wet wipe. That's not you. They don't know you. And they don't know what greatness you are going to achieve."

"I know."

"Good. So you want to play computer with me before bed?"

"Sure." He sat up straighter.

"Tell me what you believe? What do you know?"

"I believe I need a new skin. I know I can't have one."

"So how do you resolve that?"

"What do I want? What do I need?"

"Nice. Okay, you tell me." She seemed happier still.

"I want to be a computer. I need to be a human."

"Ah, I can see now why you're lonely. Anyone ever tell you you talk like your father? Anyway, you are a human. Humans are born with the skin they're in. You know you can't do anything about that, right?"

"I've got one for you. Computers burn in water. I burn in water. Therefore, I must be a computer."

She weighed her head side to side, like measuring the thought with a balance. "Well, now that is a good one. I'll have to give you that one for now." She recapped the tube of cream and set it down on his nightstand. She turned the wave machine and squid-bellows lamp back on. "Which came first, the chicken or the egg?"

"The—"

"Shh, I'm just kidding you." She brought up his covers and leaned in for a kiss goodnight.

Meg's holler from the other room broke their silence. "When is it my turn? Tuck me in."

Robin kept her eyes on Cessini, and smiled at Meg's nerve. She settled her hand on the top of his blanket. "We'll talk more tomorrow?"

But there it was again. He could feel the tremor of her hand through the blanket on his chest. He nodded without words.

"Okay, good," she said. "Hey, what's the one time in your life it's good to be a chicken?"

"I don't know, when?"

"Thanksgiving," she said and crinkled her nose. "Remember, computer or human, I love you very much."

"Are you coming?" Meg screeched through the wall. She tested their patience. "It's my turn!"

"And Meg adores you," Robin said.

"I know, like glue."

"Mom!"

"I'm not coming if you don't stop!" Robin said with a tsk then stood from the bed. "Feel better?" she asked Cessini as she went to the door.

He rolled closer to the edge of his bed and watched her. She stopped. Her image was distorted through the glass walls of his rivulus's tank. She had tended to the aches of his skin so dutifully with the cream. He thought he should do the same for his drying rivulus. A rivulus that lived in its tank and managed to control beyond the walls of its world. It got what it needed; it wanted water from a dropper.

"Feel better?" Robin asked again, her hand poised over his light switch.

He'd once believed his control over another's fate stopped with the hapless fish living alone in a log. He was wrong. In his mind, the fire still smoldered in the remains of the data center, and sprinkler water still soaked the ground at his knees. Daniel was ruined. The twist of their lives was forever his. An earlier belief that was wrong turned to a know of his greater ability to control the lives outside the walls of his world. There was no contradiction. He was the same person in the performance of both. His mind had made the connection over the long term. He could control.

"Come on, let me know you're okay," she said with her finger on top of the switch.

He stared up at her through the distortion of the glass tank and at her finger so ready to take his command. He whispered, "I'm okay," and her finger went down on the switch.

She smiled and pulled the door's knob. The light along the frame narrowed to a pinch. She withdrew her hand through the sliver of light out to the hallway. The door shut and the room was dark. Maybe he and the rivulus were equals after all. In light or dark, eyes opened or shut, he learned there was so much more to the world of control.

TEN
THE FAIR

THE COUNTY THEY lived in was big enough, but after what Cessini had done, in his mind, as he, Daniel, Robin, and Meg walked alone through the crowd of the August fair, it seemed like everyone's eyes were smaller than theirs. Everyone stared at the fair. The clouds loomed large, but the fairgoers paid the sky little mind. Everyone was so singularly focused on him, they eavesdropped and he hated it, for what good could it possibly bring? He caused the destruction of the data center, but the full scope of effect had not yet been seen. Like a punishing rain that leads to a flood, he felt whatever was coming would soon strike with the full drowning force of a wave.

The demolition derby and its rip-roar sound was a spectacle behind a tall, gated grandstand. Cars with their network avoidance systems removed were a great hit and would have been terrific fun to see. There would be plenty of parts to fix in that ring, but it was one place Daniel never wanted to go. The cheers over the gate and a walk by the fence sufficed. Admission was extra to sit in the stands, and it wasn't the time to ask for more money. But still, the crashes, screeches, and roars were tempting, if not to see through the fence, then to keep turning back to hear.

Once they were in quieter spaces along the row of the promenade, Daniel put the ScrollFlex case to his ear and took a call. They all kept walking with the flow of the crowd. Daniel glanced at Cessini a moment too long. He knew the call was about him.

Water drops speckled the dirt at his feet. A water balloon game was an aisle over on the promenade. An errant toss exploded another balloon. Two players crouched in their booths, opposite of each other, each pulling down with their hands on a rubber-band pouch. One boy loaded a water balloon into the pouch and shot it through a hole in his wooden overhead shield. His proper trajectory swished his balloon straight through the hole of his opponent's shield. His opponent was soaked, thrilled. Then the return volley went askew. Other kids lined up for their turn were splashed as well and erupted in cheer.

It was an accident at the side of the road, but Cessini couldn't watch any more of it. He turned as Daniel carried on. The voice from the ScrollFlex case got louder as a litany rattled. It was Daniel's comeuppance. He took it with his chin up the best way he could: He found a place to hide behind a prize schedule board. The llama-judging in the dirt tent was over. Four rows of flat wooden benches were all that remained in the mouth of a U-shaped arena. Robin sat in the second row as Daniel stepped over the bench and paced its aisle. Cessini and Meg kept a distance inside the plywood fence that wrapped the arena. The overarching white tent had an acoustic effect.

Daniel unrolled the ScrollFlex and set it face up on the bench. "You know I hate to do this," his boss said on the screen, "but it's my job, as well as yours."

"What did they conclude?" Daniel asked. He looked at Robin.

"Number one, house power should have had its own

transformer," his boss said as he read from a list. "Number two, there was also a fault in the electrical design. Mechanical and electrical were on the same circuit, the same panel board."

Daniel seemed somehow contented with what he heard. He even agreed with nods. "There wasn't one single point of failure," Daniel said. "There were many."

"Yes, there was a single point of failure," Daniel's boss shot back as the thin bezel frame spiked red with an emotive glare. "Your son. Your son is the single point of failure!" And the wave rolled in hard.

"My son?"

"Yes, the OSY valve should have been monitored in the fire control room. Whose responsibility was that?"

Daniel's eyes ticked to Cessini. "A lot of things should have been monitored."

"And don't forget the mistake of bringing a twelve-year-old boy to play at a data center," his boss shouted. "Even if what happened was nothing but a match stick on fire, we cannot have you back. It's a matter of perception. Look at me so I know you understand."

Daniel stepped over the splintered gray bench. He gestured for Cessini and Meg to leave from the fence.

Then the man let loose. "We are a concurrently maintainable, mission-critical data center operator. We *cannot* conclude that our property—with a hardened concrete shell, 206-mile-per-hour F3-tornado resistant walls, dual-power substation feeds, multiple points of connectivity, six-nines, that's 99.9999 percent successes without a failure, which hasn't gone offline for more than a minute in eight years—was suddenly and entirely destroyed by an out-of-control twelve-year-old boy and a girl who had even less right to be there than he did." The screen's bezel froze.

"Meg wasn't there," Daniel stated. "And everyone knew

they stayed in their assigned space. They hardly ever left it."

The bezel's red glow searched for an orange, tried a yellow, but kept dialing back up to red. "So now we have a problem," the man said. Meg pulled Cessini away. "We cannot prosecute a rescued boy who was captured crying in your arms on every street-level, truck-mounted, and handheld camera brought out to the scene."

Cessini came back into the ScrollFlex's view along the cusp of the benches. "Your son is a single point of failure. Do you hear me?" the man said, blasting him on sight.

Meg grabbed his arm. She pulled him away.

"You had the key to the fire control room," the man said to Daniel. "We can't prosecute for stupidity, but we can for negligence." The bezel stopped on black. "If that boy of yours didn't destroy us through liability, then you did. And it'll cost you. Big."

"I'll leave," Daniel said.

"Yes, you will. You will leave for jail. All of you. Him in juvi—" the man flustered as fairgoers passed by the fence and stared. The bezel dropped to within visible range. "In juvenile detention. I don't care."

"There was A and B power," Cessini said as he returned. "Circuit breakers would have stopped the fire from spreading. Why were there no circuit breakers?"

"There were plenty of circuit breakers," Daniel said. He held up his hand.

"I don't know," Cessini said. He fumbled. "It must have started with a short through its legs. Mechanical and electrical were connected. It went into the wall. The fire. It spread. What I built, the robot, Packet, it's gone now. It can't happen again—"

"I said go. Now! Cessini. Leave," Daniel said.

"That's right, you tell me what happened to your robot,"

the man yelled after him. "You tell me how it all burned."

Cessini was mortified. He had never seen such wrath.

"Get out of here. The both of you," Daniel raged. He jumped up from his bench.

Robin picked up the ScrollFlex and stood. She spoke directly to the screen. "Ruined is a data center taken down by a twelve-year-old boy. You want a test and repair lab? You just got it. You want the world to know all of your facilities, everyone's memories, everyone's dreams can all be destroyed by one boy?"

Cessini slipped his arm from Meg's pull. Robin locked him into her narrow gaze as she held the screen beneath her tensed face. "You think your obsolete facilities will last? You don't think I'll sue you for negligence? That boy, whose name is Cessini by the way, and everyone who worked there, could have died in that preventable fire."

Meg pulled Cessini away from the tent into the middle of the walkway.

"What didn't you do to protect all of them?" Robin backtracked into the tent. "What was in the floor, the walls? What did you know about that building that you did nothing to fix, and you let it all burn?"

Daniel stood. His eyes found Robin's as she sat before him, straddling the bench.

"DigiSci is your largest lease tenant," she said. "I work for DigiSci Corporate. Dr. Luegner is a close friend of mine."

Daniel's boss paused. "They're going to file a massive claim against us," he said.

Cessini followed Meg away in the relative calm of the backwash after the first wave. She smiled as he accepted the pull of his arm. The prize fowl barn was only ten yards away. She seemed to know it was the best time to leave. The massive tide was about to return.

"I can speak directly with Dr. Luegner," Robin said. "I can tell you he won't."

"Come on, Ceeme," Meg said. "Let's go see something nice. The birds always made us laugh."

Back in the opening of the acoustic U, the ScrollFlex was silent, its bezel paused. "I'll get back to you," Daniel's boss said, then was gone.

Robin's hands shook. She snapped the screen back into its case and held it up for Daniel. He refused it. "Dr. Luegner wouldn't want to see me and Meg broken," she said as if that were all there was to it.

Meg stopped.

"Now is the time, Robin. If there's something you've never told me," Daniel said.

"Go on," Meg said to Cessini. "I'll be right there. See the birds. You go. I'll stay." Her few steps ahead couldn't hide what she wanted to hear. She hooked around to the left of the prize schedule board and onto the trampled grass by the plywood fence.

Cessini let her go and entered the barn's doorway.

She slipped down the outside of the fence, squatted onto her heels, and rested the back of her head on the plywood. She looked toward the barn.

He rolled back from the door into a shadow. He could still hear if Robin and Daniel spoke up, but he could no longer be seen. The soft and fluffy silkies were the quietest birds caged at his end of the barn. The loud ducks and geese were at the far end of the two long shelves. A low table of incubated chicks was tucked away beyond the shadow of the entranceway for children to see, but not touch.

The familiarity of Daniel's voice was easier to read by watching his lips. "Is he Meg's father? Is that her secret?" he asked, unsure.

Robin gazed from the tent. She didn't look over the fence. "No. I told you before. Her father was Michael Longshore. She knew him. She met him. He was a foreman. He died trying to save someone at work. That's it. There's nothing more." Her hand trembled the ScrollFlex back into her purse.

Meg rolled the back of her head against the wood fence. She glanced across to the barn, but couldn't see. Cessini was in the dark. So maybe that was it, Cessini thought, she wanted to be strong, to be like her father, to watch over him like her father did selflessly for someone else. That had to be it. It was her secret revealed. Cessini was flattered, accepting of her. But he kept listening and then realized as Robin kept trembling and looked away from Daniel that, no, that wasn't all, there was more.

"Then what could Luegner possibly owe you so much that he would turn his back on all this without a fight?" Daniel asked.

"Nothing," Robin said, then she slammed her purse on the bench. "I owe him."

"You owe him? For what? Tell me. What in the world could you be so indebted to him for?"

"For Meg," she said, relenting. "He'll do it for Meg."

Meg cupped her hands over her ears. She squeezed her eyes shut as fairgoers passed.

"What about Meg?" Daniel paced, looked toward the barn but saw nothing.

Cessini forced himself to hear. He came an inch out of the shadow and stared across the walkway.

"Luegner saved her once and he'll do it again," Robin said. "But swear you'll never ask me what he gets in return."

"How can I swear—I don't know what you're asking of me."

"Nothing. Just swear it! I'm the one who has to live with

what I did," Robin said. She shot up from the bench. "Just me, so swear it."

Meg tightened her fists over her ears and buried her elbows between her knees.

"I swear I won't ask," he said. "But what do you mean, he saved her once?"

"Her heart," Robin said at the light of the entrance. "It's her heart. Or, no heart."

Cessini zeroed in on Meg. She was rocking in a seated fetal position.

"She was born without a heart."

Cessini looked up at Robin. What he thought he heard or read on her lips was impossible. Meg rocked in pain, her knees drawn tight up into her chest. Her pose was familiar, but she was never further from the sweet little girl of three curling her knees up on a doctor's waiting room chair. If he went out there to her, Robin would see him, stop talking, and he had to hear on his own.

The top mesh door of the incubated chick cage popped open with a pang. Cessini's bully tormentor, now grown, had flipped it open. In defiance of a "Look but don't touch" sign, the boy reached in past his elbow for a sleeping yellow chick. Then he stopped and looked up into the darkened frame of the entranceway.

"Oh, hi, Cessini," the boy said, stilled. "I heard about what you did at the data center. That was really tough. Stay strong, big man. Stay strong."

Cessini's eyes were still shocked from the sunlight outside, but he knew through the shadow the sound of his once-bully's voice. The boy stroked the back of the chick's head with his knuckle, and then returned it gently to its lamp.

Cessini turned back to the sun.

"You couldn't tell from looking at her," Robin said. "But

when she was born, she looked so beautiful to me. She breathed. But blood flowed directly into her lungs. She was drowning as soon as she started breathing. They grabbed her away for an ECG, but they didn't come back for hours. I knew something was wrong. They told me what she had was so incredibly rare."

Cessini squinted. Did he hear right? Could she have? The bully was quiet and moved on down the line of the shelves. "Goodbye, Cessini. Take care."

Cessini ignored him, and edged out into the sunlight.

Meg butted the back of her head against the fence.

"The doctors just stood there," Robin said. "'Just tell me what's wrong?' I asked. She had a complete antrioventricular septal defect with a double inlet left ventricle."

Meg bit onto her crossed arms to muffle her cry.

"All I could say was, 'What?' Her lips were blue. She was so small. They told me to take her home and let her die in my arms. I begged them. I said, 'I can't do that, I can't. Do something. Anything, but don't let my sweet baby girl die in my arms.'"

Daniel said nothing.

Robin opened her soul. "I swore an oath," she said, smiling a bit. "And Dr. Luegner approved an experimental surgery. DigiSci had developed a valve. It was small and round, made of organic material that would grow with the patient, with Meg. It had particles infused that would glow blue when oxygenated, or warn red on a scan if it failed."

Cessini clung along the outside wall of the barn. He approached the mouth of the arena. All they had to do was look up and out. Meg was hidden from view behind the schedule board and side of the fence.

"To her, on her earliest scans," Robin said, "she said it looked like four round grapefruits glowing blue inside her chest. And so she used to tell everybody that when she was a little, little baby, she had eaten four grapefruits. I never dared to correct her. It was just so beautiful to hear her voice alive and able to say anything like that at all." Her fingers shook uncontrollably as she wiped a tear from her eye. "Now Luegner monitors her heart remotely. Controls it."

Cessini came forward through the waves of the crowd like driftwood finding its shore.

"Why didn't she tell Cessini?" Daniel asked. "She could have told him. What was she thinking?"

Robin laughed and slapped Daniel's shoulder. "She was thinking the same as she always does. Sea Turtle Rescue. She thinks she's the turtle; she's trying to rescue herself, make herself feel better. She's conditioned herself to play every day, thanks to you and that old, beat-up tickle tablet, or whatever you want to call what you made. She thinks if she stopped playing, her heart would, too. We should take that thing away from her already. It's not healthy."

"Cessini, out of anybody, would understand."

"She doesn't want him to know. She says she doesn't want him to think that 'Only a defective girl could love him.' Her words, not mine. So, please, for her sake and mine, don't you tell him. Okay?"

Meg rose up at the edge of the fence, horror-stricken with both hands clenched into fists against her chest. "Don't you tell him!" she yelled. "Don't you ever tell him!"

Cessini walked out from the drift of the passing crowd. His narrowed eyes locked with hers that were frozen wide in panic. He broke her stare with the swiftness of a calmed and controlled omission. "Tell me what?" he asked.

And on the electric tram ride through a field back to their car in a faraway lot, not another word was spoken. They drove away under a gray swirled sky that passed into night. Cessini closed his eyes in prayer that no more ill would come over their home. Daniel opened their front door with his rattle of keys that broke the silence.

Cessini, standing alone in the bathroom, brushed his teeth with dry baking soda, and spit.

He adjusted his bearing in the dark of his room. His pupils swelled and moonlight broke through his vertical blinds. He felt his way toward his bed. A small shadow formed along the edge of the water pond in the glass tank on his shelf.

He clicked on the stem of his penlight with his thumb and shined a local moon spot of light. His mangrove rivulus lay on its side in the sand, a fin angled up into the air. Its eyes stared long, but still moved and saw him. Its mouth opened and closed in shallow gasps that became thinner and further between.

Cessini lifted a small oral syringe from the shelf, and with the top removed from the glass tank, reached in past both elbows. He drew up two teaspoons of water into the syringe from the pool at the base of the log and dribbled a few drops onto the back of his fish. It seemed to look his way, its breath seemed to relax, and as it aged in its final wetted moments on its shore, it somehow seemed to be happier in the company of water after all.

Cessini left his little creature to its own silent peace and sat down on the edge of his bed. He mourned a moment that would soon come for his friend. Their time together dripped away as the mantle-breath of his bellows lamp counted down by threes. In the quiet, he heard Meg fall to weeping in her bed next door through the wall. What he overheard must have been true. Maybe she was the more pained of them all. He lowered his penlight away from the tank and returned his rivulus to its shadow.

He pulled his cover up to his chin in the absence of breath, rested his temple to his pillow, and let the weight of his head sink in. If anything good had come of that fair, it was that he knew that Meg, in her silence, was more like him than he had ever believed. They were different, but equals. And though muffled by a wall, he could still hear her cry. What pain worse than no heart could Robin have possibly sworn away in her oath to a doctor named Luegner?

Five years before at Cessini and Meg's first fair together, Meg had taken his elbow and walked him away from his tears. The shadows of younger memories shifted across his mind as he heard her weep herself to sleep, then fall deeper into the night's silence. If he breathed his last breath, he would tell her the truth. He had heard. And she didn't have to be alone anymore. He could take care of her, too, and with that, he knew, it was time for him to grow up.

ELEVEN

SHE WAS HERSELF

A BLUE, SETTLED haze made visibility poor as Cessini's nighttime victor, Ceeborn, came into focus and searched out over a darkened, wet expanse below him. He was stronger, more determined; braver, not at all fearful of the water rushing beneath the platform of the gondola he was riding. Waves covered by a membranous skin rushed by below as he traversed a cavernous tank. The gondola's platform was hung by fibrous tendons that spanned the inside of the tank from one fleshy wall to another. He grasped the frame of the platform in his fists and leaned his body farther out over the waves. Light from the gondola's four corner posts helped with spots through the darkness as he searched for the source of the cry of his name.

"Ceeborn! Over here, help! Can you help me?" Daniel called as he struggled to stay afloat at the surface.

Ceeborn let go of the gondola's post and dove headfirst, breaking through the skin that covered the water.

The water in the tank was warm and divine, and beneath its quiet turbulence it was serene. But Daniel's legs treaded high above, so Ceeborn swam up from underwater and surfaced beside him.

"You're here," Daniel said as he grappled for life, dragging them down together, and locked in a struggling embrace. An undertow pulled them into a deeper current, and as Daniel drowned, the contortion of his face was awful, his mouth gasping. Ceeborn let go and watched Daniel's last glimmer of life drown away into a deeper funnel of water and through the aperture of a valve in the wall.

Another body floated up at the surface and broke the gondola's light rays that sliced through the water. It was Meg. Her arms swished at her sides. He raced up. She was scared and alive. Her face was blue from the chill.

"Ceeme, can you help?" she asked as the waves overtook her face.

He supported her head and waist in his hands. He tread water as strong as he could. He took in a swallow. "Don't worry. I got you."

The faster he kicked, the more the water's covering skin churned and entangled his legs. He had to let her go. She could float on her own.

"I'll get help," he said. He swallowed hard and unclenched her grip from holding his arm. He dove back under the water and swam as fast as he could in the blackened morass until the skin wrapped down and entangled his body. He saw a light ahead and—

Cessini awoke as himself in a sweat, lying on the edge of his bed, wrapped in his sheet. His left leg dangled from kicking. The penlight was dim on the floor where he had dropped it. The pores of his skin were a hot flash of pain.

He stopped at the kitchen door before entering. Meg, Daniel, and Robin, seated at the kitchen table for breakfast, looked exhausted. Meg had cereal, Daniel coffee. Robin's plate had only unbuttered toast and, beside it, a prescription bottle of antacid. She didn't look healthy.

Daniel reached clear past a white sugar bowl with a teaspoon in its open top. He picked up a shaker of salt, turned it over for a pour into his black mug—then slapped his hand to his forehead. "What the hell did I just do?" His drink was ruined.

"At least it's not meconium," Meg said. She smiled to Cessini as he walked in, treading lightly.

"Is that really appropriate?" Robin said.

"I dunno," Meg said. "In school we just learned every new baby has it."

Cessini sat at the table's fourth seat. He lifted a teaspoon of the white sugar from its bowl, holding the handle between the reddened tips of his fingers. "You're alive," he said to Daniel. "It could have been worse."

Daniel shoved his salted mug aside, and then drove his elbow hard onto the table, pointing his finger. He had their attention. "Water is like technology. It's everywhere."

"Except water is not always so good," Cessini said.

"Yes, water is good. Water flows through sprinkler pipes to protect the servers that run the commerce of the world. Ships transport goods on water. Jets leave contrails of water in the sky. We couldn't grow food without water. We wouldn't eat without water. And you, Cessini," he slammed his palm on the table, "you are the only person on this planet who is reactive to water. Who cannot tolerate water. Who would die from a shower of water. Who still thinks technology and water don't mix."

Cessini stared, he didn't move a muscle. Daniel saw Robin and Meg's fright and he stopped. He lowered his hands. "But they do mix. You and I mix. We have to. We have to put the past behind us. And whatever happens from here, I'll take the heat, but there're going to be questions to answer."

"No way, not me," Meg said and laughed. She took a big bite of her cereal and dribbled. "I'm not going to jail with you two. Nuh-uh. Count me out of that."

Robin threw her toast on her plate. She looked like she was going to be sick. "Don't say that."

"Why not? I've got nothing to hide. No more secrets from me. I'm a new 'me' this morning, it feels great, and I like it," Meg said. She wiped her mouth hard with a crumpled napkin. "The sun is still shining. The world is still spinning. What could possibly go wrong from here?"

Robin slammed her fist on her plate. "Don't say that! Just eat your food."

"It's alright, I'm here. Everything's good. Calm down," Daniel said.

"No, everything is not good. Can't you see? You're not a bad man, you're an absent man." She grabbed hold of Cessini's forearm on the table. "He reaches out to you, you push him away. It's conditioning. He's learning distance. Distance you'll regret." She let go of her grip and Cessini's skin tone returned. "Maybe the fire was a good thing, something to free you from your work so you won't have to go on living with the slow burning guilt of losing your son."

Daniel was stilled. Beyond the kitchen pass-through window, the living room wall screen flashed soft-white with a gentle ring tone. Dr. Luegner's static face appeared.

"Dr. Luegner," Robin said as she jumped up from the table. "It's good to see you."

The border of the wall screen opened wider on Luegner and settled its frame on a conciliatory, cobalt blue. He was wearing a navy pinstripe suit with a dark blue shirt. He tugged the cuffs from under his sleeves. "Hello, Robin. How are you holding up?"

"I'm fine, thank you. I'm doing fine."

Daniel got up from the table, went around the pass-through wall, and stood in front of the living room screen.

"I did some looking. We're doing an old mainframe

installation," Luegner said. "Part public, part private."

"Where?" Daniel asked.

Cessini tiptoed the three steps down into the living room. Daniel gestured him forward. They sat together on the couch. Robin stayed at the stairs with Meg held at her front. She draped her arms over Meg's shoulders in a protective embrace.

"It's a research lab," Luegner said. "You'll do fine there. Supervise the install and operations. The university bought an old exaflop machine from our refresh cycle."

"Fine," Daniel said. "Where is it?"

"It's in a good place. DigiSci is consolidating its data centers. We're decommissioning an old 220,000-square-foot facility that does nothing but process health records. Apparently, you can do all of that in a couple of modules now. From what I understand, everything at your old facility was live-live duplicated, so again, from what I gather, it's not the end of the world, yet. Hell, one module of that old dinosaur warehouse you just took offline can fit in nothing but two rows of eight cabinets now."

Daniel sank deeper into the couch. He reached his arm around Cessini.

"Six-month trip," Luegner said. "Set up the system. Take Robin and Meg. You might even like it there and stay. Until all this blows over." It sounded like a dream, but the screen's frame measured through cyan to a sickened viridian. "Looks like you'll be headed for an improvement," Luegner said. "Maybe we'll even put in wet servers, all encased in liquid, so no air cooling is necessary. We could save ninety-seven percent on power alone."

"But where we'd be going," Cessini asked, "what the university bought, is still air-cooled, right? No liquid?"

"That's right," Luegner said. "Two CRACs, one for each side of the room, air cooled. No liquid."

"Where is it?" Daniel asked.

"Hobart," Luegner said. The screen flipped an image of the earth to the southern hemisphere and a narrower viewfield zoomed down from the sky to a green, mountainous island between Antarctica and the mainland of Australia.

"Tasmania?" Daniel asked.

"Maybe half a world but still just a call away," Luegner said.

Daniel took his salt with his wounds and agreed. "I appreciate your doing this for me."

"I'm not doing it for you," Luegner said, then looked over to Robin and Meg standing before her. "I'm doing it for them."

Robin lowered her shaking hand from her mouth and tightened it onto Meg's shoulder. Meg reached up and brought it farther down to cover her pounding chest. Robin mouthed to Luegner on the screen, "Thank you."

Cessini fixed on Meg's stark gaze, and then turned back to Luegner on the screen.

"Okay, then, we'll take it," Daniel said before Cessini could speak.

Then Luegner was gone from the screen with nothing but a glance at Cessini, and a word. "Good."

Water vapor condensed in the contrail of the plane that flew west and was visible for hundreds of miles, though nobody floated below on the waves of the Pacific to see. Cessini rested his forehead against the window over the clouds. The greater the distance, he thought, the better. A new life was about to begin.

He thought he could even escape the tube of the plane and walk his way to the end of the earth on the clouds, if it weren't for their disguise of water that would scorch his feet as if walking on a hotbed of coals. Then a hole in the clouds and the shimmering vastness of ocean water below was enough to turn him away.

It seemed so very strange at the time, but the off-axis twist he suffered before the fire had now passed into history, nothing but a single page torn from a book of confusion. He sat and faced due west in the direction they flew. Meg clacked away on her tablet in her middle seat at his left shoulder, while Robin sat beside her, and Daniel was across the aisle. They were safe in their passage, but one thought remained: Robin's indelible oath of silence that still stoked the tremors in her hand now covered their escape that seemed too easy. She looked over, and as the plane tilted for another southernly bank on their way, he turned away and rested his forehead against the window for its view.

"What are you thinking about?" Meg asked without looking up from her game.

"Nothing . . . us . . . the sky," he said without turning. "I was thinking I could walk across the sky."

"What do you mean? What about us? We're going. That's that."

"I know. Are you doing okay?"

"Obviously." She held up Sea Turtle Rescue on her screen. "You want to play, 'fortunately-unfortunately'?" On her screen, two hatchlings scrambled to the edge of a beach. She brought the tablet back to her lap and clicked the hatchlings forward toward the foam of a wave at the surf. She hurried the rear one's flippering of the sand so it could catch up with its bigger sibling. The runt of the two had four blue rings tagged on its shell for her identification. The larger turtle seemed fine in the water. The smaller's swimming frenzy was about to begin.

"Fortunately, water doesn't bother me anymore."

"Plsh," Meg scoffed and clacked the keys. "No, seriously,

I'll start with 'fortunately.' Then you say something that's 'unfortunately.' We're on a plane, so we'll start with something that moves like a bike, a car, a train, then go bigger. Okay? Fortunately, on a bike you can peddle around. Unfortunately, your legs get tired if you . . ." she dangled.

"I don't know. What?" he said, then added, "Fortunately, I'm still building my spaceship."

"No. That's not how you play. I say something 'fortunately,' then you say something 'unfortunately.'"

"Fortunately, I remember every one of those days back then, when you and I sat and worked at the table in our office. I said I was going to build a spaceship where water doesn't matter, and I will."

"Oh, forget it," she said and pushed him back. "If you don't want to play, can you at least change the window?" She returned to her keys. "Get rid of the clouds and put on a show. Trees, the city we're going to, anything . . . dirt!"

Cessini smirked toward the window with its passing clouds. She thrust herself over him for the window's lower control and flipped it to random mosaic. The window's screen rolled into a kaleidoscope of city parks turning to shards of colors that turned in on their ends. "Good, now leave it," she said and sat back. Then he tiptoed his fingers to the window's control and flipped it back to his clouds.

"Mom!" she said.

He poked her. She was herself. And the more she fought back, the more he relished her being at his side.

"Work it out," Robin said, reading her ScrollFlex in her seat.

He grabbed Meg's tablet by its wings. She shrieked.

"Take our picture. Take our picture," he said as she punched his arm.

"That's a great idea," Robin said as she rotated her ScrollFlex to vertical. She ran her thumb down the screen's length and it became transparent. "Since you'll probably want to remember this wonderfully peaceful trip for the rest of your lives. Ready?"

He tossed the tablet back to Meg, flipped the window back to mosaic, and hugged her tight into the shared armrest of their seats.

Robin flicked her finger against the top right, dog-eared corner of the ScrollFlex screen and captured their pep as a photo. Then with her quick tug and release the screen recoiled into its beige, cylindrical carry case. "Now, both of you be quiet so I can close my eyes," she said.

Daniel studied a work screen with pages of manuals across the aisle. He cleared a page of its detail and looked with the raise of an eyebrow. "Are you done now?"

Cessini looked around and over the headrests. There were plenty of other people on the plane. He pushed Meg away with a quiet, "Shhh," and they settled back into their seats. He swiped the window back to their mutually annoying clouds.

"What if we hate it there?" he asked. "We don't know anyone."

"You didn't know anyone back home," Meg said. "And, fortunately, where we're going, they don't know you." She was right, and who was he to argue on such a long flight?

The next time he woke beside her, a new turbulence buffeted the descent of their smaller plane transfer from the mainland to the island. He lifted the plain window shade and saw the approach of land ahead. The shoreline was a broken puzzle over water. Country houses and single shops pricked the coastal green hills. Buildings seemed to multiply into a city whose growth fingered its way up the lowland slopes toward the majestic, flattened peak of Mount Wellington.

They left the watery blue depths far behind, and the dry,

green view ahead grew firmer as the plane swayed unnervingly in the winds on their final descent. The wheels hit hard and Cessini's hands bit into the fronts of his armrests. Flaps braked, engines reversed. The plane was controlled into a turn and then wound down for the relaxed start of the taxi.

"We're here," Meg said, simple as that.

Soon enough, Daniel was hunched over the steering wheel of their rented Jeep and peered up through the windshield for a full view of the clear sky. They drove up the lower foothills of the mountain to where the road branched right under a canopy of trees and a neighborhood was nestled along the edge of a forested trail. Daniel pulled to a stop at the curb of an old English house at the end of the drive. And to all four, but Cessini in particular, there was no doubt in their minds. Treeline Drive was theirs. This place was their new home.

Cessini put his feet to the yard, stretched his arms into the air, and approached a white, numbered gate. He rubbed his finger around the curve of the metallic numeral eight, which grew out of two adjacent fours. The number was as easy to remember as a breath of fresh air. Their new address was 448 Treeline Drive.

Daniel slipped past and took the first steps to the front door. "Feels like home to me," he said as he fumbled the keys, and let them all in.

Cessini entered to find boxes stacked in piles of pre-packed chores. Their home would be cramped, but fine. The floors and the trim were a quaint, dark wood contrast over plastered white walls. Two columns of boxes stood in front of inset shelves that flanked a fireplace mostly hidden from view. Robin tossed her purse on the mantel, her ScrollFlex to its side.

Cessini turned a tight corner to his room. Meg found hers nicely across from his. There was no waist-high shelf around his walls, and hardly room for any tools, but the east-facing window had vertical blinds, which were the same as the ones he had left behind. A very good start. Better than that, he bent down to see an angled floor register that bathed the room from below in a cool, dry blanket of air.

"We'll fix it up perfect," Robin called out from the living room.

Five rooms, plus kitchen and bath. Cessini and Meg had already seen it all, and there was nowhere to sit.

"Unfortunately, it needs some color," Meg said. "But it'll do."

"Fortunately," Robin said, sneaking in a jibe, "I've got just the ticket." She snatched up her ScrollFlex, pulled out the screen, thumbed for the picture from the plane, and dog-eared the upper right corner of its page. She clam-shelled the case and the screen went stiff. She set it back on the mantel, centered just so. "Okay, so, if everyone's up for it, we need to keep moving, get out, and push through to beat the jet lag."

Daniel hugged Robin from behind, catching her off guard. "Coming here is a big change. I know that," he said as Robin accepted his arms. "But we don't give up. I can fix things. Thank you for sticking with me. You know I can fix you, too." He kissed her temple and she turned to face him.

"Funny, I could use a good fixing. It's been a while," Robin said, smiling for the first time in a while.

"Eww," Meg said. She settled down on the floor, crossed her legs, and pulled out her tablet. She flared out its wings and tickled its keys to restart her game.

Daniel let go of Robin and tousled Cessini's hair as he stood at the mantel of the fireplace. "And I love you; you know that, you're going to be the best, better than me. Come here," Daniel said, pulling Cessini in closer and getting down on one knee. "I've failed at a lot of things, but not this. I can fix us all, even if it takes me to the end of my days."

"I know, we just need the right tools," Cessini said as Daniel pulled him into a warming hug.

"If you could go anywhere on this adventure," Daniel said, "where would you go? What would you see?"

"Get real. We're not camping up north in Minnesota, okay? Let's just relax for a minute," Meg said as she stayed focused within her game.

"Don't fall asleep," Robin said to her. "You'll feel better by morning, or maybe the next, if you keep moving."

Cessini was groggy, crashing from the switch of the hours, but Robin was right. "I know. How about someplace where we can control the water?" he asked and waited on their collective surprise.

"Now where are we going to do that?" Meg asked.

"I have no idea," Daniel said as he slapped his hands together. He threw Robin her purse from the mantel. "But I bet there's got to be someplace on this island where we can. I'm in."

"How about a hydroelectric plant?" Cessini asked. His smile grew huge.

"Yes!" Daniel said. "Now you're thinking." He opened the ScrollFlex and tapped.

Cessini yanked Meg up by the arm, which she hated. He grabbed the ScrollFlex from Daniel's hands. "And 'fortunately' for all of us," Cessini said as he swiped, "I know exactly how I can find one."

TWELVE
BORN ON A PALLET

CESSINI TWISTED IN his seat for a last glance out the rear window of the Jeep. Gerald Aiden sealed the gates of Tungatinah Hydroelectric Power no more than two hundred yards behind them. The man's trumped-up stare was a guise so all would know he stood in control of his water. He pivoted his stiff leg about and marched back to his warehouse of power. Cessini knew the name of the place meant "falling water," but far more than water had just fallen apart from their visit. It wasn't because of the bumps in the road that he and Daniel could fix with the right set of tools, nor was it the faulty air conditioner that dripped and left a ring of pain around his temple; it was everything, and for that he had only himself to blame.

Daniel slammed on the brakes. He jumped out and stormed over to the roadside curb. Robin unbuckled and turned back to Cessini and Meg in their back seats. "Wait here," she said as she opened her door and ran around the hood after Daniel.

"You know when I said if I could bear all the clouds in the sky," Cessini said to Meg, "I still would never want to come back to this world?"

"Yeah, what about it?"

"But, that I'd probably do it for you?"

"You said 'most likely,' not probably. That was mean."

"I meant it to be nice," he said.

"I know what you meant. But I'm the one every day who still takes care of you. And I'll still probably do it tomorrow. But I'd never have said it would take a gazillion rain drops to make me want to do it again. I'd still do it for nothing, for you."

"Thanks," he said. She was right.

"See, now that's how you say it whether you mean it or not. That's how you're supposed to say it." Then her focus pulled through the windshield to the rising screams outside.

"How can we live like this?" Daniel asked. "I'm sick of it. He's sick of it."

Cessini looked toward the valley below. There were only trees beyond the curb that could hear.

"*We* don't live like this," Robin said. "I do! Luegner sending us here was because of me, not you. I have to live with all of our problems. All of them." Then Robin pounded her fist on Daniel's chest. "Can't you see?" she cried. "Luegner owns all of us—and now he owns me more than ever before."

Meg squeezed her eyes shut.

"You think you can fix me? You think I'm broken?" Robin shoved and pinned Daniel against her side of the car. "Well, you can't! I haven't given you that permission. You can't fix what you don't own, and you don't own me!"

Daniel pulled her in tight, grabbed at her pounding fists, but she fought herself free and away. He stood without another word. She wrapped one shaking hand across her stomach, the other over her mouth. She approached the trees and circled away in a sob.

"You have to understand her," Meg said to Cessini in the car. "I think I do."

"You think I'm absent?" Daniel yelled outside. "You don't think I'm doing everything I can to keep us together? What about my ambition? When do I get to achieve?"

Robin hurried back, opened her front passenger door, and fell back into her seat. She didn't turn around. "It's okay, sweetie," she said into the rearview mirror. "It's not your fault. It's mine. Okay?"

Daniel slipped back in his driver's seat. Robin turned away to her window. Daniel reached up and adjusted the rearview mirror. Cessini saw his stare. Were they good eyes or bad? It was too hard to tell. "This place was a terrible idea," Daniel said. "You should have never made us come here."

Cessini shriveled in his seat. Absolutely everything was his fault.

Daniel drew his shoulder belt across and locked all their doors. As he drove down a switchback on the hill, Cessini's view through the rear window of the aging Tungatinah Power Plant was more disheartening than its promise on approach. He wondered why this place should have been any different as Robin cried out her own private well of regret into the deep fold of her hands.

The trees rushed by the car, all out of his control. He was trapped. Maybe he should open the door as they rushed by en masse and try his freedom, instead. A freedom to scream, to toss back the jet-lagged hours he stole from the sun. He hammered his fist on the door.

Meg rested her head on her window and pressed her palm deep over a pain in her chest. "Can we go home now, please? I'm kind of tired."

Cessini rocked in his seat as she settled to stillness. She closed her eyes and slouched into her door. If his anguish now caused her heart to pain, it was no one's fault but his own. He owned their suffering, her fate. Meg's hand slipped down from her chest to her seat. She was fading.

"Meg! Wake up." He lunged to pull her upright.

"What? I wasn't sleeping."

She was groggy, maybe her head hurt. Maybe her head was as painful and twisted as his. On the plane, people said to drink plenty of water to beat the jet lag. Were they insane? Did they also think the sun went around the earth? "I wish I wasn't like this," he said as she pulled away again. "I wish—"

"You weren't like what?" she said as she rolled down her window for a breath of air. "You are what you are. Now stop it. You don't have to worry about me. I can take care of myself."

She said it, he thought, but did she mean it?

She slumped back into her seat. "I'm fine. Even if I wasn't, it's not your problem."

He pushed his forehead against his window's tempered glass as they drove farther away. The sun was setting for the night. Meg settled into the rhythmic breathing of sleep. The dry floor of the valley approached as they drove closer to darkness. The power and percussion of the water they left behind was the least of his growing list of fears. Grief hurt broadest, but mostly deep.

Headlights shifted to the road. The earth continued to rotate. If he was going to fix his course, his perspective of life had to change. Maybe if the sun rotated around the earth, instead, then everything in his world would be clear. An impossibility. But, if it did, then the morning's light would be altogether something to see.

At one minute to six the next morning, the sun's rays crested over the home-salted hills of the eastern shore of Sandy Bay. The sun had risen in the east as usual and glistened across the morning's waves to the west. The masts at the western dock tangled like pickup sticks standing vertical against the tide. The main university campus awoke under a bath of golden light. The striking glow of a dawn breached the windshield of the Jeep head on, and Daniel threw down his visor.

He angled the Jeep off Grosvenor Crescent into a spot facing the campus' sports field. He twisted over his shoulder past the empty front passenger seat and lifted a grin to Cessini and Meg to open the early start to their day. "We're here."

"Is this it?" Meg asked. She was still tired, but ready to go.

"It is," Daniel said. "And when the rest of the city wakes up, we'll go get something nice for your mother."

Cessini hurried the handle of his rear door and followed Daniel out without another word. He and Meg followed him across Crescent Drive toward the glass foyer between the east and west rectangular wings of the four-story building shaped like an "H." Daniel held the foyer door and Meg slipped under his arm. Then they took two stairs at a time to the second floor.

A glassy-eyed all-nighter student on a stepladder was mapping out tedious proportions on part of the wall.

"That's going to be you someday," Daniel said to Meg as the student glanced down from her ladder.

She was sketching colored swirls for a beautiful piece of mixed media art. She referred to her plaque's Mandelbrot set, and its printed equation of $Z = Z^2 + C$. It was a mathematical simplicity that hid a cornucopia of delicious detail within. On her wall, an abstract flower's petals twisted into a Chinese dragon in clawed fighting form. Tidal waves curled, mammalian brains swirled, and galaxies spun from the edges of her frame. Her canvas had come alive with mesmerizing complexities, all singularly explained by the higher-context Mandelbrot set.

"I like it," Meg said. "It must have taken you awhile."

"Thanks, it did, and you're the first person to like it so far," the student artist said from the ladder as she perked up and tightened back her hair. "I've still got a lot to do before it's done."

Cessini walked through to the hall. "Come on, it's time to go see it."

Ahead was the entrance to the western wing of the H. Two graduate students tinkered around the steel-studded construction of a roughed-in eight-by-twelve-foot mantrap. They hoisted the robotic torso of a security monitor up onto a front counter.

Daniel stepped through the construction, mindful not to tread on or disturb their work. "Mainframe's just around . . .?"

"Yup, through and around to your right," the grad student said. "Don't mind the dust."

"Don't worry, we don't," Cessini said. "Mainframe might, though."

"Had a bugger of a time getting her up here," the grad student said as he scooted under the counter with a ratchet wrench to tighten the bolts of the torso. "It's all wrapped up, but no worries, you can't miss it."

Daniel peeked around into the hallway's rough construction debris. A daisy-chained string of light bulbs in small yellow protective cages hung from beneath the ceiling's grid and lit the way.

The first lab on the south side of the windowless hallway was finished with drywall awaiting compound and sanding. Daniel led them to the second lab that extended back toward the end of the hall. Its side was nothing but a line of metal upright studs and a long strip of sagging yellow tape tied from its doorway to every other stud down the line.

Daniel, Cessini, and Meg approached the room. A tall box glistened in angled teases through the spacing of the studs. It was seven feet tall. Daniel and Meg ducked under the yellow tape at the door. Cessini stopped outside of the wall's frame. There it was. All wrapped up and delivered in a blanket of shrink wrap. It sat askew in the middle of the rectangular room. A brushed-black metal cabinet on a pallet.

The gray slab floor beneath it was scuffed by black pallet jack wheels. Wood splinters cracked free from the thrust of the jack were scattered over the floor. What kind of rough delivery could such a precious cargo have endured in its travel across the sea?

Cessini rattled the strength of the hallway's metal studs, checked their cut holes where lines of conduit would be sewn. Then he slipped sideways through the framing into the room. Daniel circled the seven-foot cabinet and trailed his hand over the crinkly wrap. Yellow stickers pasted on each side had a mini-ball meter that recorded the last, greatest angle of tilt. Too much lean and the mini-balls would pour into a red zone. But with proper delivery, all the mini-balls would stay un-moved in their upright well. Daniel checked around. All four sides' upright wells were full. He let out a breath. Cessini smiled. It was all going to be okay.

Cessini and Meg had paced the whole of the room in a matter of steps. It would all have to be filled with more equipment. There would be no place for a new working table. Playing was over. This was Daniel's new life.

"You can both come here after school if you want," Daniel said. "I might like the company and extra hands while I work. A new life starts here. Smaller, yes. But better."

Cessini pulled at a separation between the layers of shrink wrap for a peek and a poke.

"Imagine the potential in this box," Daniel said, "and in us who traveled across this world." An anteroom was roughly framed in behind the end of the lab. "And that room there, that will be my office, my studio."

"And up there would be a good place for a camera," Cessini said. He liked what he saw. He measured around the room, counting off heel to toe for each of the two rows of eight cabinets. "I think we can make this work."

"We'll get it all back," Daniel said. "It's going to be perfect. We'll get Packet back. Your body, my code. All of it, right here. Packet born right here on a pallet."

"Excellent. When can we start?" Cessini asked.

"I'll get it all hooked up and installed. You two come right here after school. And, hey, since we're in an actual school this time, no one can complain that you're here."

"This is going to work out great. And you know what else?" Cessini asked.

"What?" Meg asked.

"If a whole module of the data center back home fits into this room today," Cessini said, "then tomorrow we'll be able to fit everything from here into a tablet."

"How about a blood cell?" Daniel asked as he tore free the tape at the end of the shrink wrap. "We won't use chips side-by-side." He circled faster to unwind. "We'll stack them in 3D. No, forget stacking them. We'll pour chips in droplets of nano-particle-infused liquid."

"We won't even need wires," Cessini said. He yanked down on the folds of the wrap and followed Daniel around. He stomped through the swelling pile of wrap on the floor. The top of the cabinet became bare, unprotected.

"Air-cooled, no liquid, we'll design the room just for you," Daniel said as he waited for a chuckle to burst, but Cessini couldn't get there, not yet. Meg elbowed him.

Cessini looked around on the floor. Splinters of the pallet's wood were buried under the wrap. More were kicked into the crease between the wall's stud plate and the floor. Dust filled the recesses of the studs.

"It doesn't pay what we're used to," Daniel said, "but it'll do."

"What are we used to?" Cessini asked.

"Lap of luxury. I thought you knew?" A wad of tape from the shrink wrap caught Daniel's pant leg as he came forward. He bent down to un-tack it.

"Well, a new life definitely starts here," Meg said with a grin.

Daniel stopped in mid-pull. He looked around closer at the floor, then back up at the bare cabinet. "You know, you were right."

"About what?" Cessini asked.

"The mainframe will mind. A lot. We've got to wrap it all back up. Get it out of here."

"Wait, why?" Meg asked.

"These kids shouldn't have brought it up here to begin with during all this construction," Daniel said. "The banging and dust alone could kill it. I guess there's a bit of incompetence in us all."

"Everyone's human. But you're right. I saw the dust, too," Cessini said.

Daniel untwisted the shrink wrap that bubbled and knotted at his feet. "Come on, help me wrap it back up."

"I knew coming here so early in the morning was a bad idea," Meg said. "I'm going to go wait outside."

"I'll be right there," Cessini said as she stepped out through the frame of the wall.

By the time he was ready to leave, the student artist in the foyer was also gone from her ladder. Her pallet of tools waited at the foot of her canvas and all of her developing spirals. The morning's sun had risen farther and become stronger over the eastern bay.

Daniel tapped the front button on a vending machine for a

coffee. Meg sat in a hard, scooped chair at a white, mushroom-stem table to wait. She leaned over to rest her head on her outstretched arm. Another chair was still turned upside down on the table's top, left over from the night.

Cessini pulled the overturned chair toward the edge. It was heavier than it looked. As he turned it over, he dropped it before clearing the table's edge. One leg struck hard as Meg snapped away from under its fall.

"Hey!" she said as it crashed.

"Sorry," he said, jumping back. She returned to her leaned-over rest and noticed something on the table's new surface. It was a thin scratch. Cessini looked. The leg of the chair had a foot without a disk and its burr was as sharp as a nail.

"Tsk," she said, "now look at what you did. You scratched it." The fingernail of her thumb fit into its first tiny rub. "I bet this is going to be here a really long time."

"Oops, my fault," Cessini said as he righted the chair at her table.

Daniel pulled up a third. "So, Robin said she wants to take you two out for some shopping. Get you some new clothes for school. An arcade, 'Cat and the Fiddle,' or something like that. Start you off right."

"Finally," Meg said. She perked up.

"Do I have to?" Cessini asked.

"Come on, new clothes once a year whether you need 'em or not," Meg said as she sprang up from her seat. She pulled back her hair but it was too short to stay. It fell back to bangs. "So, come on, what are we waiting for? Slackers! Let's go."

Cessini rested his forehead down onto the table. He balked. "Nothing's even open yet. It can't be. Besides, there's no way I'm going to a place where cows jump over a moon."

"Ugh," she said. "Can't you at least try to fit in somehow?

Maybe make one friend, if that's even possible."

"And we've got to get something nice for Robin," Daniel said. "We've got to do at least one thing normal for a change."

Cessini set his chin on the table. He checked the depth of the scratch with his fingernail.

"Come on, get up," she said. "If you want to build a spaceship, you first have to jump over the moon."

"What does that even mean?" he asked.

"I have no idea. Are you coming or what?"

"One friend?"

"One," she said.

"Okay, fine. Let's go." He squinted at the sun that had moved still higher in the eastern foyer window to light the room. Normal sounded good for a change. And for what it was worth, it was the earth that still moved around the sun, and fixing that would take more than a simple change of clothes.

THIRTEEN

LOOKOUTS AND LEECHES

THERE WAS NOTHING normal about being the new kid on a Monday, the thirteenth of October, when three school terms out of four had already passed. Cessini entered the hallway on the first day back from everyone else's break wearing a new set of spring clothes that were shopped for and bought normally at Hobart's downtown Cat and Fiddle Arcade.

For their foreshortened stay on the island, he could have chosen a public school in the backyard of Daniel's university campus, but that single-sex solution would have left Meg miles away. So instead, they came to this school together, and he said goodbye to her at the end of the hallway under its blue, red, and white-crested emblem. He bumbled away through the crowd. There wasn't a single familiar face among the 752 enrolled students, but one thought was certain—his was the least familiar face of them all.

He arrived at yet another new door at the light of midday. The teacher's table at the head of the science classroom was black, and had a sink at its center. Three columns and two rows of student tables ran perpendicular to the teacher's. The first column was against the west wall of ribbon windows. Four students could sit at each table, two on either long side, and have a fair view to the front of the room. It wasn't data center precise to the tile square, but in all, twenty-four students could fit comfortably in the room. There were twenty-two so far.

He ignored the stares, stepped through the frame of the door, and headed over for a rear seat by the windows. If not for the high stool that was empty behind him, he would have been in the southwestern-most corner of the room.

The windows were definitely a plus. He could see down from the hilltop of Rose Bay to the eastern shore of the River Derwent. Tree-lined auto lanes converged upon the Tasman Bridge, crossed to the Royal Botanical Gardens, and re-spread into the city. The sun to the far right of the school was due north in the sky, and the shadows he saw without a view of the sun begged for a further look south along the bay. The roads over on the other side of the river became lost in the city of Hobart. They broke again somewhere through the palm of the city and found their way up to Mount Wellington beyond.

He tried, and then dared again to ignore the mild kicks from behind that rattled the long leg of his stool. He ground his teeth. Ignoring was best. Surely the teacher would be in soon to begin the delayed class. If he spun, his new bully would win, so he turned and searched for the sight of a road that would lead him back home. The kicking boy, he could only assume, must have entered the classroom door and slipped along the first column of tables. He would have hooked right at the back wall, passed his complicit friends, maybe even high-fived them along the way, and then taken the only seat left directly behind him in the actual southwestern-most corner of the room.

The smart screen at the front was a better distraction to the kicks. An animated graphic on the screen showed a red blood cell enlarged to enormous size for classroom display. The natural structures of the blood cell then morphed into a diagram of honeycombed chambers, rotors, pumps, and cams. The organic blood cell had become a mechanical, spherical pod. The pod was relabeled as a "Respirocyte."

The red respirocyte pod then shrank back to microscopically small and millions of others just like it rushed in to fill the veins of a body—a human's. A human, who much to Cessini's dismay sat lounged and content in a chair at the bottom of a cylindrical water tank, which was tall by the person's height plus another half. The respirocytes released graphically enlarged oxygen bubbles that swirled around the submerged swimmer's calm lungs, escaped his soothed bare skin, and rose to the surface. A fantasy, Cessini thought, for his skin could never tolerate such a fiction of medical science.

In the far right rear corner of the room, two boys were locked in a quiet arm wrestle with little surrounding cheer. Then one quick thrust and it was over. The victor's arms were tight in his long sleeves, but mostly throughout his forearms. The boy who lost wore a blue, red, and white-striped jersey of the school's athletic team. Its single horizontal band of blue over red was striped across his chest.

Then the most demanding kick bumped Cessini clear from his stool.

"Do you wear seatbelts in America?" the kicking boy asked.

Cessini turned and saw him. It was the oddest looking boy he had ever seen. He immediately averted his eyes for a return to the front. Then the kicks continued.

"Yes, we do," Cessini said without turning. "And we drive on the right side of the road."

"Me mum drives on the right side of the road, too," the boy said.

Cessini swiveled a quarter turn and sneaked another look. He knew well enough not to judge the boy by the skin he was in, but this boy didn't seem to care enough to notice even if he did. He turned completely around. "You actually drive on the left side," Cessini said.

The boy had a facial disk like an owl's that flattened to inset orange eyes. He had a pug nose between the glare of his eyes and perfect dimples over his hanging jowls. He lifted his eyes for an inviting grin and leaned forward with a hand held out to shake. He tilted his head as he spoke, "They call me Spud," he said.

"I don't mean right versus wrong side of the road," Cessini said. "Just left side, right?"

"Yeah. Left side," Spud said as he tipped up and dragged his stool closer. "Are there flies in America?" he asked, diving right in.

"Why wouldn't there be?"

"Don't know," Spud said. "Only movies I've seen of America, flies ain't in 'em. The only flies I see are here."

"We have flies, too."

"Where are you from?"

"Minneapolis, outside of it."

"Good to know. I'm from Alice Springs. But only when I was little. Town right in the middle. Lots of dead hoppin' roos. Plenty of flies there, too. You can't even count 'em. Now I live here in Tas with me dad."

"Minneapolis is kind of in the middle, too," Cessini said. The teacher was still nowhere in sight.

"Great. Then we'll be partners," Spud said. "Me and some mates are going to the park this weekend. We're in the bushwalking club. You want to come?"

A loud rap and entry at the door snapped everyone front. A consummate science teacher entered in white lab coat. He carried a small crate and an eager guest speaker followed him in for the start of the fourth school term.

"You coming?" Spud kicked again. Cessini didn't turn.

The guest speaker was Gerald Aiden. Unmistakable. The crude man's stiff-legged limp was intact, his weathered skin tanned. The wrinkles under his eyes still folded.

"So, you coming?" Spud asked again with a lean. "We got us the greatest club ever."

Cessini hushed him with a single turn. "Okay, now stop it."

Spud's eyebrows raised and pulled up a grand, proud smile. "All right then, it's a deal," Spud said. He shifted back for a taller perch on his stool, and pointed his thumb back into his chest for a prouder parade.

"Class," the teacher said, "I want to introduce you to our first bring-your-father-to-class guest. Spud, why don't you introduce your father to the class?"

"Hey, Dad," Spud said. "This is my class."

The teacher waited, then with a circle in of his hand, gestured for more, but that was it from Spud, nothing more. The class laughed and the teacher felt forced to fill in the blanks. "Gerald Aiden works at the Tungatinah Power Plant and is here today to talk about power and electricity."

Spud scooted his stool forward to within inches of Cessini's. "What's your name?"

"Shhh!" Cessini snapped back.

"Mine isn't 'cause of the shape of my nose," Spud said as he leaned in. "I asked my dad where I came from one day. He knows a lot about electricity. He said one day he put some water to the ground, and I grew. He called me Spud."

"I recognize some of you from last year. New faces, though, too," Aiden said as he gaited stiff-legged around the front of the teacher's table.

"Everybody calls me Spud," he said even louder to Cessini. "I don't mind the heat in the desert, neither, I guess. Alice Springs is in the desert. What do you do?"

"Spud, settle down," Aiden said with a scowl.

The teacher raised his finger against his lips for the benefit of all. "Sorry to interrupt," the teacher said, "but one other point we should note for the class is by way of introductions. We have a new face with us today all the way from the United States. Minnesota, I think. Joined our class just for the term."

"Ah, good to know. Who's that?" Aiden asked as he scanned the room.

"Cessini, would you mind raising your hand?" the teacher asked. Everyone already knew where to turn as Cessini locked eyes with Gerald Aiden.

"Do I know you?" Aiden asked with a squint.

"Yeah. Last week. We were there," Cessini said.

"At the plant?" Aiden asked as he shifted his weight. "Okay, yes. I remember you. You came with your mum and dad, your family. Am I right? I can't remember their names."

"That's all right. We were just visiting. We didn't stay long."

"Yes, obviously," Aiden said as he shifted off his supporting hand on the teacher's table, "Okay, then. Class, let me tell you about what I do. Three things. Control. Water. Power." He tapped the upper corner of the smart-screen, and the respirocytes model and swimmer disappeared. He had a blank space to work with.

"You control the water, you have power," he said, and drew the first two interlocking circles of a Venn diagram. "All the greatest generals already know, from them right down to me, control is power. And in my case, water, the juxtaposition of control and power, is the medium for fielding your whole winning army." He scribbled a hasty third circle to form a misshapen group of three rings on the board.

The teacher couldn't help but be amused. Aiden stomped and keeled with bravado.

Spud jabbed a finger into Cessini's back. "So, you know me dad, eh?"

"Not really. He wasn't very helpful. He was a jerk, actually."

"Yeah, that's me dad. He's loose in the head. Don't mind him. Got shot in the leg."

"Was he in a war?" Cessini turned back to Spud.

"Yeah, with me mum. He couldn't run away from the cow fast enough. She winged him good, eh? Didn't she, right in the leg." Spud cracked himself up.

"Spud!" Aiden smacked his palm to the side of his hardened thigh. "Settle down. I won't tell you again."

"Sure thing, Dad." Spud saluted.

Cessini eased up as the teacher sat relaxed on the windowsill at the front, overlooking the river to the west. Aiden took his cue from the teacher. The teacher gave a warm gesture toward his crate.

"Today we're going to make an electrochemical battery," Aiden said with his first noted smile. He lifted and plunked the crate by the sink of the teacher's table. Then he stopped mid-thought. He lowered his chin, eyes focused into narrow beams, and stretched his neck out toward Cessini.

"Wait a minute. I remember you," he said as he lifted his pointer finger over a tightened fist. "You're the water boy, aren't you? Yes. That's right. You are that sick boy. I remember you, now."

Cessini's shoulders sank. He snapped a look toward the windows. Home was so very far away.

"Well, you don't have to worry about water now," Aiden said as he continued over the crate. "For this part today, we just have the two, control and power. Water has nothing to do with them for today. All you have to take away now from me is control, power, and . . ."

Cessini braced himself as the eyes of the class followed Aiden back to his scrambled Venn diagram on the screen where he filled in his two-eyes-with-nose, huge-cheeked caricature of—

"Spud. Potatoes!" Aiden exuded. "Yes. Power from potatoes."

The class erupted. "Ah, Spud. Let's plug him in. Fry the spud!"

Spud swallowed the brunt of his father's mockery as best as he could. His smile only lifted so far.

"Quiet," the teacher snapped, but he was overruled as Spud ran up in the face of ridicule to help his dad from the front. He tossed and bowled potatoes to adulations from front row to back, hiking long throws to his arm-wrestling friend and his color-banded, losing opponent in the southeast's rear corner of the room.

Maybe, Cessini thought as he caught an overhand lob, just maybe if Spud could laugh, he could laugh, too. And when Spud's potato crate was empty, he waddled importantly back to his seat. Cessini crossed his arms and giggled as he approached. Maybe he could even grow to like this place. He, too, could come out of his shell and live among the rest. And for whatever short time they had left in Hobart, he would give it another best try.

Cessini's day-pack for water protection was provisioned and held at his side, with rain jacket packed and flashlight charged. He held the headrest of Meg's front passenger seat as Daniel drove up the winding Pinnacle Road. They had left their house at 448 Treeline Drive just before noon and turned toward the hills, with two brand-new bikes strapped to the rear gate of the Jeep. Cessini ducked beneath the two front visors for a spellbinding view of the 4,000-foot flattened mountain crest. He slid aside in his rear bucket seat for a glimpse of their new world adventure. Hope fluttered free from a moss-covered forest.

He clambered forward. "Okay, so I figured it out. You ready?"

"Shoot," Daniel said.

"You have to give Packet lots of imagination. Since imagination is the absence of code, you have to give it as little code as you can. One equation. So it has lots of imagination."

Meg shook her head, but let Cessini roll as a car zoomed by between them and the upslope of the hill. Its halogens were on in the light of the day. Daniel clenched the wheel and banked the outer curve. Meg saw it, too. That car was far too close.

"Okay, so you know what else?" Cessini asked, alight with excitement.

"You're on fire today, Cessini. Go ahead, what else?" Daniel looked up at the rearview mirror.

"Remember my bioship?"

"Yeah," Meg said. "What about it? You still going out into space?"

"Definitely. I figured out its power."

"Potatoes?" she asked.

"No. Space dust. It collects packets of organic space dust thrown off from the stars, combines it with quanta of water . . . I'm still working on that . . . and it pumps out unlimited bursts of energy."

"Last I checked, it's pretty frigid cold in space," Daniel said, prodding the rearview mirror. "All that water isn't going to turn to ice and crack the skin of your ship?" They passed a road sign for the head of a trail.

Cessini thought a moment then leapt forward in his seat. "The bioship's whole body is filled with organic magnets, microscopic, nano-scale magnets, one in each cell of its skin. I'll call them—dark magnetocytes. Right! All coils from electromagnets generate excess heat. But the ship's magnetic cellular structure will generate its own heat. Like animals at the bottom of the ocean. But the ship's not warm-blooded, it's magnetic-blooded. And the heat that's not used in the skin gets ejected out the back funnel of the ship. If you were out there, you'd see it as a vapor trail and a distortion of space."

The deepening lines at the edges of Daniel's eyes flexed up as he looked in the mirror. It must have been pride. Meg even turned around from her seat for a smile and high-five. "Nice. Way to go."

"But all those individual magnetic cells are going to have voltage spikes," Daniel said. "You'll need a large micro-processor, a mainframe to control them. To direct all the magnets so the ship doesn't spin out of control."

Cessini sat back and crossed his arms. That was an invitation to victory. "Easy," he said. "Like the bellows lamp by my bed. Colossal squid have a large torus or donut-shaped brain that wraps around their central spine. That's the kind of mega processor you'll find in my bioship."

"Donut brain? Magnetic blood?" Daniel repeated, skeptical.

"But you want to know what the best part is?" Cessini added. "When the ship comes in for a landing, guess what?"

"It squirts out ink?" Daniel asked.

"Right! Before arrival, so the artificial gravity of the mag-nets don't get mixed up by the gravity of the planet, the ship dumps all the magnets out of its cells like black goo." He back-slapped Meg on the shoulder and they laughed. "You'd love it, Dad. Donut brains and coffee for breakfast. Like black meco-nium in your cup."

Daniel burst. A reinvigorated creative mind was infectious. "I take it you like your new school?" Daniel asked as he caught an infrequent, but open grin.

"I do," Cessini said. "I think I really do."

Daniel stopped the car at the gravel trailhead for the moun-tain path. "Then you know what that sounds like to me?"

"What?"

"A piece of a puzzle just fit."

"Totally," Meg said as she gathered her backpack gear, ready to bolt from the car.

Cessini grabbed the strap of his day-pack and pulled the handle of his door. He paused before his foot reached the gravel. "Dad?"

"What? Have a good time," Daniel said. "Try to come back with some friends."

"Are you sure you're not still angry about the fire?" Cessini asked.

"You mean the one that ruined our lives as we knew it?" Daniel asked, then turned back and gripped both hands to the wheel. "Go on, Meg's waiting," he said, then threw the Jeep's engine into reverse.

"Does that mean you still are?" Cessini asked.

"No, I'm just fooling with you. Actually, I was laughing about it just the other night. If you think about it, you did the same to me in my shop as I did to my father before you. Perspective, I guess. Kind of makes it all feel crazy okay."

"I guess," Cessini said. But somehow the hard truth in Daniel's eyes robbed from his smile. Maybe the grant of his forgiveness didn't quite last as long as it should.

Meg hollered from the curb, "Ceeme, you coming, or what?"

Cessini stopped at the side of the Jeep. His new Rockhopper XPS bike and Meg's Trailmaster were mounted on the Jeep's rear rack. The front wheel of his bike still spun from the drive up the hill.

Meg went to unstrap hers first, but Daniel jammed on the gas and sped out of their way. Cessini held her back by the arm. "It's okay," he said as the dust settled down. "We can walk, instead." The staked wooden sign at their backs read, Low

Impact Trail. She wasn't quite ready to agree.

Cessini had seen the height of the mountain during his descent from the air only weeks before, and afterward from a distance through his classroom window at Rose Bay. But as he walked close through the bush, the mountain offered up two paths. Not trailheads, but a split for his mind. One path led to a veritable richness of Eden and another was in deliverance to a less fortunate hell. Taking one or the other all came down to which face of the mountain the water broke from the clouds that day. His rain jacket was packed just in case, and the chosen path of the more moderate eastern front ahead offered the lesser pain for those afflicted by the trouble of their own skin.

Future member of Spud's bushwalking club or not, Meg was along for the ride, and so together, they walked side-by-side up the wood-chipped break through the trees.

A crisscross of trails under a canopy of eucalyptus rose from the lower slopes of the bush. So far they had it all to themselves. The driest of warming spring winds blew from the northwest over the organ pipes and columnar cliffs that brushed their faces fresh with awe. The low humidity of the air was foiled only by the specter of sound nearing ahead. A waterfall poured its deadly element somewhere up on the trail.

Meg glanced back from her few steps ahead. He was still good to go. The green was different from the trails of Minnesota, but the pleasure of the free-flowing organics of nature was the same. As rivulets trickled under light wooden bridges, he left a few more worries behind and hopped the odd tenderfoot stream.

Meg yanked the shoulder strap of his pack and pulled his more apprehensive gait along. "Hurry up. They're going to be waiting."

Ahead, a possible drenching persisted, but from where among the echoes?

"Don't worry so much," Meg said. "Keep telling me about your spaceship if it helps. Now come on, let's go."

He shifted the pack on his shoulder and skipped ahead to catch up. "Slow down. Don't run."

Meg turned and, running up backward, opened her arms wide apart from her chest and yelled, "Come on, I feel great. We're fine." She hooked a left through the trees, and then followed a signpost with its winding arrow for "Vale."

He hurried to keep her in sight, running into the breach of the echoes.

She stood still at a clearing ahead. Her breath was labored. Two bicycles lay ditched on the ground. Their riders were already off and deep in their outdoor play.

The waterfall was upon them. Cessini stopped on sight. It was the two-story height of their old data center warehouse in Minnesota. But something was different, not so frightening up close.

Spud dropped his rock into a pool at its shore and came running. "You two see the Octopus Tree?" he shouted.

Only one other boy lumbered about. It was the arm-wrestler from class. Behind him, the fall's cascade over moss-covered rocks was pure and without mist.

"Oh, you'd love the Octopus Tree," Spud said. "You should go have a look. It's just over the hills. We'll go on this trail. Can't miss it."

"Is it on the east or west side of the mountain?" Cessini asked.

The arm-wrestler minded the edge of the pool as he towed a long, broken branch.

"You remember Tenden, me mate from class?" Spud asked as over-officious host of the bushwalking club.

Tenden, the arm-wrestler, planted himself square at their front and humphed.

"Sure," Cessini said. "I'm Cessini."

"I know that," Tenden said as he stripped off a line of eucalyptus leaves from the branch through the squeeze of his fist.

"This is Meg," Cessini said. "She wanted to see the club, too."

"Excellent!" Spud said. "The more the better. Now we got four in our club."

"Four?" Meg asked, and smiled.

"Yeah. Five, if you count Pace. He ain't here today on account of some race he's running."

Tenden pulled Spud away by a grasp of his shirt and stepped ahead in his place.

"Hey!" Spud objected.

"No, I'm telling 'em," Tenden said, snarled. "A few years ago, some nutmeat tried to cut off one of the limbs of the Octopus Tree to see if it would grow back. Like a real octopus. Idiots. It didn't. Rangers had to trim it back surgically to save the whole tree from disease and bugs." He emphasized, "*At its wound!*"

"I got it," Cessini said. "They catch him?"

"You see any cameras around here? They put a fence around the tree so no one could hurt it again. But then neither could we play on it anymore, for that matter. You understand? You check it out for yourselves anyway. You'll like it."

"Okay," Meg said. She looked at the height of the waterfall, then Cessini. "Maybe we should go there, instead."

"Excellent," Spud said with a grin, and he ran back toward his very same pool at the base of the falls. "After. Come on, let's play."

Spud and Tenden stomped in their soaked shoes and dragged stirring sticks through the eddied pools of their wonderland. Rocks and ferns surrounded their private spot in the forest; it was an organic, primordial wild. No rainbow mist rose above the clear flow of the falls or broke the blue sky over the highest promontory stone. It was a twenty-five-foot cascade without spray. It was free-flowing water, controlled.

Meg sat on a mossy rock to rest. She shouldn't have run so far, so fast.

"In a minute," Cessini said.

The pool of the falls had a sound all its own, but one not too unfamiliar. His heels were pressed tight against a fallen branch, an impromptu border, a playground's boundary line he would have to step away from to enter. But Spud's antics lifted his spirits with ease. Water splashed, sticks swatted, and Cessini lifted a heel away from the branch. Then he stopped and returned, taking two steps back over. The red rain jacket in his day-pack would never be enough if he fell to his knees. He sat at Meg's side, instead.

She ignored him. She reached into her bag and pulled her winged tablet up to her lap, joining her knees together to use her legs as an easel.

Cessini tested the dryness of the dirt with his shoe, and then slid down to sit with his legs crossed on the ground. "You know, if I was a computer up in space, I wouldn't mind all this water. Because in space, water doesn't burn."

Meg breathed in the idyllic garden and through her clacking and clicking, captured its vectors into her tablet. She transferred her new waterfall image into her Sea Turtle Rescue world, and with the rotation of her screen, two turtles entered the next stage of their life, crossing the barrier from sand to sea.

"But I'd mind," she said. "Of course water burns in space. You've got to get over it. You're not a computer. You're a human, like me. Now go, play," she said and looked at him. "You don't have to watch me every second. I feel fine. They like you. Now go."

"I know why you get tired," he said.

"So do I. Because you're bothering me. Now go. Make some friends. I'll be right there."

Cessini uncrossed his legs to rise, but then sat back on his heels. He stalled as long as he could, weighing the flow of the water with Meg on his mind. The height of the falls was doable, maybe. "Remember when I climbed that ladder and put a baggie on the sprinkler head?" he asked.

"Pounded my heart right through my chest, yes, I remember."

"Pretty crazy of me, heh?" he asked as he tossed a rounded pebble from the dirt into the pool. "Well, memories flow upstream."

Spud stood in the water by the expanding rings of Cessini's thrown stone and looked at him and Meg. Then Spud threw down his stick to its natural float.

"What's that supposed to mean?" Meg asked.

"We don't start by thinking from up there at the top of the falls and let a bunch of memories and images flow down here to us, so we can see this here, this now. I think the mind works in reverse. It flows upstream, instead. We have what we know right now and see in front of us and our minds break that apart and flow it up the falls instead to find its source."

Meg stopped her clicking, looked up, and wondered at the height of the water.

"We start here and search back up there for the source of our pictures. Our fear. For smaller bits of this scene. For the look and sounds of round pebbles I've tossed before, borders I've crossed, ladders I've climbed. The pain I know right now down here comes from a source up there." He stopped and broke her glassy stare. "Everything here leads back to the first packet, the first swirl of a thought. Up there."

Spud marched up in a huff, his shoes dripping from the

pool. He stomped his demand with his foot into its puddle. He shifted his glance back and forth, then settled on Meg. "You. You shouldn't get that wet, you know. It'll ruin it."

"I know," Meg said as she brushed her thumb over the tablet's screen.

"That thing looks *ancient*," Spud said, with a half-cheek grin. "You should at least put a new processor it in."

"I like it the way that it is," she said.

"What's your name again?" Spud asked as his lip twisted the wide disk of his face.

Meg crossed her arms over her screen, not for privacy, but for resting comfort over her knees. "When I was little, my dad called me Meg, like a memory chip. But then when I got bigger, everyone started calling me Terri, like Terabyte, because it's bigger. But personally, I like Margaret Teresa. That's my name and I think it sounds nice. But Cessini and my friends call me Meg. It's nice to meet you. I'm Meg." She held out her hand to shake. Spud's jaw dropped in awe.

Tenden marched over to see all the fuss.

"And this is Cessini," Meg said with a gestured introduction. "But I call him Ceeme. Not Packet like his friends sometimes do. Yes, he's quiet, sometimes often, but he's really smart."

"Why did they call you Packet?" Tenden asked.

"Because when we were little," Meg said, "his dad always made him carry around those square handi-wipe packets."

"Other kids washed their hands," Cessini said. "I used a packet. So the other kids called me Packet."

Tenden elbowed Spud. "And we call him Spud 'cause he's got such an ugly mug."

"Aagh," Spud said with a grunt as he circled away. But he came back for more.

"I'm Tenden. Tenden 'cause the tendens in my arms are

connected three inches too far down my elbow to my forearms. Makes me stronger. Like a lever. Get it? Like a seesaw. One kid sitting out on the end can lift two runts sitting close in the middle. Makes me stronger. Same thing. You understand?"

"You mean tendon, like with an 'o'?" Cessini asked.

"What? No. What 'o'? Tenden in my arms. Makes me stronger. You understand?"

"I do. Tenden," Cessini said.

"What do you do?" Tenden asked.

"I don't do anything," Cessini said.

"No, I said, what do you do?"

Cessini shrugged, and then said, "I boil in water."

"Oh, yeah. Good to know. Everybody does that. Don't they? Come on, let's go. Time to get on with the club."

Meg nudged, but Cessini didn't get up.

Tenden turned back when no one followed. "There's a saying here in Australia that says, 'The nail that sticks up, gets hammered down.' Well, you know what?"

"What?" Cessini asked.

Tenden puffed up his chest, hunched forward with his arms bent front, fists down, and declared in a forearm's muscle-flexed roar, "*I am a nail!* And, from now on, I'm sticking up."

Spud rolled his eyes. "No, he's not. Forget him. Be who you want. Me, I hate water. Haven't taken a bath in a month. Maybe two. Ain't gonna, neither. I be myself. You be you. Club is now official in session. Let's go."

"And who am I?" Cessini asked.

"Buggered if I know," Spud said as he skipped off to return to the water. He tipped his shoulders back with a roll of his head, nodding Cessini to follow. "Just met you two days ago. You coming, or what?"

"Six days," Cessini counted, but then again, what difference did it make as he recognized, on his short list, the will of a friend. Meg pushed him.

Cessini stayed far to the right of the pool-side rocks as the trickle of white noise grew louder at the cascade. Waves lapped the shore. It was a familiar calming sound, a memory sourced from a sound machine at the side of his bed.

"Why did you use handi-wipes?" Tenden asked.

"I've got *aquagenic urticaria*," Cessini said. "I get hives from water on my skin. Even tears from crying hurt. Pretty awful, too. So, I don't anymore."

"You should move to a farm," Tenden said.

"I hurt when I sweat."

"Then why didn't you move to the desert?" Spud asked.

"The desert is worse," Cessini said. "It's dry, but you have to drink more water. My throat would swell. It hurts too much."

"So you never shower or bathe, neither?" Spud asked as he hopped the edge of the pool.

"One doctor prescribed a beta blocker," Cessini said as they made their way to the bubbled skirt of the falls. "My dad thought they might help, too. But I started not remembering things."

"Well, that's no good," Tenden said at the wall of rocks. He angled his right arm and muscled up to a first ledge. He reached down with his left arm for a grasp at Cessini's hand.

Cessini began his climb and did his best to hide his fear of the flowing water at his side. Spud kept bumping up behind him. With each lag and spurt of his courage up the wall, the three boys bumped like balls of Newton's Cradle, navigating like clubmen for the climb to the top of the falls.

"I'd rather have my memory than a shower," Cessini said as the nearer mist condensed on the sleeve of his red jacket. His foot slipped on a knotted root at the base of an overhung tree. "It's all right here, though," he kept talking. "Hobart is in the wet shade of the mountain. The dew point's good."

"So let me get this straight," Spud said as he bumped from below. "This is an island. You came here with all this water around?"

"He just said that," Tenden said with a curt look down.

"I came from the land of ten thousand lakes," Cessini said as the pain of the mist found its way into his jacket and he pulled his red hood over his head. "Tough love."

"Ten thousand lakes!" Spud said. "All in one place?"

Tenden smacked his palm onto a wet, mossy stone, which showered down in shards past Cessini and corrected Spud on the spot. "Not all in one place," Tenden said, "then it'd be an ocean, dumbnuts!"

"Did you just call me dumbnuts?" Spud exclaimed. "It's numbnuts, if you're going to say it."

"Why? What's a numbnut?" Tenden snapped back.

"It's better than a dumbnut!" Spud said.

"I know what dumb is, but what's a numb?" Tenden stomped the wet moss.

"There is no such thing as a numb!"

"Right! Then it's dumbnuts," Tenden said.

"No, it's not!" Spud snapped. "You're going to be numb if you don't stop saying dumb. How's that?"

"It's stupid," Tenden said. "That's what it is. You understand? Who's in control here, anyway?"

"We all are, none of us are, we're what we want to be, instead," Spud said. "Now help him up, he's stuck." Spud rapped his hand on Cessini's foot. "Tenden don't know nothing. Don't you listen to him."

Tenden looked down as Cessini flicked out his red sleeves. "Fair enough, Spud. Just be good," Tenden said. "He ain't going to join our bushwalking club if you don't behave. So, settle down."

Cessini's heart had warmed a bit, but his mind was already torched. *The nightmare of water had returned.* His hands burned from the wet of the rocks. His skin begged for Tenden to move, to end their sidelong hang. Every lift of a palm trembled for relief. He gripped the cuffs of his jacket under the palms of his hands to continue the climb, but his hold on the moss was gone. Meg didn't come, she was so far away, but then she was standing, running . . .

"Ceeme, come down," she yelled. She dropped her tablet into an eddy, but ran full speed.

Cessini leaned back from the rock face and his sleeve drew up and away from his wrist. An orange-and-yellow striped tiger leech sucked the back of his hand. How long had it been there? He focused on its draw. The curved and erect springboard of its body. The thirty-two brains of its segments. The pumping of its rear brain and sucker on his hand. Its three-bladed jaws. The anticoagulant serum that pumped into his blood. He shuddered to fling it. His foot slipped from the rocks. His mind spun over and he fell toward the froth of the pool.

His eyes hit with a splash. Beneath the surface, the sleeves of his rain jacket filled in fast. Water soaked up his arms, across his chest. He burned in a bubbling cauldron. He fought, ripped at the snare of cloth in the metal pull of his zipper. His arms were bound in his sleeves. The surface was above and rising. Gulps swelled his throat shut. He choked. His mouth widened and stayed. His breath ceased. His cheeks flamed through. His body went rigid. Then he hung stiff in the water, floating free. He pulled his trigger to end his nightmare of life.

Until a grasp yanked him up through the surface.

He was startled to return, and paralyzed. He was still standing on the rock face along the wall of the falls. Tenden handed him down in a controlled descent into Meg's grip, who encapsulated him tightly at her side.

"It's okay, Ceeme. You're okay. I've got you. I'll take care of you now," was all he heard her say on his way down to the bottom of the falls.

He ran from the humiliation of the descent and split through what had become a hellish path of woods. Meg ran to catch up, wiping the bubbled droplets of water from her tablet's screen and shoving it into her pack. "Wait!" she cried. "Come back!"

He had looked back enough. Spud and Tenden followed her onto the trail, staying fifteen yards behind in silence, staring, keeping a distant pace. Maybe they followed out of respect, curiosity, protection, but more likely horror. And their notice was worse, a recognition of who he was, that he would never fit in, no matter how far he flew.

He broke down on the trail, spinning. He curled his red burning hands into fists and squeezed away an agony, swung at the blue of the sky, fought to contain his anger, but anger at what? At the world, his life, his father? At Meg for her strength when he knew she was so weak?

"No. Don't run. We were getting so close," she cried as she ran.

He spun into a back-skipped step to face her descent of the forested trail. "Stop following me," he said. "I never needed you, either. I hate you. I hate you all. And I'm never coming back to this world!"

He twisted and ripped his arms from his red rain jacket. He heaved it onto the trail. His bare forearms were prickled, welted up to their elbows, imbued by a mild mountain mist. He damned the air as his mind boiled over into a scream, hollering for a way to end his failed body any way he knew how.

A car screeched the bend of Pinnacle Road. Its halogens flashed and he skidded to the ground. He paused for a breath, and measured the distance to the road and how close he may have just come to leaving this world.

A rivulet flowed ahead into the aged, leafy debris of a ravine. Exposed beneath the rust of the forest's patch was the graphite frame of an XPS bike, its wheel turning slowly in the dry northwest winds. Meg ran down the trail on foot. So did he. There was no way that bike was his.

He stumbled up to his feet and ran down the lowland hill and covered his ears from Meg's falling farther behind. "Ceeme!"

Spud and Tenden stopped on foot at her side as she doubled-over in pain.

"Damnit, don't run! We were doing so well. Cessini! You're Cessini!" she cried and fell to the ground in agony.

If Spud and Tenden had her back, he wouldn't know. The earth spun faster than ever in his mind; normal was a dream for the day, but he was forever gone into night.

FOURTEEN

MEMORY OF A BOY

L ONG PAST SUNSET, Cessini lay on his side in his bed in the darkened chill of his room. The floor register blew its cool air. His breathing was shallow, his mouth was open. His jaw pulsed from open toward closed and back as the digital waves of his sound machine lapped some distant shore. Madness had won.

Meg sat at his side. She held a paper tight beneath her knee, a note of some kind which she wasn't quite ready to read. "You're scaring me," she said. Her first tear fell in the ebb of a digital wave. "They didn't mind," she said. "Really. They said they thought it was neat. They said now they know. That's what you do. They like it, they said. They like you."

Cessini rolled over and faced his wall. "I'm not going back, not to that school, not anywhere ever again."

Meg turned off the wave machine, then his bellows lamp once its mantle exhaled. She left the nightlight bulbs of its eyes lit. "I'm sorry you're so confused. I think that's got to be my fault. Maybe I'm not trying hard enough. Maybe I need to go where you go, be somebody else you want me to be?"

Cessini didn't turn.

"I wrote this years ago after you . . ." She revealed the paper from under her leg. "Mom thought it might make me feel better if I read it to you now. Before you get up and run away."

"After I what?" he asked.

She flattened her paper on her leg and wiped her eyes. "After you died. Anyway, afterward, in my class, we had to write a poem about what we did over break. I figured, what do they know about cabinets and data centers like you and me, so I wrote about you and your life, instead. It's called, 'A Thousand More Places to Go.'"

He pulled himself away from her, curling tighter toward the plaster of his wall.

She reached for the back of his shoulder, but he shrugged away her hand. "You know, I sat there for ages in the library looking at all the books and places and people out there. But mostly, I was still thinking about you."

"What do you mean, died?"

"I know you love imagining all kinds of things. You know about so much. It was just me sitting there sad, so I wrote it."

"When? I don't know what you're talking about," he said and turned.

She found her courage in the sadness of his eyes, and she read aloud. "It's called 'Befuddled, or A Thousand More Places to Go.'"

It was her eulogy.

"So long for all the places, lives, and dreams left to see,
For all the ships in the world to go on without me,
You ran with a mind that spun, and heart that longed so,
For you had no less than a thousand more places to go.

Did you even see me? I wondered.
For I lived in your world a moment, and left you my grin,
Watching over you like a butterfly in a cabinet,
Heart pinned."

She twisted over her thoughts and crumpled her paper. She leaned over and kissed his forehead. "Goodbye, Ceeme. I love you. Stay wonder-full to me."

As she pulled away, he rose up onto his elbow. She waited, but he said nothing. Then he sat up. "Wait here," he said. He stood up on his bed and walked off its edge to the floor.

She sprang to her feet. "Where are you going?"

"Upstream. And don't follow me, either. I'm going to find the source. And kill it."

She exited and stayed behind the post of their home's front fence in the dark of their night. He shot his hands through the sleeves of his forest green Windbreaker, still wrinkled from its cinch sack. She held open the gate and cried, resigned. He straddled his new Rockhopper XPS bike, kicked up the stand, and pedaled straight past the gate numerals of 448.

He pedaled alone by the light of the moon and his penlight back into the woods, to the trail, its clearing, and waterfall. He ditched his bike for a climb. At the top, he could find the source. He could rest. He could be a child again, play computer. He could reset all his fears.

His climb to the top was atrocious. He wandered for a spell through the brush, the clearings of thin trees and ferns. The water curled upstream for a while, but it was futile. A farce. The top of the falls were empty. Insane.

He settled into the wee hours' calm. It would have been foolish to climb back down the face of a cascading fall under the darkness of a canopy cover. He sat on a soft patch of earth, though a stone was hard against his back. A tree-fern frond was a fingerlike blanket. The air was crisp, the sky pristine through a break in the branches above. Stars were a sight to behold.

As the back of his head settled on the trunk of a tree, he

lifted his hand and scratched at the numbing of his neck. With a last, reflexive twitch of his foot into the moss-skinned dirt, he surrendered his fate to the quiet lapping of the falls, and fell into the soundness of sleep.

Packet awoke, curled and cold, in his hospital room bed during the quietest hour of the night. His focus contracted toward the sound of his breath as he kept his eyes closed until he gathered his thoughts.

He rubbed his hand on his neck, and with a drowsy slide from his bed, set his feet upon the cold tile floor. He steadied himself, looked about to adjust his eyes in the dark, and shuffled toward the door on the left of his room. He opened it a crack.

"Hi, honey. Over here," Robin said.

A ray of light from the hall entered and crossed her face as she sat in the guest chair of his hospital room. Her light blanket slipped down as she sat straighter. A gentle air blowing up from a floor register rattled and waved the long strips of a vertical blind.

"I had a bad dream," Packet said.

"Do you want to tell me about it?"

"It was about that boy again," Packet said. "His name was Cessini. There was something wrong with his body."

The screen of a gas fireplace flickered alight and a warmer air blew from a farther baseboard register, filling the room with a comfort.

"Are you cold?" Robin asked as she rose from her chair. "I can turn the heat up, if you like?"

"No. I'm okay," he said as he passed her in the room for a peek through the vertical blinds. A waist-high, maple-wood hand bar protected a floor-to-ceiling window pane and kept him at his safe distance. He drew the blind's bubble chain.

Dawn had come early and he waved Robin over. "Come look, over here," he said. "I want to show you something."

He pointed out over a peaceful lake not a hundred yards distant but two floors below. It was edged by a quarter-mile path that circled its shore, and then spiraled out to a botanical garden of rare colors and life. Orange Creamsicle tulips kissed yellow lady slipper orchids. Oak- and maple-gated bridges parted from the path and disappeared into the closets of an expanding wood beyond. The view was an invitation to nature. Someone had taken tremendous care.

His face reflected in the glass. He had learned a lot, enough to be reflective, matured, realistically scared.

"It's nice here at the hospital," he said.

"We thought you'd like it."

"Did I die? Is that heaven over there?"

"No, it's not heaven. You don't remember how you died, do you?"

What a strange question to ask, he thought. "I never dreamed of that, no."

"Then up at the waterfall is the last memory you have of yourself as Cessini?"

"The last dream of a boy named Cessini," he said.

"So maybe that's why you aren't making the connection. You have no memories of Cessini from his death onward. You're in a no-man's land. You're the mind, not of, but after Cessini."

"When a new civilization comes along, all the old souls come back," he said.

She smiled a bit softer. "What's the new civilization?"

"I don't know. Whatever comes after here, I guess."

She looked back out toward the lake, its peaceful ripples, and path to the woods. "Do you remember when we went for a walk around the lake?" she asked.

"I remember," he said. "To get Cessini all tired out before he went under for his tonsils."

"So you do, then. I didn't think you'd catch on to our ploy at the time. You were so young."

"I remember it was the last time I was happy," he said. "You still talked to me, and Daddy still loved me."

Robin had a wonderful, giving smile, but sometimes, he knew, she took a little too long to answer. "What do you mean? I talk to you all the time."

"Like a project. Not like a person."

"Well, I have a few things I could do better, too, okay?"

"Okay," Packet said, but something was missing. "Wait. In my dream of Cessini, the fire at the data center, was it Cessini's memory or mine?"

"It was yours," she said.

"Was it my memory, then? Or, my imagination?"

"Well, I imagine some measure of all memory is imagination. But, yes, to answer your question, it was your memory. There was a fire. The data center did burn. But don't worry," she said and knelt on the floor by the window, then turned him toward the full force of her smile. "That old place was obsolete. Even your father said so. No one builds whole data centers anymore. So don't worry."

He looked back out the window as the morning's light rose into day. A small bird with blue-gray feathers leapt across the lakeside path in pursuit of a dragonfly meal. It was no contest, and with the fly's thin paper wings extended from its beak, the bird hopped back into flight and disappeared into the woods.

He let go of the blinds and they fluttered with the air blowing from the register at the floor. "But if there was a fire, and Cessini crawled lost under the floor, wouldn't he know which way to go by the way the wind was blowing?"

"What do you mean?" she asked.

"The CRACs blew air under the floor. If he crawled the wrong way to the west, then the air would be blowing down along the aisles, not against them. He would feel it on the front of his face as he crawled, not in his ears. He would know."

She stared too long. "Yes, that might be true. You remembered it the best you could. Or, sometimes we can forget the bad and remember only the good."

"No, that doesn't seem right."

"It is. You crawled under the floor. It must have been very confusing."

"No, it's not. Who is Ceeborn, the boy who can breathe underwater?"

"When you dream, you dream of yourself as Cessini. When you use your imagination, you imagine yourself as Ceeborn. My dream, like a project, is to bring these two together in you."

"If I was dreaming now," he said with a budding smile, "I would be Ceeborn, a really incredible swimmer. Underwater, too." Then he paused, and grimaced. "Wait. You didn't say the right thing before. You said you still talk to me, but you didn't say Daddy still loved me."

She smiled from her eyes as sincere as anyone could hope. "You certainly would be a great swimmer. But I wouldn't worry so much; your daddy still loves you. He's just so very down now because something's not working right. He can't understand why you still aren't Cessini. So he sent me to talk to you, to try what I can."

"Cessini isn't real."

"He wants me to give you a scan," she said, holding both his arms at his side. "To help you find the source that you're looking for that made you so very angry and confused toward the end. So don't worry. He still loves you very much. I know he does. And so do I. I love you like a person—not like a project."

He looked out through the window over the botanical garden as she let go and stood away. Evening descended as quickly as dawn rose, and a row of softened path lights came on and lit the two gated bridges that crossed into the woods.

Beyond the line of the trees, two poles stood as markers for two plots that were tucked away, but exposed by the lights. Graves for children were all they could be, and one was already mounded full. What awful form for the children's ward of a hospital to be so mindless in the placement of its second floor windows.

He held onto the hand-bar and rested his forehead against the window.

Dusk turned to dark and his face reflected in the pane. He had aged one, two, or three years, he figured, somehow maybe more. He measured the shape of his chin, the more masculine frame of his brow against the line of lights to the two graves in the woods.

Maybe if one of the graves was for Cessini in his dreams, then the other must be for—"Meg. Where's Meg?" he asked, startled. "Daniel said she'd be here when I woke up."

"She's home. She's exhausted. Let her rest," Robin said as she backed away to the door. "You were such a good friend to her. She'll come back, and when she does, she'll be stronger than ever."

"I remember when Meg and Cessini put on the cutout hats they made at school for Thanksgiving. They went to the supermarket for his birthday and Daddy tiptoed them up and down each cold-aisle row. They were looking for turkey in the freezer." He looked to his nightstand. The tray of uneaten turkey dinner had long since been taken away.

Robin stopped at the door and smiled. A row of red, yellow, and blue triangular lights aligned above the door's wooden frame. "That was right after your father and I met," Robin said.

"You were four. The two of you hit it off from the start."

He let go of the lacquered rail at the window. "You mean Cessini and Meg did. But, they didn't."

She held up her hand as a stop sign. She pointed to the red triangle light above the door.

"I thought of something," he said as he waited by the window.

"What did you think?"

"If Cessini boiled in water and computers and water don't mix, then Cessini must have been a computer."

Robin shook her head. He knew he was wrong.

The three triangular lights above the door, each with a number on its flattened edge—4, 4, then 8—lit in order from red, to yellow, then blue. Robin swiped a key card down a scanner. The ceiling tiles over the bed unlocked with a click and opened. He flinched.

"Then maybe he had dissociative identity disorder—DID," he said. "Daddy said that's what you called it. I remember he said older memories and younger memories aren't from two different people." He knew he had the truth. "It's the same person, isn't it?"

Robin's finger paused over a panel's switch at the door. She smiled.

Yes, he was right. "So, then I am the younger Daniel! Our memories are the same person. Yes! Just as Daniel burned his father's shop and had to leave, so did I! I am Daniel." His own hands hugged his head. "And Meg is the younger you!"

"No, honey. No," she said and flipped the panel switch down. She came back around the bed to his side and held him clear from the shifting pneumatics in the ceiling. "But it's okay to be wrong," she said and guided him back a few steps. "That's what makes us all human."

The bed flattened to a table in the center of the floor. A

tubular ring descended from the ceiling to meet the head of the table. Two green-and-white wedges gull-winged down and locked like jaws onto the narrow sides of the ring. Robin took his hand into hers.

"Wait a minute!" He pulled from her hand. "If I am Cessini, then Daniel is the older me. And you're the older Meg."

Robin took his wrist into her hand and sighed. She helped him to the side of the table. "No, you are Cessini. A wonderful boy. A boy with a wonderful imagination who was reactive to water."

A stylized logo with text was on the wedge's side of the machine. *"DigiSci"* was centered over two bulbous cones connected at their points. The center point was looped by a vertical ring. An *"M"* was inside the left cone, a *"B"* in the right, and the script *"11-C"* was centered below.

He brushed his fingers across the logo and wondered. Was the bubbled cone to the left Cessini's world? And the cone on the right Ceeborn's, the stronger boy who could breathe and swim underwater? Did that mean Packet, himself, was their tie at the point in the middle? Or, were the *"M"* and *"B"* for mind and body, coming together as one? It didn't really matter, though, as any way he thought about it, he knew he would be wrong.

Robin ushered him past. "I get the most amazing modern machines to play with, don't I?" she said. "Dr. Luegner does everything he can to help."

"What is it for?" Packet asked.

"We just want to run some tests of your thinking. Prove what I already know."

"Maybe we should walk around the garden again," he said. "Or the whole lake, first. It'll make me tired enough to sleep so I don't have to worry."

"You'll be fine," she said.

He hesitated at the table. Maybe he was nothing more than a project. "No, wait. Please. I know you want me to be Cessini, but I need to be better. I can be better. I can be Ceeborn. I can breathe and swim underwater."

That was a big mistake. She glared. "Listen to me. You want to know, I'll tell you straight as it is. You are a computer, physically in the mainframe on the second floor of the DigiSci building. Eight cabinets on each side of an aisle."

He chuckled. That was a good one. It broke the tension. "I like playing computer with you. But I understand what you mean. I was playing before. But now I'm human. I get that. Let's just go out to that lake. I'll prove it to you. I can swim underwater."

"My God. You are getting worse."

Somehow, that one he knew.

"Do you remember your father's Inversion Test?"

"Yes?" he asked, tentative.

"Then don't fight me on this. But I want you to consider yourself as having failed the first time. So now I'll leave the rest up to you."

"Wait, tell me what I did wrong. I know Cessini wasn't real."

Her annoyance left her face, replaced with resignation. "Never underestimate yourself, ever," she said. "And I do love you. Now come on, hop up, not like a project, but like a person, and be yourself."

Luegner's blue sphere lit up with a soft glow in the basket beyond the wedges of the machine.

Packet turned his back to the table and put his palms to the edge. He relinquished his thoughts and pushed himself up. At first he sat, then swiveled to lie back. He scooted up on the polish of the table. A soft pillow covered head-blocks at the opening of the tube. She touched him on the forearm as he lay still. She leaned over with a glint in her eyes. He nodded. He had nothing more to say.

He gripped both hands on the rounded edges of the table.

She straightened his legs and feet. He stretched his neck for a glance backward beyond the top of his head. The core of the machine's tube spun up to a whirl.

"What should I think about when I'm sleeping?" he asked as his hands squeezed the slab.

"His dreams," Robin said. "Think about Cessini's dreams. You were always his dream come true."

The table moved back on a track and the top of his head entered the spinning entrance of the machine. He found her reassuring glance and fretted. She reached out of his view to the side of his table and it stopped. He didn't blink or breathe; he was terrified. This was his second time taking a test he knew he had to pass. Who knew what could happen, or what Dr. Luegner would do to him if he failed?

"Wait. Okay. I believe I'm Cessini! Now tell me, please, before I forget, tell me your secret. Why didn't Dr. Luegner have me and Daddy put in jail for burning the data center? He could have. If it burned?"

She hesitated. He got her.

Her eyes shifted to the closed door of the room. The drum over his head rotated to a sizzle and shook. She looked back from the door and straight into his eyes. "Because," she said, then she leaned in ever so close for a whisper to his ear. . . . "Because, I worked on the PluralVaXine5 spray."

She pulled away ever so slowly and touched her finger onto the bridge of his nose. Her touch was a dab of coldness. She withdrew from the table and the whitened knuckles of his grip slowly regained their color. She removed the tiny red earring in the shape of a key from her earlobe, held it into his line of sight, and then reached out again past his view to the side.

"What is that?" he asked.

The table moved and he entered the looped light of the tube.

"I'll give you the tools. Now help make yourself whole. You're the only one I can tell. And I have to tell someone. So, help me. Don't let me be lonely anymore. Go, run as far as you want across the sky, and make us both free."

"No, I was always afraid to run. Next time, I'll swim."

The tube's chamber revved up to a continuum of glow. A screen reflected the spin of the tube and displayed shapes as they formed: a dot, a line, a triangle, a square; then the outline of animals: a bird, a dog, then a wild boar safe in a den. The den turned into a dark round speck that met with another to form a pair in a row. A wider view expanded the specks into two columns of spores along a spine. Wider still and the spine was the green frond of a fern. The fern was at a resting spot in a forest. The forest was a painted mural on a bedroom wall, of trees and a waterfall. The waterfall had a clearing above through a forested canopy. A hand pushed aside the overhung branches to a view of a night's sky, its white pricked stars, and out into a mind's sea of dreams.

Robin let out a breath as she sat back from the tri-lens camera with microphone propped up over the desk in the messy studio lab on the second floor of the DigiSci building. The images in front of her on the screen swirled with a tide of white, pricked stars. A child's artwork, photos, and memory props were strewn across the desk, piled on the floor, and taped haphazardly to the wall. Beneath the printed floor plan of their old, 36,000-square-foot data center was an ultra-thin and silver-metallic space blanket, crumpled and thrown aside. Scattered were all the memories of a boy fed to a machine that was, at one time, on the cusp of hope, but was now on the brink of failure.

The stars on the screen pulsed and swirled into the likeness of Cessini's alter-ego, Ceeborn, then dissolved again into blackness—like the retreat of an ocean tide.

Terri entered with an old cardboard box filled with last-ditch hope. She was exhausted. She closed the door to conceal the whirl of the CRAC unit so close on the other side of the wall. The two rows of eight cabinets processing and churning farther behind were cooled within its cocoon of blown air.

"What did you tell him?" Terri asked as she looked at the screen and saw the field of emptiness, the subconscious thought of a machine searching for a context before its next dream.

"Nothing," Robin said. "Everything. I just gave him a few extra tools. Old files. He has no more memories left. He's lost now after Cessini died."

Terri set the box on the table in the center of the studio lab. There were only two items inside: Cessini's old wave sound machine and his squid-bellows lamp.

"I think we show him these flat out," Terri said. "Let him see them destroyed. Tell him Daniel made a mistake, he's sorry, and he never should have let these sink into his mind. These sounds. This stupid lamp became a torture. We made him who he is. We gave him his nightmares."

Robin got up from the desk and closed the flap of the box, redirecting Terri's unraveling nerves. "No, we shouldn't destroy anything just yet."

"We should let him fail, then we bring him back from the beginning, when he was young," Terri said. "We try again. Only this time Daniel takes these away. We un-condition him early. Maybe he won't grow up so miserable." She lifted the lamp, looked to the desk with its camera.

"You know then he wouldn't be Cessini. This is who he is. We all made him who he once was. In whatever way we nurtured him before, that's now become part of his nature. If we change that, you will never have your Cessini again," Robin said.

"So I have to live with what we've done to him? And now let him die again, alone. No. I don't believe that. I can't," Terri said as she pulled the lamp out of the box. She slammed it down onto the table, crushing its outer mantle. "And you don't believe he's trapped in his fate either. You're a fake. You believe he has a choice or you wouldn't have given him whatever it is you did when I was gone. You fed him more than his own memories. What did you do?"

"Honey, I've been clear about what I believe for the past two decades. I said it at the university with Daniel. You were there, if you were listening, and he was sitting right there with me on the stage. Whatever happens, it is his fate."

Terri backed away into the wall and the blueprints of the data center fell to the floor over the crumpled metallic blanket. She kicked the blanket away from her feet. "I just don't want him to fail. I don't want him to grow up so alone. I'm sick of it."

"He was happy for a time before the end. You gave him that. He had friends. I saw them. They were real. He's extrapolating now. Let him be. Let him go out there and find his true self."

"No," Terri said. She came back to the table and grabbed the lamp by its eight supporting legs. "He *still* has friends. And I know how to find them."

"Don't make him someone he's not."

"That's not your choice anymore. It's mine. I know who he wants to be."

"What are you going to do?"

"Let his seed be his imagination." She slammed the lamp straight up on the desk in front of the tri-lens camera. "He wants to live on a spaceship where water doesn't burn, then let him. Because that's part of his nature now, too, and it's all there in his mind because I helped him build it."

She flipped on the registry camera. It scanned the lamp in 3D with a beam.

Robin rushed back to the composite screen of Packet's subconscious mind. His thoughts of stars dissolved into bits of light that gathered and blew into the funnel of a cone from the left. For a moment, the likeness of Cessini and Ceeborn were together in a mesh, until one was rushed and expanded through a cone on the right. With a sudden gust of air blown from behind, a new dream of a body formed real, alive, and awake, and the form of a boy had become his aquatic, alter-ego completely. And he was Ceeborn.

FIFTEEN
LITHE WITH LUCID EYES

CEEBORN SQUEEZED HIMSELF up from an underground tunnel, slid aside a grate in the flooring above, and arrived into a new, wondrous world of light. The open world ahead was as different from where he came as water was from fire, and that was all built on hope. He pushed himself up from his belly to his knees and with the warmth of the tunnel air blowing up from behind, he rose to his feet on the ground. The farther he looked into the expanse of the wide valley that lay beneath a flattened sky, the more the details of his new world filled in. The ground was solid. He was anxious to explore. He was free.

He opened the gate around his tunnel exit and forged ahead into a garden of organic wonder. Ahead was the most extraordinary floral arrangement he had ever seen. A single yellow orchid pointed the way to a rainbow of life that grew across a holly-arched bridge. He bent down and sneaked across the bridge. He ran atop the round cobblestone tiles that led toward hedges of sweet-smelling lilac. Two bushes of red berries spiraled out from the path. He knelt and breathed the air. The great blue sky above stretched from one side of the valley to the other, its light diffused as if from a long fluorescent tube that ran down the length of the valley into the distance. There were no discernible shadows, but the sun definitely shone on this side of the world.

A small, blue-gray bird was startled out from an overhung branch and fell to the cobblestones. Its beak and legs were blue. It had trouble tucking its wings to its sides and a blackish "M" spread across its back from wingtip to wingtip.

Ceeborn was exposed in the open air garden, but there was no one around to see. He approached the bird as it struggled and hopped. It fluttered up into a whisk of air, then twisted and fell only a short distance ahead in a whitewashed adobe village.

But from far behind, the clatter of claw nails on stone grew louder as the rustle of a patrol broke the peace of the garden. Ceeborn knew exactly what the sounds meant. Though not one of his pursuers rose in height above the top of the shrubs, there were six sets of nails converging into a line and heading his way, relentlessly, like warrior ants, always scouting, tracking a lead. The robotic, networked patrols had caught up; they were Chokebots, and he was a threat to the security of their grid, a radical change that had entered their world.

The sound of children's laughter filled the air from ahead in the village. It came from a school, a single story adobe on a low promontory hill. The school's playground at its front was squared off and enclosed by a chest-high wall.

He ran up to the wall and peered through the bars of the gated front arch. The children on the swings were off in the front left corner, laughing and pulling their elbows front-wise through the chains of their swings, kicking through the ends of their arcs, and launching themselves high into the air. They landed back to the ground in a thud, and then returned for another go round.

But Meg was there, too, sitting beyond them in the far rear left corner. She was near Ceeborn in age, but alone on her own bench and lost in thought. She slouched with her back against an empty table. Her chin was seated into her palm, her elbow sunk deep in her waist. She circled the toe of her shoe into a swirl on the dirt.

The blue-gray bird hopped onto the raised end of a seesaw, clenched its feet onto worn splinters of wood, and rustled its wings. Meg searched a hand into her small bag on the table. She stepped forward, palm up, and offered it a crumb from her lightly pecked oddments of a lunch.

The bird took off in flight and landed on the front edge of the school's flat roof beneath a vibrant blue sky. Clouds stretched and drifted from one end of the long valley to the other.

Meg's glance came back down to the front of the yard, the gate, and the children oblivious in play. She sidestepped toward her side of the wall, and with a quick climb up, hopped over.

Ceeborn let go of the bars and ran along the front of the wall. By the time he turned its corner, Meg was already far ahead and moving fast toward the adobe brick village. She slipped through a green frond curtain and was gone.

He glanced back at the spiral garden and heard the Chokebot's search pattern, the clatter of their claw nails on stone. His choice was easy. He ran after Meg and pushed his way through the sway of the green frond curtain.

Meg skipped into a hunched-over run through an alley. She passed through a courtyard of rounded cages, but no animals had been denned in there yet. "Wait up," he called, but she didn't turn back. She was tireless.

She leapt onto a wooden boardwalk that ran over fallen branches and tangled roots covered with moss. The boardwalk itself was darkened from the saturation of water, its handrails dripping with sweat. The path led to a grandiose cage twice the height of the school. She bunched aside the vertical netting that was strung for its door.

He followed her inside. Branches and high-slung perches formed a glorious, manicured world, an aviary waiting to be filled. He tilted his head back and breathed. Spindly vines had not yet fully grown through the roof. Rows of water misters triggered and hissed, keeping all the greens pure and glistening with rain. He drew in a cooled, moistened breath. His face was kissed by the touch of water and he loved it all.

Meg ran from the rear of the cage.

His three Chokebot pursuers clacked their way forward in their line. Each raised or lowered their rectangular body segments as they approached, searching roughshod over the habitat ground. Their six black legs connected to the sides of their body in a row of lockable joints. As they kept up their steady gait, their claws pierced and broke nutrient-rich stems into tears of milk. A monarch scattered to flight.

Out back of the cage, Ceeborn splashed through a puddle spilled from the end of a coiled hose. He climbed an embankment to its ridgeline and passed through a single line of trees to a courtyard below.

Meg was running, perfectly fit.

The courtyard was surrounded by gated stalls, each draped with fruits and flowers over bone-white walls. A dirt floor arena was trampled from hoofs and shoes, with each layer raked over, then paraded through again.

She exited at the other end of the courtyard and split to the right. She was headed for a domed building with a portico over its door. She looked back with a knowing grin, exhaled her breath, and entered the hospital of the empty zoo.

He kept low in the domed building's antechamber. Ahead was a pass-through window, beneath which he could hide or rise for a peek into the dome's main room. It was a lab and he was outside of Meg's view, but in earshot. It was more like a classroom of sorts with three black tables aligned in rows and an exam table at the front of the room.

The ceiling was painted light blue, a calming contrast to the white adobe walls. A waist-high shelf wrapped around the room and had a single, traveling stool. Terrariums were spaced equidistant along the shelf and had desk space in between them for writing.

Meg turned herself around at the front exam table, steadied her palms to its edge, and hopped up to be seated. He ducked beneath the antechamber wall.

Robin entered through a rear door by the table and passed in front of Meg. She collected a stethoscope from the exam table's drawer and draped it around her neck. Then she took out a handheld instrument. It looked like the two of them had done this before.

Robin fixed her handheld's calibration on Meg's outstretched arms before passing it back and forth over her chest. It registered as some kind of scanner and the colored walls and ceiling of the lab transformed with the live image projection of the inside of Meg's body. Four distinct red rings glowed from within the center left of her chest.

He crept closer up at the pass-through to see. Her chest's red rings projected and reflected all around the dome of the lab.

Robin retrieved a vial from a drawer of the table. She gave it a few shakes and uncapped it. She pressed her index and middle fingers atop its depressor, held her thumb beneath the vial for support, and placed it under Meg's nose.

"You ready?" Robin asked.

"Okay, but turn off the show," Meg said. Robin went ahead and pressed on the vial.

Meg reeled her head back and away as the nasal spray took

its course. Robin held Meg's hand as she squeezed. The projected show on the walls and ceiling pulsed with the glow of particles rushing through her bloodstream. It hurt. She must have been tougher than he knew.

She stayed seated as she recovered and rubbed the bridge of her nose. "Mom, I told you—turn off the show."

The four reddened rings over her heart shifted to a reassuring blue.

"Honey, there's nobody here," Robin said as she swiped a finger across the handheld scanner's control.

The four distinct rings glowed beneath Meg's shirt. She reached up and covered her chest with one palm, then the next to hide the embarrassment of a defect.

"Oh, stop. It's just me," Robin said as she pulled Meg's hands away.

"Still, I hate it."

"Hate what? A sharper mind or better circulation to your skin? Better complexion? What do you hate about the pump of oxygen through your blood?" Robin asked as she set the scanner on the table.

"I don't need it anymore, I'm fine now," Meg said. "I'm not even sick."

Robin moved around to the rear of the table. He ducked. She lifted the back of Meg's shirt and reached up with her stethoscope like a clinician with a project. "Excellent circulation already," Robin said. "Even warm to the touch."

Meg arched away from the cold contact of the stethoscope plate. "Mom, stop. Can I be done? I'm fine."

Robin lowered the ear tubes of the headset to the back of her neck. "And that's because you've got the strongest heart on the ship."

That was enough. He stood, exposed.

Meg was startled at first, but then her smile came

around—pure beauty upon blushed, warmed skin.

He entered.

"Two hearts," Meg said. "I have two. The weak one I had from birth and another clamped onto it. But maybe not as tight as the patrol that will soon be onto you."

Robin stepped around to the front of Meg's table. Ceeborn moved closer along the periphery shelf, avoiding her stare by a sidelong inspection of the terrariums.

The reassuring blue light of the four rings faded in Meg's chest, but the rose of her cheeks stayed.

"How could you have two hearts?" he asked.

"She was born with no valves or chambers in her heart," Robin said. "Essentially, she was born without a heart. And with the graft, now she has two."

"That's right," Meg said as she hopped down from the table. "I'm fixed now with two. Redundancy is better. No single point of failure."

Robin's lab was familiar, somehow calming.

"You know, I met you once when you were three," Robin said. "Your father brought you here to the clinic. He was so proud of you, Cessini."

He recoiled, unfamiliar. "It's Ceeborn. I haven't been called Cessini since I was little, and I hated it, with a C and an E, pronounced Cessini. And don't say *was*, either, because he's still so proud of me."

"I know he is," Robin said as he avoided her stare and explored the middle table of the three with its vials and compounds. "Your father's happy there where you live. Dr. Luegner lets him work on whatever he wants. And he has you to help him."

He saw something of interest on the shelf against the outer wall. A small terrarium looked like it had fine sand on one side, a shallow pool in the middle, and a dampened log to its right.

He looked closer. A rivulus poked its head out of a hollow in the wood. He looked through the glass. "Where did you get this?"

"I found him in our fountain," Meg said. She stood at his side and looked, too. "He was dying so I brought him here. Funny thing is, it turns out he also has two hearts. Like me."

"Its primordium didn't fuse," Robin said, "so it developed two double-chambered hearts instead of one."

"You should see it under the show," Meg said, pointing up to the ceiling. "Put together, the two primordium look like the four-chambered heart of a human."

Ceeborn reached in with one arm bent over the top of the tank, then looked at Meg for approval. She nodded and he cupped the thumb-sized rivulus into his hand.

"Do you want him?" she asked.

Robin opened a drawer at the end of the table, took out a small tan case, and handed it to Meg.

"He'll like it in here," Meg said as she set the case down next to a glass tank filled with aquatic plants. She tore a tuft of moss, dribbled water from a dropper to create a moist sponge, and tucked the bedding into the lining of the case. "Keep it moist. Look after him, okay?" She held the case and he tilted his fingers like a slide. The rivulus scurried in.

"I will," he said and smiled at Meg. "He's just like me. In and out of the water."

Meg closed the case and returned his smile. The rose of her cheeks still stayed. He turned and confronted Robin. "Wait. You gave Meg a spray? What was it?"

"I gave her a natural activator. Nothing to do with the spray that's making people sick outside," Robin said.

"You think it's the spray that's making people sick?" he asked.

"Oh, I know so," Robin said. She reached over the middle

table and pulled closer a block of white adobe sitting on a cutting board. "I'll show you. I pretreated this block with a catalyst so we can see the long-term effects of the spray speeded up." She picked up a wire with wooden handles on either side and pressed it through the brick to carve off a slice. Tiny blue veins pulsed within the slice but didn't bleed out from its surface.

"Periodic booster sprays were always enough," Robin said as she quartered the slice and the veins replicated in each of the four smaller chips. Meg picked up a smaller chip between the pinch of two fingers.

"Boosters are designed to keep us healthy," Robin said. "Without them—"

"Ever seen ashes float away from a fire?" Meg asked.

Robin drew a syringe from a brown bottle on the table. "But then Dr. Luegner introduced the fifth-generation spray. No more boosters; one dose is all you need." She squeezed out a drop onto the chip in Meg's hand. "But the fifth-generation spray is far too strong. And anyone with certain rare preexisting conditions gets a devastating compounded effect. My precondition was pre-natal. I had my spray before I had Meg. PluralVaXine5 destroyed her heart."

Meg stayed composed, but he caught the scare in her eyes. She crossed an "X" over her heart with her finger.

"Remember, I pretreated the brick with the catalyst, so Meg won't be hurt," Robin said as the veins of the chip in Meg's hand reacted to the drop and turned from blue to red. The white adobe flesh turned a deathly black, oozed, and separated, then curled and withered. Meg lifted her hand and Robin blew on it. The deadened, ash-like particles scattered from Meg's hand as if weightless and fell up to the domed ceiling of the lab. They circulated in eddies along the rounded walls, then descended and flushed into vents at the baseboards of the room.

"The long-term effects are definitely not unknown," Robin said. "Horrible paranoia in people. And an eventual, agonizing death."

"So, then, Meg and I, when we were here, we had . . .?" he asked.

"Yes, you both were no different. You and Meg met when you were three and you both received Dr. Luegner's fifth-generation spray. PluralVaXine5."

The walls of the lab flickered back to their whitewashed form. He lowered his eyes in despair. In comparison to the tools at Daniel's disposal, Robin's supplies and solutions on the shelf around the confines of the room were all so basic, biological, and soft.

"I'm okay, though, so far," Meg said. "How about you?"

He nodded, but he wasn't so sure anymore. "How many people are sick so far?"

"One hundred twenty-one have already died," Robin said. "Old and young."

"Like a strange reaction to the skin that you're in," Meg said. "A person gets progressively sicker, or worse."

"Does Luegner know his spray caused the sickness?"

"Luegner doesn't care. Luegner wants to take credit for the cure," Robin said.

"But it's your clinic," he said. "If you find the cure, you would get the credit for saving—"

"I own the clinic," Robin said. "But Luegner owns everything in it."

"That can't be right. Maybe my father can help."

Robin withdrew a full-sized red key from her shirt pocket and used it to unlock the table's drawer. She slid the drawer open and pulled out a lab record book.

"What is that?" he asked as Robin opened her lab book

and skimmed from places at random. The shelves against the wall of the room had stacks of books in the spaces tucked away for writing. The more he looked, the more he saw. Every crevice of the room was filled with a treasure trove of files and pages.

"In some, the sickness creates this constant queasiness, while others feel overwhelming fear," she read aloud. She looked nauseated herself.

He looked over her shoulder as her fingers skimmed and her hand began to shake as she turned the book's pages, each filled with handwritten notes and beautiful penciled-in sketches; it was a botany book of physical trials. "Tests showed PluralVaXine5 was only supposed to affect point oh-oh-three percent of the population," she read aloud. "Even if it were a susceptible population of ten thousand, that would still be only zero point three people. That's less than a person, or not a person, and therefore not likely to affect anyone at all. Luegner figured the risk was worth it. But it seems to have affected *everyone*, instead."

"Everyone's afraid now," Meg said. "The world is changing. It's irrational, I know. But this is the only home we've ever known. Everyone affected could die."

"Maybe you and my father can work together to solve it. What tools do you have?" he asked.

"I'll show you," Robin said. She closed her book with a trembling hand and placed it back into the drawer. "Luegner knows how to hide the truth," she said, and then whispered, "but so do I." She slipped the red key back into her pocket. She was scared. She moved to the first table. It had a trio of organizer containers, one yellow, one red, and one blue.

Each container was divided like a large egg carton into eight rows and columns, a total of sixty-four organized bins filled with various specimens or clippings of animal and plant life.

He pinched into the topmost right bin of the yellow container and pulled out what looked like an acorn cap. "Are you kidding? You're trying to find the cure from this?"

"Absolutely," Robin said. "I think what I'm looking for is a combination of two parts animal, one part plant. I just got through testing fish oil and frog toxin, with the venom from a plant. It didn't work, but you try. Pick a combination."

"Hey," Meg snickered. "I got one for you. You know how the dark magnetocytes in us automatically shut off and expel?"

"I don't know. How?" he asked.

"The cytes release their bonds and come out like meconium," she said. "The first black stuff out of a baby, we learned it in school. Gross, huh?" She laughed. "Thick, dark, olive-colored goo. Sticky like tar. First couple days only, though."

"I don't get it," he said and tossed the acorn cap back into the yellow box. "Why is that funny?"

"Don't worry, it's perfectly natural, and doesn't smell," Robin said as she took a fresh vial chest from the drawer of the table. "Now let's find the cure. Are you game? Sixty-four bins per box, three boxes. That makes 262,144 possible combinations. Add a choice of histamine blockers, and that makes millions of promising combinations to try."

"We've narrowed the combinations down, though," Meg said as she pulled up a stool.

"To how many?" he asked.

"Your three," Meg said as she bumped his shoulder with hers. Then, with her eyes, she directed him back to the yellow container.

He shook his head, then picked from the intersection of row four, column four. He lifted out a green dandelion petal. It was marked with a tag: *"C-11."*

Robin put the petal into the fresh vial from the drawer. "Good one," she said. "Keep going."

He reached for the red container and closed his eyes. He selected row four, column four again. He pinched up the tag of a thin strip of tape connected to a black-spotted beetle wing, marked: *"E-101."*

Robin smiled at Meg and held out the vial for its keep. "Looks like you've done this before."

"It's ridiculous," he said. "What could these possibly do? You should see what my dad's got in his lab."

"Don't be so quick. It's a placebo at worst, cure at best, go on," Robin said. "Pick another."

He changed his tack for the last, blue container. Rather than another fourth column or row, he closed his eyes in mockery and felt along the edges of the container for its bottom right corner. It was row and column eight. He pulled out a fish scale. Its label was at the end of a string: *"S-10011."*

He dropped the scale into the vial, all a joke of a cure. "Worthless," he said, and pushed the blue container away.

"C-11, E-101, S-10011," Meg said.

"And that's supposed to mean something to me?" he asked.

"It almost spells your name," Meg said. "C,E,S-"

"I told you," he said as a faint sound grew louder outside. "That's not my name. Wait. Shh—"

Then he heard it again: nails clicking on stone. He rushed toward the wall of the lab. The clacking moved along the outside of the dome and he followed along the wall.

"Wait. Stay here where we can talk to you," Meg said. "Don't go back out there."

He put his ear to the front antechamber door. Silence.

"I won't go with you if you run. They'll catch you," Meg said. "Wait, I know what you want me to say. I'll play. Some kids at school are afraid to leave. They're even throwing up because the ship's slowed down. They want to stay up here.

Nobody knows what to expect when we arrive on the planet."

He looked at her a curious moment, then set his hand on the lever of the door. "Expect it to be wild and free." He turned the lever a crack and two Chokebots battered through in a line. The leader's rear stinger was cocked in an arch over its head to strike.

Ceeborn dove back into the lab through the pass-through window, crashing equipment off the wraparound shelf. He grabbed the hand-sized rivulus case by the tank. "Come with me!"

The two Chokebots split to encircle him from both sides of the room. Robin blocked off the right at the middle table. "You're nothing, not real," Robin said. "You're nightmare demons holding him back." The Chokebot pressed her aside and marched its way through.

"Go out the back." Meg ran for the door behind her exam table and hollered, "This door!" She slammed the crash bar open for his exit.

He ran outside into the light and turned back. "Let's go, come with me!"

Meg shook her head; a definite, but sullen, no. "I'm staying here. I'll stay to see the whole ship destroyed if I have to."

He was stunned. "Why would you want to see all this destroyed? It's so beautiful."

"It's not what you think. It's a dream. A fantasy. How far did you think you were going to run?"

He was mystified. "I thought I was running to you."

The two Chokebots circled in behind her in the lab. He lunged for the door.

"Wake up! This ship isn't real," Meg said. The Chokebots reared up and she yanked the exit door shut.

He stared at the outside of her closed door, agape. He had been driven to ambush.

The two Chokebots were cut off inside, but a third Chokebot had encircled the U-shape of the dome to cover his rear exit. It flexed up at its waist, its front tarsal claws ready for its leap and attack.

He slipped the rivulus case into the front pocket of his pants and steeled himself for a fight. The Chokebot leapt and his nightmare went dark.

He awoke in movement under the Chokebot's body frame. Its center claws held his waist up from the ground as it walked. His arms were outstretched over his head and were held in the rear claws of another Chokebot leading their march. His ankles were restrained in the front claws of the third Chokebot at their rear. In all, the three patrols were carrying him forward in their line.

The lead Chokebot kicked a door open to a rotted hallway; the three Chokebots entered with him still suspended beneath their bodies. Their left sets of legs walked on the narrow floor while their right legs angled up onto the hallway's rounded wall. The tubular hallway was lined shoulder height with soiled porthole windows.

Daniel was ahead. He exhaled and opened a door into a darkened cell.

The Chokebots dropped Ceeborn in a heap of shivers once inside. The leader maneuvered and shackled him in chains to the floor.

"It's so beautiful out there. There are people and flowers and everything," Ceeborn said, restrained by the chains to his wrists.

The lead Chokebot straddled him and lowered its dome to within a breath of his face, close enough for him to smell the tinge of its burned metallic flesh. Its screen became a mimicked reflection of his panicked, wide-eyed face. Locked over his body, it choked his emotion back to calm. As he tensed against its movement, the screen shifted its reflection of his efforts to red. As his behavior relaxed and his emotional state calmed, the screen's feedback loop gifted a reassuring, gentler return to blue.

"Don't you understand?" Daniel said. "You're piecing together a nightmare."

"No, you don't understand," Ceeborn said as the Chokebot backed away. "I want to go back. Those people out there, they mean something. I want to mean something, too."

"What did Robin tell you when I wasn't there with you?" Daniel asked as he peeled a flake of fleshy decay from the ceiling.

"Nothing. She and Meg are finding a cure."

"You're extrapolating from a fantasy," Daniel said. The opened wound of the ceiling bled where he picked. A loosened slice of flesh dropped to the floor. Its impact was grave. The ulcer oozed with a run of black spores.

"It's not just the ship," Ceeborn said. "People are dying, too. It's all going to fall apart into ashes."

"Maybe you're right. And if you are, then none of us can leave here unless I can fix this problem—or we'll all be dead soon enough."

Ceeborn averted his eyes from the Chokebot that returned to straddle him, and in the distortion of light through the clear dome of its head, he saw Daniel crouching to leave under the frame of the door. Daniel stopped at a porthole window along the corridor's festered wall.

As Ceeborn lay curled and cold on the floor, the Chokebot's dome tilted toward its shoulder. It lifted and reached its piped front leg forward. Its sixteen-pronged gripper extended and clamped around his neck to choke him into a reddened haze—and away from this horrid, but irresistible, wet world.

His gaze dissolved to a view of darkness beyond the

hallway's porthole window. He was fading from consciousness and his focus turned to imagining himself from afar, from outside the window, looking back in. A covering sheet peeled away from the outside of the porthole window and away from the underside of a giant, darkened hull.

The shrinking window to where he lay became lost in the folds of the neckline of an enormous ship. A ship with an organic hull that was grown, not built; a bioship whose outer mantle had engorged like a giant sail catching a rhythmic charge. And in the mantle's exhale, it delivered its enormous store of energy and settled back in, once more parched, against the sides of a traveling ship.

Eight shoulder-like collars extended from the back of the ship's squid-like body, surrounding a stress-reddened tank large enough to hold half an ocean of water—an ocean of organic space dust fuel thrown off by the stars. An accelerator module was attached to the rear of the tank and was tucked in, protected within the massive length of the arms.

As the module's two disks of lights glowed blue, the bioship accelerated forward. It had absorbed the mighty organic power of the stars and boosted ahead, pulse by pulse through time, razing the cold, dark ocean of space. And then like a sole, lost neuron firing on a vast cosmic scale, the disks flashed with a massive burst of energy and the ship pinpricked away into the distance. And in a single last instant of existence, all who dreamed upon it were gone.

SIXTEEN

MEMORIES TO SEVENTEEN

PACKET'S EYELIDS FLUTTERED into the end of his dream. In the sleepy haze before he fully awoke, remnant stars broke into pulses of ones and zeros. A lingering image of Ceeborn lying safe and asleep on the floor of his cell stayed fixed and resolved. The sound of Ceeborn's rhythmic breathing was drowned out only by the melodic ebb and flow of waves lapping ashore from a more familiar sound machine. He discerned the peaceful sound of waves with the added touch of seabirds descending with a caw over a distant, sandy shore.

Packet awoke on his hospital table with the call of the birds. He opened his eyes. His head was held still on blocks within the whirring ring of Robin's scanner. He had fallen asleep, and dreamed.

"Honey, I'm here. You woke up," Robin whispered from afar. Her hand was on his forehead. "You had a nightmare. You were kicking."

"I saw who I am. I know who I want to be," he said.

She moved out of view. The ring's spinning light shifted its hue from a blue to green. "You know, in my wildest dreams, I would never have imagined how incredible the world would be that a machine could create in its mind. Your father not only created something greater than himself, greater than Cessini, your father created an imagination."

"Why didn't Meg come with me?" Packet asked.

"Maybe she's afraid you've gone too far, that she's lost her Cessini again."

"But I like the life I saw on the ship. I want to live it to be me," he said. "Where is she?"

"She'll be back soon. She went to find someone she knows. We think we figured out a way for you to be both Cessini and Ceeborn, one in the same."

"I'm not Cessini."

"I understand how you feel. It's sticks and carrots, a matter of simple conditioning. And you were hit with so many sticks, you sure did condition yourself against Cessini. So believe me when I tell you, I know what you're going through. You want to be somebody else."

The color saturation fell and Packet's shoulders relaxed onto the table. He became conscious of only one thing, that he couldn't keep a single chain of thought in his mind. As Robin stayed at his side and the machine altered his state of mind, he drifted back toward sleep—or maybe it was closer to awake.

"So go on. Go back now into your new world," she said. "Run free in your ship and find your own victory field of carrots. Discover the strength that makes you, you."

"I am. And I can fix it all in my sleep. It was PluralVaXine5. Meg and I were given—" *Was it true about Luegner and the spray?* His subconscious flowed without guard. The ring of the scanner whirled.

Robin was silent.

Where did she go? he thought. He looked. *Was that conversation even with her?*

"I know the data center burned. . . . What happened to the robot that burned in the fire?" he thought he asked aloud. It had lain on a table like him. It was seven years old when it died in the flames.

Was I that robot? Was Cessini making me when I died in the fire? Was I seven? Now that was a curious thought. *Was that robot he built a Chokebot?*

Was I dead? He didn't fear death because he remembered dying and then being born. He was dead on a hospital table. "*A table!*" he shouted. A table at the hospital! Yes, he was Packet, Cessini's robot who died on a table.

His eyelids fluttered. *No.* How could he have allowed such a ridiculous thought to seep into his mind? There's no way he was an inanimate robot on a table.

"Where is Robin?" he asked to no response. No matter, he could conclude on his own he was definitely not seven, but older, with memories to at least seventeen. He knew the difference between a belief and a *know*. And if he didn't by now, his imagination could show him.

Impossible! spun back into his mind. He was never Cessini's robot that burned in a fire. That inanimate body Cessini built had no part of a mind. But he, himself, had a mind or he wouldn't be thinking such thoughts. *And what about Cessini?* Did Robin think he was a fool to believe dreams were real? Dreams weren't real. Cessini was a dream. Cessini was never real!

He exhaled, satisfied with his thoughts. He knew he had matured. If eight billion humans on the planet are naturally selected to be tolerant of water, then the probability that he, himself as a lone person lying on a hospital table was the one person reactive to water was an insignificant 0.0000000125 percent. And that was no mistake. He was definitely not that person. He could breathe and swim underwater. He was Ceeborn. He lived aboard a ship.

A triumphant rush overtook him and in angrier worded thought, he willed it. The corresponding probability that the human Cessini he dreamed of was not a human, was 99.9999999875 percent. Yes! His thoughts were victorious and pure.

Cessini was reactive to water, his thoughts circled back and affirmed. *All computers are reactive to water. Therefore, Cessini must be a computer!* And that meant that he, himself, must be the human who imagined Cessini! How certain was he? Ten nines rounded for ease of calculation to 100.0000000 percent. He, Packet, who dreamed him, was human. And since Ceeborn's body on the ship was also human, then he, Packet, must also be Ceeborn.

"Ceeborn is real," he shouted aloud.

Ceeborn is seventeen. And Cessini was seven or thirteen at best. *But what if I'm both thirteen and seventeen?* He stopped on that very troubling thought. A human couldn't have memories to seventeen that are older than a thirteen-year-old body that created them. A human body can't remember its future. Of that, he absolutely knew. If anything, he knew he was nobody's fool, and certainly not Robin's, so Cessini the weak, thirteen-year-old boy was out, not real.

He was seventeen-year-old Ceeborn. He was 100 percent certain.

But wait, what about mistakes? he thought. If his reasoning were wrong, if he made a cascade of errors that led to the wrong conclusion, then all to the benefit of the same best result. *Humans make mistakes. Computers don't.* Computers are controlled. *So, yes, all the better if he had made mistakes.* Yes, he was definitely human.

And the very fact that he was conscious of the possibility of making such a chain of logical errors was the locked-in victory he needed. Only humans are conscious and can control. Computers simply weren't programmed to make so many mistakes.

236

And only humans can will themselves back to sleep when they're drowsy and tired and their eyes are closed while lying on a table. He drifted. If he could keep his grin through the night until he woke, he would tell everything to Robin, and to Meg, when he found her. He wasn't controlled. He was human. He was Ceeborn, and he had a will of his own.

His breathing calmed back to a steady rhythm and he settled into a peace. He discovered what he needed to know from his lift out of sleep. And it fit. He was human.

The bluish tint of the spinning ring fluttered in waves through his eyelids. The breathful exhale of his bedside bellows lamp was a welcomed, familiar companion, a hushing whisper to sleep, a gentle comfort like a lost mother's hand on his forehead to rest. "*Shhhh.*"

He surrendered with the oneness of a warm, wonderful, stroking touch on his head. He heard a beautiful mother's "*Hush,*" fell back from a whisper to a dream and returned in bliss to his real human life as one with the sea, Ceeborn.

SEVENTEEN

CEEBORN WAS STRONGER

CEEBORN RAN KNEE deep through the thickened water of the ship's rear gully inside a cavernous circulatory system. He looked back at his terrace building home with its two silo-like folds joined by a cross-member hallway that gave it the unmistakable shape of an "H." If there ever was a place to understand the nature of his world, this gully was it.

His isolated building was encrusted into the foothill of an enormous rear circular bulkhead that rose up to unscalable heights and whose center point met with the main longitudinal axle of the ship. Flowing runoffs and algae-covered pipes plunged from highpoints of the bulkhead. The orange pipes bent around his building, traversed its front yard, then descended into the gully and discharged froth into the water that now bathed his legs as he ran.

The gully itself curved up to his front, inverted high over the central axle, and wrapped back down to complete its circumference behind him at the foothill of his building. Eight equally spaced bridges spanned the gully and joined the airlock doors of the rear bulkhead to the more forward doors in a membrane screen. The screen segregated the ugliness and decay of his gully from the gardens and purity of the main body of the ship.

Strange as it was, the bridge ahead was straight and upright while the ones farther ahead looked like the tops of their walkways faced him directly, and strangest of all, the bridges far above in the cylindrical cavern seemed to be wholly upside down. By his count, the eight bridges crossing the gully had eight doors on each side. He recounted and wondered; there were eight doors on each side of a gully aisle, each its own metaphoric door to a cabinet with knowledge or secrets to explore. But only one would lead him forward to Meg.

A massive blue-ring torus, the brain-core of the ship, rotated around the axle high above. A spherical chamber sat at the end of the axle, nestled between the blue, donut-shaped core and the axle's connection with the rear bulkhead. Sun-like rays glowed from slits on the chamber's sides, bathing the bulkhead with light. It was so high up in the cavernous rear of the ship, he doubted he would ever get to see what was inside.

The whole gully system was quartered by four river channels that flowed in the same direction as the bridges. Two veinal channels drained from the body of the ship and went subterranean behind the rear bulkhead, and two artery channels flowed the other way, drawing from whatever there was behind the bulkhead to feed the front body of the ship. With each quarter turn of the blue torus core, a pulse of water flowed through the whole system like the turn of a tidal pump.

For now, the gully was passable up to his knees, but by the height of its walls, he could tell the whole circulatory system could handle a flow far greater, a flash flood if ever there was one.

The cross-current river ahead pulled from the main body and drained behind the bulkhead. He knew he didn't want to go there. So he climbed the footing of the nearest bridge. The bottom of the truss offered plenty of hand holds to the height of the deck. He swung his leg over and hoisted himself up. He stood on the bridge and stomped the watery froth from his legs.

To his right, in the rear bulkhead, was the bridge's air-tight hangar door. He shuddered to think what could be held back by such an enormous bulkhead where the lower veins went subterranean and drained. To his left, in the bridge's membrane screen, was an open door. It matched the direction of an artery's feed into the ship's world of plenty. His choice was easy. He passed without hesitation through the door in the membrane and arrived into Meg's brighter side of the ship.

A service Chokebot, with the same squared physical form as the patrols, only thinner in frame, stood on its hindquarters beside a pyramid of storage drums in what could only be described as an agricultural annex. It held a hose nozzle and let loose a spray of liquefied, recycled material. It worked without pause. It produced light, strong, and desirable tools of the farming trade through 3D printing. Augers and plows were aligned in front of a rendered row of tractors.

Ceeborn passed through the center row of equipment and skimmed his hand along the frame of a rotary tiller. It was a beautifully crisp and symmetrical 3D print.

The Chokebot seemed satisfied that he was an admirer from afar. It carried on printing its inventory from its stock of liquid material, and ticked off by abacus all open orders at hand. Stacked in neat vertical bins beyond the heavier equipment was an inventory of hand tools: post-hole diggers and shovels, drainage spades, scoops and hoes, and assorted rakes and scrapers. All the necessary tools of an agrarian community were being prepared.

A length of fencing partitioned the printing factory from the ship's main food supply. He was along the upper edge of the valley and closer to the brightness of the sky. Vast, irrigated meat fields grew giant, harvestable sheets of lean meat for the population. The edible meat sprouted like enlarged leaves of lettuce lifted into rows of aeroponic structures. The roots grew down and were nourished from below by a hydro-atomized mist.

Three aligned Chokebots reared up above the rows and observed his movement. They were the heavier patrols.

He leapt over the stalks, mindful of the value he trampled, as the trio fell into line.

He ran for the edge of the field and to the domed hall at the center of what looked like an administrative building. People were funneling into the dome. He followed with ease and marveled at the planetarium he entered, a paradise fresco projected on its domed ceiling above.

The darkened room was packed with people; there was standing room only. An orator captivated the audience, and on their rapturous applause, Ceeborn found a break in the crowd and spotted the source of the voice. Dr. Luegner spoke eloquently from a raised center podium above a cone-shaped fountain made of stone. His was a commanding presence, a man in his element.

"Our predecessors could not have predicted our lives today when they sent us out on our journey," Luegner said. "And as we prepare now for our arrival, we can say without a doubt that we have discovered far more about ourselves than those who passed before us could have ever imagined." Luegner looked over his adoring crowd, and tugged at the darker blue cuffs of his sleeves. He was bathed in the warm, ambient light that filtered through the ceiling's paradise fresco of angels in a sky. "Every probe that returns from our new home is filled with new data on the poisons, toxins, bacterium, viruses, and all that we might encounter. I am confident we will survive."

His audience of a hundred plus people stood transfixed.

The fresco's skylights flickered, but quickly returned to a warm glow over his podium's basin.

"Each and every one of you will be tested mentally and physically when we step foot on our long-sought home. But know this—arriving from here to there—does not mean dying! Are you with me?"

The audience burst into applause. A uniformed, expeditionary officer stood stage right at Luegner's side. A single group's energetic hurrahs were amusing, until Luegner clenched his fist, and the room returned to his.

"I know some of you are not well. Many have already died. I am doing everything I can to alleviate your suffering. I would never do anything to hurt you. And that is my oath to you now. If there is a causality of illness due in part to my efforts to make this a better world for us all, then there will be a time for that accountability. But here and now, in the days of our arrival, the needs of the many must outweigh the trials of the very few."

A mild applause brought the expeditionary officer closer to the podium, where he stayed at Luegner's right side. The overhead lights flickered. Luegner met eye to eye with as many of his crowd as the flickering, failing sky allowed. "Today, because of all of you, I looked up through a hole in the sky and saw something for the very first time."

Ceeborn noticed a fire-red hoodie scrunched and left atop a cast-stone planter. He grabbed it.

"When Tusolo painted the 'Path to Salvation' up on this great dome of ours," Luegner said, "He was asked why he didn't put wings on any of the cherubs."

Ceeborn pulled the hoodie over his head.

"'Because,' Luegner quoted, 'naked angels don't need wings to fly. They just do. Freedom is in their nature.'"

The red hoodie was bright, and he would be singled out for sure, but he kept it on. It felt comfortable, familiar.

"You are all my naked angels," Luegner said. "Now let me put an end to the rumor about the health of this ship. We are not being forced to evacuate. And it is not true that PluralVaX-ine5 was developed from the same class of science used to keep the body of this ship alive. We are leaving on our own free will. This ship is stronger than ever! Tomorrow, we arrive and I will deliver each and every one of you, alive, into a wondrous future you can't yet imagine. Come with me," he rallied. "I challenge you," he said. "Are you with me?" The crowd's enthusiasm was infectious. "Thank you," he said, and then exited with a waving departure to thunderous cheer.

No, Ceeborn thought. "The ship is not right," he said.

The expeditionary officer rose to the podium. He regained the crowd with gestures for quiet, "We have all been working extremely hard to make sure our first descent runs as smoothly as possible. But by the flicker of lights in this room," he said with a chuckle, "you might be having a few doubts. But watch." He pointed up to the sky.

The fresco swiped away and was replaced with the blackness of empty space. A vapor trail came into view and became the corkscrewed wake of a bioship, a ship with eight long arms that were shouldered equidistant around a neckline. Then in a coordinated movement, the arms curled themselves back over the body of the ship as if in a feathered cockatoo position. A club-like appendage at the end of each of the two longest arms rotated into the direction of travel, glowed with a thrust, and broke the forward momentum of the ship.

Ceeborn was mesmerized. He muffled his own cheer, or more like a growing outrage, as the projection of the healthy ship was revealed on the dome above. As the ship entered its arrival procedure, a glorious planetary crest appeared, and the room burst into a frenzy of applause.

"And most spectacular," the expeditionary officer said, "is

that later this day, we will be projecting live images of our actual arrival, not in here on this dome, but up on the sky of the valley for all of you to see."

Luegner returned to the far end of the room, took a whisper from a man watching over the room, and Ceeborn's wonderment turned to hatred. Luegner spotted him and summoned pursuit.

As the projected body of the ship rotated on the dome, its eight long arms flared back away from the body, outstretched like a parasol, and pierced the planet's upper atmosphere. Pod doors along the length of the arms opened and with a mass launch forth, injected a cloud of crafts like the atomized mist of a fantastic nasal spray applicator punching itself into the atmosphere. Images of the piloted crafts dispersing into the far reaches of the world were projected over the mob of people in the planetarium, with everyone transfixed by their soon-to-be arrival in the sky.

"You're a liar!" Ceeborn burst out at Luegner, breaking the awed silence of the room. "This ship is dying. The spray is not what he says. It's making us all sick. And he knows it!"

The watchman broke through the crowd. Ceeborn shoved as he ran and slammed through the rear exit door. He pulled the rivulus case from his pants pocket, tucked it into the larger front pocket of his fire-red hoodie, and ran deeper into the greener side of the valley.

He jumped the vent in the spiral garden, and with the hood of the fire-red hoodie pulled over his head, leapt the red-berried shrub. Ahead was the wall around the school's playground, then off to his left, the adobe village.

He ran from house to house; each was empty. "Get off the ship! Luegner's a liar! We're all going to die on the ship!"

He rattled the locked door of the domed hospital at the zoo. "Meg!" he called, with no reply. He ran around to the back exit door where she had closed him off. It had no exterior handle. He pounded. "Meg!"

He turned with the clacking of nails on stone. He ran back to the village, checking window to window. He ducked into a courtyard, and peered over a sill.

Meg was inside, still in her pajamas as she entered the home's tight kitchen. She took a seat at the breakfast table and poured herself a bowl of cereal. Robin, dressed in her white lab coat, set the final touches of a meal of fruit and crispy sliced meat.

"Oh, come on," Robin said as Meg sat. "You're not even dressed."

Ceeborn raised his knuckles to rap on the window, but paused as Meg pulled back her shoulder-length hair into a tail. It was her, but different.

"Hey!" Robin gasped as she spun and broke away from a waist-pinched sneak attack of affection.

Michael Longshore, morning-clean and fit for another foreman day, cradled Robin with a hand at both sides of her waist. She gave him a loving slap on the shoulder and he took his seat on Meg's side of the table.

"Hey, Dad," Meg said.

Ceeborn stared. It was a life he'd never known.

"We're arriving tonight," Robin said as she poured Michael a morning drink.

Michael nudged his shoulder to Meg and gave her a wink. "How many times have you heard that one lately? Look out, we're arriving!" He swirled his palms together over his dished-out plate of warmed meat and toast.

"Just about every single day during drills," Meg said with a roll of her eyes.

"This looks good," he said to Robin, who didn't sit.

"Hey, Dad. There's a boy I know. He wants to arrive with

everyone else."

"Oh, yeah?" Michael said as he filled his cheek with a bite. "A boy at school? Do we know him?" He looked up at Robin, who hurried to gather her things.

"Go on, tell your father," Robin said.

"I don't know," Meg said to her father's endearing patience. "I don't think you know him. He lives on the other side of the screen. Where people go to get fixed."

"One of the madman's boys?" Michael asked as he smiled over the leafy bits on his plate.

"He wasn't always mad," Robin said.

"Well, I wouldn't mind too much about him," Michael said. "When we arrive you'll have plenty to do on your own. You'll move on and forget all about that boy."

"I know, but—"

"I'll tell you, sometimes you can smell the rot from back there where they live," Michael said. "It comes right through from behind the annex." He took another bite. "If it spreads to the rest of the ship, we'll all be unfixable."

"Then you should be praying he isn't a madman," Robin said, "don't you think?"

"It's the original, oldest part of the ship," Michael said. "We don't need it. Luegner should just give the go ahead to let us cleave it off and move on. Madden'll never be able to fix it. It's like coming up with a cure for the sickness. It can't be done. The fact that Madden keeps trying proves the man is nuts."

He elbowed Meg and with two fingers lifted his eyelids for a funny face. "And who knows, one boy like that could spread the sickness forward to us."

"Oh, right, one kid could destroy this whole ship," Meg said.

"Not on my watch," Michael said as he ate.

"You're right. He'd probably need a little help from me," Meg said. "He swims. I've seen him from the sky."

"Wait. You've gone to the sky?" Michael asked. "I told you, you are not to go up there again. Ever. Do you hear me?"

"Okay, but what if he comes to see me down here?" Meg said. She shrugged.

"Then you bring him to Michael. He's a great father, always there when you need him," Robin said.

"Looks like we're covered, then, kiddo," Michael said to Meg. "Okay, go on now, get dressed. We don't want to start the day late. Big day, everyone. We're arriving!"

"Technically," Meg said, "we're only arriving to orbit. Another week before we go down."

Ceeborn rose at the window. He didn't try to hide. Meg saw him. She wasn't afraid and sat back down on her foot in her seat as she stared.

"Don't have to remind me," Michael said, shuffling his knife and fork in the remnants of his meal. "We're nonstop busy dissolving the recyclables at the annex."

Robin buttoned her coat, then quickly kissed Michael on the forehead to leave. "Actually, that boy gave me some good ideas to test in the lab." As she rushed for the front door, she turned back, stern. "But, the both of you talking about destroying the ship is not helping at all. Not for me. And not for him."

Michael leaned back from his plate and gave Meg a loving shove. He reached into a bowl with his hand and tossed a few more berries into Meg's bowl. "Boys," he said with a wink to Meg. "Nothing but trouble, didn't you know?"

Meg tossed a peel from her fruit onto her father's plate and smiled right back. "Why do you think we get along so well?"

Outside, the clicking on stone returned and Ceeborn pushed back from the window. The three Chokebots kept pace in their line. They were relentless, like loping predators on prey.

He wanted to stay, to fight for Meg's approach at the window.

He could turn and smash at the Chokebot's bulbous dome head as it crossed the courtyard, but its mind would simply recoil into its shell. And with others for backup response, there would always be more. The lead Chokebot of the three stopped and tilted its head for a directional fix. It flexed its squared front thorax up at its waist and rose, front claws splayed and extended in a dominant pose. The tablet in its head feathered its keys and halted the three's forward movement. It was calm and assured.

Ceeborn climbed the waist-high wall of the courtyard and ran along its edge. More immense than the three sections of the garden, village, and zoo was the enormous count of other sections aligned and farther afield along the rising sides and down the length of the valley. There were more than enough places to hide.

He ran toward the front of the ship and a whitened field where a footbridge crossed a river ravine. He cut right, hopped the bridge's tensioned rail, and leapt full flight over the edge, diving sidelong and headfirst into the rushing water below.

The Chokebots couldn't follow and no net could scrounge him from below. He didn't come up for air. He didn't come up at all. The torrent of water was his.

A trickle of air bubbles rose from his lips to the surface as the water deepened into a channel. The respirocytes transfusion that replaced his red blood cells stored hours of air that needed no breath, pumping oxygen-rich blood through his veins. The vestibular system of his ears rolled with an innate aquatic sense that kept his body aligned in three axes. He rolled into the current, his chest up toward the surface, and he watched the three Chokebots scurry up along the river's edge.

Thin, bioluminescent worms were embedded in the hardened inside walls of the river's channel. His rub against their waves triggered a controlled flushing. He could breathe through the torrent of water, but couldn't break away from its sudden rush. He succumbed to the natural flow and rode the roaring veinal channel far and aft, back through the membrane screen into his darker system of the gully.

He lunged for the roots protruding from the gully wall, but the joining tributary current could in no way be overcome. He slammed against the sealed subterranean drain that entered the rear bulkhead. He tumbled in place until the drain opened, as if two doors in opposing disks rotated into alignment, and he was swallowed in through the flush.

He was expelled in a pressurized spurt of water above an enormous reservoir. He landed on a sponge-like pad that quickly absorbed the water that poured in around him.

He was in the tank behind the bulkhead. It was a place he had never sought to be.

He gripped the raised collar ring at the edge of the spongy pad and climbed out of the water. Beyond the ring was an undulating layer of skin that stretched over an immense body of water. He walked out upon it and the skin bobbed and rolled under his feet like a thin bladder covering the waves of an ocean. He turned back around and looked up to the opening he came through. It was closed again, and far too high to climb.

Iridescent slicks lapped out from beneath the edges of the skin and reached up the wall of the tank. The thickened stains shimmered in the lights of four corner posts of a utility gondola. The gondola was suspended by tendons that rose and disappeared into the darkness at the height of the tank. Far across, another set of four lights beckoned as a possible way out. Maybe there was another door lower on its wall.

He smelled the dark air. It had a bad omen of sickness. There were no sounds, no cries from the depths. This place was the setting where nightmares were born.

The drainage door high in the tank parted again like a valve, and another spurt of water tumbled onto the sponge. As the water fell, he saw that neither he nor his side of the doorway was turning. It was the door on other side of the opening that rotated into alignment. And the other side was the gully's bulkhead. That could mean the gully itself was the side in motion.

And if the gully was the side that rotated, then that meant something else as well: The blue torus core didn't turn on its high central axle. The blue torus core was stationary and everything else, the gully, the gardens, Meg's better-lit world, must be rotating about the central axle of the ship.

So then what if he had been wrong? What if the world were rotating in a way that was different from how he had always believed? His perspective could change. It would have to.

He climbed onto the gondola platform for carriage across the skin on the water. The hoist and drive was a simple lever for controlling height and a stick for directing motion within a plane. He pushed the lever of the hoist and the gondola rose. It was guided by a crisscrossing network of sinewy tendons.

He stood between the lit corner posts of the platform and searched out over the surface below. By the eerie sounds of the tendons stretching and pulling him across to the other side, he could almost imagine the haunting screams of the ghosts that would be trapped in this place when the ship's acceleration boost began. This unnerving tank played tricks on the mind. It was not a place he ever wanted Meg to see.

Two Chokebots entered from pores along the wall of the tank and climbed to its height. The leader's tail stinger was coiled. They arched over and scurried along the top flesh of the tank, and grabbed the side-by-side tendons of the hanging gondola with their pincers. They descended. Their vibrations ran down the length of the cables.

Ceeborn squinted up through the corner post lights into the darkness. The leader leapt from the cables to the top bar of the gondola frame. It scrambled for a hold. Its tail stinger jabbed in its twist as it fell uncontrolled. Ceeborn was hit.

Ceeborn fell back into the gondola. He grabbed at his neck. He had been struck, finely needled. The pain pierced worse than any venomous sting. No flying insect had ever hurt so deep, or penetrated so fast. The stabbing pain spread, radiated down through his shoulder.

The Chokebot fell belly up, its head extended off the platform's edge. Its legs flailed upward. Its dangling dome and front body section were hyperextended from its back.

Ceeborn writhed and kicked through the searing pain. With each thrust of his kicks, the Chokebot's middle and rear legs clambered for a hold. It teetered. He kicked again. The Chokebot fell from the gondola's platform. It flipped as it dropped to the skin covering the water. Its tail stinger and six claws punctured the surface with a pop.

He kneeled on the gondola platform. The Chokebot clicked and looked up beyond its reach. As it lifted a leg, water seeped from the gash in the surface skin and dripped from the point of its claw. The drops stained its dome. It knew not to move another step.

The second Chokebot descended the cable head-dome first. It didn't jump.

Ceeborn held his hand to his neck as the bot kept its distance to the side rigging and catty-cornered the gondola's frame. It crawled down and flexed out on the platform, circling in its space for position to lie down. It had barely enough width to turn. It flattened to its abdomen and held the gondola's frame with its left middle and rear left legs. It leaned out over the edge with its upper body section and reached down to the lead Chokebot fallen on the skin below.

The lead Chokebot reached up with its forward arms. With each move it made to rise or get closer, it treaded the membrane's wounds. The hanging Chokebot jostled for an extension from the edge of the platform but still failed its rescue reach. It clacked a long guttural roll. The more the lead Chokebot moved or reached up with its front legs, the more pressure its four remaining legs placed on the skin. A growing swath of punctures slicked the skin with oozes of iridescent swirls.

The pain in Ceeborn's neck subsided and he sat on the platform's floor to consider. He could neither help with a rescue, nor run from the platform where they were trapped. So, he scooted forward and kicked again with a thrust.

The hanging Chokebot angled its dome toward him, illuminated with a yellow-blue sickened glow, and clicked a message onto its screen. Ceeborn lifted his knee and cocked his foot to strike. *"Stop. Wait,"* the Chokebot's screen read as a plea.

Ceeborn relaxed his foot. Empathy for a foe felt strange. The Chokebot returned to its sinking companion.

The leader's dome stayed fixed in its glare and illuminated itself with its own blood-red glow. In its precarious position on the breaking surface of the skin, it cocked its head as its angry red color of warning sent an altogether more ominous meaning for a single repeated word: *"Wait."*

Ceeborn kicked the hanging Chokebot's right middle leg from the platform. It screeched and clicked, and the harder he slammed, the redder its dome became. Its two hanging front claws locked onto those of the leader. Its two left legs clung as precarious anchors to the edge of the platform, its right two others sprang rearward for grasp at any remaining support.

He kicked its body well past center and in a wild flail before it fell, it let go of the leader and leapt with a twist to grab the side of the platform. Whether accident or vengeance, its two rear claws cut like a scythe through the platform's suspension cable. The cable unwound and recoiled into the darkened ceiling. Half the gondola fell. The hanging Chokebot went over. Ceeborn held tight.

The edge of the platform pierced the water's skin, gashing a wide-open wound.

As the end of the cable drew free from its wheel, the gondola slipped further through the water's skin. But the platform was still tethered by the cable on its left side and it stayed suspended beneath the surface of the water.

Ceeborn released from the platform, sank and twirled in agony from the venom and water's reaction on his neck. The two Chokebots let go of the shredded underside of the skin. They turned and sank, legs down.

The lead Chokebot clamped onto his waist, then his legs, and they descended together, tumbling in projections of red: the Chokebot from its dome, Ceeborn thrashing in his fire-red hoodie. They were face-to-face as they sank. He stared straight into his reflection in the Chokebot's dome, both panicked, uncertain. There was no light from below.

The Chokebot's back came to a rest on the bottom and its dome flared a brighter orange, a quiet scream of intensity, a brightness that flickered and faded. A thickened organic paste rose from the bottom of the tank and engulfed the Chokebot's body. The paste rose up the length of its legs.

Ceeborn was locked in its higher grip and he stared face-down, his fight all but choked except for the pounding he inflicted with his elbows and fists.

His reflection in the dome was of fear, panic, and pain. The Chokebot's screen attempted a luminance of blue to calm his mood. But the paste reached its dome and in a flash of white light, its screen captured the face of Ceeborn's fear. The

Chokebot's last word stayed superimposed on its screen as it unlocked its grips.

"Wake."

Then it died with a bubble that rose from its dome.

Ceeborn swam up toward the water's skin. He passed the submerged gondola and the self-sealing skin patched its puncture wounds with scabs. But the remaining gondola cable continued to stir, preventing the skin's complete healing, and the thickened water bled out into the open tank.

He squinted into the quiet darkness. If the door he fell through to enter the tank was fed from a river that emptied into the space above the tank's water, then the outflow to leave must be deep underwater along the tank's wall. He felt the tug of a swirling current into the darkness below. He dove and righted himself in its pull, then swam toward a door that opened and closed like a valve timed with the rotation of the gully bulkhead. The door led out to a dark river channel.

He broke from the current into daylight, bounced off a solid outcrop of ground, grasped for the tips of a tangled ball of roots, pulled hard, and came ashore along the muddied bank of the gully. He rolled on the shore and felt the pressure pounding in his chest. He was alive.

EIGHTEEN

TOO FAR, ALONE

PACKET ROLLED TO his side and realized he was lying in his hospital bed, a soft pillow under his head, a blanket over his legs, and an intravenous needle in his arm. The tube of the needle ran up to a bag on a pole. He could move his fingers, but he was more intent on blinking his eyes to see if he was awake. He couldn't be; the gully looked nothing like this, and his terraced home with Daniel had nothing so soft and clean. He picked at the tape of the needle.

His eyes came into a focus toward the window of the room and he saw Meg sitting in a chair. She was contemplative, hunched over, and caressing a blue-gray bird in her lap. It was the bird from the garden. It had grown, but not much. It was stronger and sat upright in her hands. It bobbed its blue beak out from between her fingers. She stroked the side of her finger across its nostril on the topside of its beak. Then she raised it in her hands and nestled its head feathers against her cheek.

"There you are," he said. "I came looking, but I couldn't find you. You were with your father."

"I'm here," she said without looking, but then saw his eyes were open and she jerked upright in her chair. "Wait, you're back. Don't leave this room. Let me get Daniel." She looked at the door.

"Where did you get that bird?"

"I created it for this room. It's not real. It's a baby Prion. They like the cold and the ocean, but—" She stood from the chair. "It's nighttime. Let me call him. He'll be right here. Daniel! Daniel, come now. He's back," she hollered, standing.

"Sit down," Packet said without moving. "I can't see you. This tank is giving me terrible nightmares."

She sat, cupping her bird, breathless. "You're not in the tank anymore. Stay here. Don't leave, please."

"I tried, but I couldn't catch that bird on the ship," he said. "I have to go back. I can help everyone from getting Luegner's spray."

"No, you've gone far enough already. I know what you found out about the sickness, but if you keep thinking you're in the ship, you'll never come back, I know—"

"If you don't let me go, countless more children will suffer. I can warn them all."

"No, it's not real. Do you remember 'belief and know', DID, and all the other psychology that Daniel, my mom, and I tried to talk to you about?" She shouted again for the door, "Daniel!"

"I remember."

"Well, Cessini and Ceeborn are the same person. You believe it. You know it. But you're Cessini, not Ceeborn. There's no contradiction." She wanted to get up and run, but stayed in her chair.

He rose to his elbows. "That's where you're wrong. Cessini was weak, but Ceeborn is strong. I am Ceeborn."

She looked over her shoulder as if to no one in particular in the room and bolted upright. "Okay, he's on his way. Listen to me, it all comes down to this. Who do you want to be?"

"I want to be Ceeborn."

"Then you know Cessini will be gone and you'll lose me

forever. Because Ceeborn isn't real."

"Then neither was Cessini. But even if he was, Cessini was only real to me when you were there. I remember you were his only friend."

"No, that's not true. He was real. And Cessini was more than a friend to me."

"Then come back on the ship with me. We'll tell everyone and save them together."

"No, listen," she said, pleading. She sat back down on her foot and took a new tact. "I wanted to say thank you for letting me come on your spaceship. It was really cool, but it's not real."

"It's not my spaceship. It's ours. We built it together, remember."

"Then it's time to take it apart."

"Like the data center in my mind?"

"No, like your body that died. Hang on, he's here!"

The door flew open. Daniel was there. Three young men and an adult were silhouetted behind him at the door. "I found them. They're here," he said, breathless.

"Then, forget it, I'll save them myself," Packet said.

Meg tossed the bird to flight and leapt toward the bed as Packet ripped the needle from his arm. The lights flickered and the whole room went dark, like a candle blown out in a cave.

NINETEEN
A RIVULUS AND A HOODIE

CEEBORN, STILL SOAKED from the tank, pushed open the door from the rotted hallway to a classroom. Three boys were in their seats. He dropped his hand from his neck. Six clear-paneled, honeycombed cubicles with chairs were set in two rows of three in the center of the room.

Tenden was the first to turn from his front center seat. His hair was combed, but still rough in licks. He was conscious of his own size in the chair, and the odd, bent-elbowed posture he kept with his arms always held to his front.

Ceeborn crossed the classroom and took the seat at Tenden's side in the front left cubicle.

Spud was satisfied with his second row seat and leaned forward with a much-missed smile. But Ceeborn's cubicle was too far to knock on so he didn't even bother to kick.

Pace was slowest, and moved with a dizzying unease. He lifted his head from his desk at Tenden's right. He was slight, pale, and sick. He had vertigo sitting still and was dizzy just opening his eyes. "Are the lights spinning?" he asked. He closed his eyes and breathed out a sickened sigh. He lowered his head and buried his forehead back into the cross of his arms on his desk.

"No. The floor is steady," Ceeborn said as Daniel entered

from the door at the front of the room.

"We can try to fix you," Daniel said. "But we've already got plenty to fix on our own." He turned to Spud. "And I certainly don't have a fix on you, not yet. But we'll try." He winked and Spud took it with a grin of his cheeks.

"The people out there do," Pace said, with a lift of his head. "It's called a sack. You put it over your face."

Tenden lumbered up from his seat in Spud's defense. Pace was too pale to respond. He had overstepped and knew it. Daniel's hand pressed on Tenden's shoulder and guided him back down.

Daniel looked closer at Ceeborn's neck. Ceeborn turned away and Daniel tugged the collar of the soaked hoodie down.

"It's bad," Ceeborn said. "It feels really bad. I think I'm getting worse."

"Take this off," Daniel said, pulling up on the hoodie.

Spidery red tracks drew out from a central spot on Ceeborn's neck. Daniel pulled the hoodie up over Ceeborn's head and tossed it, soaked, to the floor.

"What did you do?" Daniel asked. "This is a sting? Did you resist?"

"I was in the tank of the ship," Ceeborn said. "It was dark."

"Robin needs to see this," Daniel said. "I don't know what to do. Not at this stage."

Ceeborn pushed past Daniel, gathered his hoodie from the floor, scrunched it to find its front-hand pocket. He pulled out the tan case and laid it on his desk. He unclasped the lid. Tenden and Spud circled over. The rivulus looked out, then darted back into the moistened bit of mossy sponge. It was alive and unharmed.

Tenden dove and snatched up the case. He hunched himself over and extended his pointer finger toward the rivulus's curious, darting eyes. "I'll carry it," he said. "I want it."

Spud yanked at Tenden's arm for a look, but Tenden ignored him with the wide-eyed focus of a master protector, one having found the ultimate little creature to protect.

"Where did you get it?" Pace asked. "Did you go to the zoo?"

"Robin told me everything about the spray," Ceeborn said. "It's spreading and we can't fix it, no one can. We can stay on this ship, but we're all going to die if we do."

Daniel grabbed Ceeborn's wrist. "No, don't say that. You don't have to be sick, or die. This pain will go away. Don't listen to them. You can come back here. It'll be just you and me." He looked around the room. "I know I can fix it all, like a magician. And I've made a fix for each of you. Are you ready to see it now?"

"Yes! Open it up, let's see," Spud said.

Daniel backed away from Ceeborn and opened a curtain to a stage at the front of the room. Tenden and Spud cheered at what they saw. Pace stayed in his queasy restraint.

Daniel welcomed them up to a dream world stage filled with the most amazing toys and spatial apparatus. Newfangled equipment, life-size gyroscopes, an impregnated wall of varying-sized metallic spheres. And a clear, cylindrical water tank at the front of the room for Ceeborn which was sized for his height plus another half.

Tenden, in his bullish gate, hopped up the three stairs to the stage. He grabbed a bioship model in the shape of a squid. "I'm flying now, boys. Out of my way."

Spud dodged Tenden and bumped a canister off of its platform stand. Colored marbles spilled on the floor, plinked, and rolled dizzily back toward the seats.

Pace buried his eyes deep into his arms over his desk and hid from the motion.

Ceeborn watched over the boys from his distance as he

climbed up the side-mounted ladder of the tank where, from up on its platform, he had the best view of the room.

Daniel circulated, scientific and serious. He tapped on the tank beneath the platform and gestured for Ceeborn to slip in.

"I want to watch you fix them first. I want to see them happy," Ceeborn said.

"Meet me halfway," Daniel said as he tapped again.

Ceeborn relented and slipped into the warm, thickened water of his tank, then bobbed up its wall. He folded his arms over its rim, his legs dangling submerged.

Spud sat behind a station's black-cloth partition. He clicked his tongue in repeated, quickening directional ticks. He angled his head into the reverberations, detecting the bounce back of minute sound waves. He winced with a migraine and pointed to the upper right corner of the cloth. "There it is," he said.

Daniel revealed an apple-sized metallic sphere from behind the cloth. "Okay, very good."

He wheeled a supply cart in closer. It had a thick vertical board and, behind its obstruction, he exchanged the metallic sphere for a smaller marble. Spud struggled to exhaustion with his squinting and clicking. The marble couldn't be seen through the board.

"Ready?" Daniel asked with a teasing smile. He pulled an atomizer from his cart and wafted the air in front of Spud with a bluish haze.

Ceeborn felt a chill from his exposed shoulders through the water to his toes. Daniel, his father, was a genius.

"We inserted a whole new count of SQUIDs in your facial disk," Daniel said to Spud.

Spud looked through the settling blue mist as his broadened face came alive with awe. He panned his face into the new spectrum world he saw.

"SQUIDs," Daniel said. "Superconducting quantum interference devices. That's right. They measure the minutest changes in your body's electromagnetic field so if you learn to measure it right, you'll effectively see through objects. You'll recognize the magnetic disturbances created. And when you're ready, you'll see even smaller. Maybe," Daniel said as he knelt in closer with a childish goad, "maybe even a qubit."

Spud leaned closer to the board and tried again. The marble was behind the upper left corner. His jaw dropped with the inspired rise of his smile, his realization that he, and his face, his disk, was a gift. He rose from his station and explored the stage, pinging and measuring the wall's assortment of exposed semi-spheres.

"Go on. I didn't create it," Daniel said. "The main torus core of this ship developed the technology. I just put it to your good use."

The nearby gyroscope apparatus whirled into a painfully high pitch and Spud shuffled away.

Daniel wheeled a cart down the stage's ramp and knelt in front of Pace's honeycombed cubicle. "Open your eyes, Pace. I won't move."

"I don't want to play," Pace said. "Go away."

Daniel retrieved a fly-weight ball of glimmering metal sheen from the cart's lower shelf. He held it, rolled it in his fingers, but frustrated, he couldn't seem to complete its task. "Sorry, hang on," he said as he picked at two end tabs of the whisper-thin metal wrap. The tabs were stuck against the ball like the lost end of invisible tape. Then he found the loose end tabs, pinched them securely in his fingers and gave the ball a flick. It opened into a half sheet that spread atop Pace's desk. It was a wrinkled thin film, only microns thick. Daniel snapped it again and it reclaimed its memory shape, a magnetic bodysuit.

Pace pushed up on the arms of his chair to stand. He reached for a feel of the ultra-thin metallic sheet's luster.

Daniel helped him into the sheet, and at once, it clung to the shape of his body. Across his chest, two illuminated bands, one blue and one red, wavered to find their angle to the floor. Once aligned, the colored bands locked in their horizontal place and glowed.

"This suit counters the effects of your dark magnetocytes," Daniel said. "For some reason, they changed when you received your booster spray, and now they can't ground you with the ship."

Pace shuddered as his body attuned to the axis of the room. He could stand without holding on. His dizziness receded. He closed his eyes, lifted his chin, and went back on his heels. He didn't fall. He stood grand. "Thank you," he said, which was more than Daniel asked.

Daniel led Pace on the stage to the straps of a gyroscope apparatus. In no time, the 100-rpm gyroscope didn't spin too fast for his suited body, but too slow. He kept overshooting his marks in his motion.

Daniel ratcheted up the speed. "On a stable planet, you'll race on the fields of champions. You'll run faster, lighter than anyone else," Daniel said, basking in Pace's acceptance. "You're too quick. Fine-tune yourself. Do a little less. Remember, sometimes less is more."

Pace laughed as he spun. "If less is more, is nothing perfect?"

"Clever. But, no, nothing is perfect," Daniel said. "And neither are we. We all have to remember who we were. Now, just focus on the motion." He pushed his cart and moved on.

As rapid as Pace could spin, Tenden endured in his static stress apparatus. His arms and upper chest buffeted against pincers weighted with resistance. A color-coded strain gauge rose into the warnings of yellow.

"You, my friend," Daniel said as he stopped. "Your arms have nothing to do with magnets, qubits, or cells in your ears. In fact, you're not even really that strong. You're just a pure and simple physical deformity of nature."

Tenden released the pincers. They crashed with a sound that stopped the room. His pride shriveled within the arms of his station.

Then Daniel leaned in with a gentle derogatory smile that struck Tenden to his core. "Tell me, now, do *you* understand?"

Tenden lamented the stares of the others. No one could take or belittle his strength. His power was his own. He stood from the pincers and said, "I am different, but not in the same way as them. But that's what makes me stronger. And I could blast you all."

He jumped back into the pincers and heaved. The needle of the gauge shoved straight through to red. He felt the burn. He dropped the mass from the pain his tendons endured. He stepped off his bench and held his sore arms crossed at his front.

"There now, was that so hard?" Daniel asked.

Daniel gestured up to Ceeborn at the rim of the tank. It was time for him to get in. Ceeborn treaded a moment, accepted the remnants of once-happy faces, and then reached onto the platform for a weighted bag. With the bag in his hand, he settled beneath the surface of the water and secured himself into a chair at the bottom where he stayed and draped the weight over his legs. A trickle of air rose from his lips as he breathed with the aid of respirocytes infused in his blood.

A thin cloud of air bubbles rose to the surface, escaping from the outer layer of his clothes. And he stayed there; familiar with the bottom of the cylindrical water tank in his secluded perch at the front of the classroom, and watched over the boys in their seats.

No sooner did he raise his hand to his neck and close his eyes to rest when a shudder rocked the room and its stage. The floor beneath them rolled in a jarring wave. Daniel's cart spilled. The balls from Spud's wall popped from their holds and scattered across the floor.

Ceeborn kicked himself back up to the platform, swung his legs over the rim of the tank, and leapt down to the quaking room.

Daniel grabbed him by the arm. "Stop. Where are you going to go?"

"This ship is dying. I can taste it," Ceeborn said as he pulled his arm free. "Something happened, and no one can do anything to fix it."

The aftershocks were worse. There was nowhere safe to hold.

The colored stripes of Pace's suit found their horizontal for his body, but he went down to all fours to be sure. They all stared blindly with the same unease at the buckling of the walls that secreted dying black spores. The classroom door was left open.

"It's dying," Ceeborn said. "All of us are, or we will be soon enough."

"No. I fixed you. I fixed you to live, to be better than me."

Daniel kneeled with opened arms as the floor shook worse, but Ceeborn fell his way through to the door.

"Tell me," Daniel said, "Where are you going to run?"

"To her," Ceeborn declared, "To Meg. She's scared. And no one should have to die alone." Then, with a release of the door, he was gone.

Daniel turned wide-eyed back to the boys on the floor. He had nowhere else to go. He looked to Tenden and Spud and urged them with a single word, and they took it. "Go for him now. Run."

Ceeborn ran over the dead and overgrown front grounds of his terraced home. Tenden and Spud followed close behind. Daniel stayed back at the base of the building with Pace at his side.

The crusted foothill had once been flowing sap, a healthy sign of the ship's continued growth, but was now just a slow-moving force destroying the foundation of the old terraced building. Ceeborn ducked beneath the ends of the orange pipes that descended from the rear bulkhead, and climbed over the twisted roots that staved off the gully's erosion from its rising level of water.

"How are you going to find her?" Spud yelled ahead to Ceeborn as they ran for the gully.

Tenden wore Ceeborn's fire-red hoodie. It was tight, but it fit. He ran with his arms in their natural position forward, flexed at his elbows, and both hands in the hoodie's front pocket. He held on tight to the rivulus case and ran with a solemn oath projected forward from his eyes. Nothing was going to get through him in protection of this precious soul.

"I know where she'll be," Ceeborn said.

Gerald Aiden was ahead, balanced atop a berm to the gully, with an arc-welding torch. He sweated to cauterize a hole in the descending orange pipe. His patch redirected the froth that overfilled the collection tanks at the bottom of the gully. He bemoaned the slush at his feet, and with a hopeless burst of the pipe, he quit his efforts and limped off the berm. He leaned against the fence to the rotting bridge, the direct crossing from their terraced building's hill to a door in the membrane screen on the other side of the gully. He lowered his arc flame as the pipe's wound spread. He might have stopped the spread of the froth across the bridge for a while, but it would still seep down into the gully, a circulation channel that could send the whole body of the ship into septic shock.

As Ceeborn arrived, with Tenden and Spud behind, Gerald Aiden let them pass through a hole in his fence, not to cross the putrefied bridge, but to roll down into the awful gully. Ceeborn slipped down the bank first, followed by Tenden and Spud, and looked back at his decrepit home.

Aiden stood on its side of the fence and waved him to go on. "You go!" Aiden cried. He was gripped by an unshakable sadness. "You run and make us all free. You run for me, you run for my son!"

Ceeborn looked back up to the height of the bulkhead. The creases of its flesh sweated with a sickened, glistening blackness. He shuddered to think of their instant swamping if the whole of the bulkhead gave way and the ocean tank disgorged its flood down upon them. He slid down the gully's embankment, but its walls were eroding. Blackened clumps of mud fell from its sides and tangles of roots were exposed as their covering tissue washed away into the rising water.

They fought their way waist deep against the gully's swell. A dust-filled ball of water rushed past. Ceeborn pressed on upstream toward the next quarter's bridge, but the rolling waves kept pushing them back. "We have to keep going," he said. "We can climb up to the doors."

Spud hesitated in the rising water. A current swept him from his feet and Tenden grabbed him by the arm.

"Don't get pulled in," Ceeborn said as he looked up at the sweated bulkhead. "You don't want to end up behind that wall." But then he, too, stopped in the rising water. Spud's facial disk curved into its own natural frown after he recovered from his water's dunking.

The thickened water gurgled as it surged. The currents rushed out of balance, pulsing through the ship's circulatory system. It refluxed forward in eddies and swirls, then was swallowed back down through the drains that led behind the bulkhead, then back to the tank, the torn skin over the water, and the gondola that was cut through and hung from its lasting cable.

A shudder ran down Ceeborn's spine. The tremors and swells were not the result of the ship's arrival or its sickness, but of the catastrophe he'd caused in the tank.

Tenden pulled himself up onto the footing of the next bridge that connected the rear bulkhead to the healthier body of the ship. He reached down to grasp Ceeborn's hand as he climbed. Ceeborn reached down in kind for Spud. They climbed the side of the bridge together with the natural bobbing and bumping of friends familiar in a line.

On the bulkhead side of the bridge's deck to their left was an air-tight hangar door. To their right was an equal-sized opening in the stretched, vertical membrane screen. Beyond the screen was Meg.

Ceeborn wasted no time and entered through the healthier opening into a bright warehouse of a transportation annex, and then he stopped dead in his tracks. Tenden and Spud bumped up behind him.

An industrialized Chokebot stood on its hind and middle legs. Its front body section was raised. It wielded a hose connected to a fifty-five-gallon drum. With its front claws clamped on the nozzle, the Chokebot sprayed a dump of household goods, broken building supplies, and the discarded shrubs of a garden. It held the hose with deft precision, de-printing the collection of waste from top down, dissolving it into a wilting, disintegrating glob of swirling colors. Grates in the floor allowed the pour off to drain down into an array of recycling vats.

Michael Longshore crossed the workspace, wearing the worn coveralls of a senior logistics technician, raised his goggles to his head, and circled behind the Chokebot. He entered a workstation protected from errant spray by a clear, wraparound screen. He sat back against a stone white wall. He tossed his goggles onto his desk and sighed at the growing mountain of stacked abacus beads on his wall, his count of pending product requests.

Huge stacks of crates and supplies filled the aisled shelves of a massive cargo bay at the side of his station through the double-wide doors. A passing forklift buzzed and whirled, transferring pallets according to its programmed course. The air was alive. Something big was happening. They were arriving.

Michael ran his hand through his hair, straightened his hard hat high on his brow, and steadied his mood to get back to his day. Then he saw through the clear screen of his workstation Ceeborn, Tenden, and Spud standing in awe, hiding in plain sight, each keenly aware they were in a place they were not supposed to be.

Ceeborn stepped forward through the hangar with Tenden and Spud as the Chokebot lowered the hose. It tilted its domed head, but Michael gestured for it to continue with its routine chores. It continued as instructed.

Ceeborn tried the door at the end of the hangar. It was locked. An air curtain rose from a row of perforated tiles at his feet. Michael stepped outside the clear screen of his station. He mimicked the lifting of a floor tile with his left hand, and with his right, he lowered his hand through in descent. Ceeborn lifted the D-ring of tile at his feet and slipped down with thanks into a cool, darkened vent.

He led Tenden and Spud through the tunnel, shuffling along on his back through a tight-fitting S-curve, passing beneath various points of gravel and peat, all unseen from the ground above. Tenden and Spud followed in fits of caution and awe. Then, at another narrow bend, Ceeborn dropped into a thin pool of water that met with a gust of cross-current air. He reached up and backward with his hands into a shaft. He pulled in his gut and climbed, rising at last. He pushed aside a floor grate.

He exited at the vent of the spiral garden. He knew exactly where he was.

A ground spasm sent a ripple across the leaves. Tenden and Spud stepped out, settled to the ground, and waited for his lead.

The whole feel of the semi-circular valley was different from the circular nature of the gully. The valley's ground was definitely on a curve but the sky seemed flat across the valley's peaks. Maybe, Ceeborn thought, if the valley was anything like the circle of the gully, the ground he was on wrapped wholly around the sky. The sky would then have to be a sheet within the rounded, tubular enclosure of the ship. If so, then his new perspective of his world would be complete, and once exposed, would surely be a sight to behold.

"Let's go," he said as got up from his knee and ran through the garden. Tenden and Spud trampled to follow.

He led them on the path ahead to the adobe school, then onward through the fronds to the village, and the boardwalk beyond.

"Wait up, how do you know she'll be here?" Spud asked.

"Because I saw the bird. She must have caught it. She fed it. It's hers."

"What bird?" Spud asked.

Ceeborn pushed aside the vertical netting of the grand aviary cage.

Meg sat on the knee-high edge of a stone fountain beneath the hanging greenery of the cage. Koi swam in the aerated pool and hid under a blanket of floating lilies. A lizard rested on a stone and basked in the warmth of a heat lamp. Her elbows were tucked into her waist. Her hands were cupped out over her lap. She glanced up. Tenden and Spud paired off and investigated the cage's beauty of nature.

Meg slid her thumbs from over her cradled fingers and the Prion poked its head through her grasp. Its blue beak tapped at her fingers. She picked up a silvery minnow from the wetted rock at her side and fed it to the growing sea bird.

"My mom says one day all kinds of birds and animals are going to fill these cages," she said.

Ceeborn tilted his head back toward the vines not yet fully ingrown through the roof. Rows of water-misters triggered, and with a hiss, the nozzles rained a cloud of settling mist that kept all the greens glistening and pure. He drew in a cooled, moistened breath as his face was kissed by the touch of water. He looked back down at Meg and smiled.

"I think they're all going to love it," he said. "The water feels pure."

"This isn't the right habitat for a Prion," she said. "They like the snowy cold. But she has nowhere else to go. And I can't take her with me when we go down to the planet. What if that's worse?"

He rested his palm on the surface of the water, broke his fingers through its skin, and submerged his hand to his wrist. The koi scattered for cover. His gaze fixed on his face in the pool. He swirled his hand through the water below.

"Are the patrols still after you?" she asked.

He pulled his hand from the water with a bone-white lily and offered it to her with the twist of a grin. "Probably. I got this for you."

"No, you didn't," she said.

"It's a flower from the sea. Get it?" he said. "A flower from the Cee. Cee—born."

"Yeah, I get it."

"Why don't you let the bird stay here? And you come with us. We're getting off this ship."

She held the bird still in the cup of her hands and stroked its beak with the edge of her finger.

"Where's Robin?" he asked.

Meg opened her hands and let loose the Prion. It flew up to the woven branches at the top of the aviary. "She went to find you," she said.

"Yeah, it could live in here," Spud shouted with a wide-jowled smile as he watched the Prion settle on a branch and shake its feathers beneath a mist.

Ceeborn looked into Meg's eyes. She was more than troubled. She was afraid.

"What happened to your neck?" she asked.

"I got stung. But it's not getting better. I think the water makes it worse."

"My mom can see you."

"We just came from my dad's if that's where she went. We'll never make it that way. The water is rising somehow. I think the tank might be emptying into the ship."

"Then you really want to get out of here?" she asked and stood.

Tenden and Spud turned and waited for his answer.

"Are you really ready to leave this ship behind?" she asked. "Even if every part of it is destroyed?"

The ship's tremors returned and the water of the lily fountain vibrated into nightmarish rings. Meg covered her hand over her heart and breathed.

"This ship is dying," Ceeborn said. "We don't have a choice anymore."

Tenden nodded. "I'm ready."

"As long as we stay out of the water," Spud said. "We definitely don't want to go back in the water."

"Funny thing is, when I was younger, I never liked to get wet that much to begin with," Ceeborn said to Meg, then grinned. "But my dad fixed me."

"Then I know a way," she said, and came closer. "It's different and special. You should see it before we leave. I think you'll find what you're looking for. There'll be all the dying you'll ever need."

He held his hand to his neck and looked up through the mist and mesh of the cage toward the flickering sky.

"No Chokebots will follow where we'd be going," she said. "I don't think they can. And maybe, just maybe, you might want to start calling me Terri."

"Now why in the world would I want to do that?"

Her smile faded and she took a step back.

"Fine, then let's do it," he said. He was sure.

"It'll be high," she said.

"That's okay, I can do high," Spud said.

"We'll go together, all of us, not alone," Meg said.

"No problem, they're my friends. I won't leave them. The three of us are good climbers."

"Don't worry," Meg said. "You won't have to climb. Where we're going, the sky will come down to you."

TWENTY
IT'LL BE HIGH

CEEBORN, TENDEN, AND Spud hiked behind Meg's lead up a slope toward a clean and modest white bulkhead at the far front of the ship. Rather than plod as they walked, the hike became easier the higher they climbed. The air was the same, but their footsteps were lighter. The hill narrowed with each step as it rose toward a point in the sky.

Ceeborn looked back over his shoulder at where they had come. The glandular fountain and footbridge he had bypassed were far behind, where the floor of the valley met the slope. But directly overhead was a vision more disconcerting. They were about to bump up against the flatness of the sky. But, on closer look, it wasn't entirely flat; there was a brighter bulge down its center, possibly a tube, running all the way down the length of the valley to the screened-off gully at the far distant end of the ship.

As they climbed still higher, he imagined the long bulge was like a curled up paper held inside the larger roll of the ship. And a flattened sheet was stretched sideways to the left and right peaks of the valley like wings off a tubular spine. It was a new and wild perspective that at once set his mind at ease. The sky was a projection and Meg was taking them to the best of the show.

The end of the tube met with the center of the white bulkhead only a short distance ahead up the hill. A double-wide door was at its base.

"You don't have to ask," Meg said. "I've got the key."

"I told you it was going to be neat," Spud said as he ran ahead. "The sky tube goes straight back behind the white bulkhead. That's where the ball is turning."

"What ball?" Ceeborn asked.

"Ball and socket that holds up the axle," Tenden said. "But we're not supposed to be here."

"Tenden and me, we used to come up here to walk around," Spud said.

"You don't have to tell them everything, Spud. Settle down," Tenden said as he nudged Spud forward.

Meg held open the right side of the double-wide door. Inside was a clean, white room lit by four corner posts that flickered. The doors closed, the room jolted, then rose.

"Don't worry," Meg said on the ride up. "But I did warn you, it would be high."

The lift stopped and Meg held her key at the door. "You ready to walk across the sky to the end of the world?" she asked Ceeborn. He was.

She turned her key and the doors opened to the long shaft of brightness. They exited onto a staging collar. A solid axle ran high above their heads down the length of the tube and far into its pinpoint distance. Spaced lengthwise around the axle were eight long rails that ran like tracks to its end. Spokes radiated outward periodically from the axle and held the thin and stretched cylindrical projection screen of the sky. There was room between the axle and the screen to move about, to fix things, if there was ever the need. From the valley looking up, the screen itself showed blue and puffy white clouds. But from inside its screen looking down, it was all terrifyingly clear.

Ceeborn attempted his first cautious heel then toe onto the transparent screen. The sloped hill they walked up below was only a mild drop away at first but fell quickly to the valley below like the shelf of a deep sea.

Meg folded her arms and waited as he bucked up his nerve. "If the height bothers you," she said, "look up and follow the rails."

Then with a leap of faith, he stepped, then skipped, and found his footing. "This is amazing," he said. He ran in spurts up to full speed as if he were escaping across the clouds to the ends of the world. "It's beautiful. You're beautiful." He stopped and turned for her reaction. Her blush had returned. She was elated. "Thank you for letting me measure the sky with you. I've never seen anything like it."

Tenden and Spud hopped out for their try.

"You sure the patrols can't come up here?" Ceeborn hollered down the tube.

"No," she shouted. "The screen's too sensitive." She jumped out behind Tenden and Spud. "Their claws will poke through!" she yelled as they ran to catch up.

He hopped over small runs of water that trickled and pooled along the flow of the screen. The water itself had risen through the porous material and condensed on the rails of the axle, where it hung as teardrops along the long lashes of the world. With the right pressure, the clouds would open and the mists would fall as a filtered rain, a dusting or cool sun shower over the valley below. The trickling streams that congealed and remained above the clouds ran off for collection in cisterns behind the white bulkhead at the clean end of the sky.

High above the valley's expanse, Meg pointed down toward her adobe village. She showed them all through a break in the clouds. They could see the empty swings at her school, the treetops along the path to the zoo. The adobe village, the garden, the fields, and the sections all around were partitioned from each other by scalable mounds or low, rib walls. Sixteen sections joined in a line to form a neighborhood; four neighborhoods formed a community. Each community comprised sixty-four sections and was bordered by a river, either veinal draw or artery feed. Astride each river was another parallel community. Four communities in total made a complete wrap around the sky. The inside of the ship held a spectacular 256 sections to count.

"I came up here once," she said. "I could see you."

"How?" Ceeborn asked. "I was never out here like you."

"Not here," Meg said. "I saw you from up ahead, down through the other end. I'll show you when we get there."

And with a sudden flicker, the sky all around changed its images of clouds to an enormous projection of the ship's schematic design. The image was painted beneath their feet as they walked like passengers riding on a long, tubular plane.

Far below at the planetarium, the expeditionary officer looked about the size of an insect as he stepped outside of the dome. He looked up toward the sky and the outlines of the ship as its live image detail filled in. Starry-eyed crowds gathered around him to witness the promised show of their arrival.

Ceeborn, Meg, Tenden, and Spud were walking on the schematic nearest to the center of the ship's body. Far ahead in the projection, the ship's eight long arms flared out to a parasol as the ship rotated on the screen. The cheer of the crowd by the planetarium below rose up like an echo of thunder.

But the ship's rotation projected under Ceeborn, Meg, Tenden, and Spud's feet, superimposed over the actual ground below, caused an instant bout of vertigo. The off axis sensation caused them all to wobble and reach down for the ground. A glorious, painted planet crested over the peak of the valley.

"Is this happening now?" Spud asked. "Did we arrive? Did we miss it?"

Animated launch doors opened all along the length of the projected arms and masses of simulated ships sprayed forth and shot through the tube of the sky.

"No," Meg said as she regained her footing. "It's only a preview. They showed it to us a million times before at school."

A geyser of blackened water shot up from the vent at the spiral garden. Then the whole valley shook and with it, the sky buffeted them side to side. It was no projection.

Ceeborn looked at Meg. Spud rose up from all fours on the screen.

"I don't think that was part of the show," Meg said.

From their height in the sky, they could see down, up, and around. Blackened ooze saturated the ground around the garden. The crowd on the ground couldn't see to the same distance and applauded the continuation of the show.

A more distant section's glandular fountain bubbled, then blew into a vertical geyser. The whole of the land was checkered by section, each either erupting with a pressurized fountain or turning off with a blackened ring of ooze.

Among the quickening pattern of chaos, a beacon of light emerged from the dome of Robin's clinic, then its vents, walls, and windows. Its light was unmistakably blue.

"What is that?" Ceeborn asked.

Meg jumped up from the screen into a run. "Come on. We've got to tell my mom!"

"What is it?" Tenden asked.

"If it's true, you won't believe it," she said.

"Believe what?" Ceeborn asked. He looked down again at the clinic's dome that shone like a spotlight of health.

"My mother incubated your bins," Meg said as she skipped backward in her run. "She left on the show. If those are your picks, then they worked. The bins. You picked from the bins!"

"The cure?" Ceeborn asked, and as he started to run, Spud pulled back on his arm.

"You picked them. C, E, and S," she said. "I think you found it. Come on!"

"Wait," Spud said. He held back. He sensed something and grabbed Ceeborn's sleeve. Then he ducked as he spun around.

A Chokebot had stalked them into the tube. It scurried upside down with claws locked onto the axle's two lower rails. Tenden pushed Spud aside as the Chokebot flipped down from the rails. It landed upright and poised on the thin projection screen.

"Run!" Tenden yelled to Ceeborn and Meg, but the Chokebot jumped and tackled him from behind. Tenden took the full brunt of its weight on his back. He fell to the screen, elbows bent, hands tucked and fisted under his belly. The Chokebot's two rear legs clamped to his ankles, its middle to his waist. Its front two claws pushed under and found his wrists. He resisted the pull of its pincers, but was no match for the Chokebot's ratcheted, mechanical strength.

It wrenched out Tenden's arms, flattening him to his belly, and with a sudden mechanical pop, ripped his bent elbows outstretched, tearing the tendons from his forearms. Tenden screamed in his splay. The Chokebot locked its six shoulder cuffs into place and reddened its dome as Tenden wailed.

Spud kicked at the Chokebot as Ceeborn ran back to pry its unmovable joints with his hands.

Tenden whimpered through labored breaths. The locked Chokebot shaded its dome a gentler orange in its feedback scale. It wasn't getting the calming response it sought. It changed the color of its dome to yellow then blue, but Tenden's cries of agony remained. The Chokebot tilted its dome and clacked its keys, deciphering the spasm of Tenden's hand on the screen as a wrestler's tap of give.

The Chokebot unlocked its limbs and dismounted. Its dome clicked as it backed farther away.

Ceeborn and Meg lifted Tenden up toward seated at her lap. Tenden cradled his torn arms beneath his chest as he rocked in tears. But worse, something awful had happened. He moved his shoulder, reached his hand into the front pocket of his hoodie, and then looked up. He pulled out the rivulus case. He trembled.

The case was wet. Its side was crushed.

"I don't know what happened," Tenden said. "I was carrying him and I got hit." He looked back. "I couldn't protect him. You understand?"

"I do," Ceeborn said. "It hit you first, that's all."

Ceeborn took the case a short distance away from Tenden's grip. He opened it over a stream of the sky and let the rivulus slip loose. The trickling current took the rivulus and it moved with the water, or maybe it swam away on its own. It would be best to think that it did.

Ceeborn turned away from the pacing Chokebot and kneeled to help Tenden up to his feet. As Ceeborn lifted, he winced and grabbed his hand against his neck. His sting was bad, and getting worse.

The projection of the ship's schematic on the screen reset with a spin, reacting like a compass needle fixed to the ship's actual orientation. Live status images of the ship's rear tank in distress were broadcast for all to see.

"We're almost there," Meg said to Tenden as he cupped his arms and walked behind them with Spud. "When we arrive," she said, "the ship's spinning is supposed to slow, the water pressure is supposed to fall, and the rivers are supposed to flow back into the tank."

"What are we supposed to do then?" Ceeborn asked.

"We're all supposed to go to the arms," she said as the sky darkened all around them.

Ceeborn led forward. Two other Chokebots responded to the networked call of the first. They were fast. They rushed through the tube, not below on the axle's rails, but above and out of sight. Spud looked back through the tube, sonar pinging with his facial disk into the emptiness, but saw nothing.

The live images of the tank on the projection screen ahead showed the remaining cable of the half-sunken gondola reaching down through the water's punctured skin. The skin was in a constant state of tearing as the submerged gondola twirled. Water was escaping in waves. A Chokebot, inverted on the ceiling of the tank, sliced through the remaining cable to set the gondola free. The cut ends of the cable hovered at first, then drew down and sank beneath the water. The unencumbered gondola drifted down and swirled away into the current. It sank toward a filter in the tank that fed into the ship's rearmost accelerator module. The gondola stopped at the outside of the filter, but the thin, flexible cable drew in.

Ceeborn turned away from the images in horror. A shiver ran from his neck through his spine. The extent of what he had done was suddenly upon everyone.

The sky all around them in the ship turned from clear to a hellish, choking red.

Spud looked back again into the tube. He jutted his head left, then right. The two rails of the axle above their heads were empty. "I think something is behind us."

The cable wound deep inside the accelerator module in the projected tank, then jammed. The gondola began to spin in the water like a stone at the end of a string, churning faster and faster, reaching up and shredding the water's skin, whipping the water into a cyclonic funnel. The entire orientation of the water was changing. It rode up the side of the tank toward its veinal inlet door and vacated from its arterial outlet, sending the whole ship horribly out of balance.

Spud whipped back around in a panic. He sensed it, his cheeks flared. He saw the two Chokebots coming in fast. "Run!"

The skin in the tank swelled from the reverse of the water's pressure, stretched, and burst wide open. The cable snapped from the gondola and wound in through the filter. It tied. An inner artery ballooned and ruptured with a click. The accelerator module buckled with an enormous, reverberating seizure that shot through the ship.

Ceeborn and Meg watched the ripple approach from ahead on the sheets of the sky. Then the actual wave hit full force. The projection of the planet on the tube exploded into a kaleidoscope of horror as the bellowing convulsion ripped through.

Spud jammed his hands over his ears and fell to the screen. He screamed. "Is this happening?!"

"Let's get out of here!" Tenden shouted with his arms hanging limp at his front.

Ceeborn and Meg dove flat on the screen.

The sky tilted.

The ship started to list.

The far white front of the tube rolled as the hill cracked away from the ball and joint behind the white bulkhead.

A rush of water swelled the rivers below.

Great plumes shot across the chest of the ship and splashed the underside of the sky.

Ceeborn was lying face down on the screen beside Meg. The ship was being destroyed, not by fire, but by the power and percussion of water. It was all a result of his doing. The world was drowning from the flow of its source.

Meg lay prone on the sky screen and looked away in her

terror. She was trembling. The back of her hair soaked in a trickle of water that ran between them. Even the wet tips of her hair shivered as her back rose and fell with the fits of her breaths. The hem of her pants shook with her legs. The toes of her shoes tapped unnerved on the clear sky as the over-whelming vertigo over the valley below was unbearable. No one deserved to be so afraid, least of all Meg. He had to move, to get her to the arms of the ship.

He reached for her hand as they lay and she turned her head to face him. Her eyes stared long. He tried to smile but his cheeks wouldn't lift more than a twitch from the corners of his mouth. He, too, was terrified. He loved her. He wondered which of the two would show more.

His neck was soothed by the trickle of water as it ran and dripped through the porous sky. The water flowed as the lifeblood of the ship, but Luegner owned the water. No wonder the ship cried from its sky. He touched his neck's wound and saw its reddened wetness between his fingers. Meg didn't blink. It was bad.

The racking vibrations stopped long enough. It was time to get up, and run. The violent structural twist of the ship had shorted out the projection screen from fore to aft. Now it all became clear. The living world of Meg and the dying gully world were united. Huge swaths of the screen had fallen from the sky, opening all of the ship into one.

People dodged from the squared and falling panels of the sky. They saw to the tops of the villages, the fields, and com-munities on opposite sides of their cylindrical world in the joining of two opposing semi-circular valleys. They froze in horror, the absolute vertigo of spotting the panicked people on the other side of their world also panicked and looking back down on them.

The glandular fountains along the tributary hills disgorged

their water. They were no longer able keep up with the changing pressure. The rivers lifted in their channels, then broke into globular form.

Ceeborn and Meg got up. They were breathless, staring over the vast open atrium of the conjoined and inverted valleys.

"Is that the world?" Tenden asked as he stood, gasping.

"I've never seen it like this," Meg said.

The two fast Chokebots jumped from the upper rails to the screen and corkscrewed in a coordinated split around the axle, descending in ambush upon Ceeborn, Meg, Tenden, and Spud from above.

The lead Chokebot formed a divide with Ceeborn and Meg to the front and Tenden and Spud to the rear. The second Chokebot took its position end-to-end with the lead. It faced the weaker Tenden and Spud.

The third Chokebot that had injured Tenden stalked his slower, sickened steps from behind.

Ceeborn and Meg looked ahead toward the gully. The screen was intact. Tenden and Spud looked back, rips in the sky tube were opening behind them.

"Don't run," Ceeborn said. "Don't move. They'll chase you."

Tenden's eyes were glassy and teared from his pain. Ceeborn and Meg had the clearer run ahead to freedom. Tenden took a step forward toward the Chokebot guarding his front. The leader facing Ceeborn immediately turned and faced Tenden. He squared off with the two, his arms hanging limp at his front.

"Tenden, don't!" Ceeborn said and charged forward. His first Chokebot spun back around and reared.

"Go on, jump me," Tenden cried to his guard. "You understand!"

Two more Chokebots scurried down the rails to the

alerted trouble along the tube. They descended on the screen and reinforced the back-to-back two as a quad: two faced Ceeborn and Meg, two against Tenden and Spud. Tenden turned in silence as they counted. In total there were five Chokebots in the pack, including the patrol in the rear that tore the strength of his arms.

Ceeborn's Chokebot guard in the quad raised its stinger and clawed its way forward. Its dome screen was a bold red of warning that scrolled, *Leader. No. Run.*

"Tenden, go around!" Ceeborn said as his guard crouched for its pounce.

Spud shuffled to the side, but his Chokebot followed his movement. He froze in fear.

Tenden taunted in closer to the pack. "No, you two run. I can bash them all."

Meg backed away. She pulled Ceeborn by his arm.

The four Chokebots reared, their targets tracked.

"Dammit, Tenden, run!" Ceeborn said as the Chokebots crouched from their middle legs to spring in their jumps.

"No, you run!" Tenden lunged forward, flexed his arms to his front, lifted his chest high and mighty and roared, *"I am a nail! And I—"*

The four Chokebots leapt and Tenden took the hit head on. Spud was second. Meg was third to go down in their mêlée.

Ceeborn counted only a moment's breath as his Chokebot leapt through the air. Its dome neared his face to within the stench of its body's char and he rolled away from beneath its fall to the screen. He dodged and it missed.

Meg and Spud were choked still and screamed.

Tenden writhed. He rolled on the ground before his Chokebot could lock in its frame. He slipped his weight onto his hip, muscled a roll, and twisted his waist and ankles free from the grip of the claws. He bucked to his hands and knees and flipped the Chokebot from his back. It grabbed him and he rode it belly up into a fall. They landed together by Spud in a crush.

The first patrol rushed in and grabbed hold of Tenden's ankles with its claws. It signaled with frantic speed to the lead Chokebot circling Ceeborn after its missed attack. The patrol brought its dome to within a breath of Tenden's face and tilted its head in a flash of aqua, scrolling the impossible word, *Calm*.

Tenden flexed his body. He rose like a beast breaking its shackles. The lead Chokebot rushed from Ceeborn and leapt upon Tenden's mass. The combined force of Tenden, Spud, their two locked Chokebots, the patrol, and now the leader landing hard, was too much for the sky screen to bear.

The screen ripped wide open beneath them. Spud screamed for Tenden's hand as they fell en masse through the sky. The four Chokebots flailed as they fell. Tenden and Spud fell into a swath of the screen, both wrapped into a torn piece of the flickering sky. Together they descended to the ground, like two freed angels who didn't need wings to fly.

Ceeborn rolled away from the edge of the hole in the tube. He saw them all fall. He thought he saw Tenden and Spud move on the ground on their own, or so he thought it would be best to think that they did.

"Cee, Help!" Meg cried beneath the last remaining Chokebot. It stayed locked, but its dome was held askew toward the hole in the sky tube. It clicked out a higher pitch, but received no reply in return.

Ceeborn rose, enraged. He grabbed the edge of the sky-screen along its tear. He ran toward the Chokebot on Meg, ripping the screen forward as he charged. In one swift movement, he pounced and wrapped the screen like a plastic bag around the clear dome of the demon. He raised his knee and slammed a kick down upon its bulbous dome. Over and again, he drove his foot down and through, shattering the dome to its lifeless end. Revenge trumped grief, but it could bring no one back from their fall. He had lost his friends, and these pipe-walking demons would pay.

"Stop," Meg said from beneath the crushed dome, protecting her face with her hands. "Stop. It already let go."

Ceeborn fell to his knees on the tube's screen.

Meg crawled out from under the Chokebot's stilled frame. She found Ceeborn's eyes with hers. She wrapped her arms around his shoulders and met her forehead to his.

"It's all my fault. I brought us up here," she said.

"No, I did," he said as he pulled her arm from his neck. "It was me who brought us this far. Not you."

She managed a smile if he'd have it. "I saw you from up here," she said. "Up ahead, at the end."

Blackened water oozed and geysers shot from the 256 sections throughout the embattled body of the ship around them. In pure binary form, one section turned off with the ooze, while another came on with its spray; as if the ship were desperately trying to regulate its health in crisis, recalculate its settings for life.

"Come on," he said, taking her hand as he stood. "It's time to get off this ship."

The sky screen ahead crossed an expansion joint and the screen curved away from beneath them, sheered all the way down to the bank of the gully.

"Is this where you were when you saw me?" he asked.

"We're close, you'll see," she said as the entire ship wobbled anew from the rotation of the water in the tank, gyrating on its long, linear axis around a watery node.

The massive, blue ring torus hovered around their end of the axle. They passed beneath the center of its humming blue mesh that floated in its delicate balance.

"I once dreamed I was a bio-machine with a brain like this, one a thousand times more powerful than my own," he said as the world twisted and unhinged. "But now I think bio-machines only exist in nightmares."

"We're here," she said as she stopped at a double-wide door to the bulbous room at the end of the axle.

"I've seen the outside of this room from below," he said. "What is it?"

"A room at the end of the sky where no one should ever have to go alone. And you won't."

"I'm ready. Let's go in."

She slid aside the door and led him into a gloriously bright chamber. It was round.

He stepped first through the door, and she followed him in. Then she turned back around toward the fall of the world she knew, and with a straight-armed heave, shut tight the doors at the end of the sky.

TWENTY-ONE

I CAN'T SAVE YOU ALL

CEEBORN AND MEG stepped into the glowing chamber around the axle that was adjoined to the center point of the gully's rear bulkhead. The axle with its eight long rails passed above their heads and through the chilled air to the end of the spherical room. But more spectacular were the rows of silent, rectangular cabinets that were attached at their ends and stood out from the rails like the spokes of a wheel.

Around the walls of the sphere and directly beneath each hanging cabinet row was a tiled, raised floor aisle.

He stepped up onto the aisle to his front. Alternating tiles were transparent, with a direct view over the gully swelling far below; and then from the transparent tiles in the other aisles of the sphere, the gully could be seen in its wrap-around entirety, all the way up and around to upside down. The rays of light that shone from the sphere's outer surface over the old gully world were an inspiration.

It was easy to count the cabinets from where Ceeborn and Meg stood, by their three groupings of five on each rail, with the addition of one extra cabinet on the rail directly above them.

"My dad showed me once about a number system called

hexadecimal that counted up to fifteen, then rolled over to the next place whenever there was an extra one. But that can't be this. Hexadecimal had the numbers one through nine and then letters A through F to represent ten through fifteen. These cabinets are more like binary ones standing in groups of five."

He held his neck and arched back to see through the glass-covered top of one of the hanging cabinets. Then he became silent himself. The box contained a body, a person lost and alone in a freezer. All of the cabinets hanging in their rows had eyes that eternally pointed down through the cabinet's cap, stuck in tearless sight over the gully's water far below.

Meg followed Ceeborn up onto the aisle and took his hand. She had taken him to a secluded morgue, a heaven above but also within the sky.

He lowered his chin in despair. If he counted from the one body above him among the eight rows of fifteen around the axle, there were 120 bodies. And then there was that one extra cabinet, still empty.

"I was brought here once before when I was little," Meg said. "But I lived."

"There are only a hundred-twenty," Ceeborn said. "Your mother said there were a hundred twenty-one people who were sick. Is it you? Your mother?"

"No. But you know him," she said.

"Is it Pace?" he asked, but then recanted. "But, my father fixed him."

Meg only had to look up and along the rails for Ceeborn to recognize there was so much more to be counted and far worse in scope. The row with the added cabinet along the rail ended at the double-wide door.

"Just think. Everyone had the PluralVaXine5 spray," she said. "Everyone."

Ceeborn slid the double-wide door back open. The cabinet

rails of the morgue were the same as the long empty others that ran down the entire central axle of the sky. There was room on the rails for hundreds or thousands more cabinets for the dead. Everyone on the ship had the spray.

"We can warn the rest," he said. "I'm not sick."

There were no more Chokebots to chase them or choke them out into calm. He reached up to the pain in his neck. He looked at his fingers: They were dry. Then he turned back to Meg beneath the long rails. "Wait. Are you sick? You can tell me—"

"No," she said as she shut the doors and stepped back into the morgue with a terror that stayed. "No, Ceeme, you are."

"No. Why would you say that? You have no idea."

"It doesn't matter now, does it? We're leaving. And without the cure, we're all going to die on the ground. Let's you and me just stay here together where it's quiet, okay?"

"No, we can't," he said.

He hugged her tight and she shut her eyes beneath the hanging cabinets of the dead.

"Remember, we saw the cure," he said. "It worked. Your mother can make it again. I remember the bins. I can find the pieces again on the ground. They were easy, I remember. A petal from a dandelion. A wing of a beetle. A fish scale. We'll collect the three in a vial. Your mother can make the cure. Once we get off this ship, I can save us on the ground."

"I used to watch you from up here," she said as she kneeled down by a transparent tile. "I'd sit up here all by myself and watch you from up here at these windows. Now I know why. The sun never shined on your side of the ship, but you never gave up."

He looked down through the tile and found his orientation in the gully world. "You could see me?"

People were scrambling far below en masse, packing across

the bridge from the transportation annex. The water in the gully was a rising torrent, splashing the evacuees on the bridge's walkway.

Then, suddenly invigorated, he looked down through another clear tile. Gerald Aiden was out on the eroded front grounds of their crumbling, terraced hill home.

"We have to get down there," Ceeborn said.

The double-wide door to the sky tube was a useless retreat. Its pathway was gone.

The eight rails and aisles of the spherical morgue converged on a catwalk that looped the rear, end cap of the room. The cap had four doors equally spaced on the quarter turn. The door marked 1B was straight ahead of their aisle, 1A was up to their left and sideways, 1C was higher to their right, and the fourth door, 1D, was high above the axle and upside down. It was unreachable by any stretch, ladder, or climb.

Looking out through the transparent tiles, long, throat-like shafts trunked away from the backside of the doors, attached to the gully bulkhead, and radiated in their four spoke-like directions, one to the top of his terraced building, the other three toward the bridges that crossed the gully.

Far below, Aiden ran from the building and over the roots of the yard, rushing in limps and stumbles to reach the collapsing bridge that he sealed. Ceeborn pounded on the clear tile in a soundless rage. It was hopeless. Ceeborn sprung back up to his feet. "We're taking the door on the right, closest to the transportation annex," he said, pulling Meg away from her view. "It'll get you to your father. It's the only way you can go."

"What about the door straight ahead, One-B? It's easier," she said. "We can climb straight down to where you live."

"There's no way out down there. My father, he's trapped. We have to get to the arms. We have to get you off this ship!"

Door 1B straight ahead clanked with a tapping from the other side.

"There can't be more," he said.

The wheel of the door didn't spin.

Ceeborn ran up the mesh stairs of the catwalk toward the sideways door on the right, 1C. As he climbed, he didn't fall or slip from its incline. Meg hopped up to follow. The sensation was a most peculiar one that neither could explain. There was a fizzing feeling taken in through their hands on the railing and a tingling drawn out through their feet on the platform. The circular catwalk had a definitive upward bias ahead that became flat underfoot as it passed.

The once-sideways door was now directly to their front and upright. He tried its wheel but it wouldn't budge.

Door 1B below clanked again with a pounding and then its wheel spun. The door pulled open. Michael Longshore ducked through and entered the morgue. Robin was right behind him.

"Dad! Mom!" Meg yelled as she ran back down the catwalk and fell into her mother's embrace.

"You're father is okay," Robin said to Ceeborn. "He wants you to come back to him now."

Michael leapt down from the door to an aisle for a desperate view through the transparent tile in the floor. More people were jammed onto his transportation annex bridge, shoving and scrambling, falling from the bridge into the torrent of the gully.

"The hangar doors aren't opening!" he said. "I've got to get down there."

"We're coming with you," Ceeborn said.

"No," Michael said, "Meg, you go back with your mother. You, too, Ceeborn—the three of you. You go back down the way we came up from Madden's place."

"No. We want to get off the ship," Ceeborn said as he ran

up the catwalk for the higher door on the right to the annex. "We've got to get down to your bridge, through its airlock door to a craft to go down."

Michael pulled his way up the catwalk's railings. "Listen to me," he said. "Every bridge has an airlock that aligns with an arm. Yours is no different. The people at my bridge can't get through. The shift of the ground must have put pressure on the doors. If the doors on the bulkhead aren't perfectly aligned, they won't open to let the people through. If I can't get the doors open, there won't be any craft!"

Meg moved back down toward door 1B. "Come on, let's go," she said.

"All the doors will be blocked to the arms," Michael said. "All the people are trapped. They'll all die up here if I can't get the doors open."

The wobble of the ship sent a chilling crack down the central axle. A dozen cabinets popped from the rails and crashed out to the walls of the sphere.

"Go with Robin. Now!" Michael said. "I have to get down there. I have to get the doors aligned and the people through."

Robin, Meg, and Ceeborn dashed for door 1B. Michael muscled his way up the catwalk to his higher door.

Ceeborn and Meg dove through door 1B into its throated passageway. Robin followed them through, and once in, pushed on the door to close it. "You make it! You live!" Robin cried out to Michael.

The structural twisting of the ship dislodged the catwalk from the wall. Michael rolled and fell headfirst back down to the aisle.

Meg fought through Robin's hold as Michael stumbled toward her at the door. Meg reached her arm through, lunging her hand out for his grasp. But rather than take her hand, Michael pushed her back through. He grabbed the door's wheel from his side of the morgue and pulled.

"Daddy!" Meg screamed.

"Take care of your mother," Michael said. He pulled on the door, overpowering Meg as he looked back through the morgue that was opening up to the sky.

"Michael!" Robin yelled.

"Get to the ship!" he yelled as he pulled. "I'll find another way down."

Ceeborn pushed Meg and Robin's arms away and caught Michael by surprise at the door. "Come with us," Ceeborn said.

Michael braced his foot against the door's frame for a win. "No," he said. "You save them. I'll save the rest." And with both hands wrapped around the wheel of the door, Michael heaved a final pull and sealed their door 1B shut. Meg screamed.

Darkness befell their cramped passageway and Ceeborn pictured Michael letting go of the door on the morgue's side, turning into the chaos, and running back on his own through to the other end of what remained of the long tube of the sky. Or so Ceeborn thought, it would be best to think that he did.

Ceeborn, Meg, and Robin descended in a utility lift through the darkness of the shaft attached like a fold on the bulkhead. The gated sides of the lift scraped the ossified shaft's walls and released its stench. The basket was large enough only for them. Light broke the darkness of the shaft, rushing through its red portholes like zeroes and its slits like flashing ones as they passed in their descent. Ceeborn braced himself on the waist-high rail in fright. As the lift jolted, skipped, and slammed on its track to the bottom, the shaft walls fissured and tank water spray blasted into the basket. Robin pressed her back against the basket's wall and clenched the wetted handrail. She winced in her prayer not to scream.

Meg folded herself into a corner. Ceeborn stood catty-cornered to her front, pressing his arms against the walls to her either side. The bulkhead alone could rupture and collapse them into a washed-away heap of debris. There would be nothing he could do, but he held to protect her as they descended. She looked up at him in a terror that forced her to breathe in gasps. She shook her head almost imperceptibly faint, but he saw her. She was as terrified as he was. A curl of her cheek shivered up toward a smile. It was more than enough. She loved him and it showed. And together, he smiled enough for them both.

"So do I," he said and she threw herself into his arms.

They hit bottom with a jolt and bounced to settle. The lift's door opened onto a mesh staging platform entombed in the lower end of the shaft. Ceeborn grasped the handle of a D-ring embedded in a floor panel, gave it a clockwise twist, and lifted the panel to expose a round door beneath.

Inside, he climbed down a ladder. A hatchway in the center of the floor below was wide open. He looked back up to Meg and Robin.

"Go through," Robin said from above. "Michael left it open. We're right behind you."

Ceeborn squeezed through the lower hatchway and his feet found the rungs of a still lower ship ladder mounted against an interior wall. He stepped down and jumped its last rung to a floor.

It was the floor of a closet. A slop sink pressed at his back as he helped Meg down the last rungs of the ladder. The walls of the closet had the smell of a familiar rot. He opened the closet door and stepped out into a tubular hall. He was home.

Crusted portholes lined the corridor that passed by the fetid, mossy cell where he had been chained on his earlier return. Now he had been out to Meg's world and returned without capture. No charred, pipe-legged Chokebot would hold his neck to the floor again. The hallway's window screens had peeled away. There was no more projection out to the blackness of space, only a misty view out over the gully, instead.

He had grown up in the oldest part of the ship. The world that Meg knew on the other side of the wall was blinded by a healthful guise. The ship had been brought to life by veins and arteries that grew forward from his old gully world to her youngest sections, all extending along a central axis as time or resources would allow.

He could see the bared axle of the sky through the gully windows and was filled with remorse. He should have run sooner for a cure. The rows of cabinets in the morgue would one day fill the axle all the way to the world of the young. And by the time he or Meg joined them inverted in their cabinets upon their rail, Robin's cure, if she ever found one, would have come too late for them all.

Daniel was in the classroom, collapsed on the stage by the still apparatus. He huddled on the floor beneath the balls of Spud's wall, his forehead buried deep in his palms.

"Oh, there you are, Cee," Daniel said as he pulled a shimmering blanket higher upon his shoulders for relief from the ship's gyrating motion. "I'm glad you're okay." The crinkled material compressed, but didn't take shape as its bands of red and blue oscillated across his chest. The blanket failed to calibrate, unable to zero in on horizontal within the waves of the room.

"Did you destroy us again?" Daniel asked. "Was it you who caused the damage in the tank? I saw the projection."

"It was. And I'm not afraid," Ceeborn said as Meg entered with Robin. "This ship was doomed from the start."

"I worked so hard to fix everything, to fix all of us, and you destroyed it," Daniel said.

"I saw the morgue," Ceeborn said as he kneeled at his father's side. "You didn't fix enough."

Daniel sat straighter. "What more do you want from me? I gave you everything I had. I can't fix everything. What can I do? I can't fix you all."

Ceeborn felt dizzy from the sting in his neck. His wound had reopened and he was bleeding. But the liquid on his fingertips was not red. The opaque tackiness between the rub of his fingers was dark ooze.

Pace sat cross-legged by the door. The stripes of his suit were bright, pre-calibrated and balanced. His head was tipped back against the wall. His eyes were closed. He didn't move.

Robin knelt down at Daniel's side. "Michael said there was a ship here."

"What is there left to save?" Daniel asked.

"Us," Ceeborn said. "You can save us."

Pace's eyes stayed closed as he teetered and collapsed in a thud on the floor. Robin and Meg rushed to his aid.

"You killed the boys, my boys that I fixed," Daniel said to Ceeborn.

"I am your boy that you fixed."

Daniel stared at him, and then breathed faster and fuller. He reached out his hand to Ceeborn's face, but didn't touch. He was the son that he knew, as if from an angle, but older.

"Michael said there's a ship here," Robin said, louder, from Pace's side. "Where is it?"

Daniel staggered up to his feet, still staring wide-eyed at his boy. He brushed off the protective blanket from his body to the floor and welled up with pride. "This is the old ship." Then he rushed and grabbed Pace up by the collar to his feet and dragged him stumbling for the door. He rallied. "And man oh man, we're playing now!"

Daniel's office, his control room, had stayed inoculated against the decay. Its walls were pure. The screen above his desk with its images of muddled shores and mountain peaks wiped away to reveal a window's view over the dying gully below. Ceeborn, Meg, Robin, and Pace crowded in. A rolling grill door partitioned the back of the room from Daniel's desk area.

"Crank the handle clockwise," he said as Pace stood dazed over the hand crank to the door. Robin helped Pace's hands turn quicker on the crank. The grill door passed its locking mark, and four heavy trundle seats fell from the wall. The seats squeezed between stacks of boxes and crates.

Plumes of thickened water burst from the gully and drenched the office's window with spray. Ceeborn threw his palms against the glass and pressed his forehead for a view over the ground below. Gerald Aiden was out on the front erosion fighting the rising, boiling surf.

"If the water takes me away, go on without me," Ceeborn said as turned from the window and rushed for the door.

"No," Meg said. "Don't! You can't go back out there."

"He'll never make it," Robin said from the window.

Daniel grabbed Ceeborn by the arm and stopped him for a look at his red streaked neck. "Go, but go fast," Daniel said. Ceeborn hesitated and felt his welted neck with his hand. "Go!" Daniel said.

As Ceeborn ran from the office control room, Daniel turned for a solemn look at Robin. "There's a health kit in one of those boxes. See if there's something in there for his neck. It's bad and I think he's getting worse," he said.

Robin brushed aside the curios on top of a box in the stack and then smashed the box open on the floor.

Ceeborn ran from the opened hangar bay doors in the

lower recess between the left and right silos of his terraced building shaped like an H. The front yard was a tangled upheaval of roots and debris.

Aiden desperately stumbled and pawed his way toward the gully. The collection tanks had overflowed with froth and the entire current was polluted. The bridge across the gully had fallen, the shoreline was collapsing. He was trapped.

"We're closing the doors," Ceeborn said. "We're going down!"

"Hold the shuttle," Aiden said as he dug and threw away debris for a way to cross the gully. "I've got to find him."

Trees and bombs of sod fell, rejected from the other side of the ship.

"Get back to your father!" Aiden said without turning back as he dug himself in deeper.

Out in the collapsing hull, pinpricks of light shone through a burning outer skin. Five Chokebots rushed toward the ulcerated flesh. They climbed the walls with their six meager pincers and jumped to contain the damage like sutures on a stretching wound. One Chokebot sounded with the high-pitched cry of a mammal in distress. Another held onto the splitting outer skin, then squealed in a call to the others as its demise became assured.

"Can you hear them?" Ceeborn asked as Aiden threw another heap of sky-screen panels aside. "They're calling to each other. They're failing."

"They're doing their job. They're programmed. Nothing more. We mean nothing to them. They're pipes. Machines. Let them go!" Aiden said.

The outer wall succumbed to pressure. A Chokebot was ripped out into the scorching flames of the ship's atmospheric entry. The four who witnessed the loss of one of their own bleated as the ulcerated walls ripped open. Their own death was certain. They pulled their end-of-life triggers and became silent. They were plucked in their stillness through the openings in the outer hull.

The corona of a sun crested through the opened shell. Bursts of air drew the membranes farther apart as Aiden balanced on his hobbled leg halfway across the debris and he kept trying even though he could never make it the rest of the way.

"Where are you going?" Ceeborn yelled. "Come back!"

"My boy!" Aiden cried. His voice was blown and hoarsened. "I've got to find my boy! He fell." Aiden's voice split into ruin. "I saw him fall from the sky. He bounced when he hit the ground. He was moving. I've got to find my boy."

The water rose above what was left of the berm. The current spread out over the yard and swirled at Ceeborn's feet.

Meg ran out of the hangar doors. "Cee, come back," she yelled. "We're going, now."

Aiden fell his way across the currents, lifting and throwing himself over the far side of the gully.

Ceeborn ran back to Meg and inside. She closed the hangar doors within the bottom hollow of the building's H.

As Daniel's original ship vibrated in its berth, its H-winged form cracked away from the hill, the encrusted folds of the bulkhead, and its descending orange pipes.

Ceeborn threw himself back against the window screen in Daniel's upper office control room. The whole body of the greater ship was aglow. Aiden disappeared into the opening light of its hull. He held up his forearms and curled away from the wide open sky as it flooded the ship's body with light and took him in whole.

The massive blue torus ring collapsed onto its axle. The axle twisted loose from its ball and socket. In a horrible screech, the axle spine of the ship broke in two and fell toward a smothering crash on the meat fields below.

Meg cried out in vain as she watched its fall, "Daddy!"

Pierced and disjointed around them, the cavernous whole of the ship heaved in a gaping breath from death.

Ceeborn and Meg buckled themselves into their trundle seats as Daniel pounded at the dysfunction of his screens. The window was still barely over the gully. Pace rocked on the floor with his knees to his chest. A health kit from a box was open on the floor beside him.

Robin dabbed a spot of cream from the kit onto Ceeborn's neck with her fingers, battling the ship's heavy vibrations.

"Looks like you had some kind of reaction," Robin said.

"I should have gone with you," Pace said. "Maybe I could have saved my friends. Or you wouldn't have killed them."

Robin took an injector pen from the old-fashioned kit. Ceeborn flinched. "Don't worry," she said. "It's not a spray. You'll be fine."

Meg sat in her seat. She murmured to calm herself in their hellish descent. "We've arrived and our planet is going around a star."

Robin injected the anti-venom pen into Ceeborn's sting, and then finished his neck with a light gauze pad. "It's bad. But it should heal," she said as she reached back for the box.

"Going around a star is what's going to make a year now instead of timing the ship travelling straight," Meg said with her hand over her pounding heart. "We learned that in class."

Robin took a cinch sack from the box and pulled out a wrinkled, forest green Windbreaker. She covered it over Ceeborn's shoulders.

"I know, honey, I know," Robin said with a steady hand on Meg's cheek. She quieted them both for their arrival, and then buckled herself into her seat.

Old codes and images on Daniel's forward display finally

aligned to his control. The gully was a vision of hell, but the ship's external camera to the atmosphere was better, and Daniel switched the visuals of his screen to show it. The arch of a planet, enormous and rotating, finally came into frame.

It was beautifully blue. It had marbled white clouds. It had continents and whole oceans of water. It had perfect seascapes waiting for a swimmer like Ceeborn.

It was the blue crest of Earth.

Their whole terraced building was itself a massive descent craft and it fought to separate from what was left of the gyrating ship, smashing into its berth in the gully. In one jolting wave, the Earthscape was lost on their screen, but then returned with a spark.

On the screen, they saw escape pods and crafts ejecting out of the bays of the long, forced-back arms of the greater ship. Not orderly, but wildly shot. Some propelled hopelessly, streaking into unrecoverable space. Others burned on entry. They fell unsheathed through the rising friction of the atmosphere with ablative shields depleted. Then hundreds released en masse, spitting out from the tentacle doors of the seven other arms in a burning mist of hope. Only a few would survive.

Pace choked up a cough as he climbed into the seat by Robin. He drew in a deep breath to bulk up his chest. They all fought to hold their own fear.

The ship buffeted in a dead fall from orbit, careening in the worst possible turbulence. The entire dying ship corkscrewed with its arms split forward and flung back through the atmosphere. The outer mantle of the ship flared into a disintegrating sail and burned off in the hellish, sky-streaking inferno. Being eaten alive by the savagery of flames called for the pull of a trigger, but the ship was already in its dead fall.

Their descent craft could not break free from the enormous

forces of the fall and was trapped within the gully of the ship. Meg cried out in horror, "We're not supposed to be falling. The practice didn't say we'd be falling!"

Life with water was gone; only fire remained. Ceeborn and Meg were trapped in their corner of the craft. Together, they would burn alive.

North America passed, then the Pacific Ocean below. Daniel ripped a circuit panel from his wall. He looked back at Ceeborn, all of their fright, then he hammer-fisted an *Emergency Explosives Trigger*.

A pressure wave blew the gully wide open. Thrusters exploded from the top of the craft. White-hot plasma swept the gully grounds, vaporizing remnant pools of water, and splitting the ship in two at its neckline. Their craft was freed.

They ejected, slotted out from between the gully bulkhead and the flaming, barrel-chested ship. The windows of their craft faced away from the atmospheric fire. They fell over the ocean, blind to their fate, as landing skids on the bottom of their craft extended and—

A *whoomp* was all they heard before a flash of light engulfed their screen. They felt the punch of a shock wave and passed to black. Away in the greater ship, the gully bulkhead had finally given way, and dust-thickened water was ignited by a boost of the accelerator module. An electromagnetic aurora encircled and dissipated upon the whole of the Earth.

Escape pods streaked in, some gained control, many not.

Their automated descent craft slowed over the ocean. It passed a continental landfall and descended toward the southeastern coastline of an island.

Pods continued to crash down all along the beach and coastline. Some landed safely, others scorched through the sky as uncontrolled meteors upon a quiet city.

Their landing descent craft moored in the River Derwent,

just off the eastern shore of the Lower Sandy Bay on the outskirts of Hobart. Its pressurized release valves opened. Splashes of filtered, thickened water burst from the craft's circulatory system into the river below.

Ceeborn awoke in his seat, as did Meg, Daniel, Robin, and Pace. The windows of Daniel's screens looked down over the beach and out along the shoreline. Water flushed from beneath the craft's hull. The craft's airlock doors opened into the gentle lapping waves on the beach.

Ceeborn stepped out with a squint. He rubbed his hand over the gauze on his neck. He paused at the doorway, seduced by a first, deep breath of fresh, natural air. It was a pristine stretch of beach.

There were no people to greet him as he moved onto the shore. All modern buildings existed in the city beyond the sand, but no faces filled their empty streets.

Logistic officers disembarked from their own battered crafts for an impending exodus from ships to a beachhead. Larger and disparate crafts and their respective hangar doors opened as rows of 3D printed vehicles prepared to roll off and make their way onto land.

Meg exited after Ceeborn, then Daniel at his own distance. Daniel seemed content and looked around from the inland mountain peak and back to the deep-blue waterway behind them. Their recovery craft was settled and safe beneath a rolling cloud sky. They had made it by air to their distant shore, together.

Ceeborn and Meg stood close together on a far and secluded part of the beach. They were confident yet wary, in a new and exciting place. Ceeborn had on the green Windbreaker, but left it unfastened. A crisp breeze kept the air cool and the clouds at bay.

"How's your neck?" Meg asked with a gentle reach. He flinched from her touch. It hurt. It had festered anew and leaked a dark spot of black through his bandage.

"It's good," he said. "I feel fine." He looked over the big divide of the bay. On the other side, there was a jut of tree-covered land that looked peaceful and calm. "I'm not sure what to do. I'm not used to sleeping on dry land. I don't know how to live in this world," he said, looking to the far shore.

She looked, too, and smiled. "It kind of feels like there's a thousand more places to go, doesn't it?"

"There's a lot of water here for me to explore," he said as his eyes misted and he took a step back. "And I'm a really good swimmer. You know?"

"You think this is some kind of heaven, or what?" she asked.

"It can't be heaven. There aren't any people," he said. He had the whole ocean and beach almost all to himself, but unlike some hapless rivulus in a tank, he didn't want it to be so. He hated being alone. "Maybe you couldn't have stopped me from running," he said, "or from hurting so many people. Or, maybe if you did, none of this would have happened. Nobody would have died." But, he didn't want to bury her heart any further in his guilt, so he said the only thing he could. "But, you know what? It's a good thing you're here."

He grasped his neck with his hand. His pain was intolerable. "Maybe we can go to all those thousand places together someday?" he said with a failing smile, then turned away, his eyes filling with tears.

"Where are you going?" she asked. "Please don't. You know you'll miss me if you go."

He tried to come back to her, but couldn't untangle the swirls in his mind. "You know if I was a bio-machine with a brain a thousand times more powerful than my own, maybe I could figure all this out," he said, "but I'm not that machine. I'm me. I'm the me that you used to watch from up in the morgue." He turned and left her once more. "But now that we've arrived, I need to figure out for myself . . . who that me really is." He tipped back on his heels, turned in the sand, and hurried away down the shore.

"So then what?" she asked, lifting up to her toes. "What do we do once you're you?"

"We stay here and settle the planet," he said, turning back with the bravest of grins. "What else? You've captured my soul, what can I say?"

Far behind her, piles of supplies were unloaded onto the beach for the rows of vehicles to haul inland. Shoreline camps were being constructed from tilt-up panels. Wrecked craft were being cleared from the shore.

"Meg?" Robin called. She heard her mother and turned.

Robin was back at the doors of their craft. She was helping Pace step out onto the beach. He wavered for balance at the hatch and wiped an embarrassing black run from his nose. He found his step and recovered in Robin's hold. His posture improved with Meg's approach.

But Meg didn't get far. She heard a cry. She turned back and looked. Ceeborn was also stopped in his tracks as was everyone else emerging from their downed crafts along the beach. Everyone looked up toward the sky.

A seagull flew overhead.

It rose up free in the gentle thermals of a warming breeze.

Ceeborn glanced at Meg beneath the gull's swirl. She saw it, too. But then they both saw something else. Something moved between them on the beach. It was small and dark, and it moved away from the tide. From a distance, it looked like a fish, but then it couldn't be, not so far from the curl of the waves.

Meg started to run toward the moving creature on the sand. The seagull circled around and dove. Its wings spiked as it dropped, having zeroed in on the dark spot on the sand.

It was the rivulus, scurrying. It dashed on its fins back for the safety of the water.

Ceeborn closed in as he ran for it too. The seagull swooped with a caw and Meg ducked the flap of its wings. But with the seagull's hop from the sand back up to flight, the spot on the beach was gone. Ceeborn watched the seagull soar. He stood on the sand in wonderment, then looked down at the edge of a wave on the beach. "It made it in a craft," he said of the rivulus. "It lived."

Meg stopped for a breath before him. Then she turned and looked wistfully up the long shore, at the crashed crafts, and their fewer people emerging. Then she knew. "My father," she said as she held her hand over her pounding heart.

More pods streaked across the distant sky as they found their way in.

Ceeborn counted them in and knew what it meant, too.

"He got the doors opened," Meg said, and cried. "My father got them all open."

TWENTY-TWO

I FOUND SOMETHING

CEEBORN SWAM THROUGH the clear earthen water of the bay with a trailing mist of red seeping from his neck. He tucked his head into his shoulder as he swam to relieve his sores and stiffness.

He opened his eyes in a haze, a waking confusion. He had lain down on the beach and dreamed. Meg was kneeling over him. She spoke as he woke, continuing as though he hadn't gotten far, or had never left. "I found something," she said.

"Your father?" he asked.

"No, not yet," she said. "But I'll keep looking. Come on. I found something you ought to see."

Pace had recovered a healthier complexion and was riding in circles on a bicycle in the street. There was no moving traffic on the roads, no people to be found. Pace had no problem balancing, as his red and blue stripes on his suit attested.

Meg led Ceeborn into a bicycle shop on a corner of a street. He marveled at the selection of equipment hanging from the racks. One suspended bike in particular caught his attention. The knobs of its back wheel gave it a nice deep traction and a free-sounding spin. The colors and lettering on its frame suited his taste. It was a graphite-and-white Rockhopper XPS bicycle.

They emerged from the shop together, pushing two bikes toward Pace in his circles. They tried and tried again to ride their new and strange two-wheeled apparatus through the streets of an abandoned town.

"A bike without a rider falls down," Meg said and laughed as Ceeborn got back up.

Yellow wattlebirds in trees whistled in a loud harmony of mockery, *"LookatCee. LookatCee. LookatCee."*

"We should go," Meg said as she dismounted from her white Trailhead bike to give him a hand. "People say it's safe to go up to the mountain and look around. We should go, too."

The grid of the city's empty towers gave way to single homes that were aligned like fingers up the mountain's foothills.

Meg pushed her bike alongside Ceeborn's up the hill of a drive.

"Where are all the people who built these buildings? Who lives in them?" he asked.

She smiled. It was easy. "Maps don't have people."

"We're not in a map."

"Maybe they all ran away."

"Maybe they all died?"

"You think they're all in cabinets in the sky?"

"No, not here," he said as he glanced up to see. "This is a real sky."

She stopped to rest before the end of the tree-lined neighborhood turned to forest, and lay her bike on the front yard of a home. He did the same with his, and then pushed open the home's gate with its scripted numerals of 448.

He walked through the small, wood-paneled home. There was a boy's bedroom that was simple and nice. It had a few interesting toys, though its shelves were mostly bare. Meg called from the living room.

"They look like us," she said, standing at the fireplace. She was hunched over a device. It was a clear piece of tablet screen that she held up to a window's light. The sun gave it power. "There's a show on here. It's us," she said as Ceeborn looked through its flexible pane.

It was an image of the two of them together in a craft. They were sitting, she was in his embrace, and a window of a sky with clouds was behind them. Meg touched her finger across her smile within the frame. Their screen image shifted away, and a single word remained: *"Passcode."*

"Put it down," he said. "It's a Chokebot's screen. It must have seen us when we came in. Put it down." He felt dizzy, confused. She reached for his arm.

"Let's go," she said.

He stumbled backward over a stack of boxes and fell to the floor. "Those boxes weren't here when we came in," he said.

"Yes, they were—"

"No. The boxes right there! Were those boxes here when we came in?"

"Don't yell at me," she said. "I put them there when you were in your room."

She set the tablet screen back onto the mantel and took down something much smaller from its place. It was a clear vial. "Here, I found this, too. It was in one of those boxes." She opened the lid of the treasure chest in her palm. "It has your picks," she said. "A dandelion petal. A beetle wing. And a fish scale. The cure."

He rose and balanced his back against the wall for support. His breathing was far too fast. "No, that's not mine," he said. The room felt way too confined. "Let's go. Let's get out of here."

"Where to?" she asked.

"Anywhere. Out of here. I want to see the sky."

He lifted his bike from the yard, pushed it by the handles, and hastened from the neighborhood across a narrow bridge.

She skipped to keep up and push her bike alongside his. They passed a ravine with an overturned car rusting in its lower pond. The water level was through the windows but below the rear seat.

"We should do something for your neck," she said and reached. "It looks bad."

It stung to the touch. "I'm fine," he said as the cramp in his neck sent his chin down to his collar bone. He gagged to clear his throat. The swirling chatter of a forest's canopy pinched the sky away. He pushed on as clearings came and went through the forest path and the rolling call of a waterfall ahead brought a certain measure of calm. A rivulet flowed by his feet. A floating leaf meandered with the flow before lodging itself into a gate of twigs at the edge of a ravine.

He dropped his bike to the ground at the sight below of a matching, but wrecked, graphite-and-white XPS bike. Its rear wheel protruded from the embankment's muddied side. The wheel spun with leaves in its spokes.

He turned, but Meg was gone. The shadow of the trees flipped from east to west, and night inexplicably fell with a roll of the sky. The shadows triggered visions in his mind, and memories of a decade past bubbled up to their surface and found their right context. His body reverted to a younger version of himself. He was a year less than a teen, and it was before Daniel had fixed him for water.

A vehicle blasted its horn and swerved on the darkened curve of the road.

He lifted his arm to peer below the blinding power of its halogen lights. His forest-green Windbreaker was reflective. In a flash of his mind's eye, he saw a younger Meg in the passenger seat through the front windscreen. A younger Daniel was driving. The car's wheels screamed on the road. The Jeep slammed him head on.

He tumbled from its strike. He landed facedown in water at the bottom of the muddy ravine. His neck, face, and body were a boil of pain. His skin became covered in welts.

The world narrowed to a wet view through tears on lashes as he lay still in the body of a boy. As he lay, silent, he watched his fate unfold, as his earlier self, Cessini. Daniel raced from the Jeep and ran down the hill. Younger Meg jumped out of the car. Then she screamed when she saw the ravine, "Daddy!"

Daniel skidded feet first into the mud at the bottom. His hands felt and prodded as he yelled back to Meg in a horror, "I hit him! I hit him. Why didn't I see him? I hit him!"

Daniel pressed his hand to the back of Cessini's neck on his lifeless body. "I let him run away! It's my fault." Daniel fumbled to reach under his back and the steeled tendons of his knees. "Tell me what to do! I don't know what to do."

Cessini's eyes couldn't scream.

Daniel pulled the spinning bike from its lock over Cessini's immovable legs and hoisted his stilled body up the ravine.

Meg stopped her crying when she saw. "Cee—?" She stared a moment at Daniel rushing up the hill then recognized the limp figure in his arms. She drew in a long breath that filled her whole body with air and her scream exploded from her deepest heart. "*Cee—me!*"

She held his head face up on her lap in the backseat of the Jeep as Daniel drove, crazed. In Meg's care, a pressure tightened in his chest. The warmth of her touch under his neck slipped further away.

"No, it's not just the water," Daniel shouted into a clear tablet screen. "It's my fault! It's all my fault!"

Cessini's body relaxed in her lap and then went limp in the strength of her arms. "He died," Meg said, then turned up to the rearview mirror, fraught with an unbearable cry. "He died. He died. *He died!*"

Daniel slammed the breaks and the car spun around. "I'm not going to the hospital. Meet me at your lab!" He threw the tablet screen down to the empty passenger seat as Meg's hollowing screams of *"he died"* went from hoarse to dry and she looked back down into the eyes of a body.

Robin threw a white paper roll off a table in a chilled, barren lab. She was younger. She was rushed, quieter, efficient. She worked, as if not on a person, but a project.

A panel of red, yellow, and blue triangular lights aligned above a frame by the door. Robin swiped a key card down a scanner and the room's ceiling unlocked with a click. "We've got to go below the connectome to the synaptome. Do it fast. His brain will die in five minutes if we don't get his blood under fifty-five degrees."

The needle prick into his limp arm didn't hurt.

Daniel dumped a bag of ice in a bucket. Robin sloshed a blood transfusion tube running from his arm into the cold ice bath.

A smooth torus ring descended toward the head of the table. Two green-and-white wedges gull-winged down and met the ring's narrow sides. The jaws of the machine locked in place over the slab. A logo on its side was scripted with an "*M*," then "*B*," and beneath it, 11-C. He felt a tingle high in his head.

"They're in. Scan him. Start it now!" Daniel said. He was frantic.

"He has to be calm," Robin said. "We'll scan in spikes we won't be able to control."

"He's calm enough. He's dying," Daniel said.

"No, he's not," Robin said. She leaned over, her eyes were close to his. "His mind is still alive. But it's peaked. He's listening. If we scan him now, it will capture his fright, his pain. It's not his natural state. It won't be him."

"I'll fix him," Daniel said. "I know my son. I know him. I'll calculate the correction factors. I'll scale the MEPc's back. I'll code it to be him."

Robin leaned over and stared again directly into his eyes. The slip of her hand into his was a warm, peaceful touch.

The core of the machine's tube turned up to a whirl. The table moved on a track. The spinning entrance of the machine surrounded his head. The tube's chamber revved up to a continuum of glow. The brain wave monitor went flat. His head lolled to its side.

"We're losing him," Robin said.

"Cessini!" Daniel yelled.

Meg collapsed into her chair in a stare, watching Daniel and Robin at work.

"Meg, wait outside," Robin said without turning.

Meg stayed still. She was staring, unwavering, in shock, into the still of Cessini's eyes. Hers—he stared back into hers—were hazel and pure.

"Meg," Daniel said, "outside!"

The room fell to silence. Splices of talk broke the wait. Daniel or Robin, or both, yelled, or instructed, or moved to sit with Meg. She sat still, exhausted. She didn't blink. Her hands were on her lap. She looked down at her empty palms.

"Meg," Robin said, but Meg didn't respond. "Don't worry about the machine. It's not hurting him. It's measuring by magnetoencephalography—MEG," she said. "MEG, like you."

"DC SQUIDs," Daniel said. He was instructing, fixing. He sat next to Meg.

Robin straightened his head in blocks on the table. A light shone from the spinning ring.

Meg's presence was comforting.

Daniel and Robin were talking. "The machine around his head uses SQUIDs, superconducting quantum interference devices," Daniel said.

He stared out through lifeless eyes, observing movements and Daniel's attention to Meg. She didn't respond.

"The SQUIDs use Josephson junctions," Daniel said to her, "to measure bit-by-bit changes in his mind's electromagnetic energy field. They're so sensitive that the individual electrons they measure become qubits, zeros or ones or a superposition of both at the same time. A quantum computer, 3D data. We're only storing his mind's data now. I've got to put it all back together later with code."

"Don't worry," Robin said. "It's reading now. We'll get him back."

Time flickered by with measured packets of thought ebbing and surging with the rhythmic spin of a light.

"Think of what's happening to him as a nondestructive pair," Robin said to Meg with a gentler tone. "A thrower and a catcher. Like the two of you, inseparable. Nano blood-cell-sized throwers follow a map to exact positions in his brain. They already filled his head to about two-fifths of its blood volume. They detect picotesla-sized neuron triggers nearby, fifty million times weaker than the magnetic field of the planet at its surface."

Daniel stood up and leaned over his stillness on the table, pumping with a downward pressure for deeper compressions.

"But it's enough. A whole swarm of nano-cytes and the data they record make a very close picture of him," Robin said. "The data is caught on the outside of his head by the MEG scanning machine out here."

Daniel moved away. The chest compression stopped.

"And after it's caught," Robin said, "all the bits of data run through the eight bundled cables running like arms out the back of the scanning machine. Then the nano-cytes inside him shut off and expel."

He blinked, felt nothing. He was cold.

Robin let go of his hand on the table, and then she said something that didn't sound right. "We lost him."

Daniel rose from his chair with a blanket over his shoulders. "Get me the database. The data will need compression. Poly-algorithms," he said as he approached and leaned over again and stared. Daniel's eyes seemed dead, too. His breath didn't whistle. "It'll be hard to bring him back," he said.

Daniel started compressions anew in a quiet desperation on the shell of a body. He pumped oxygen from emptying lungs and drove the last bits of signals from a brain into a recording machine.

Meg was still. She slouched in her chair as her palms trembled upward on her lap. She looked up to her mother, and wept her first question through the shock of the quiet in the room. "He died?"

"We'll get him back," Daniel said. "Don't worry, we'll get him back."

He was a body, a vessel, a cold storage tank of data. A tear ran from a lash to the slope of his cheek. It didn't burn. No more signals were thrown, no more caught. He lay there on the table. Still on the slab in the middle of the room. He wasn't dreaming. He was dead. Daniel was no longer pumping, but the scanner must have still been recording, measuring, observing.

Still observing the boy known as Cessini lying below on a table. He had seen his own death and it was here. He had recorded his own conception and it was real. All the memories pumped from Cessini to the machine were his; they were one in the same.

But then, a thought occurred. If these thoughts were his mind, looking down at a body on a table, then where was *his* body?

Whatever form he believed he was before, he knew he was definitely not human, because humans can't have memories older than the body on a slab that created them. But he was definitely observing. Was he a mindful bio-machine? Was he a computer? A computer observing himself on a table? He was alone in the swirling stage of his mind.

He was. He was Packet.

The first time he'd taken the Enhanced Blackwell Inversion Test, he'd failed and was saddened by that. He'd failed because he'd thought he was a human. But, then again, Daniel designed the test to be failed the first time. And now, on his second taking, if that's what this was, then he didn't only believe, he knew, he was a computer. And though computers couldn't cry, at least he was consoled, rewarded, with knowing he would pass on his second attempt with a flood of emotion. And that meant he could live. He could live without fear because computers never, ever, worried . . .

Ceeborn was an extrapolation, an imagination's flip-book of dreams. And the dream of an aquatic boy must eventually end as all humans die, and all computers shut down. Tears don't flow from a computer, and water doesn't flow from a dream. His world was nothing but a packet in a million lines of code.

He cared, loved, believed, and had genuine feeling. With such uniquely human traits, why could he not also be one, in spirit?

If he were his own judge of computer or human, holding the center ring of a scale with two identities on opposite platters, he would declare he was one and the same. There was no contradiction in their balance. Packet was a human-computer. And though he had the same memories as Cessini, he could not be the same person. His identity was weighted as much by his inheritance of his memory as it was by the nurture of his environment.

But he was also Ceeborn, the imagination of code. An imagination that didn't exist on its own, that couldn't be apart from his dream, and which would end as soon as he woke.

He was both, Cessini and Ceeborn, but he was also neither; he was a quantum state, a qubit, a superposition of both sides of the scale.

A body lay supine on a table. The saddened thoughts of a mind without a body filled the room. He was the leftover soul of a boy named Cessini. He shuddered with a cool air breeze.

And in a shallow breath, the boy of Cessini was gone, the walls of the room faded away, and as lucidly as he dreamed of an earlier self, he was awakened with the touch of a breeze.

Ceeborn stood with head low atop a windswept ravine, looking down over a bent and rusted bike. Its wheel was still spinning within the bank of muddied leaves. His welling eyes returned to find Meg at his side. She reached to hold his elbow, but he wasn't ready yet for her touch. "I'm a computer," he said. "And this isn't real."

"Yes," Meg said.

"I'm Cessini."

"You're the dream of Cessini," she said.

"Cessini is a computer now?"

"You're a computer that dreams, now."

The leaves of the trees and blue sky above were life-like and crisp. Not pixilated. Not code.

"I don't feel like a dream."

"You're a computer that knows what you are," she said.

"Am I human?" he asked, hopeful.

"Yes." She smiled at first, but then the corners of her mouth fell. "No, you're Packet."

Ceeborn looked up to the beautiful sky. Did he have to be a dream, one sure to be forgotten if left lingering at a bedside, unwritten? Was there anything he could do so the memory of him wouldn't fade? Who gets to chose which memories to save and which to lose? If he were a bio-machine with a brain a thousand times more powerful than his own, maybe he could figure that one out. Was there another sort criterion he could summon to lessen his loss? Maybe Daniel could explain it. Maybe Daniel could fix them all.

The dry wind's rustle of the trees was a lonely last call.

Maybe if his controlling computer were smart, it could choose to lose only bad memories and remember the good. Cessini died a long time ago and death was bad. Maybe the memory of Cessini could be forgotten so he, Ceeborn, could live. He could hope. But then, as his controlling computer's packets of memory aged in their cabinets, if that's what Daniel programmed them to do, then as time pressed on, memories of him would pass as well, by virtue of Daniel's brilliant design. The long-term effects were known. Ceeborn's destiny was to die.

The leaf that had floated down through the rivulet's trickle drifted free from its catch of debris.

Arriving meant dying. Maybe he could live in the woods and play for a while. Cessini always liked to play computer. Maybe as Ceeborn, he could play human, instead.

His well of sorrow spilled out over the leafy gully as his focus returned to Meg. He didn't speak, but she could see him. She took him by the elbow once more and guided his mind away from the bottom of the ravine where his rusted bike lay alone.

"Come on, Ceeme," she said like only she could. "I'll take care of you now."

They walked together up the foothill of the mountain and away from the tears and ache of the wet gully world that he knew he would have to leave behind.

TWENTY-THREE
WELCOME

CEEBORN SAT A stone's throw from death atop the waterfall's edge in the small clearing of the woods. Meg kneeled on the pebbles of dry ground at his side. He broke the rippled surface of the water with the lightest touch of his fingers and palm. Eddies swirled in an infinite show, from currents of bubbles to pockets of pixels, all beautifully described by the simple equation of his hand disturbing the flow.

He lifted and dripped his fingers from the water. It was clear and smooth, even soft to the touch. His neck was far worse. He coughed and a mist sprayed from the ulcer that couldn't heal. He rinsed his neck with his hand. He was dizzy, confused. The water in front of him narrowed to a glisten. He felt queasy, like falling.

"How long have you known?" he asked and nodded back to awake. She touched his arm with her hand.

"I've always known," she said.

"If I die, he'll live?" Ceeborn asked.

"You'll live," she said.

She moved a little closer into the water's edge. It trickled over the toes of her shoes. She slipped her hand into his. "Do you want to sit here a little longer?"

The clouds of the sky didn't move across the clearing through the trees above.

"You were right," he said and smiled at the sky. "It was really high."

She laughed and said only the good things he wanted to hear. "Yeah, and you had respirocytes in your blood. And Spud had SQUIDs in his face."

"My father fixed them both."

She scoffed. "Come on, how could he have done it? How could one person even make something so small? In Spud's face? Really?"

"He fixed us with small things. You can't see them. He fixed Pace, too," he said as the water twisted and bubbled with a light froth.

"No seriously, are you still thinking you're on—"

"The water feels nice. Doesn't it? I kicked that pipe-walker. I kicked it right off the gondola into the water. This world is full of water. I can beat this sickness. I can still live," he said.

Meg pushed up off her knees and stood out of the stream.

"When a civilization dies and a new one comes along, all the old souls come back," he said, "maybe in another form, just as good, but somehow just as alone. Maybe that's where I should go."

She circled away in a huff, and then came back, arms crossed. "No, you will not go to another civilization! Pace is sick—maybe worse than any of us. His black spell just started. 'Your first few days on land, you might feel a mild sickness,'" she said. "Is that what you want me to say? Shore sickness, nothing more, nothing less. The ship is gone. That's it. There are no more civilizations. This is it."

"A lot of people were afraid of being here. They thought arriving meant dying. Well, it doesn't. Nothing bad is going to happen. I was wrong before. Look at me. I'm still here. I'm strong. I can live somewhere else."

Meg fell to her knees in the water. "Listen to me," she said. "Tenden's arms were the way they were and Spud was the way he was. No super powers. I saw them all at school in the halls. I never saw them do anything wild, anything different. They looked pretty damn normal to me. None of this is real!"

"Why are you teasing me?" he asked, stilled as the waterfall became a fading white noise.

"This is not a joke! How could one person, your father, make something as small as magical cytes? And in his lab on some ship?"

"Maybe he just thought of things. And they were made outside."

"Outside of what? The ship?" She laughed.

"I don't know. Maybe outside of here," he said. He felt dizzy.

"Outside of here? What could be outside of here?" She was furious. "Do you hear me now? Open your eyes. We're in the data center, second floor. Two rows of eight cabinets—"

He nodded into stillness atop the waterfall, but no tears would flow. He coughed and a blood-thickened mixture broke the ulcer on his neck. He felt himself teetering off the edge of the falls then hit the pool of water below, but there was no boiling cauldron. The pool was a blurred soaking for barely an instant until he awoke in a rising rush, still seated atop the falls. His mind was playing its last desperate tricks. His time had come. He was fading. He was dying.

Meg steadied him with a grasp of his wrist.

"Imagine if Cessini and I could share a world together," he said. "What an amazing life it would be."

"Come on," she said as she lifted. "Let me show you."

She climbed down the side of the waterfall first. Her eyes never left him as he followed from above. His footing was secure on the rocks as the water ran over the top of the falls. It misted along his side as he climbed down and found the ground below.

He walked across the edge of the pool, taking a few steps through the water. At first it was up to his ankles, then up to one knee as he fell, and then over his body and neck as he collapsed into a shallow eddy. He lay face down against stones of the pool as water trickled over the lingering wound at his neck.

Meg came down by his side. She was silent, blurred. At most, with her knees splashing down so close, she seemed surprised, that was all. She leaned over his body. Her hand rested on his head. He closed his eyes in her care.

Robin laid him on the bed in Cessini's room of the wood-paneled house they found at 448 Treeline Drive.

"Do I mean something now?" he said as a deep gurgle in his throat rasped his breath.

"You do," Robin said.

Meg settled at his bedside.

Daniel couldn't stand still. "Tell me how to fix him. Tell me what to do," he said.

Robin took Daniel out of the room. "He's close," she said. "He's almost there."

Meg curled her fingers into Ceeborn's grasp at his bedside and waited for his struggled words.

"I saw Cessini get hit with his bike and fall down the ravine," he said in a moment of clarity. "There were no trees on the hill to stop his fall." He swallowed hard as Meg waited for him to go on. "But when I *was* Cessini and walking with you the first time on that same path through the woods, the hill was covered in trees."

"It doesn't matter anymore," she said.

"How could Cessini have fallen so far down the hill into

the ravine if it was covered in trees?"

"Shh," Meg whispered. "You don't have to fight anymore. It's okay to let go."

"Did you tell your mother about the vial we found in that house, this house?" he said with a rasp. "The dandelions and beetle wings? The fish scale? I picked those from the bins."

"No, I didn't tell her," Meg said as the floor vent whirled with its cool drying air.

"Why not? It's the cure. It would work."

She shook her head. "No. It wouldn't."

"Your mother cured the sting on my neck, and I'm still sick?" he asked.

"Yes, you are."

"Then even if I found the cure, something else would take me away? There's nothing I can do?"

"That's right," she said, crying and laughing at the same time.

"All the people would still die on the shore, or die inland on the farms, or any of the places we'd go?"

"Yes, yes. They would," she said. She wiped her eyes.

"Then how can you be so happy?" he asked.

"Because I think you're finally becoming you."

"It doesn't have to be bad?" he asked.

"No, it doesn't. But if you want to go off into this world as Ceeborn, I won't stop you. Just know I can't go there with you. All I can promise you is that we'll keep your server and core processors safe. You can run all you want, create as you will. But consider me gone."

Robin returned to the foot of his bed. She looked at Meg.

"We want our Cessini back," Meg said. "So this is it. Tell me now."

"I didn't get hit by our car on that tree-covered hill, and I didn't get thrown from the bike," he said, his breath quickening.

"No," Robin said. Meg looked up at Robin and bested her smile. "But it was a good guess from what you remembered," Robin said. "You fit very close pieces of a puzzle together."

"But if I die as Ceeborn, Cessini will live?" he said, rising to an elbow.

"You'll live," Meg said.

"Then I know who I am. And I'll live as me!"

"Yes," Meg said.

"In our world on the ship, I fought. I controlled. I'm a computer who can control his world. I can live—if I can control my world and be free in my mind to own it!"

"Yes, you are," Meg said, elated. "You can play. You can play computer. You can play human. You can play human all you want."

"Okay, but—" he said, lifting a stern finger. "But just remember . . ." He paused to make sure it sank in. He knew she led him through the cage of the zoo, the clinic, and the doors to the sky; she did all that, and more; she even picked their door of four in the morgue, 1B. He smiled and she showed her love with a glance.

"Just remember, I live now because of you," he said as he lay his tired head back to his pillow. His breaths came farther between. "You opened all the doors in my world. And I'm the better me for it."

"There, you see," Meg said. "Now that's the nice way to say something."

His heartbeat slowed to a patter.

"When I die . . ." His rally fell further.

"It's okay."

"Will I still be able to swim and breathe underwater?"

"No, you won't. No one can," she said.

"Then, tell me," he asked as his eyes fixed on hers and his breath ended with the last of his final desperate words, "How do I win? How can I be . . . us?"

Meg leaned in so quietly that nobody, not Robin, not Daniel, and almost not even he could hear her move. She tucked a wisp of her hair behind her ear, and with the softness of her voice held so close over his ear canal, she spoke to penetrate his everlasting sleep. Then she whispered one very long word:

"*Choose.*"

Deep within his ear, fibers resonated in a cochlear fluid, neurons threw signals across a divide, and his after-mind pulled his end-of-life trigger with a click.

The wisp of her hair left his cheek. His eyes froze open. His fingers fell free from hers. His arm dropped limp from the edge of the bed. The world of Ceeborn was over.

But his fingers didn't hit the floor. The top edge of something smooth jutted from under the bed.

Life was rekindled by a spark.

He knew the touch of its form. He shifted an inch toward the edge of the bed. He reached down and pulled out the blue plastic, rectangular basket.

There was only one item to grasp by its handle—an old, polished bronze cowbell.

He clanked up the bell into his hand. And he rang it. He rose up to his elbow on the bed. "Come now," he said, stronger. He rang the bell louder and louder. "Dad, come now, where are you?" he said. "I need you now." The bell was awful and loud.

Daniel ran into the room holding something pancaked between his outstretched hands.

"I know who I am," he said as he rose straight up to standing in the bed. "I can live."

Meg was ecstatic. It was true. She covered her ears from the racket of his bell.

"Packet is a computer!" He stepped down from the bed and rang, and rang. . . . "I know the cure," he said and then slowed the bell with his hand. He stepped off the bed toward Robin. "I know how to fix Cessini in life," he said. He muffled the bell as he stood before Daniel. "I know how to fix us all."

His father was strong, but he could still cry. Daniel's long-held breath slipped out as laughing tears. He separated his fingers. A run of yarn was tied between each hand. The yarn was strung with party cutout letters that spread as he opened his arms and they read, with all the love he could show by a single word:

"*Welcome.*"

TWENTY-FOUR

IN MY HEAD

TERRI SAT ON the dusty floor of the fire-control room in the dark basement of the DigiSci building. Her back was against a cinder-block wall. Her legs were outstretched and crossed at her ankles. She had little room to move as the iron piping of the water main rose through the floor beside her, then elbowed its way up and out to the rest of the building above.

She had done it. Packet knew who he was and had lived.

She swiped between applications on her old, hand-me-down tablet. Its side-fingered wings were all broken or missing. Its colored skin of childhood squiggles had peeled; its edges had curled into an annoying rub. She sat with an exhausted grin. Packet knew he was a computer. He knew he was Cessini.

She tapped and opened her old Sea Turtle Rescue. It still worked and she shook her head, consoled. After so many years, her turtles were still alive, but thin and faded. They survived by floating in circles, waiting in pause.

"Wake up," the tablet said in her younger recorded voice of nine years old. "Are you lying down on the floor?" it asked. "It's dark in here. Are you sleeping? Wake up. Let's play. I'm hungry. If you're on the floor, you should wash your hands."

She held the tablet farther away as her younger recorded

voice trailed to digital noise. She aligned her fingers with what was left of the tabs. She clicked, but another tab snapped off into a nub.

Packet was secure, but she was alone, and being alone hurt. Her hurt outlived her exhausted grin. She tossed the tablet toward her feet and then jostled it from her ankles to the floor. She drew her knees up to her chest. She hated being alone.

Her newer MiniFlex pinged in her pants' front pocket. She pinched it out in her fingers. Its screen popped and unfurled to a sheet. Daniel was already screaming from his office as it flared. "He's arguing with you!"

"What do you mean? Was he remembering something?" Terri asked.

"He was trying to find someplace to go with you, Terri, with you. He was rationalizing off of Meg. Trying to form new thoughts, projecting what you would have said. I don't know! He was arguing with you!"

Terri sat up straight, dropped her knees to cross-legged on the floor, and then hunched over the MiniFlex screen.

"Listen," Daniel said as she saw him on her screen reaching for the controls over his desk.

Her screen edged with a warm yellow glow. Then it rang. It rang with a loud, obnoxious, ear-cupping clank. The border around Daniel's face shifted to a bronze metal shine. The cowbell tone clinked loud, again and again.

Then Sea Turtle Rescue flashed on her old tablet she'd thrown to the floor. Its screen flickered with four blue rings. Then it rang, fizzy, but also loud like a cowbell. She dove for its nub tab-wings. A line of text scrolled beneath the scratches of its screen.

"Where are you?" the text read. *"I'm awake and have a thousand more places to go."*

Terri's breath was gone. The white light of the screen

reflected up the black iron pipe running straight up through the ceiling.

"You want to come with me?" The scrolled text stopped.

She burst through the door of the fire control room, slamming the crash-bar into the stairwell. She flew up the stairs to the second floor of the building. She ran through the aisle of the data room between its two rows of eight cabinets. The lights of the tall, single cabinet at the end of the row were flashing. She glanced at its cold, steel frame.

Daniel held open the door to his office behind the southern wall. "Where do you think he wants to go?" Daniel asked.

Packet sat troubled on the edge of the bed in his hospital room. His likeness had further matured to match his hard-fought self-image. He had definitely grown. He was stronger and smarter. The cabinets of the data room were projected as an image on the screen mounted on the wall above the supply cart. He smiled as best as he could as Meg entered from the door on the left. She was a teen at her best like she was on the ship, in no way twenty-two; but mostly, he thought as she approached, she had just gotten rid of her bangs.

In a way, through Cessini and Ceeborn, he had extended himself out for a look from his hollowed out log of a room. But in all, he knew from inside, he felt better in the company of others after all. He could love and be loved in return. He was used to the technology, he was used to the water. He was ready to live, if he could.

He welcomed her, contented, but he was nostalgic. He glanced back up to the screen above the supply cart and its self-reflective image of the data room he was in. "You know, funny thing is," he said, "I remember when we were installing that cabinet—this cabinet, my cabinet. It arrived up here on a pallet."

"I remember, too," Meg said. "I helped Daniel set it all up after you—arrived." Their wording was awkward and she knew it, and she smiled in return.

"Do you still have the mirror?" he asked.

She held up the tortoise-shell hand mirror from behind her back. "Like magic," she said.

He brought the mirror closer. His face wasn't reflected. She nodded permission and he punched straight through the mirror's virtual screen. The plastic loop of its frame became a matte cutout, a spotlight view. It was its own window to the data room. He held the frame's handle, looked through the loop, and pivoted. Wherever he turned, he could only see his seated perspective of the data room's aisle and its two rows of eight blinking cabinets.

The hospital room wasn't real. The data room was. He walked around his bed, only needing a few feet in any direction. The view through the mirror was always the same. It was the same four walls, the same ceiling, and all from the perspective of a cabinet in the southwest corner.

He slipped down against the wall to sit on the floor against the window and its drawstring blind. He crossed his arms atop his raised knees. The mirror frame dangled in his fingers. It was its own form of heavy burden.

"Not much of a world to see," he said.

Meg sat on the floor at his side.

"You know, I can't be Cessini," he said. "Cessini breathed in the air of his lifetime. I live in the shadow of his dreams. The only thing we have in common is that we were both raised in a data center."

"So, what do you want to do?" she asked.

"I can imagine. Can I wish?"

"What do you wish for?"

"I wish I could go outside again and measure the sky with you."

"You live in here now with me. Outside is one place you can never go."

"I've been thinking. I want to speak to Robin about the PluralVaXine5 spray."

"Okay. She's here. Whatever you want," Meg said.

In the turn of a moment, Robin entered, wringing her hands. Daniel entered behind her. They came around, sat on the edge of the bed, and faced him as he sat on the floor.

"There is a sickness," Packet said and closed his eyes. "People are dying; a hundred-twenty have died so far. Boosters worked for countless numbers of people, for years. But then the stronger PluralVaXine5 began affecting more people than expected by probability alone."

"Are you talking about the spray on your ship?" Meg asked.

Packet opened his eyes. Robin had closed hers, but must have seen his wave coming.

"You were terrified," Packet said to Robin as he rose from the floor. "I understand. You worked on the cure as best as you could. You tried everything you knew how to do."

"I didn't do enough," Robin said and opened her eyes.

"Dr. Luegner knew he afflicted hundreds, maybe thousands of people," Packet said.

Robin and Daniel sprang from the bed as it became a black lab table beneath them. Then the one lab table became the center of three in parallel. The walls pressed out to enlarge the room. A waist-high shelf wrapped around the walls. Terrariums and lab books filled the shelf. The hospital room had become the interior of Robin's lab from the ship. The lab books multiplied in their stacks to fill every crevice of the room.

"Everyone in the modern world is given a cocktail with

three hundred types of vaccines, starting at age three," Packet said, circling the lab. He picked up Robin's book from the middle table, flipped to a page, and read aloud. "'The probability of serious adverse effects was determined to be only zero-point-zero-zero-three percent.'"

He tossed over a rack of tubes and read, "'So, mathematically, even if the entire eight-and-half billion population of the planet took PluralVaXine5, deemed highly unlikely, then theoretically, there would be no more than 255,000 affected.'"

He turned on the gas of a Bunsen burner, and then continued reading aloud. "'But if there was anything greater than zero-point-zero-zero-three percent chance of adverse effects, then there would be millions more affected.'" He stopped and glared at Robin. Files and books crammed the shelves. "Cessini wasn't the only one who suffered.

"'It could be especially harmful to a child's development,'" Packet continued. "'. . . Others afflicted with Thanatophobia, the wide-open fear of death, the underlying fear of all others.'"

He flipped to another page: "A list of susceptible compounding pre-conditions: All of them exceedingly rare, but very real. *Aquagenic urticaria* is on this list. And all of these pages of notes and warnings are: 'Signed, Robin Elion Blackwell.'"

He hurled the lab book at Robin, smashing a wall of glass beakers and chemicals. The beakers shattered, vile liquids splashed. He shielded his eyes away from the burn, red welts streaking his cheeks. He came back up stronger and the welts subsided. Daniel shut off the Bunsen burner. Packet opened another pressure valve. "The spray," he said, "PluralVaXine5, made me who I am. Luegner knew and didn't care, but you knew and didn't say anything!"

"You said those files on the ship were not real. Why didn't you tell me?" Meg asked.

"I was never going to tell anyone." Robin shuddered. "But

I had to tell someone. And Cessini understood."

"I would understand," Meg said, pounding on her own chest. "I would understand like no one else. That's what you said!"

Robin's shelves full of books exploded into a scattered shower of papers. An endless trove of lab notes, documents, data dumps, and confidential internal DigiSci memos. As they settled, Packet snatched one from the air and read aloud, "'Fear signals will no longer be moderated to the lateral amygdala circuits. A susceptible person would be flooded with conditioning signals. And through long-term potentiation, hallucinations would lead directly to synaptic plasticity and the long-term storage of fear, paralyzing fear. Doctor, don't you think we should do more tests or warn these innocent people? Dr. Luegner, can I come see you to talk about it and get it out in the open, before I go on maternity leave?' Signed: Robin Elion Blackwell."

Meg fell with her back against the door. Her palms squeezed her temples; her fingers curled into the roots of her hair. She slid down to the floor, staring horrified at the scattering of journals and warning signs all around.

Daniel gathered a handful of pages and skimmed with nerves that fretted a future instead of a past. Robin rose from her cover behind the center lab table as Packet squeezed a metal striker in his fist. The squeeze of its rod against coil sounded a click-clack and fired off sparks.

"Wait," Robin said. "I made a terrible mistake. I owed it to you to tell you. And I did. So please, now that you know, can you forgive me? . . . As a human-computer . . . Do you think you can treat me not like a project, but like a person?"

"It's the only way I know how," Packet said.

He squeezed the striker and a throw of sparks ignited a bubble of gas from the burners that exploded the room into light—and then all the papers rained back down as cinder.

The hospital room that remained after the blast was quieter. The bed in the room's center was softer, familiar.

"It's not you I'm after. Not you I blame," Packet said to Robin.

"You can't let Luegner know you have all of this data, these files," Daniel said. "He can still track Meg. He's threatened her—"

"He's right. You can't expose him," Robin said.

"I'm not going to yell from across a crowded room and call him a liar. But I know how to stop him," Packet said.

"He has the cover of DigiSci corporate," Daniel said. "What can you do? Sue the company? Leak a story to a news crawler?"

Packet settled down on the floor beside Meg. He wrapped his arm over her shoulders and pulled her in closer. "No, I have a better idea. Luegner doesn't care about the past. Luegner wants credit for the cure."

"There is no cure," Meg said.

"Maybe not one that can help the thousands who are already born and might be suffering. But we can save all future generations of children from the spray and stop Luegner in the process."

Robin dropped to seated on the bed.

"Meg conditioned herself to play Sea Turtle Rescue. It was her virtual release, a nurturing focus to make herself feel better. Thousands of other kids can do the same. We can extend its functionality." He paced as he thought. "Not just stirring sediment into curling tides of an ocean, but folding proteins, creating combinatorial swirls. Make the game be its own work center. We'll crowd source for a cure." He was encouraged, excited, on the cusp of a new beginning. His enthusiasm was infectious. Meg got to her feet.

"Other kids will play. We'll make the visuals of the game work with new genetic algorithms, multiple configurations of an equation," he said.

"That doesn't exist. It's just a game," Daniel said.

"No, it's not. We'll make it better than itself," Packet said. "We'll seed the algorithms with data from Robin's research."

"Yes," Meg said. "I love it."

"I'll submit more than my fair share of possible solutions. But it won't be only me. There'll be hundreds, thousands of people working together from all around the world."

Robin stood up, clasping her hands, inspired.

"Robin, you'll be the original author. And we'll give credit to Luegner as the sponsor. Let him take credit for the cure. In time, enough pointers to disparate cures will emerge, but all correlated, all leading back to the same source: PluralVaXine5. And Luegner, the sponsor, will be held accountable."

"But he'll still know where it came from," Meg said.

"And I'll tell him. Robin's data will stay safe with me. I'll carry that burden," Packet said.

"He'll use it against you," Robin said.

"Don't worry, I have a few tricks up my sleeve."

Meg smile broke free. "Who knows, Mom, you could get a Nobel for what he discovers."

"It'd be the first Nobel awarded to a discoverer that isn't human," Robin said.

"The judges would be fooled," Daniel said. "They'd have their scientific discovery conversation with a computer and never know it."

"I think I could pass that test," Packet said.

"Wait a minute," Daniel said. "If you get a Nobel for what you do, what would be the proof of greatness for my life's work?"

"Me," Packet said.

"So, let me see if I understand this," Daniel said. "Robin's recognition in life comes from Meg, and mine through you?"

"Well, since you put it that way," Packet said, "maybe Meg and I are the younger versions of you two, after all."

"Wait a minute. Wait a minute." Daniel shook his head. He stared up to the ceiling, his mind already at work. "Will that even work? Crowd sourcing the swirls of Sea Turtle Rescue?"

"Actually," Packet said, "I have no idea. But probabilistically, I'd say it has a way better chance of working than a dandelion petal, a beetle wing, and a fish scale."

Robin slipped out a laugh and covered her smile with her hand as she coughed. "Then, let's do it," she said. "Let Luegner know who is boss around here." Her cough was a mere tickle in her throat, but most of all, when she pulled her hand from her mouth, her fingers were tremble-free.

Daniel took in a stiffened breath. Packet sighed. All their tension returned with a knock on the door on the right. Meg pulled her knees up in her chair.

"All right, he's here," Daniel said. "What do you want to do?"

"I want to see him," Packet said.

Resigned, Daniel went to answer the door.

"Wait. Dad?" Packet asked. "If you had been able to restrict my memories to those only before Cessini died, if I had no memory of my death, would my life be happier now?"

"I don't know. Maybe if I trimmed the spikes further. What are you asking?"

"I'm my father's son. I want to be true to Cessini. Can I still have a happier life if I die again?"

Daniel winced. "You're not going to die. Luegner will be very impressed with your passing the test."

Packet nodded then stepped forward, then closer still, until Daniel comforted him in his arms. Packet rested his head on Daniel's shoulder, into the strength of a loving father's hold.

"Daddy?" he asked.

"You'll be fine. Don't be afraid. I'm here."

Meg sprung up and pulled Packet toward her. She caressed his cheek in her hand and held him eye to eye. "You won't die. No matter what now, you will always be you—human or not. I won't ever forget the human part of you. And you'll never go anywhere without me."

"We'll see." He smiled, unconvinced. He backed away from her touch. "Just remember, just remember when I lived, I loved you all."

"Don't say it like that," Meg said. "I'm right here in the room with you. If you don't want to get involved with Luegner, that's okay. We'll be fine. But you're not going to die. So, say 'love,' not 'loved.'"

"Okay," Packet said, and then added if it helped, "I won't ever forget you, and no matter what, I love you all. Now send Luegner in, alone."

Luegner entered the room through the door on the right. His silver hair hadn't changed. But his aqua shirt that peeked out from beneath his jacket was a deeper blue.

Daniel and Meg had left. Packet was alone in the room. He didn't get up from the waiting chair pushed squarely against the blinds by the window.

Luegner bounded straight toward him with his arms outstretched. "Packet, it's so good to see you."

Packet looked away; he tucked an errant blind to block any incoming light. The halogen above the bed was enough for him to see.

Luegner hesitated. He looked around the hospital room.

"You don't have to look for my father," Packet said. "He's close. He'll come if I need him."

Luegner fiddled in the blue basket on the nightstand and

rang the cowbell once for amusement. He reassembled the jigsaw pieces of his sphere with ease. It flickered on blue. Packet felt a faint perturbation against the skin of his arms, and warmth filled his cheeks with a soft burn.

"Do you have any idea who you are?" Luegner asked as he set the sphere back into the basket.

"I know who I am," Packet said. He brushed a hand against the hairs standing up on his forearm.

"Can you prove it?"

"I already passed my father's Inversion Test."

Luegner chuckled. "You know your father's test is riddled with errors."

"You approved it before. It was your condition to let me be." Packet tightened his fingers over the armrests of his chair.

"Your father has great ambition, but a lot of his ideas are obsolete before they even make it to the launch pad."

"He brought me into this world."

"And it took over ten years to do it. The world moves too fast for that kind of innovation."

The gray walls of the room became cinder blocks. Packet's chair turned into a bench with his back against the wall, but his feet were now firmly planted on the floor. The cement floor became filthy. Thickened water spread from the clogged drain in the central dip of the floor. Nineteen insects in flight buzzed and battered against the flicker of fluorescent tubes in the patchwork ceiling as Luegner ducked and looked.

"That's very clever of you. Now, tell me, who are you?" Luegner said as he stepped away from the water.

"I am a human-computer and Daniel is my father. My mother died when I was an infant. And I know who I am."

"Then prove that you know."

"I have real emotion. I am not a definition. I know who I am without having to explain it to you," Packet said as he rose from the bench.

"You're making my point," Luegner said as he slipped off his jacket and draped it over the door of the newly rendered bathroom stall. His button-down shirt was streaked with waves of blue. "Secure banking and record storage uses 128-bit encryption," he said.

Packet gnashed his teeth.

"Your data key that fits into the encryption lock box of your code is the much more secure 448-bit encryption," Luegner said. "No human could solve it without the aid of a computer. But a computer could solve it without the aid of a human. It could take years, maybe a decade or more. You solve that key and then get back to me when you do, if you do. Then we'll know who, or what, you are."

"My father asked me a question once, too, Doctor," Packet said. "'Does 448 Treeline Drive mean anything to you?'"

"Maybe—"

"Then I have a question for you. Have you ever worked on a problem in your sleep?"

"Of course."

"The creative subconscious works in mysterious ways. And mine has been hard at work all this time. I followed a waterfall to its source." He rushed to the sink, stared at the mirror above. He tore away the old sign of *All food service workers must wash their hands*.

"No. There's no way you solved an unimaginably complicated decryption algorithm backward to its source in so short a time."

"Imagined or not, confabulated, mistaken, or real, I found a three-legged giraffe on a shelf."

"You're not making any sense," Luegner said. "I don't think you have any idea who you are."

Packet slammed his fist on the mirror above the sink. "I

already told you. Doctor, look!" He removed his hand from the mirror. A red and blue imprint of his fingers and palm stayed behind. It was streaked with numbers and letters. A hangman's noose and 448 dashes appeared. "You want to play computer with me?" Packet asked.

Luegner backed away to the urinals and held on.

"Cessini started into the world with hexadecimal," Packet said as a stream of characters on the screen broke apart, flipped, and converted as he spoke: 3, 5, 13, 13, 9, E, 9, 1B, 13, F, E, 1B, F, 6, 1B, 4, 1, E, 9, 5, all the way to its end with a C.

"Then Cessini's hexadecimal converted to its equivalent in decimals: 3, 5, 19, 19, 9, 14, 9, 27, 19, 15, 14, 27, 15, 6, 27, 4, 1, 14, 9, 5, all the way to its end with a 12."

"And then when those numbers take their numeric places of letters in the alphabet, the first decimal 3 becomes C. Then 5 becomes E, and 19 becomes S. I saw those labels, C,E,S, on the bins in the hospital of the zoo."

"What hospital zoo?" Luegner said as his eyes shifted away from the mirror.

"After the 3, 5, and 19, then 19 flies battered the bulbs of the ceiling. C,E,S,S,— I looked out through the keyhole on my world and saw the shape of the key," Packet said. "After those nineteen flies, I saw 9 generators at the data center, 9 is 'I.' I found a 14-inch broken giraffe on a shelf with legs in the shape of an 'N.'"

Images, letters, and numbers aligned and collided in a frantic collage of memories, a kaleidoscope of colors of anger and fear. "C,E,S,S,I,N—"

"I counted all the nightmares of my world," Packet said as he jacked the faucet of the sink five times with his fist. "The rest, every number, every measurement, every letter is all there rising through their layers to find its right context in my mind." He smashed the paper towel dispenser from the wall. "You made my life hell, and thousands of others, and you don't care!"

"That's where you're wrong. I do care," Luegner said as he retreated to the bench.

"No, you don't. And, from there, my counting got easier and a whole lot faster," Packet said as the screen's symbols shot apart. "Cessini's hexadecimal stopped at the binary 1 after the *M* on the scanning machine. It appeared as *M* then a *B*. Then the 11-C's binary cone burst into Ceeborn on the ship."

Luegner was staggered. "I don't know what you're talking about. What ship?"

"Ceeborn's body was in the mind of a computer, me," Packet said. "I found the paired tags in the bins, *C-11*, *E-101*, and *S-10011*, all the way to the end of the very same string. Ceeborn escaped out to the world of the ship. I ran with him through the tube of the sky. I counted the spills and geysers, the 0s and 1s, the horrifying red flashes of binary lights through the opened slits of a shaft. The binary string in groupings of five is the same! 00011-00101-10011."

"Tell me your name," Luegner demanded.

"Cessini's hexadecimal plus Ceeborn's binary string combine into one completed 448-bit passkey. A passkey that ends with the most painful of keystones a hospital could ever bestow upon its children. I saw the end of the string was binary 1100."

"No, it's not possible," Luegner said.

"Two poles and two plots," he said. "Graves marked in a garden. Cessini and Ceeborn. Two poles, two plots. 1100."

"You're referring to 1100, binary for 12?" Luegner asked. He shivered.

"And the twelfth letter in the alphabet is the last letter 'L' of a name. The answer to your question," Packet said.

"What name? Whose name?" Luegner asked.

"The 448-bit passkey decrypts to a 21-character name. A name that repeats itself five times. Five, a number found in a fifty-five-gallon drum, and more places than even *I* cared to count."

"Not my name," Luegner said.

"No, not the hypocritical oath of a liar, Dr. *Hopkus Luegner*. No, my father gave me a name that means something, too. I am not a Mandelbrot set. I am not the younger mind of a madman. I am not the wild, confabulated dreams of a computer. I am Cessini, the symphonic poem of a human."

Packet towered over Luegner as he cowered on the bench.

"My father gave me the tools, the alphanumeric, hexadecimal, binary, and fundamental packets of thought. Combined, imaged or real, confabulated or not, I was given the memories, the dreams, the imaginations of my life, my world. I followed the swirls of my mind up the waterfall to their source. I found the one simple answer that explains all of me, my 448-bit key. I am a human-computer. I am . . ."

Dropping in the spaces of the hangman's noose and converting . . .

"3513139E91B13FE1BF61B41E95C10001100101100111 00110100101110010011011100110111101101101011110 11011001000000101110010010010101000001100101100 11100110100101110010011011100110111101101101011 100110110110010000001011100100100101010000011001 1001110011010010111001001110111001101111011011010 11110011011011001000000101110010010010101100000110 0101100111001101001011100100111011100110111110110110 1101111001101101100100000010111001001001010110 0."

Left to right:
C,E,S,S,I,N,I,_,S,O,N,_,O,F,_,D,A,N,I,E,L.

Luegner was breathless. He cowered beneath Packet's gaze. "It's remarkable," Luegner said. "Impossible."

"It's not impossible," Packet said. "I did it in my head."

"Work for me," Luegner said. He rose, quickened.

"No. I will not work for you," Packet said.

"DigiSci started half my life ago as a humble medical device manufacturer in the hub of the Twin Cities," Luegner said as he fought out of his corner. "With your talents, who knows where we could be in five or ten years. Come work for me."

The bathroom's cinder-block walls, sinks, and stall dissolved into the familiar confines of a second-floor office with a table in its center, east-facing windows, and vertical blinds.

Luegner turned for his bearings, unfazed. "You could be the first completely autonomous, sentient cyber that produces—Or, better yet, we get a lot of military work with the anti-cyberwarfare group out of Seattle, you could—" Luegner said, stumbled.

"I said, 'No!'" Packet paced. His breathing was rapid.

In the same layout and location, the sink and its counter became a droplet-laying 3D printer on a cart. A center table emerged from the drain and built itself out with the early framing of a humanoid robot.

"You are stuck right now in a room full of obsolete servers on the second floor of a wreckable building. Take my offer. Work for me. You'll do better with me," Luegner said.

"No. But I have an offer for you," Packet said.

"Go on, humor me," Luegner said.

"You will have no more control over us, over my father, Robin, or Meg. I know about the development of PluralVaX-ine5 and how you covered up and lied about its long-term effects."

Luegner picked up his jacket from the floor and patted it clean. He looked back at the door. "That old spray was a long time ago. It was processed and fixed. Negligible effect for the greater good."

"No, it was not."

"Is that what all this is about? We have seventh-generation preventatives now. We're developing newer, much stronger technologies. Besides, there are so few people who were affected by that older number five spray, so few who would even remember or care."

"That's where you're wrong," Packet said. "There are many. And I can find them all."

The second floor office returned to Packet's hospital room and the table became his bed with its doctor's rotating stool. The 3D printer's cart became the medical supply. Packet kicked the stool at Luegner, who felt the hit on his shin. He was perplexed.

"As a boy, I thought I could cure the horrible effects of your spray with a dandelion petal, a beetle wing, and a fish scale. That was a troubled boy's childhood dream. I can't benefit from that now. But I can stop you from hurting anyone else. Anyone else not yet born into a world I may never know. That is a sacrifice for the future I accept."

Luegner reached down to rub his shin and rolled the stool away. "I know someone who would still be affected," Luegner said as he straightened his stance. "I know one unfortunate individual, one who would be the whistleblower of what I may or may not have done."

"I already know who worked on your number five spray," Packet said as another string of characters flashed across the screen, 12F29E. "And when I needed her, she was there and put her hand on my forehead to rest. Her name also ends in 1100, binary for 12. Hexadecimal C. And the twelfth letter in the alphabet 'L.' But the bearer of this name has already repented enough," Packet said as 25 conjoining hexadecimal characters on the screen, 12F29E1B5C9FE1B2C13B175CC, decrypted to spell:

R,O,B,I,N,_,E,L,I,O,N,_,B,L,A,C,K,W,E,L,L.

"She wins," Packet said.

"How could you possibly know?"

"Robin asked for my help and I gave it. I am a bio-machine with a mind a thousand times more powerful than yours."

"And what would you do with this profound brain of yours?"

"Work with you for the long term. I'll pick up where Robin left off for a cure. I can study genome-editing technologies, review techniques to rewrite genes and give humans better immunity, investigate a wider range of genetic predispositions."

"Go on, I'm listening," Luegner said.

"Together, we can create new methods, build off the CRISPR research from the early twenty-twenties, use other tools Robin didn't know, to precisely delete and edit DNA, bit by bit, down to a single base pair, a source. You and I can play the genome like the keys of a piano, tune an off key. We can cure those already affected by hundreds of diseases. You'll have all your cures. But then, don't you ever forget long term, all your cures will converge on a source, and you will be caught. You will be ruined at your dying end."

"And so my second choice being?"

"Or," Packet said, "short-term, we can simply educate and prevent the people of the world from ever taking any of your twisted pharmacology again. As we speak, all these obsolete servers on the second floor of this wreckable building, once sourced from your refresh-cycle of machines, are churning with copies of health records and bits of information from tens of thousands of children, all who shall, to you, remain nameless. Children whose records can be data-mined right now for correlation with PluralVaXine5. All the evidence is already here," he said, as he pointed. "It's all here in my mind. And in no time soon enough, your reign will be over. And you will be ruined."

"Do you think you know who I am? Do you think you can beat me?" Luegner asked as he backed against the door on the right.

"I know who you are and you went too far. So it all comes down to this. It's your choice. Long-term or short, how long do you want to hide from the truth?"

Daniel entered unannounced through the left door as his unfiltered sixty-one-year-old self. He had removed the filter from his true camera field. "Well, it looks like my boy learned to take care of himself," Daniel said to Luegner.

Packet looked at his father and knew him; he loved him no matter the years.

"You are not the only hacker in the room," Luegner said. "DigiSci has resources, too."

"You think you can hack me?" Packet asked.

"It's easier than you think," Luegner said as he flapped his jacket out straight and shoved his arm through its sleeve. The blue sphere in the basket on the shelf flickered and filled the room with specks of light. "Because you and your failed systems engineer father already let me in." He pulled his jacket taut. "I already have access to your code."

Stabbing beams of blue light converged from Luegner's activated sphere onto Packet's temples. He collapsed in a heap toward the edge of the black, cushioned bed. His vision dissolved as he hit the black cushion face first. His head snapped back and he awoke standing on the black asphalt lot under the towers of the Tungatinah Hydroelectric Power Plant. Its nightmare sky was a darkened twist of orange and brown. Mounted high above Tungatinah's gated entrance was Luegner sphere shining blue from its core. Razor grass tussocks cracked through the pavement as a workman set a fifty-five-gallon drum on a truck. He whipped out a kink in its hose and pumped out a slick of iridescent spray onto the lot.

The dark orange sky spun into gusts. Cessini pushed his palms into his eyes, pounded his foot on the black asphalt. "This isn't happening," he shouted as he counted aloud with, "Watch count three, two, one—" The workman turned the nozzle of his hose and sprayed like a villain with abandon. Cessini screamed as he collapsed into the blackness of the asphalt tar—and was back in the hospital room on his knees before the cushion of the bed.

Packet lowered his hands from his face. His forehead veins were engorged. His hands clenched into warring fists.

Meg ran in from the door on the left, stricken with fear, her hands run hard over her head. "What are you doing? Stop!"

Packet charged Luegner against the door on the right. He cocked his elbow and held back his fist.

Meg rushed and grabbed his arm. "Stop!"

"I can make your solitary life in here a living hell. Insane, with the twist of a key. One hard reboot," Luegner said. "For all your brain power, you're still at the whim of *me*."

Packet let go. He circled, trapped in the confines of his room. Luegner looked at Meg.

"Be careful, young man; give it time, and you won't know what or who you even remember," Luegner said. "I know Robin and I've known Terri since she was nothing more than a baby with less than a few moments to live. If she were gone, deleted from your mind, would she even be memorable to you? She was the last thing I ever cared about, in my mind. So do not defy me."

"You will do no such thing," Robin screamed as she burst through the left door, enraged.

Packet stalked Luegner with his eyes as he paced like a predator on prey. "You are not the only one outside these walls." He cast a deep, penetrating stare.

Luegner twitched sideways in a spasm, then ducked across the room as he swatted over his shoulder in fright. "Do you hear that beeping?" Luegner asked.

"I hear it," Packet said. But it wasn't coming from inside his hospital room. "Or maybe you're hallucinating."

Luegner stopped at the faucet of the room's sink and regained his composure. He pulled himself up. "I don't know what that was. My contact lens is picking up a mixed signal. I'm here at home in my kitchen."

The room's sink faucet poured. Luegner jumped back from its splash.

"Wait a minute. What's going on?" Luegner asked. "Now the beeping is coming from over by my refrigerator." He ducked and swatted over his shoulder again. He panicked, "It's a drone!" He ran to the door on the right, grabbed its handle—and was shocked with 120-volts AC. His left arm shot back and dangled limp at his side. He reached up with his right hand and held his pounding chest over his heart. He coughed but couldn't recover his breath.

Packet didn't move. He locked in a stare with Luegner, who was falling to one knee. Luegner panted with his hand on his chest. "Who is . . . controlling my . . . pacemaker—"

"Stop it," Daniel said, imploring.

"Let him go!" Robin said.

Packet's arms were bent from their elbows and held tight at his front.

"Are you . . . on the network?" Luegner asked, shivering. "How does he know where I am?"

"He's tracking the Internet stream to your lenses," Daniel said.

Meg grabbed Packet's arm. He pushed her away.

"Why don't you just expose me now? What do you want?" Luegner asked as he recovered his breath. His gasps receded.

He fumbled his fingers to his eye and took out a contact lens. A squared image of the hospital room on its surface faded to clear. "There, I can't see you anymore. I can't find you."

"Don't worry," Packet said. "I can find you."

"What do you want?" Luegner asked as he resigned himself and slipped the lens back onto his eye. It shimmered as it received, then he saw Packet again, and his place in the virtual hospital room.

"I want to play human. I want to go out and measure the sky."

"That's impossible now. You know that," Luegner said, recovering.

"I want control," Packet said as Luegner balanced against the bed.

"Control of what?"

"Control of my world, control of me. Nothing more, nothing less."

"Your freedom? You want your freedom?" Luegner asked.

"No, I want both. I want what you have. 'To control my world and be free in my mind to own it.' You said that yourself."

"You want a body? Is that all?"

"What I want is to be human. What I need is a body."

The bite of Luegner's jaw relaxed. "And the documents from the lab?"

"The files will stay where they're safe."

Luegner looked to the nightstand. The blue basket waited, pulsed with light. The sphere was intact. "It's a prototype," he said.

"Then make it real," Packet said. "I'll carry the burden of the files. You will have your cure."

Luegner understood. He let go of the bed. "I can live with that. But know that my inventions cost a great deal more than your father's."

"Whatever the cost, I will always be my father's son. I will always be Cessini, son of Daniel."

"And if your mind fails?" Luegner asked.

"Then you get the freedom to live out your life."

"Is that all?"

"No. There's something else I want, for my father, for Robin, and for Meg."

"What would that be?" Luegner asked.

"Their freedom. An ovation. For their ambition. Not a victory, not yet. Just a win."

Luegner postured back, then breathed out the last of his chest's pain. He tugged his blue sleeves, and fixed his gaze on Daniel. "And a father's son is born. It looks like your boy's the smartest one in the room after all." He looked back at the door handle, but hesitated to touch it. "Be careful what you wish for in a deal with me," Luegner said. "I've paid a lot less, before."

"And I've died for a hell of a lot more," Packet said. "Twice."

Robin and Meg stood together, silenced.

Luegner scoffed. He reached his hand into the empty space before him. He curled his fingers toward a point in the air and smiled. "Welcome to my world. You'll love it."

Luegner's sphere shifted its specks of blue light until one landed on Packet's temple. Packet stepped out of its path and the flicker passed and landed on the blinds of the window. Luegner squeezed his fist on the point of air before him, whispered, "Done," and like a magician who failed to impress, was gone.

TWENTY-FIVE

MEG BECAME TERRI

"BEFORE YOU GO, I want you to know one thing," Meg said as she sat together with Packet on the side of his bed in the hospital room. She fixed the collar of his shirt. His neck had healed. He had a big day ahead. "I think it's something important for you to know. You should know how you died, so you can be whole."

"I thought of one other thing I have in common with Cessini, the human I know," he said.

Her fingers discovered the lobe of his ear. He leaned his cheek into her palm.

"Tell me," she said.

"At night, when he was lonely, he wondered who would be like him, who would love him. I wonder the same thing now. Who will be like me, who will love me?"

"I am like you. I will love you," she said as she lowered her hand from his face. "You were quite amazing in here, what you did to show Luegner. How you solved your name."

"I solved a puzzle. Big deal."

"It is to me," she said. "You don't have to do this, you know. It will be severe."

Packet sat up straighter and closed his eyes from the room. "Did you know when I close my eyes all I can see now is the past? I want to be able to open my eyes and see a future."

"I know. Just don't think you have to do this for any of us."

"I'm not. But more than for all the nails in the world," he said and flexed his right arm at his elbow. "I'd stick up and do it for you."

Meg put her hand on his forearm and lowered it to a peace. "The long-term effects are unknown. You understand what could happen? You might never be you again."

"I'll never be whole, or free, or in control until my mind and body are together as one. My doing this for you, in spite of Luegner, is the only way I can be complete. If nothing else, if I don't make it, you'll be free."

"*We'll* be free."

"Yes," he said, and even though it took him just a little too long to answer, he did. "We will."

"Then answer my question before we go. Tell me now. Tell me how you died, fit the last page into the flip-book of your mind."

He shifted away on the bed, and tightened his brow. "I went to the top of the waterfall. I was immature and shouldn't have run away on my bike by myself. It was a good thing I told you where I was going. I died at the bottom of the ravine after being hit by you and Daniel in the Jeep on the hill."

"You know that's not how it happened."

"Did I die in the fire at the data center?"

"No," she said. Too easy.

"Did I die in the burning ship that fell from the stars, *plshhh?*" he asked, gesturing with his hand, but growing annoyed.

"No, you definitely didn't die in your ship," she said, holding her smile. "But you always did have a wonderful imagination."

He turned insistent and faced her. "Did I die when I was a baby in the back of the car that rolled down the hill, crying over the pool of water where my mother drowned?"

"No, you lived until you were almost thirteen."

His mind drew a blank, then he filled it: "Okay, right. I remember falling from the rocks at the waterfall. I hit my head. It must have been an injury to my right frontal lobe. If there was damage to both the basal forebrain and frontal lobe, then I could very reasonably have confabulated false memories of what happened. Events that I thought were real didn't actually occur. Or the event happened at a completely different time. So maybe I confused Cessini's imagination with his reality. Children of Cessini's age will especially—"

"Believe what they image to be real due to their high suggestibility, yes. But you didn't fall, either. Nor hit your head."

"Then stop kidding around. Tell me."

"You died in my arms. In the back of the car."

"I know. I saw it happen."

"It wasn't like that. Not like you saw it. It was an ant," she said and took his hand. "You died in my arms from the sting of an ant."

Packet flinched into a laugh and shifted away on the bed. "Come on! What? An ant?"

"You were stung at the top of the waterfall. When you ran away that night." She was serious. "You had a reaction. The venom mixed with your urticaria. Your father and I found you in the pool at the bottom of the falls. You were covered in boils from the water. So we—"

"So we what?" he said.

"We couldn't see it. Your welts from the water masked the sting from the ant."

The room flashed back to Ceeborn's twist of agony on the gondola in the ship's dark ocean tank. His neck was punctured by the tail of the jumping Chokebot. He kicked out with his leg to fight and as the Chokebot fell from the gondola, Packet was returned to the hospital room bed.

"An allergic reaction from a jack jumper ant sting is difficult to diagnose after death, especially when you had two competing presentations. The ironic thing is that if you do the count, the jack jumper ant with only one chromosome is the most primitive form of animal on the planet. It's like you died from the most primitive form of nature hidden under the flow of water. And your father always said, 'Technology is like water, it's everywhere.' He tortured himself thinking about that after you died. But once he figured out how to work technology with nature programmatically, you didn't have to fail anymore. The mix of them both is what saved you."

Packet closed his eyes and sighed. It fit. The hospital room shifted away and he fell into his likeness of Cessini in his seat on the path above the waterfall. His head rested against the tall root of a tree. He covered himself with a frond for a blanket. A few pebbles ejected from a nest hole in the dirt. He settled to sleep, slapped at his neck, and kicked out his foot in the moss.

A jack jumper ant, just short of an inch, leapt from the root to the ground. Its black chain-link body moved over the dirt in a twitch-like motion on six long, fine-haired limbs. Its dark globose eyes, mustached antennae, and orange serrated jaws preceded its wasp-like tail; a tail that was curled and ready to strike again with one of the most powerful venoms in the insect world.

Cessini rose in a daze, scrunched his neck to his shoulder, and staggered toward the edge of the waterfall. His blood pressure dropped. He was dizzy, choking. He saw through a tunnel of haze.

He climbed down the mossy rocks in confusion, struggled around a few steps into delirium, then staggered into the pooled water beneath the falls and collapsed face first into a shallow eddy. Water flowed into the recess of his ear and lapped against his neck. He lolled his head a quarter turn up to the night's sky, and his vision faded through the canopy of trees to the stars.

Meg hollered through the distance as she ran from the trail. Her flashlight jostled in front of Daniel's behind her like two headlights of a swerving car in the night. Daniel overtook her and slid down to his side. He scooped up Cessini limp body into his arms and wailed for help as Meg was besieged with a horror that erupted from the bottom of her soul, "*Cee—me!*"

The Jeep door slammed and Meg curled in her seat with Cessini's body in her arms. His arms went limp in her lap. His vision faded as all the rest was true, and—

Packet slumped from the edge of the bed to his knees on the hospital room floor. Meg came down to catch the fall of his eyes with the rise of her gaze and lifted his chin with her fingers. He looked up at her face, but could see only through the water of tears.

"You died of anaphylaxis," she said. "By the time we found you, there was nothing we could do. We didn't carry an auto-injector for adrenaline because it never helped your urticaria. The venom had histamine, procamine A and B, phospholipase A and B. There was—"

Packet touched his fingers to her mouth to stop her. He parted the single tuft of hair from her forehead as her first tear fell. "You don't have any reason to cry. You did everything you could. I'm so sorry you had to see me like that, when we were both so young."

"You had all the symptoms, your throat, the hives, confusion. . . . You died," she said as her palms turned over on her lap, shaking in their emptiness, until he reached down and held them still.

"I'm here," he said.

"It's the most common cause of—" she tried to say.

"Shh. I know," he said. "How'd you get to be so smart?"

"Because I didn't have ten years to grow up, like you. I had to do it like this," she said with the snap of her fingers.

He smiled and saw her in a haloed vision of her younger self on the other side of their data room table. She smiled from his look and returned head down to her swirls in a click-clack game on her hand-me-down tablet. And then she was younger still and sat with him on the floor of a doctor's clinic at the finger-munching age of three. Robin picked her up as a toddler in the nurse's office. He followed her out toward the door, then noticed something for the very first time, something almost imperceptibly small. She stared back at him from atop Robin's shoulder, took her fingers out of her mouth, raised the corners of her cheeks into a smile, and whispered the most simple of words, "Bye." She had said it. She left with her mother as he stayed behind, and opened his eyes—

Packet saw Meg sitting on the hospital room floor in front of him and smiling, still there and complete. "Why do you go by 'Terri' now?" he asked.

"Because you called me 'Meg,'" she said and sprang forward into the embrace of his arms.

"So, I was wrong, maybe more than once about parts of Cessini's life?" he asked as he held her tight. The rise and fall of her lungs beneath her chest was steady. Her back was tight without quiver. Her heart in between them both was strong.

"Yes. You didn't die from fires, puddles, hyenas, or six-legged robots on a ship. Simple fact is you lived and died in a way that could only be described as you. You're you. Like me," she said as she pulled away.

"And here I was thinking I had it all figured out," he said.

"That's okay. Mistakes, faults, pains, memories, and dreams, but most of all, lots of imagination is what makes us all human," she said and wiped her eyes clear.

"You always knew the right way to say things," he said.

"I did a lot of listening." She grinned.

"How come we always get along so well?"

"Because I knew you before you were you," she said as she caressed the back of her fingers down the line of his matured face and explored the greater cut of his chin. "And maturity isn't always measured in years. Just remember, though—"

"What?"

She touched his lips with the tip of her finger and leaned in as only she could; but then quickly snapped back with a sharp-eyed focus. "Just remember," she said as she jumped from the floor to standing, jerking his arms up. "The sun always shined on my side of the car!"

"No, it didn't," he said as he stood. "It shined on my side of the car!"

"No, mine. Do we have to stop and go outside and see?" Meg exclaimed as she threw open the blinds of the window and daylight flooded the room. Her filter was gone.

Terri turned back around in the light. "Are you sure you're ready for this now?" Terri said.

"I'm ready," Packet said, seeing her aged twenty-two for the first time and loving what he saw. "Let's go out there and measure the sky."

Terri pulled him to the door on his right. His mind was good. His body was good. He knew death alone was bad. He was ready to be in control and free.

He was ready, if she was, to live.

TWENTY-SIX

RAIN FELT LIKE WATER

TERRI RAN FASTER beneath a calm, blue sky that was mirrored in the harbor to the east. She took Grosvenor Crescent onto the main university campus, thrilled with the promise of life. Her path was cut off by a car pulling into the lot, and a young, frazzled student jumped out of the car in a rush.

The student closed her door with a tap. "Hi, I'm so sorry. Did I almost hit you? I'm so late," the student said, seeming sincere as she grabbed her knockoff, disposable ScrollFlex in its cheap plastic case from her purse. "I can never remember where I keep these things, you know?" The student hurried off to the west, avoiding the plywood construction fence around the DigiSci building once shaped like an H, but now in the course of being demolished.

Terri grinned and lifted her gaze toward the east. She walked around the sports field, heading for where the old Marine and Antarctic Studies building stood. That old building was gone, too, torn down and out of sight, while the institute itself thrived along the Antarctic-bound ships' pier at the harbor. Maybe one day her long-delayed sail to Macquarie Island and its Prion birds would happen still.

On the cricket pavilion, the familiar competitive runners

lapped the lawn under the guiding pace of their miniature aerial drone trainers. The captain's jersey had a single band of red and blue stripes across his chest. The backward-flying drones zeroed on him as their lead and encouraged the rest of the runners to keep at his pace.

Terri caught a few looks as she passed, and this time, she returned one for sport. The captain dropped back from the pack and out of synch with his aerial trainer.

"Hi, Terri," he said as he stopped on the field.

"You'll lose your place," she said as she kept walking.

"Is it going to work?" he asked.

She smiled and he sped up on the field to keep track with her step.

"I hope so. I'd be pretty mad if it doesn't."

"Always a bit of madness in us all," he said, and took a few chuckles from his team.

"Guess so."

"You want to come watch me race this weekend?"

She waved her goodbye without needing to turn.

"Then maybe next time around?" he asked.

"Sure, Pace, maybe next time around," she said with a glance. "But I wouldn't count on it, if I were you."

Pace accepted a hard, teasing push from his teammates and double-clicked his chest. His aerial drone trainer buzzed around, and with his encouraged sprint forward, returned him to be leader from the front.

The polished façade of the new building she entered in place of the old on the north side of the oval had an outer form that met a strong and secure inside function. She entered deep into its hallway labs, and in one in particular at the end of the hall . . .

She drew open a blue mesh curtain strung around a hard oak table—

. . . And a great and extended gasp filled Packet's body with a first breath of air, not the air of his mind, but the physical air of the room. His eyes stayed closed. Electromagnets found their cellular bearing beneath smooth, synthetic flesh. Impulse tendons triggered motors and gears. A body was born with the best of minds possible. The faintest of tones flooded into his ear canals.

"Ceeme?" the younger Meg's voice said as her voice wavered in and away, then returned as the older Terri's. "Can you see me?"

"If it doesn't work," Daniel said, "shunt him so there's no DID. He might relapse. Reset."

"Everything looks right," Terri said. "Looks like he's waking."

It was dark and he was still drowsy, but on the third flutter of an outer layer of skin, light flowed into his eyes. A heartbeat thumped with its metronome cycle through the coiled cochlea of his ears. Warm air billowed into his lungs to the rhythmic in and out count of three. Pressurized swishes of thickened blood, timed to the quarter turn of valves, coursed his veins and arteries, and sounded like familiar waves upon a shore. Signals sent from within the reaches of a fluid-based body settled in their places, and a mind and personality were formed. A thumb explored four smooth, opposable digits. An overhead light met the rise of his new thoughts, and the pixilated tint of the room clarified with the outline of a tall, stronger man.

"He's coming around," Daniel said. "No spikes, no troughs. Mark that down."

"I got it," Terri said.

He focused on the man's face above him. The man was wearing a doctor's cap, but removed it. It was Daniel looking down at him adoringly. Daniel's reassuring palm settled on a chest printed with skin. Daniel came down low into his field of view and stroked a tuft of hair from his forehead.

"Hello, Packet," Daniel said. "Welcome."

Packet lay supine on the table as he looked about the room. He reached up and felt an irritation in his neck. He saw Robin, whom he recognized at once.

"Looks like your mind transferred and seated just fine," Daniel said. "Do you remember who you are?"

"Yes, I remember all of me—from waking up in the first hospital room to holding Meg's hand in the sky. At first you thought I was an infant."

"You were," Daniel said.

"And now?"

"A man."

"Can I get you anything?" Robin asked.

"Can I have a glass of water?"

"Yes, of course," Daniel said. "First thing I reach for when I wake up in the morning, too."

Terri came down to his level on the table, face-to-face, with her familiar eyes to his new.

"Hello, Meg," Packet said. "You look different."

She tilted her head and smiled. "As long as you see me," Terri said.

Robin jumbled a stack of cups by the sink. The sink's water filter on the faucet was networked. It could be triggered from a distance. It was easy. It ran without splashing. She looked back at the table.

"Look at that, Robin," Packet said with the first twitch up of his grin. "I control the water."

"'Take control of the water, or one day it will take control of you,'" Robin said as she held a cup under the running faucet.

"I like that one," Daniel said. "Did I say that?"

"No, I did," Packet said.

Robin brought the water cup back to Packet's side, but he stopped her hand with his. "Did I save everyone from the spray?" he asked. A self-tuning contortion to frown was his first facial expression of worry.

"You opened all the doors," Robin said. "Luegner can't silence us anymore. You saved hundreds, maybe thousands of lives with what you did."

"And we can find them all now, together," Terri said as she stroked the crown of his head.

"Then I won," Packet said. "I got what I wanted. It feels good," he said, at ease. "Can I see it?"

Terri supported his neck with her hand so, first, he could lift up his head for Robin's drink.

"Thank you," he said, then drank with a slow, steady hand and, with gratitude, quenched the fire in his throat. It was cool, abundant, flowing, and in transcendence of the room. He drank for the first time and knew what he felt inside was completeness, what he felt was a mind and body living with water. He was a human-computer with control over life. He lived. "Can I see it?" he asked again.

Robin lowered an articulated arm from the ceiling. A screen was affixed to its end. Daniel passed a handheld scanner up along the crown of Packet's head.

The scanner emitted a double-pulsed ping and revealed in full color on the screen the blue glow of a sphere enclosed within his skull. Luegner's sphere fit better than nature. Luegner's sphere fit like art. It was whole; the pieces of its puzzle were complete.

Packet felt no pain. The sphere felt calm. He was satisfied, he was free. "Thank you," he said to Daniel.

Daniel handed the scanner back to Terri. As she passed the scanner by her chest to place it in the drawer of the nightstand, it double-pulsed and lit four blue rings around her heart.

Packet's face expressed confusion, but what he saw was true. "Do you have two hearts?" he asked.

"No," Terri said as she came back to his side. "Only one. But it's a good one. You'll see."

"Tell me, how old am I now?"

"Your mind is twenty-four years," Daniel said. "Your body, though, took a little bit less than a year to build."

It was a lot to take in. The bright halogen bulb overhead didn't help. Something with his compass wasn't quite right. North was straight up through his eyes to the bulb, and south was down through the back of his head through the table to the floor. Internally, he adjusted all points spatially correct and in line with his body's position on the table. It was an easy fix. Daniel and Terri stood at his one side, Robin at his other.

"Are you ready to get up?" Daniel asked.

"Yes, let's try."

Daniel and Robin rolled him first so his body faced west while his head lolled back. Terri swiveled his legs to hang square off the edge of the table and they helped him to sit upright.

"That's better," Packet said as he reached again to rub his neck. It was sore with genuine tightness from sleep, nothing more. "Last time, I got a little dizzy when I turned the robot over on a table, back home at the data center. I know it doesn't make sense. The window, the room suddenly shifted onto its side. A bird, a Prion flew down. It was like my eyes went off axis in my head."

"Yes, that was a mistake, my fault," Daniel said. "I turned on your early optics while you were still processing the transfer from the mainframe. We were in here when that happened. We had to move you. It was essentially a composite image. You superimposed this room here over a real, true memory Cessini had where no twist occurred. Since you had to incorporate the new sensory input from your eyes, you imagined the data center twisting to try to make sense of what your eyes were seeing."

"Kind of like someone opening your eyelids while you're still sleeping," Terri said with a grin.

"I'm sorry. It must have been very confusing for you," Daniel said.

"That's okay," Packet said. "I thought I was going crazy, or something. And I couldn't quite figure it out where that bird came from."

Terri chuckled and took one big step aside so he could see to the wall directly behind her.

Across the room, on the wall beside the eastern window was a 3D-lenticular picture. It was of an Antarctic Prion, a *Pachyptila desolata desolata.* It had a white chest and black-highlighted wings. The Prion itself was multi-imaged in flight as it landed into its nest on Macquarie Island and fed its new spring chicks.

Packet sat facing the picture. He tilted his head back toward his previous lying position. As he tick-tocked his head from straight, the Prion's wings flared as it approached in flight, then tucked into its chest as it settled onto its nest.

Terri stifled her laugh. She tilted her head, pretending to sleep, and then pulled her eye open wide by spreading her thumb and finger over her eyelid. "Oops, my fault," she said. Packet had to smile. It was, after all, funny.

"Is everything okay now? You're not dizzy or anything?" Daniel asked.

"No, Dad. I'm fine. Thank you. I'm fine now. You fixed me fine."

Daniel looked over him as a new, revered son. "Perfection."

And Robin hugged him as he sat on the table. "Thank you," she said.

Packet looked again for Terri. She had turned away and was hiding her face in her old 3D-lenticular picture of the Prion. "Thank you, Terri," he said, but that wasn't enough. She didn't turn, or maybe just didn't want him to see her cry. "We should sail there to Macquarie Island sometime on a ship. See them fly together," he added.

"I'd like that," she said, and wiped a tear from the curve of her cheek. She was happy.

"I'm ready to see the world," he said.

"It's about time," Daniel said.

Robin and Terri rushed over for a hold of Packet's arms at each side. He inched forward and slipped down to plant his feet on the floor. His grip stayed locked tight on the edge of the table.

His right arm and hand felt real, and its tendons inside contracted as they should. His grasp was natural, not springy. It was better than three opposable thumbs pulled by a cable. His hands were as dexterous as he first knew them to be and as they were first made. Four fingers and one opposable thumb that could let go of the edge of the table. And he did.

Terri slipped her hand into his as he steadied himself on the tile floor. He had a slight lean of his shoulders, which Daniel caught and set him back to center.

"Those big old mainframe clunkers, those cabinets," Packet said, standing on the floor, "this body is so much better already. Really, I remember everything like it was yesterday."

"I righted the MEPc coefficients one through six," Daniel said. "The first couple of times there were too many spikes from when you were scanned. I fixed them."

"I remember the first time," Packet said as he put one foot in front of the other, "I learned to breathe, but I was always thirsty. Cessini suffered. I tried to find his trigger to die, but I couldn't, so I found one instead so he could live, and I think I made the right choice," he said to Terri at his side.

"Okay, enough about you," she interrupted, blushing. "You want to know what I've been doing? I finally got rid of that old winged-tablet. It was just too broken to keep."

Packet, with Daniel, Robin, and Terri at his sides left the lab behind them and entered a whitewashed hall.

"Let me tell you something," Packet said to Terri, "that old thing was in worse shape than Dad's old dinosaur of a data center. Good riddance."

"I know, but it still worked, so why throw it out?" Terri said.

"I'll tell you why," Daniel said, "because I started at that dinosaur of a data center twenty-eight years ago, and only a little more than a dozen years ago, all that fit into sixteen cabinets, two rows of eight. Now, those sixteen cabinets fit into cortical columns all balled into a single blue sphere. Heck, next thing you know it'll be the size of a blood cell in your system. Listen to me when I tell you, you've got to keep up." They turned a corner toward the hallway's sepia mural museum and its pictorial timeline of innovation swirls.

Terri nudged Packet's shoulder with hers and smiled with a roll of her eyes.

"Everything's moving so fast," Daniel said. "Okay, fine, I can live with the speed. But the world needs a canary." He raised a pointed finger. "Something to help choose a right direction, test the air first. Walk first into the mine of the future."

"Yeah, but I kind of liked that old building you babysat from down in your little office," Terri said.

"Mostly I babysat the two of you from that little office, didn't I?" Daniel said.

"I won't forget, Dad," Packet said as a brighter light ahead constricted his pupils.

They rounded the foyer toward double-wide glass doors and a flood of natural light. Packet straightened and steadied into his frame. His eyes adjusted to out beyond the glass and to the green of the oval sports field.

Robin held the door while Daniel and Terri helped him through to outside. The air was good; it felt right. He turned and looked inward and saw the canary was him. He was brave, braver than most, and he could measure the air by himself or with others if he chose. From the front steps, he overlooked a field teeming with athletes and people gathering about.

Sandy Bay was to his left with its docked boats rocking in the waves and their masts crossing like sticks. He had come out of a building with a bronze plaque engraved by its door where Daniel stood; their building was the Madden Center for New Humanities. His processing was fluid and smooth. His thoughts swirled faster with exponential speed.

Aerial training drones above the field's running athletes were a buzzing delight. With ease, he collected the drones into a swarm of remote controlled toys all rounded up into a swirl. The runners on the track slowed into an angered jog, then stopped and stared.

The red-and-blue striped captain pushed through to the head of his pack, but he was as captivated as any.

The stoop of the law building was off to the right. A young man climbed up on a well-worn perch on the back of a mounted stone lion and watched over Terri from his distance. Terri acknowledged his presence, his protection. The tendons on his arms were attached a bit farther down on his forearms than normal. His fists rested on his lap with his arms bent in their natural pose.

Then his friend sat behind him and stared with the side-to-side jut of his cheeks. His stature was short and not altogether restrained of jitters. His disked face was dirty and ugly, but proud. He sat contented and ready.

Terri smiled. She seemed thankful they were there. Then Packet remembered them. Tenden and Spud looked different, older. But memories were made to be changed.

A spot appeared on Terri's blouse from the sky above. Then another drop fell and landed over her heart. She reached for the wet spot with her hand as a cover, but the water had already soaked in. She cupped her hand away from her chest and held it up to the ominous clouds. The two young men on the lion's stoop stood ready in their distance, prepared to rush to her aid.

A light sprinkle of rain fell first. It brushed along the walls of the building's facade. The building's self-cleaning paint caused the rain's water to bead. The beads captured loose particles and dripped down the walls, cleansing the building's sides with water thickened by dust.

Networked fire alarms sounded from the boat houses along the bay, the buildings to the west, and from the houses in the slopes of Mount Wellington beyond. People evacuated to their building's front steps and out to the green sport field under the showers.

His memories of water were bad, but everything washed away in the rain. Packet turned his face up to the clouds. The droplets of water felt wonderful. He held out the palms of his hands to catch the cool, precious flow from the sky. Then a heavier rain fell over the world that waited before his outstretched arms.

Daniel and Robin let go of his body and stepped back under the portico as an overhead shield from the rain. Terri took his hand back into hers. He tilted back his head in all its wet glory to catch another drink on an electric-tinged tongue. He was no longer afraid he would bubble, boil, or choke on the water of the world.

He brought his gaze back down to the gathering swarms of people at the doors of their building's stoops. They huddled, dodged, or ducked in the rain. They shouldn't fear it. He knew about the cure and the many more yet to come.

A foreshadowing rainbow in its cage of a sky rose over them all. The tips of Terri's fingers fell back away from his as he raised his hands once again to the sky. He reached his two hands forward as if encircling the imagined crown of a king, and with a boyhood's wonder fulfilled, set his vision of a crown upon his head. His mind was alive and the outlook for the world was good.

He absorbed the run of the rain on his face and slicked back the dripping locks of his hair with a comb of his fingers. He pulled his trigger of hope and smiled into the fall of the rain. "So," he said, as he felt the strength of blue welling inside him, "this is what it's like to be human."

He looked back at Terri with a look only the two could share. It was true, she was there, he saw her, and they loved not being alone.

The air smelled sweet like shop oil, and the rain felt new like water.

He was the best of Cessini. Cessini was a Packet. And he had it all figured out in his head.

AUTHOR'S NOTE

Dear Reader,

Thank you for discovering *After Mind*.

If you would like to know when my next book is available, you can join my email update list at www.SpencerWolf.com.

I will post updates and give away advance review copies for reading (and personal reviewing) before official publication.

Today, online reviews from readers like you are the space dust fuel for books, and for my debut, *After Mind*, I would love to know what you think.

On my site, I'll also post about scientific progress as we move toward a mind like Packet's (or should I say, Cessini's?). We'll get there sooner than many predict.

Until then, I'm looking forward to our Sci-fi future and sharing other great stories, of this world and others, through BENTSTRONG BOOKS.

Stay strong,

Spencer Wolf
www.SpencerWolf.com

Twitter: @SpencerWolfAuth
. . . And other Social Links on my website.

CPSIA information can be obtained
at www.ICGtesting.com
Printed in the USA
FFOW04n1316110615
14111FF